HIS PLEDGE TO HAVE

THE SILVER STAR RANCH SERIES

SHANAE JOHNSON

CHAPTER ONE

"Can you believe I've never been in a long-term relationship?"

Artillery Silver could believe that about the guy who was sitting across from her. His name was Chet. Or -wait? Was it Chaz?

Whatever it was, it certainly wasn't the name he'd given on the dating app they'd initially connected on. On the popular app, MeetCute, individuals could use nicknames. Tilly had used her actual nickname of Tilly. Charles—or was it Chester?—had called himself MomApproved. Tilly was starting to wonder if the moniker boasted that the mothers of the women he dated approved of him? Or if it was only his mother who approved of him?

"Most women aren't honest about who they are on these dating apps, you know. When you meet them in person, you often get a big shock."

Christian -or maybe it was Chase?- only barely resembled his profile picture. In his current state, he sported a comb-over that barely had enough wisps to complete the trek to the other side of his forehead. He was five inches shorter than his dating profile claimed and forty pounds heavier. That picture on his profile had to be at least ten years older than the man who sat across from her at the dinner table.

All that evidence led Tilly to think it must have been his college picture… or maybe his high school yearbook photo. Whenever the picture had been snapped left Tilly in no doubt that Clarence—or maybe it was Clinton?—had been telling the truth about one thing; it was easy to believe he'd never been in a long-term relationship.

"I find most women can't live up to my high expectations."

"Maybe because they're too busy looking down at you?"

Tilly hadn't muttered the words under her breath. She'd said them loud enough for the guy at the next table to hear her. Like her, her next-table-neighbor didn't bother to mute his reaction. The dark-haired man laughed out loud. His sensual lips parted, allowing a few red droplets to fall back into the wineglass he held partway to his mouth. Most of the droplets seemed to cling to the flesh of his quirked lower lip as if the liquid was unwilling to part from him.

Light green eyes met hers. They twinkled with mirthful delight. A second laugh escaped him, sending more droplets. A few of those droplets landed on Tilly's arm.

Tilly glared at the man. He grinned back at her. She had to turn away quickly before he made her laugh too. The way he lifted his right brow in a perfectly arched upside-down V of mocking never failed to elicit a giggle out of her.

"I think you're different, Artie," her date was saying.

Tilly's attention snapped back to… whatever his name was. The man deigned to ignore her nickname and gave her one of his liking. She saw no reason to exert herself any further over trying to remember his.

"You're pretty enough." MomApproved leaned to the side and gave her seated frame a once over as though to confirm his words. "You were early for our date, which shows eagerness. You ordered a steak, which shows me you're healthy. But..." He held up a finger and wagged it at her as though she'd been a naughty child. "… you'll need to cut back on the calories before things get out of hand and you balloon up. I won't be one of those husbands who'll stand to let his wife let herself go after I put a ring on it."

Tilly's fingers pinched at her wineglass stem. Her eyes narrowed on the bright, bald spot on her date's forehead. It made an excellent bull's eye. She bet she could hit that marker with her eyes shut.

The man sitting at the table next to them cleared his throat. The sound was loud enough to bring a few of the other dining guests' attention to him. Not Tilly's date, though. He went on and on about what he expected of his wife-to-be as their next-table-neighbor began to cough.

The coughing man wasn't in any distress. His gaze was locked on Tilly's hand. Belatedly, she realized she'd raised her wineglass an inch off the table-cloth. The contents of the glass were nearly empty. But really, who could blame her with the tedious-ness of this date. Still, what was left in the glass would make a splash if the contents met with MomApproved's bloated face.

The guy next to them coughed a little louder. Tilly distinctly made out the words *Don't, Cause,* and *Scene* in the midst of his theatrical hacking. To punctuate his whooping Morse Code, he narrowed those light green eyes at her.

Tilly huffed as she set the glass back down. The man was right. She wasn't on this date to cause a scene. Her date was doing exactly what she had planned for him to do; he was proposing marriage.

Tilly needed to get married, and soon. She'd been going through dating apps like a horse quidding hay. She chomped at each straw of a man she came in contact with and spit out the wet bundles of rejects. But just like with a horse that wasn't properly swallowing his food, Tilly had to put a stop to the practice because she wasn't getting what she needed to keep her livelihood going.

Her father's will stipulated that she and her five sisters had to get married within three months of the reading of his will if they were going to keep the ranch they'd grown up on. It was the only home they'd known. And in two weeks, their time would be up. So, Tilly couldn't afford to be picky about who she would wind up rolling around in the hay with.

"I would suggest we go Dutch on dinner," her

date was saying. "But, since you ordered the more expensive item on the menu, I think we should each pay our own way tonight. Like it says in my profile, I'm a feminist. I believe in equality of the sexes, and that includes financially."

Tilly lifted her wineglass again. Her hand didn't jerk to empty the contents in his face. She pressed the rim of the glass to her mouth and took a healthy gulp of what remained of her drink and her pride.

She had to do this. Her sisters were counting on her. Already four of the six Silver sisters had married. Only Tilly and her twin Gunny were left. And Gunny had a fiancé.

"Why don't we take this back to my place," said MomApproved. "My parents will be out until midnight playing bridge, and we'll have the whole basement to ourselves."

Annnnnd cut scene. That was a wrap on this date. Because, nope, she couldn't do it. She could not spend five more minutes with this joker, much less the rest of her life. She had only one choice left. She threw up the white flag.

Not just metaphorically. She tossed her white dinner linen to the floor.

Her neighbor at the next table lowered his left eyebrow as he looked down at the crumpled signal at his feet. Where lifting the right brow was always done in amusement, lowering the left brow was a sign of exasperation. His expression read, *Are you really giving up?*

Tilly wanted to glower at him that, *Yes, she was giving up, and he'd better do something about it.*

With the same pouting sigh he'd affected when she'd asked him to watch *Grosse Pointe Blank* for the tenth time—even though she knew he loved it, Carter Shane lifted his long form from the chair. Tilly took a moment to admire the play of muscles under his fitted black shirt as his lean fingers smoothed out the fabric.

Tilly knew firsthand what those muscles felt like under her cheek. She'd fallen asleep more than once while leaning against him on the sofa as they watched old movies. She'd even woken up a couple of times, laying fully against his chest with his arms wrapped snug around her, the television blaring static at them.

Now Tilly watched as Carter bent his form to pick up her napkin. "Excuse me, ma'am, I think you dropped… Artillery? Artillery Silver, is that you?"

"I'm sorry," Tilly pressed her hand to her chest. "Do we know each other?"

"Do we know each other?" Carter turned and

gave her date a chuckle. "How could you forget me? We met at fat camp when we were teens. Don't you remember?"

There was a sputtering cough. It didn't come from Tilly or Carter. The man that only his mother would approve of was choking on his drink after Carter's pronouncement of Tilly as a formerly overweight person.

She would've killed her friend for this if she managed to keep herself from laughing. Gotta hand it to Carter. Her sister's fiancé knew how to clear Tilly's unwanted dates quickly and efficiently. After all, he'd been doing it for weeks now.

CHAPTER TWO

Carter Shane used the discarded white dinner napkin to dust off the vacated chair. He was mildly surprised that he didn't see a puddle in the seat after the occupant's hasty retreat. He was also surprised that Tilly's date moved so fast to the exit with the extra weight the man carried.

"He may not have been lying about his level of physical fitness," Carter mused as he folded himself down in the chair across from Tilly.

"You're one to talk about fitness having been a fat camp dropout." Tilly lifted her wineglass as though to down the remaining contents, only to find that the glass was empty.

"Oy, the politically correct term is Health Resort." Carter snagged Tilly's fork and speared a chunk of meat. It was in his mouth before she could swat his hand away from her plate. "You didn't think my hail Mary save was free, did you?"

"Can you believe the nerve of that guy? Not one thing from his profile was true." Tilly poured herself another glass of wine from the opened bottle on the table. She tilted the bottle to Carter, but he put his hand over the top of the glass nearest him. "Right, I keep forgetting your one glass rule."

Carter hadn't finished the glass that was still sitting on the other table. He'd never been much of a drinker. In any of its forms, alcohol tasted the same to him, like a bitter astringent that was best used to strip a car's engine. As he watched Tilly's throat work to take the liquid down, he began to feel a thirst that he knew the red liquid would never quench.

When Tilly dabbed at her lip to catch a wayward droplet of the red ambrosia, Carter looked away. It wasn't the alcohol he wanted. No, he wanted something he had never tasted, could never taste.

A tremor ran down the length of his right arm, causing his index finger to tremble. He clenched his fingers around the fork to hide it from her. Tilly was usually a very observant woman, but he'd managed to keep the occasional shakes and twitches from her over the past two months.

"You're being too hard on..." Carter paused. "What was his name again?"

Tilly opened her mouth to respond. Then she frowned. "I gave up trying to remember after he told me my figure reminded him of his mother."

Carter's gaze went from the red stains on her bottom lip to the crinkle between her brow. The little lines that drew in there formed the center point of a heart where the two halves met in the middle. Her blue eyes rounded at the top part of the heart. Her bottom lip completed the shape.

Oh no. He was back looking at her mouth again. He had to stop doing that; looking at Artillery Silver's perfectly kissable lips was mission impossible. Because he was never going to kiss those lips. He'd never know how soft they were or if they were sweeter than the wine she sipped.

"That's sad," he said. "You don't know the name of your future husband."

Tilly scowled at him, then snatched the fork away from him.

That single touch sent a jolt of awareness through him. Carter's pinky finger joined the fluttering dance of his index finger. To hide the involuntary movement, he returned to his table to grab his own cutlery. By the time he took his seat across from Tilly again, his fingers were behaving.

When he looked up, he found Tilly's gaze on him. She wasn't looking at his hands. She was looking at his face.

That furrowed frown turned into a pointed glare. What Tilly didn't know was that Carter found that her glare made her even more beautiful. Her blue eyes blazed like the hottest part of a fire, making Carter want to forget any caution and get burned.

"He probably lied about his name, too," Tilly huffed. "How can you trust someone who misleads you or keeps secrets?"

A spasm rocketed through Carter's palm. He dropped the fork, letting it clatter to the plate. Then he shoved his trembling hand under the table like the dirty little secret it was.

Tilly had been carving a piece of meat. Her gaze tracked to the edge of the table where his hand had disappeared. She pursed her lips as though she were about to ask him what the matter was?

"Was it the height or the bald head that did it?" Carter needled, trying to get her attention back on her awful date.

"I have nothing against a bald head. Look at Vin Diesel or the Rock. And what modern woman hasn't had a fantasy or two about Peter Dinklage in his role as Tyrion Lannister?"

"Peter Dinklage? I thought you would've been a Warwick Davis kinda girl."

"Why would you think that?"

"You made me watch *Willow* last weekend."

"Made you?" she scoffed. "You're the one that swore that Val Kilmer hit his peak as Doc Holliday in *Tombstone*. I had to counter that with the brilliance of his acting in the role of Madmartigan."

"Proving once again that you like the villain to turn into a hero."

The frown was back. It always came back when he'd bested Tilly in the language she knew best; filmology.

"Let's face it, you're the only woman I know whose favorite John Cusack film isn't *Say Anything*."

"Because it's a sappy 80s film."

"You and your dark heart love *Grosse Pointe Blank*."

She grinned at the mention of her favorite film. "Who in their right mind doesn't love that film? Rebel son returns to his hometown for his high school reunion, where everyone else has a family, a house, and a dog. But Martin Blank has become a professional hitman with a score to settle because he was an overachiever."

Carter chuckled. Trust Tilly to find the good in a trained assassin. She would've been perfect for his best friend Truman, who was an actual trained sniper. But the thought of Truman holding Tilly set his entire arm to shaking.

"I'm surprised you didn't go that route," Tilly said.

"What? An assassin? Unlike our hero in your favorite film, when I took the Army's psych exam, it showed that my moral compass was pointed due North."

"How lucky for Gunny."

The mention of Tilly's twin was like a bomb between them. A tremor went through Carter's entire body, and a piercing pain in his head made him wince.

"You're still on board to marry her, right?" asked Tilly. "I mean, now that Brig and Jackson are together, she's the only one of us left."

"And you." Carter pressed his lips together. He hadn't meant to say that out loud. But the two words hung between them.

"I'll be fine." Tilly waved away the inconvenience

of her single state in the face of only two weeks before the deadline to keep their family ranch. "I've got a few more dates lined up. I'm sure one of them has to be my Mr. Right."

"Yeah, sure." Carter's tone lacked any kind of certainty. "Or you could run after your date. I'm sure he hasn't gotten that far."

Tilly tossed her dinner napkin at him. Carter caught the white flag. He wished it meant her surrender.

But it didn't. Tilly saw him as a friend. In truth, that's all he could ever be to her. She was already close enough to him that she might see the secrets he was hiding from her, from everyone. At least when he married Gunny, that particular Silver sister would only stick around long enough for the ink of the wedding license to dry. Then she'd be off, returning to her quest to save the world and all its endangered species.

The upside to the deal was that Carter would have a place to stay, a place to work, and he'd still get to hang out with Tilly and watch movies or talk about nonsense. He couldn't ask for much more than that in this life. It was likely more than he deserved.

CHAPTER THREE

"What do you think you're doing?" Tilly demanded.

"Hailing a cab?" said Carter. "What does it look like?"

Tilly's indignation turned into a scowl as Carter brought his wallet from his pocket and onto the dinner table. The waiter sat the check down on the table, placing it in front of Carter, which Tilly took offense to as well.

Sure, she had just dumped a guy because he'd suggested they go Dutch. But at least... Seriously, what had his name been? At least MomApproved had brought up who would pay. Carter just took charge of the situation, swiping the check away from Tilly before she could get her fingers around it.

Carter thumbed through his wallet. Tilly couldn't help but notice that his bills were organized by denomination. A few one-dollar bills, followed by a number of fives and a few twenties. Carter pulled all of the twenties from his wallet and slipped them into the billfold.

"Keep the change," he said, handing the billfold back to the waiter

"No," said Tilly. "I can't let you pay for my date."

"Date? That was my night's entertainment, a live-action romcom. You played your part brilliantly. But I think casting got the leading man wrong."

Once again, the man disarmed her with his jokes. Carter was right, though. The wrong man had been cast in tonight's episode of her disastrous dating life. In fact, this whole past season of Tilly's Dating Adventures would've likely been canceled after the pilot episode. The only thing saving the show was the introduction of her sidekick, Carter Shane.

Carter stood and brushed imaginary crumbs off his shirt and pants. Tilly's gaze tracked the movement. Unlike the men she dated, Carter fit the profile of a man any woman would want to go on a blind date with. In fact, a few of the women looked away from their dates to appreciate the man's form.

"You're showing off," Tilly said to Carter.

"What do you mean?" The look of innocence was fake as he slid his jacket over his form.

One thing Tilly knew about Carter Shane was that the man knew how handsome he was. Moreover, he was not above using his looks and charm to get what he wanted. Case in point, the table next to where they sat had been reserved. But a few words to the hostess and Carter had been seated there just a few moments after Tilly and her date.

"You're the only man I know who women might pay to watch put clothes on," she said as he buttoned his jacket.

Carter grinned at her. It wasn't the same grin that he'd given the hostess. Carter never flirted with Tilly. Likely because soon after they met, he'd been assigned to marry her baby sister Brig. When Brig fell for and pursued another member of their unit, Carter had been reassigned to marry Tilly's twin sister Gunny. And so, because nothing could ever happen between them, Tilly and Carter became something else. They became friends.

It was their friendship that made Tilly feel the urge to hiss at each of the women looking at him. Not a verbal hiss like a cat. More of a visual hiss where she cut her eyes at them—like a cat.

Carter was taken. Not by her. By her sister.

Gunny would be thanking her lucky stars when she arrived home in a couple of days to exchange vows with the man.

When their father's will had been read a little over two months ago, and the Silver sisters had learned what they'd have to do to keep their home, each and every one of them had balked at the idea that they'd each need to hitch their wagons to a man to keep their childhood home. It had gone against everything their father had taught his six daughters. Lessons like you can do anything a man can do, and that includes building your own home.

To prove that lesson, the general had made each girl build a cabin on the ranch. The Silver sisters were no strangers to hammers, nails, and power drills. Now, all of a sudden, they each would need a man to keep what they'd built with their own hands?

It had made no sense. Until the six men of their father's unit had strode onto the ranch. As each Silver girl and President's Man teamed up, it appeared their strengths and weaknesses meshed into something that made the pair even stronger.

Except Tilly. She'd already been casually dating a couple of guys at the time. She was sure she could get one of them to marry her. Especially since

Truman, the sixth man of the unit, had no interest in holy matrimony.

Tilly hoped that Carter might be the glue to finally make her twin sister come home and stay for good. After all, Tilly looked forward to hanging with Carter each day, watching old movies and television shows, looking through magazines at fashion do's and don'ts, and people watching when they went into town.

"Hey, what do you think about them?" Carter nodded his head toward a couple in the corner of the restaurant. "First date? Or an old married couple?"

Tilly looked over at the two people Carter indicated. It was a silly game they played, one she loved. "Newlywed couple."

Carter looked at the couple anew. The pair leaned toward each other, not quite touching but near enough that they could. The man looked down at his dinner companion with total admiration. She looked up at him with patient amusement.

"Yeah," said Carter. "I think you're right."

Tilly was a good read of people. She could size up a person within the first five minutes of meeting them face to face, hence why she went on a lot of dates. Tilly had never wanted for male attention. She went out with a new guy each week. Sometimes two. Getting the first date was no problem. It was the second date she had trouble with.

People could easily hide behind their online profiles. But when they stood before her in real life, everything became crystal clear. Crystal clear that, most of the time, they'd been lying on their profiles. Tilly, and her razor-sharp internal lie detector, couldn't abide lying.

"You ready?" Carter held out his hand to Tilly. His fingers were immaculately groomed, clean, and cut in even half-moons.

His fingertips were also soft to the touch. Tilly knew that because he always offered her his hand when she was getting into or out of a car. She also knew his large hands spanned her waist because he'd helped her down from a horse a few times. She even knew the exact temperature of his palm because he'd rest it there whenever they crossed a street, and he switched sides with her, always making sure his body was between her and the street traffic.

It was old-world gentlemanly behavior, the kind her father told her a man should exhibit if they wanted to date her. Not one of her dates over the past couple of years had offered his hands in any of these manners. They mainly wanted to grope.

When Tilly took Carter's hand now, a tingle went to the center of her palm. It stayed there, sizzling and radiating warmth. The heat made her shiver.

"Cold?" Carter asked.

They had stepped out of the restaurant into the warm evening air. There were still rays of the sun in the sky. Her date with what's-his-face had been early in the evening. Tilly supposed she knew it would be a bust. Now her whole night wasn't spoilt.

She didn't answer Carter's question. She didn't want to lie and say that she wasn't cold. Not when she had already anticipated what his action would be. Not when she craved what he was about to do to her.

Sure enough, Carter tugged off his jacket. Tilly's gaze was riveted to the rippling of his muscles under that dark, fitted shirt. Then she was engulfed in his scent and body heat as Carter draped his jacket over her shoulders.

Vanilla mixed with citrus hit her nose like she'd walked in a garden of exotic plants. She felt drugged by Carter's scent. Her mind went to the scene in *The Wizard of Oz* when Dorothy and her crew walked through the poppy fields. That's what she felt like as Carter's heady scent filled her.

Tilly closed her eyes and breathed him in. She knew she had to be quick about it. She couldn't let Carter see the effect he had on her. They were friends. They were soon to be in-laws. Friends and siblings smelled each other. Right?

"Hey, look out," Carter shouted.

Tilly's eyes slammed open, guilt rising hot to her cheeks. She expected to see Carter glaring at her for what she'd been doing. But she was slammed into his chest.

All she saw was the dark color of Carter's shirt. Her gaze landed on a sliver of his exposed skin. She saw the beat of his pulse in his collarbone. She smelled that super sweet scent of him mixed with a musky note of aftershave. Men shouldn't smell like flowers. Tilly's belly grumbled even though it was full of steak and wine. She wanted to taste the salty-sweetness of him for dessert.

"Are you okay?" Carter wasn't looking down at her. His eyes were blazing as they looked after a group of kids on skateboards zooming down the sidewalk.

"Those idiots are going to hurt somebody," Carter growled

He still wasn't looking at Tilly. So she had a few more seconds to savor the feel of being in his arms. Of imagining that this was how her date would end, with a kiss from this man.

And then his gaze turned down to her. The anger was snuffed out like a match being blown out. But the flame was too strong, and it struck back to life. And this time, it burned brighter.

CHAPTER FOUR

Carter knew how to disassemble an M4 carbine rifle. He could do it in the dark with just the feel of his hands. In this moment, his hands couldn't figure out how to unlock their hold on Tilly's frame.

Instead of straightening and lifting off the woman, Carter's fingers clenched her to him. Instead of unlocking his arms and pulling away from her, Carter's muscles tensed, readying to tighten their hold.

Just like guns, Silver women were not toys. They were not meant to be played with. If one of them went off, people would get hurt.

Carter needed to disengage. He needed to step

back. The responsible thing to do would be to point Artillery Silver in a safe direction.

The problem was that her lips were within striking distance. For weeks he'd sat, stood, or walked close to her. The temptation had always been there. But he wasn't fool enough to act on it.

He was supposed to be marrying Brig, or Gunny, or one of the other sisters. But not her. It had never been Tilly. Even though the moment Carter had lain eyes on her, his heart had said *This One.*

Tilly had barely glanced at him on that day. Now he had her full attention. He knew that if he acted on what was in his heart, she would never speak to him again. That—her silence—he couldn't abide.

Still, his entire body ached to do it. To bend down and kiss her. But Carter stepped back.

He unlocked his hands. Then his arms. Finally, he managed to put space between himself and Tilly.

Instantly, he felt like he was crashing down into withdrawal. They had to get home soon, or his symptoms would become noticeable. Not that Tilly ever looked that closely at him. If she had, then she would not only see how he ached for her, she would also see the general ache in his bones when he was off his meds.

His hands were shaking with want of her, but mainly they shook as his body demanded another hit of his pain meds. He needed to get back to the ranch to get a dose in his system. He sometimes didn't think clearly between long stretches between pills.

"Sorry," Carter said. "I didn't mean to—"

"I wasn't paying attention—" Tilly said at the same time.

"You're alright?" Carter reached a hand out to her cheek. His fingers trembled in the space between them. He brought his hand back to his side.

"I'm good. You?"

Carter nodded. "We should probably head back and—"

"You want dessert?"

Carter couldn't finish his sentence. He choked on his words. Had she heard his thoughts? Did she know that the only thing he wanted to curl up with and sample were her lush lips?

"I have a craving for something sweet and salty," Tilly continued. "I want to satisfy that craving before heading back."

He could only stare. His green gaze latched onto her blue, and he swore he smelled scorched earth from the heat coming between them. But no, someone had just tossed a cigarette butt into the street.

"So, how about it?" Tilly asked.

Carter opened his mouth to shout yes. Yes, he wanted to satisfy his sweet and salty craving for her.

"How about some ice cream?"

Carter gulped down his desire. It stuck in his throat. "Sure."

That was the only word he could manage. He had to put all his energy into concentrating on walking. His whole body was on fire, the fire of an unfulfilled desire along with the fire of the need for his meds.

Carter pushed the fire of the withdrawal down. The longer he stayed in town, the longer he could be with Tilly. They wouldn't get this much time alone in a few days. Her sister would be coming, and then Carter would be beholden to the vows he promised to make to Tilly's twin.

They walked to the end of the block where an ice cream shop was. It was a quaint one-story shop, like most of the establishments in the small town square. Everything in the town was within reach. The grocer in the center of the square. The police station at the edge of the block. The courthouse right next to it.

It was the kind of place Carter had grown up in where everybody knew everybody. It's also why he was in no hurry to go back to the home of his birth. He didn't want anyone in his current business.

His parents would inevitably find his medications and question his use. It had been nearly a year since the incident. But pain would forever be his constant companion. Not the physical pain, something deeper. An ache in his very bones that never quite went away and pestered him in his sleeping and waking hours.

The men in his unit understood. That's why they asked no questions. His civilian parents wouldn't understand that. So it was better for him to stay on the ranch with a wife who would leave soon after their vows were stated.

It would be the perfect relationship. Not only because Gunny wouldn't hassle him over the pills. Because Carter would have an excuse to see Tilly every day.

Carter kept his hands to himself as he crossed the street with Tilly. He made sure to keep her on the inside of the sidewalk. Though he worried about the pedestrians on the walk as well, now that they'd almost been run over by a reckless kid on a skateboard.

His reactions had been slow after the blast that had taken his team down and killed the general. Carter had walked away with no limbs lost. But everything in him constantly ached. The doctors had prescribed a low-dose pain killer. Unfortunately, the pain kept creeping back. So Carter had doubled and now tripled the dosage. Looked like soon he'd have to make his daily pill regiment into quadruplets.

"I'm buying the ice cream," Tilly said as they came inside the establishment.

"Seeing as I'm a feminist," Carter pressed his hand to his heart, "I'll let you pay my way."

Tilly snorted. "I can't believe I lasted as long as I did on that date with a straight face. Do men really think like that?"

"I'll have you know that men are a very diverse breed of humans."

Again, Tilly snorted.

"Some of us even do our own laundry," Carter went on.

Tilly threw back her head and laughed. Carter didn't tell her that he still messed up his white and color loads sometimes. He'd let her believe some men were more evolved than they actually were.

"He was all wrong for you," Carter said. He didn't mention that most of the men Tilly chose from the dating app were wrong for her. It was as if she was purposefully not trying to get married. "He said his favorite movie was *Psycho*."

Tilly winced. "Yeah, it explained a lot. Son who killed his mother and then talks to her corpse." She tilted her head and looked off in the distance. "You know his shirt did look a bit feminine."

"You think it was hers?"

"She would probably approve."

The two of them bent over with laughter. A few of the customers in the ice cream shop turned to stare. Both Tilly and Carter shrugged at the outsiders who didn't get their inside jokes.

"Not everyone is a Cusack fan," Tilly said once she sobered. "Too bad you don't have a brother."

"I do," said Carter. "But he's into WrestleMania as a grown man."

Tilly looked horrified. She rested a hand on his shoulder. "I'm so sorry for your family."

Another laugh bubbled up through her elegant throat. This was Carter's favorite part of every day since he'd come to the ranch. Making Tilly laugh.

Seeing her smile. Having her ruin a movie for him as she talked over the dialogue. It was the highlight of his every day.

"Gunny isn't into movies," said Tilly. "Unless it's a wildlife documentary."

It took Carter a moment to comprehend what, and then, who a Gunny was. Right. His fiancée.

"She's more of a *National Geographic Special* kind of girl."

"Well, Morgan Freeman narrated *March of the Penguins.*"

Tilly smiled, and Carter was dazzled. It wouldn't be so bad marrying Gunny. Not if she had Tilly's face.

The shopkeeper handed over two cones to them. Tilly took a bite of her ice cream. The dollop brushed against her skin, leaving her a creamy beard. She giggled and began dabbing at her chin.

"You missed a spot," Carter said. "Here, let me…"

His hand was already moving before he could think better of the motion. His thumb reached her cheek. He didn't feel the cold of the ice cream. All he felt was the silky warmth of Tilly.

At the same time as he touched her, Tilly canted her head. Her tongue snaked out of her mouth and caught the same dollop of cream as his thumb.

When her tongue made contact with his thumb, shots were fired, and Carter's brain short-circuited.

Gone was the data on the woman he was supposed to marry. All he saw in front of him was the woman he was going to claim as his own. No matter what the fallout.

CHAPTER FIVE

Tilly had been coming to Castro's Creamery since she was a kid. Old Mr. Castro had fled communist Cuba before she'd been born. The dapper gentleman made his way to the Midwest, married a cowgirl, and opened this beloved shop where people came from miles to try his flavors.

Tilly made it a point to try each flavor at least once. And because Old Man Castro kept inventing new and inventive flavors, there was always something new to try. Today's special was Cereal Milk. As the creamy concoction touched her tongue, Tilly was transported to Saturday morning in front of the television with a bowl of Fruit Loops in her lap.

She'd been reveling in the fruity sweetness of

the ice cream when a few drops dribbled down her chin and met with Carter's thumb. It was a complete and total accident that her tongue brushed his thumb in its effort to lap up the cream that had dribbled from her lips. And like a cat who'd had one taste of sweet, frothy ambrosia, Tilly wanted to go back for more.

The first time had been a mistake… Hadn't it?

If she did it a second time, it would be on purpose… Which would be a bad thing, right?

But why would it be so bad? Tilly couldn't remember? However, she knew the reason that it was bad was important.

It couldn't be that to lick another person's thumb was bad manners. Carter's hand was still on her face. He hadn't pulled away. Which had to mean he didn't mind it the first time.

If he'd have minded, he would've told her so. He told her everything. Because they were friends.

But friends didn't use each other's flesh as a topping on a sundae. Right? She was only mildly sure that was a rule.

Maybe if she asked him really nicely, he'd agree to give her another taste.

They'd shared popcorn on their movie nights. Their fingers had touched in the bowels of the buttery goodness. Had that spice been there those times she'd popped kernels in her mouth?

When they'd been out at a bar the other night, and Carter had saved her from another disastrous date, she'd had a sip of his cocktail. Belatedly, she remembered that the drink had made her eyebrows raise to her hairline. It had to have been the same spicy kick.

So it had happened more than once already. What would one more time be? It was just a small thing between friends. Because that's what they were. Since he was going to marry…

Tilly let out a low sigh. Her shoulders slumped as she set the ice cream cone in a dish on their table-top. The realization of why she couldn't have another taste of Carter punched her in the gut where there had been nothing but sweetness and spice before.

Carter was going to marry her sister. He was going to be her brother. She couldn't want to eat ice cream out of her new brother-in-law's hand. That was highly inappropriate.

She needed to back off. She needed to put distance between them. She needed to remove her face from his hand so that the temptation was no longer there.

Wait?

Carter still hadn't removed his hand from her face. In fact, his thumb swiped at her chin, where the ice cream had dripped. The cream was gone, but Carter's thumb was still there.

His thumb wiped higher and higher. It brushed the flesh just under her bottom lip. It skated along the spot at the corner of her mouth where her bottom lip met her top lip.

Tilly held herself entirely still. She couldn't have another mishap with her tongue. The problem was Carter's thumb was coaxing her tongue out of her mouth, like a snake charmer playing a flute.

Did Carter know that that's what he was doing to her? He had to? He often anticipated her needs, like having a selection of DVDs of her favorite movies after a long day of chores. He sometimes completed her sentences. True, most of the time, she was quoting a movie. But he was always there with the punch line. Always there to say the thing she was thinking. Or sometimes not saying it but clearly thinking it and nudging her with his elbow until she giggled first.

Though Tilly had been born a twin, she had never had this kind of connection with her sister. Gunny was far too serious. She was always concerned about saving an endangered animal or plant. Gunny never sat back and watched life for its entertainment value.

Gunny often didn't get Tilly. Which meant Gunny would never get Carter. Because Carter was so very much like Tilly.

If Carter and Gunny got together, it would be a bad date that would never end because they'd be married. There would be no white dinner napkin thrown on the floor to save either of them. It would be a catastrophe.

Tilly knew what she had to do.

"You can't marry Gunny," she said at the same time as Carter said, "I can't marry Gunny."

Tilly glanced up into his eyes. What she saw there took her breath away. Carter's gaze was latched onto her face, roaming over her features with a familiarity that she had never felt with another person.

Carter's gaze was both soft and fierce at the same time. Wanting something but afraid to reach out and touch it. Tilly read his emotions easily because it was exactly how she felt.

She felt his pulse quicken because he still held her chin in his hand. She felt the slight tremor in his thumb as the tension increased between them. She felt a spark, a tingling as electricity zapped between them.

"Why?" Tilly asked him. "Why can't you marry my sister?"

Carter gulped. It wasn't a gulp of uncertainty or guilt. It looked as though he swallowed down a huge helping of desire. Tilly read the action easily because it was exactly what she was experiencing.

"Because you told me not to," he said.

"You do everything I tell you?" she asked, wanting him to say the real answer that she knew to be true because she heard it in her own heart. "Because I distinctly told you not to watch *The Matrix* sequels, and you did."

Carter chuckled, his caress on her face heating. Then his other hand joined until he was holding her steady in his grip. "I would do anything you tell me." He paused and then added, "From this moment on."

The admission sounded like a national security secret he was letting her in on. He was whispering to her, even though there were hardly any people in the ice cream shop. Old Man Castro had gone to the back after he'd handed over their scoops.

"If you tell me to marry your sister because you believe it's the right thing for her and for me, then I'll do it."

Now Tilly gulped. It wasn't a gulp of uncertainty or guilt. She was swallowing down a huge helping of desire, only to have more of the sensation fill her throat, her mouth. "I think it would be the right thing…"

Carter's head dipped low. Tilly couldn't help but grin. Even in this serious moment, she couldn't help riling him up.

"It would be the right thing for the ranch," she continued in a somber voice. "But it wouldn't be right for you. And it wouldn't be right for me."

Carter's head lifted, eyes shining bright with hope.

"I think I might be in love with you, Carter."

Tilly caught a flash of his grin before she was tasting it. Sweet, salt, spicy, and heat met her lips. Tilly gulped it down and took another taste. She was greedy for more.

She wrapped her arms around his neck and pulled him closer. He was sweeter than the ice cream. Sweeter than a bowl of the most sugary cereal. And it wasn't enough. She needed more of him.

A throat cleared. It had probably cleared more than once before Carter let Tilly go. It had to clear one more time before Tilly let Carter go.

Old Man Castro stood behind the counter. He raised a bushy brow at them. "This is a family-friendly place. You two take that outside."

There was no bite to his heavily accented words. Tilly had no problem following his instructions. She wanted to be alone with Carter so that she could indulge uninterrupted in her dessert dish.

CHAPTER SIX

As soon as they were out of the shop, Carter pulled Tilly to him again. He wrapped one arm around her waist and the other he used to capture her chin. He brought her to him and did what he'd wanted to do since laying eyes on her nearly three months ago.

He kissed her.

He kissed her like it was the first time.

He kissed her like it was the last time.

He kissed her like he had all the time in the world. Because now he did. He didn't have to deny or hide his feelings any longer. The freedom of being able to touch her without pretense made him dizzy. Or maybe that was the heady, rich taste of her.

Sugary breakfast pastry to zap him with energy in the morning and the last rays of sunshine before curling up for the night. That was what Tilly Silver tasted like to Carter.

When he broke away, she grinned at him. He grinned at her. They had spent weeks together with a never-ending commentary running between them. But for the first time in their acquaintance, they both were at a loss for words.

Carter tugged Tilly into an alleyway between the ice cream shop and the tailor shop. The work day was coming to a close. It wasn't quite five o'clock, but a few workers were sneaking out early. Not that the town had much of a rush hour. People probably were simply eager to get home to be with their families.

Looking down at Tilly, there was no place else that Carter wanted to be. He kept his hand cradled at the back of her head as he pressed her into the brick wall. He didn't press his suit or try for another kiss. He simply looked down at her. His expression was unguarded as he allowed her to see everything he'd been feeling for the past two-and-a-half months.

Had she said she loved him? Or had he imagined

that? He never would've dreamed that she would, that she could. But maybe his luck was finally changing.

"I don't have much, Tilly. Just a bunch of DVDs and a few VHS tapes. But everything that I have is yours."

"Hmmm," she hummed, toying with the top button of his shirt. "Would any of those DVDs feature one John Cusack?"

"I have *High Fidelity, Con Air, Serendipity*. The theatrical releases and the director's cut."

"So you plan to keep me up all night," she grinned, "watching all versions?"

The grin Tilly gave Carter nearly unmanned him. He felt his knees buckle under the weight of his desire for this woman. He wanted to cuddle under the sheets with her, allowing her total control over the television remote, and never leave.

"Marry me," was all he could say.

Tilly's grin softened. Tears pricked her eyes. Her lips moved, but no sound escaped.

"I'd say we should probably go on a date first, but I think that's what we've been doing these past two months."

She closed her mouth. She closed her eyes, but it

was too late. A sigh escaped her lips. A single tear fell from the corner of her eye.

"There's no one else for me but you. I know that for certain." Carter caught the tear, brushing it away. "I would've married your sister to save you and your family, but my heart would've always been yours."

Slowly, Tilly lifted her head. Gradually, her lashes lifted to reveal that startling blue. Haltingly, her lips parted, and she spoke. "Carter?"

"Yes, Tilly?"

"Would you have let me marry one of these jokers I've been dating?"

His grin was one part mischief, two parts caveman. He realized then that the only reason he had let—yes, *let*—her go on these dates was because he knew not one of those jokers had been in contention for her hand.

"I think either you or I would've kept sabotaging those dates," he said.

Tilly's lips quirked upward as though she finally realized the zero-sum game they'd been playing these last two months. Then she winced.

"What is it?" Carter looked around. "Is Clifton back?" Maybe her date had come back for his doggy bag?

Tilly's wince cleared in an instance. "Clifton? Right! That was his name."

The man that only his mother could approve of was not on the prowl. Then what was Tilly wincing about?

"No, it's not about him. It's Scout."

That was worse. Scout Silver was a force that Carter didn't want to reckon with. Tentatively, he peered out of the alley and looked in both directions. He didn't see the general's oldest daughter marching on the street.

"This will ruin her plan," said Tilly. "She's going to kill us."

Oh, that was her worry. If Carter was no longer on board to marry Gunny, that left them a man down. Right now, Carter didn't have the brain space to worry about that. He pulled Tilly to him. Now that he had the right to do this, he wasn't giving it up. Ever.

"The plan is still the same," he said. "The players have changed. We get married, and we'll find a guy for Gunny on the dating apps."

"Gunny will probably do it if she gets back in time. And if the man is not cruel to animals, environmentally conscious, and drives a hybrid." Tilly rested her head on his chest. "In the meantime, Scout will argue us down."

Scout could argue all she wanted. It wouldn't change a thing. Carter would not budge from his hard-fought position. Still, weariness hovered just over his skin like a cloak blowing in the wind.

It was late in the day. Carter should be feeling the full effects of being late for his medication dose. But all he felt was the warmth of Tilly. The rightness of her. This woman was the most powerful medication. She took away all of his aches and pains and worries. She was the only thing keeping both his symptoms and the side effects at bay.

A bell tolled, announcing the half-hour. Carter's attention went to the bell tower. It sat above the courthouse. When the bell came to settle, an idea had sprouted in Carter's mind.

"She can get mad," he said. "But if we're already married, there's nothing she can do about it."

Tilly lifted her head to meet his gaze. Carter tilted his head to the courthouse. Tilly followed the direction he indicated. Her brows lifted as understanding dawned.

She turned him, a grin on her face. He didn't need to ask if she was in. He saw it there in her eyes.

Carter held out his hand. Tilly took it. It was as if

she was already shouting *I do*. They stepped out of the alley and rushed across the street. The building would be closing in less than thirty minutes. They had to make it in time. Carter couldn't spend another moment without having Tilly as his wife.

CHAPTER SEVEN

Tilly looked up as she climbed the stairs to the courthouse. The classical style of the building screamed for the people by the people. The tall marble pillars that extended from ground to ceiling were imposing as they stood solitary and independent. Above the four pillars was an ornate roof of sharp angles that boasted of stability and longevity. The two pieces would fall without the other's support.

Tilly's steps faltered as she ascended the last step. Carter caught her elbow and brought her to him. She could've managed to right herself. She'd been standing on her own two feet all her life. But having the support and shelter of him beside her, surrounding her, Tilly knew she now wanted to be permanently attached to this man.

"Second thoughts?" Carter asked, brushing a strand of her hair out of her face.

One look in his eyes and she forgot her train of thought. All she saw was him. How had she ever seen any man but him?

"No," she said. "I'm not having second thoughts. I'm eager to make this official."

A grin split his handsome face. The divot at the top of his upper lip and the twin dimples on his cheeks fairly twinkled at her, beckoning her closer. Tilly couldn't help herself. She kissed him.

The sweetness from the ice cream was still on his bottom lip. It mixed with that heated spice she had accidentally tasted earlier, that taste that had finally brought her to her senses and lead them both to this inevitable conclusion.

"We have to hurry," Carter said, breaking the kiss far sooner than Tilly would've liked. "They're closing soon."

It was almost a quarter to the hour. It would be a miracle if they made it to the judge in time. Neither of them wanted to go back to the ranch without that marriage certificate as their armor.

It looked like they were in luck. Inside there

were hardly any people in the lobby. Most of the men and women ambling about were clearly workers headed home for the day. They had coats and purses slung over their shoulders and forearms and were headed for the exits.

Carter tugged Tilly to a desk occupied by a young man who was still busily typing. The title placard over his head read Clerk. The clerk's coat was slung over the back of the chair. An open brief-case sat at his feet. He tapped a key with his index finger definitively and reached up to the monitor of the computer as though he were about to turn it off.

"We're here to get married," said Carter.

"We're shutting down," said the clerk without looking up. He pressed the button, and the screen went black. "Best to come back tomorrow."

"We still have fourteen minutes," said Carter. He held up his cellphone and waved it under the clerk's nose. "It says on the city website that it can take as little as ten minutes to get married."

"It's quarter 'til," said the clerk, finally giving Carter his attention.

"Which means we have plenty of time," Carter grinned.

The clerk huffed, setting his mouth in a grimace

that screamed denial. But then his mouth went slack. "Tilly? Artillery Silver? Is that you?"

It took her a minute which was time they didn't have, but slowly Tilly recognized Ryan Burns. They'd dated in high school. Well, dated was a strong word. She'd gone out with Ryan a few Friday nights. But she'd also went out with his good friend Dave Graham a few Saturday nights. When they found out, they demanded she choose. She'd stopped dating them both and insisted they could all stay friends. Although this was the first time she'd seen him in years.

"Hi," Tilly said, waggling her fingers.

"He knock you up or something?" Ryan chucked his thumb at Carter.

Tilly set her mouth to say no, but then thought better of it. This was a shotgun wedding, but only because they were trying to avoid Scout aiming at the both of them. So she decided to stick as close to the truth as possible.

"If Scout finds out we're doing this now, she'll kill us. I'd like to die a married woman if it's all the same to you."

That piqued his interest. So much for staying friends after the breakup. He looked between the two. Whatever he decided, Tilly knew that the whole town would know about this before she and Carter made it back to the ranch tonight.

"All right," Ryan finally said. "Hand over your driver's licenses. I can get the paperwork, but I can't guarantee the judge will make time for it."

Ryan bent over, rifling through a drawer under his desk. Out of his view, Carter gave Tilly a fist bump. After her knuckles touched his they each opened their fingers wide and wriggled them like an explosion.

It was happening. She was just a few minutes away from being Mrs. Carter Shane. Tilly Shane. Artillery Shane. She liked the sound of it.

Two precious moments later, they'd finished filling out the paperwork and, with a loud thud of his official stamp, Ryan handed the document over. Tilly's fingers shook as she took the marriage license. The lightweight of the sheet felt heavy in her hands.

Carter took the other end as though to balance his share of the weight. The paper stopped shaking. Everything felt steady.

Once again, the feeling that this was the right thing swept over Tilly. It was rash, and it was sudden, but it was exactly the direction she wanted her life to go in.

"You'll need two witnesses for the ceremony," said Ryan.

Carter winced. Tilly knew what he was thinking. Even if they called their friends and family on the ranch -which they didn't want to do- none of them could get here in time.

Tilly glanced up at Ryan. "Would you mind?"

The guy she'd went out with a handful of Friday nights all the way back in high school smiled warily, but he nodded. Then his wary smiled turned down-right mischievous as he looked over Tilly's shoulder and raised his hand as though to get someone's attention.

"Mel, wait. Don't leave yet. You'll want to see this. Tilly Silver is getting hitched."

"Tilly Silver?" came a high-pitched voice filled with disbelief and a hint of disdain. But at least it was female and not male.

It wasn't another guy she'd dated. It was worse. It was the wife of another guy she'd dated. They hadn't been married at the time, thank all that was good and holy. Though Melanie might have been dating Al Hopper at the time. Tilly had never been sure. He certainly hadn't said so.

Melanie Hopper scratched at her jaw, using her

left hand. The diamond on her finger sparkled. She looked at Tilly's bare left hand and smirked.

"This I gotta see," Melanie said, her tone laced with superior scorn.

Tilly's lips hurt as she held onto her polite grin. She needed this woman's presence for the next five minutes. Her dislike was preferable to her sister's temper.

The unlikely bunch walked down the hall and knocked on the judge's door. Tilly wanted to urge them all into a fast trot. They had just under ten minutes left.

CHAPTER EIGHT

Carter held firm to Tilly's hand as they came up to the door of the judge's chambers. He gave her hand a tender squeeze. She turned and rested her chin on his shoulder. He wanted the world to stop while he gazed into those blue eyes.

"What is it, Burns?" A tall man with snowy white hair stood in the doorway to the chamber. "I was just headed out for a dinner date."

"Sorry, Judge Blair," said the clerk. "We have a last-minute request for a marriage ceremony."

"At this hour?" The judge looked past the clerk, and his snowy white brows rose to his hairline. "Tilly? Is that you?"

"Hello, Judge Blair. It's been a long time."

"I haven't seen you since your father's..." The

judge allowed that sentence to dangle as pain crept over both his and Tilly's features. "Well, I'm delighted to see you, dear girl. Are you dining with us tonight?"

"No." Tilly shook her head, tightening her grip on Carter's arm. "I'm here to get married."

Now those bushy brows over the judge's eyes drew together. His head canted as he took in Carter. Carter remembered the first time the general had looked at him. General Silver had an uncanny way of looking right into the heart of the men who served him. As though he could see past their qualities and any sins they might possess. The judge's assessment made Carter feel as though he were back on base, squirming in his combat boots.

"I thought Haran was performing ceremonies for you and your sisters," said Judge Blair.

"Not this time," said Tilly.

"What's the rush?"

"We're in love," Tilly said at the same time as the clerk stage whispered, "She's in the family way."

Tilly's cheeks heated, her lips pursing together. She didn't correct the guy who clearly still carried a torch for her. Carter had ignored the dig earlier when he'd thought it would hurry the process along.

Now, he worried the incorrect assumption might bite them both in the shins.

"You took advantage of this little girl, son?"

The judge's eyes were laser-focused on Carter. Even though he was being accused of something he hadn't done, Carter felt as though he was standing directly in the fire. Sweat broke out at his temple and under his armpits.

"No, Judge Blair," said Tilly. "I took advantage of him."

There was a slight cooling sensation as all gazes went to her.

"Not in the way you think," she said. "He was going to marry my sister."

The brief cooling period was followed by another flash of heat. More heads came out of office doors. People stopped in their strides toward the exit and lingered to listen.

"But then we realized we're perfect for each other," Tilly continued.

"Which sister was he going to marry?" asked the judge.

"Brig," said Carter, at the same time as Tilly said, "Gunny."

Carter wondered if there was any central heating and cooling in this building. His fingers were chilled to the bone while his chest was dripping with sweat. He wanted to get out of his clothes. He wanted to get out from under the judge's glare.

"None of that matters," said Carter. "What matters is I love her, and she loves me. And we want to get married, sir."

The judge stared between the two. The court-house workers looked between the judge and the couple with bated breath. The clock on the wall ticked toward the new hour.

"If this is really that important to you and you're truly in love," said the judge, "then there's no harm in waiting."

Carter felt Tilly's shoulders deflate. They'd have to go home and face her sister. It would be tough, but they'd get through it.

"It's all right," Carter said to her. "We'll come back tomorrow morning."

"No," said the judge. "You can come back in two months."

"Two months?" both Carter and Tilly said at the same time

"That's my decision," said Judge Blair.

"There's no rule that says we have to wait that long," said Tilly.

"To the contrary, I'm making sure that no rules

are being broken," said the judge. "I heard a disturbing report that you Silver girls were abusing the institution of marriage to cheat an inheritance."

Both Tilly and Carter opened their mouths to deny it. Though they were in love, and each and every one of the general's daughters had eventually fallen in love with one of his President's Men, that was technically true.

But how could the judge know such a thing?

As if in answer to Carter's silent question, the clack of heels coming toward them sent a shiver down his spine. He turned and saw a familiar face.

Carter didn't know much about General Silver's ex-wife. The man had rarely spoken of her. But Carter had heard the general speaking to her over the phone on more than one occasion.

Speaking was putting it lightly. When the general spoke to his former wife, Catherine, he was often yelling. His normally calm features reddening, and the hairs of his buzz cut on end from scrubbing his fingers through his hair.

When Carter had come to the ranch months ago, he hadn't heard Catherine's name mentioned by the Silver girls.

Or so he thought.

Cruella was the name the Silver sisters gave to their step mom.

When Carter had met Mareen a couple of weeks ago, he'd seen a shade of her mother in Mareen's cold attitude. Though he could barely reconcile the ice princess Mareen had been a few weeks ago with the rosy-cheeked, smiling woman she was now.

Carter felt Tilly's hands go cold the moment she saw her stepmother. Even before he'd agreed to make her his wife, he'd put himself before anything that threatened her happiness. Which was why he'd insisted on tagging along on her dates. But now, just the act of wanting to marry him could be used against her. He had to do something to protect the woman he loved.

So, like any fool who thought he was Prince Charming, he threw himself into the wicked witch's path.

"Mrs. Silver."

The older woman's back stiffened. "It's Ms. Chesterfield."

She didn't turn to face him. All Carter got was her profile. Just that partial look was enough to freeze a glacier and, at the same time, melt an iceberg.

"My apologies, ma'am."

Another blast of chilly air went through the room at the use of the word ma'am. Carter wondered if he could put a right foot forward with the woman.

"I worked with your husband—"

"Ex. Husband." Her voice was clipped enough to separate the hyphenated word into two.

"His dying wish was to do what was best for his daughters."

Now Catherine turned to face him. Carter flinched under the weight of her glare. He felt Tilly standing beside him, offering her strength and support. He'd faced down men with automatic rifles, but he hadn't felt truly afraid for his life until this singular foe.

"You should know that Wilson loves your daughter," Carter said. "Mareen is very happy."

"My daughter's future has been ruined because a down on his luck, washed up soldier, with no name and no money has her living in a dirt cabin all so he and the rest of you can pick over my ex-husband's remains."

"That's not what happened, and you know it," said Tilly.

"No?" Catherine turned her attention to Tilly.

Instinctively, Carter shifted to block the icy chill

from reaching the woman he loved. But he couldn't help the shiver in his bones reminding him that he was past due for his medication.

"So I'm mistaken in believing the only way the ranch will pass to you girls is if you get married?" Catherine asked with a false note of innocence.

Tilly opened her mouth and shut it. That was the truth of the matter. But it wasn't the dirty plot that Catherine was making it out to be.

"Exactly," Catherine said, taking the judge's arm. "You're all marrying under false pretenses to steal my dearly departed husband's property from me."

"Dearly departed?" Tilly sputtered. "You hated my father."

Something crossed over Catherine's features. It was there and gone in an instant before Carter could make out the emotion. If it had been an emotion.

"What I hate are lies and deception," Catherine said. "And that's what you girls are engaging in. I won't allow what you're doing to put a stain on Abe's name. Despite our differences, he was a good man. He would turn over in his grave if he knew what his men were doing to his daughters."

Now it was Tilly holding Carter back. Those men Catherine was disparaging were all good and brave soldiers who had risked their lives to save the general. Not only that, they'd each kept their promise of checking in on the general's daughters after his death. By all looks of it, Catherine hadn't done that once in her ex-husband's absence.

Judge Blair glanced between the three of them. The onlookers moved their mouths wordlessly as though they were eating popcorn at the movie theaters.

"These are serious allegations," said the judge. "Out of respect for your father, I won't bring this into chambers immediately. But I'll be by to talk with you and your sisters soon."

With that stay of judgment, Judge Blair led Catherine down the hall. Catherine shot them a cruel smirk of certain victory as she and the judge walked out the exit.

The license in Carter's hand wouldn't be put to use today. The judge might call all of their marriages into question depending on how Catherine whispered lies into his ear. They thought they'd get an earful with their marriage from Scout. Now everything might be in jeopardy.

CHAPTER NINE

The truck came to a slow stop in the driveway of the ranch. Tucked safely in the passenger seat, Tilly could see the lights on in the dining room. She could hear the laughs of the couples inside. Once she and Carter stepped out of the truck and inside the house, all joy would cease.

Carter put the car in park and cut the engine. Neither of them made a move to unstrap their safety belts. It was as though they both knew the real ride was still in motion, and things were about to get bumpy.

When Carter's hand found hers, Tilly should've felt like she could take on the world. Instead, she only wanted to stay inside the vehicle where they were together. Where a woman who was meant to love her and her sisters like daughters would be giving her advice for her wedding night, not trying to prevent it from ever happening.

Tilly didn't have a lot of memories of her stepmother, Catherine. What memories she did have were of a woman too beautiful to be real glaring down at her. Catherine rarely smiled. The few times Tilly had seen the expression, it had brought her nightmares.

Catherine would've melted the Wicked Witch with one of her grins. Her smile would've poisoned the Wicked Queen without the apple. Instead, her Wicked Stepmother was intent on locking all of the Silver girls, her own daughter included, away from their princes.

"Everything will be alright," said Carter.

Tilly heard his words. She felt the warmth of his fingers as they squeezed hers. She also felt a tremor in his hand.

Carter's words sounded a little slurred. He often sounded that way when it was late at night. He shivered a lot, too, during the cooler nights. She supposed his body temperature always ran colder, but he was always warm whenever she'd managed to rest her head against his shoulder and cuddle up next to him.

Tilly realized she wouldn't need any more pretext to cuddle up next to him. He was going to marry her. He loved her. Pretty soon, they might be cuddling up in this car because they'd be homeless. But it would be worth it.

"You know what you need?" said Carter.

"What?" Tilly asked.

Carter brought her hand to his lips and brushed a kiss across her knuckles. "Shakabuku."

Tilly snorted a laugh at the silly, made-up word that she knew so well.

"You know what that is, don't you," Carter grinned. "A swift, spiritual kick to the head that alters your reality forever."

"Did you just quote Martin Blank from *Grosse Pointe Blank* to me?"

"It seemed fitting," he kissed each of her fingertips.

"Wow. I am so in love with you."

Carter grinned. "That's good because we might be headed head over heels in the bad way when your sister gets her hands on us."

"It's not our fault," said Tilly. "Though we probably made it worse."

"Yeah."

Carter brushed his thumb over her lower lip.

Tilly would much rather stay in the truck and let him kiss her silly. They both looked at the lights in the house. Still, neither moved to unbuckle their seatbelt.

"You know, technically, this is Mareen's fault," said Tilly.

"You have a point there," Carter agreed. "It's her mother that's causing trouble."

"If Mareen had just married Steven—"

"I think his name was Stephán."

"—then her mother would have no reason to come to the ranch. In fact, Catherine would be none the wiser."

"You make a very valid point."

"I know, right?"

"Beauty and brains."

"You're a lucky guy."

"That, I am."

Tilly leaned over the console. Carter met her halfway. With her lips pressed to his, she felt like she could conquer the world.

Yes, kissing was far better than facing her sister. What was that saying? Making love, not war. Such good advice.

"What the heck is going on here?"

Tilly and Carter broke apart at the sound of

Scout's voice. Tilly felt like she was back in high school and had been caught necking with a boy. In fact, hadn't she gone parking with Ryan Shane? And Al Hopper?

Man, karma was not her friend today.

"I can explain," said Carter, unbuckling his belt and getting out of the car.

Tilly knew she should follow him. She reached for the button of her safety belt. With a press of her thumb, she was free of the belt. However, with one look at Scout's face Tilly held the freed strap in place, so it looked like she was still strapped in. This ride was about to surpass bumpy and get downright treacherous.

"You bet you will explain," Scout was saying. "Explain why you're kissing one sister when you're supposed to marry another."

"Didn't this whole scenario just play out last week?" said Truman from the porch.

He stood next to Jackson, who leaned heavily on his walking cane with one hand while the other was wrapped around Brig. Brig and Jackson grinned at each other. Then they turned their attention back to the show in the parking area.

"I'm in love with Tilly," Carter said.

"Told ya," said Brig. She reached out her hand to

Truman, making a come hither motion. Truman reluctantly handed over a bill. Then he gave Carter a scathing look.

"My bride is the smartest of the bunch," said Jackson, looking adoringly at Brig. "Never bet against her."

"Now that Tilly and Carter are settled, that just leaves Gunny and Truman," said Brig.

"Nope," was the only sound Truman made before he leaped off the porch and blended into the night.

"Artillery?"

Tilly turned her attention from the spot where Truman had disappeared to the place Carter was standing. It was dangerous territory as he was faced off with her sister. Scout did not look in the slightest amused.

"A little help here?" said Carter.

Right. Tilly was still in the truck while he was facing off against her sister. Honestly, Tilly liked her spot. It was warm in the cab of the truck. Nicely upholstered seating. That safety belt that only needed to be refastened to hold her steady. And there was also that lovely key in the ignition that would help her make a fast getaway.

Unfortunately, she couldn't do that. She couldn't leave Carter behind to face her family. They were in this together. And so, Tilly took a deep breath and climbed out of the truck.

"You love him?" said Scout.

Tilly nodded, not sure of her voice.

Scout raised her head skyward and shook her head. She took in a deep breath, filling her lungs as though preparing for a long, loud lecture. But when she lowered her head, she let out a sigh and opened her arms.

Tilly didn't hesitate. She went into her big sister's arms. She took all the comfort Scout was willing to give at this moment. Because, even though Tilly had braced for a hurricane of emotions, she knew this was still the calm before the storm.

"We have bigger problems," said Carter.

Tilly wanted to glare at the man she loved. She wasn't ready to have her peace doused. But they'd stalled long enough.

"When we went to the courthouse to get married..." Carter began but broke off abruptly. His body shivered as though the memory was physically painful to him.

"You what?" Scout's embraced turned painful as she pulled away enough to glare down at Tilly.

"Our stepmother was there," Tilly picked up where Carter had left off. "Catherine's trying to convince the judge that all of our marriages are fake. That we're trying to pull a scam. If Judge Blair believes her, we might lose the ranch, anyway."

The rest of her sisters and their husbands had all gathered on the porch. Everyone looked around at each other with worry and fury on their faces. Tilly turned to Carter, but he was doubled over as though in pain.

"Carter? Are you okay?"

CHAPTER TEN

Carter felt like he was underwater. He felt like he was in a tub of boiling water. But he was still freezing cold.

He tried to move his feet to propel him out of the depths. He tried to reach his arms over his head to break the surface. But his entire body felt weak, weary, and worthless.

He was tired. So tired. He knew that if he just rested for a moment, he'd be able to gather his strength and try again.

He had to try again. He had to break free. There was a very important reason for him to be free.

"Carter? Are you okay?"

Tilly. That was his reason. His reason for waking

up. His reason for dreaming. His reason for breathing.

He had to break free of what was holding him so that he could hold her. She needed him to hold her, to be there for her. None of the men she met on those apps were even half as qualified as him for the job.

Except, Carter couldn't even lift a finger, he couldn't even move a toe to get to her.

Because he was drowning.

Not in water.

Not in cold.

He was trapped inside of himself. The only thing that would set him free was another dose of his pain meds. The same meds that were holding him hostage now.

"What's wrong with him?" came Tilly's urgent voice.

Were her words accompanied by sobs? He'd never heard her sob before. The sound broke the hold the withdrawal had on him. He tried to reach for her. But just like her voice sounded far away, her entire body was far away.

He was being lifted. Carried away. Away from her.

No. He couldn't let that happen. He tried to fight, but he was being held down.

Strong arms caught his feeble attempts to get free. They weren't Tilly's arms. He knew that for certain. They were bigger, rougher, and a bit hairy.

"I've got him," came Wilson's grizzly bear of a deep voice.

"Let's move him to the cabin," came Linc's directive.

"I'm coming too," Carter heard Tilly say.

He couldn't make out who told her to stay back or the argument that ensued. The only thing Carter heard clearly as he was being carried away was Tilly sob again as she said, "I'm going to be his wife."

"Just give us a second," said Jeff. "It's an old injury. He won't want you to see him like this."

Carter heard the door shut. And then silence. Linc and Wilson were speaking to him. He didn't hear Tilly's voice. Without the sound of her voice, nothing else mattered.

Well, nothing but the pounding in his head. The shivers that made him feel both hot and cold at the same time. His labored breathing where he felt like he couldn't gulp down enough air to fill his lungs. He had never let it get this bad.

"Where are they?" Wilson demanded.

Carter didn't pretend to misunderstand. "Under the mattress."

He heard Wilson's heavy boots on the floor. Then the creak of the mattress. Finally, the twisting pop of the cap coming off the medicine bottle.

A glass of water was pressed in one hand. A pill in the other. Carter wanted to tell his friends that he needed more than a single pill, but one would suffice for now.

The relief was near instant as the synthetic opioid dissolved onto his tongue, into his bloodstream, down to his very soul. His breathing returned to normal. The pounding in his head ceased. The fog retreated from his brain.

When his vision cleared, Carter saw his friends staring at him. There wasn't judgment on their faces. They each knew what he had gone through in combat to bring him here. Each of them had taken this pain reliever at some point in their military career.

Linc should still be on the medication for his TBI, but he'd declined any more refills before he was discharged. Wilson had only taken it during surgery. Jackson had come off it not too long ago. As far as he knew, Carter was the only one still reliant on the meds.

"Did you tell her?" asked Wilson.

"No, I didn't," said Carter. "There's no need because I'm going to quit."

He'd determined that the moment he'd tasted the sweetness of Tilly's lips. He'd suffer through any pain if that was his reward. He'd just needed to get through that last bout of withdrawal. This would be his last dose.

When he looked up, he was met with silence from his friends. They didn't even bother to glance at each other. They only stared at him. Still no judgment.

In the military, doing hard drugs was a no-no. Soldiers couldn't get away with it with the frequent drug tests they had to undergo. Besides, it would be disastrous to be under the influence when your life, the lives of your buddies, and innocents were on the line.

Pain medication was a different story.

"I'm going to quit," Carter said again. "For her."

"Fine," said Linc. "Then you won't mind if I take these." He held up the bottle of his meds.

Carter wanted to tell his friend that that wasn't his only bottle. He didn't need to. He was quitting. So he nodded.

"Search the cabin for another bottle," Linc said to Wilson.

Wilson was already moving before the full sentence was out of Linc's mouth. Wilson was a bloodhound. Carter knew the man would find his stash. And so Carter said nothing. Because he was serious about quitting.

"Withdrawal is going to suck," said Linc. "But it won't kill you. You've got a good twenty-four to thirty-six hours before the withdrawal symptoms kick in. You need to tell her by then."

Linc was wrong. If Carter had been taking the recommended dose, he would've had that much time. These days, if he didn't have his tripled dose, he would be feeling the withdrawal again in hours.

Already, he'd been without his normal dose all day, and it had hit him this hard. How was he going to make it through the night without another hit? But worse, how was he going to face Tilly and tell her this secret he'd been keeping from her?

CHAPTER ELEVEN

"What are we going to do about Cruella?" said Scout.

Tilly nearly voiced aloud that she could not care less about their wicked stepmother. Catherine could swoop down on her broomstick right now with a legion of flying monkeys, and Tilly wouldn't care. All she wanted to do was to get back to Carter.

In all her weeks of knowing the man, she'd seen him sluggish in the morning, irritated under the afternoon Montana sun, and drained as the moon rose high in the late night. But Tilly had never once seen Carter unresponsive.

It had been as though he couldn't speak. As though he couldn't coordinate his movements. As though he wasn't himself.

She'd reached for him, tried to hold on to him. But the weight of him had been too much for her. She'd had to relinquish her hold to his friends. And then they'd shut her out. Physically shutting the cabin door in her face.

Tilly had grown up with a house full of sisters who had each other's back without questions. A neighboring ranch filled with strong men who would back them up if they sent up their secret call. But for the first time in her life, Tilly felt utterly alone.

She wanted to march back over to the cabin, but she felt drained. Inside her chest, her heartbeat had slowed. Her throat ached. But from somewhere, she felt a soothing balm making its way through her.

Looking up, Tilly saw Mareen. Her sister's hand was stroking her back and offering comfort. Tilly had expected that comfort to be coming from Saylor, the peacemaker of the family. Mareen, who had been an outsider of the Silver clan nearly all her life, was still finding her footing now that she was inside the household.

"I'm surprised that Wicked Witch didn't swoop in on her broomstick already," Scout was saying.

"Scout, be nice," said Saylor.

"What?" asked Scout, her blue gaze blazing with

indignation before they landed on Mareen. "Oh, no offense, Mo."

"None taken," said Mareen, her attention still on Tilly. "Not if my mother is planning to do what I think she's planning to do."

"What do you think she's up to?" asked Saylor.

"She's going to try and convince the authorities that we're all pulling a scam. If she can get the judge to believe it, then he'll call for an investigation."

"But we have nothing to hide," said Brig. "All of our marriages were for love."

"True," said Mareen. "But they didn't start that way. I'm not sure what Stephán told her, but she could probably use that against us too."

Mareen and her former fiancé had appeared to part on good terms. But Stephán had taken the long drive with Catherine back into the city. Tilly was sure that ordeal was enough to turn the man's good-will to bad.

Tilly couldn't focus on Mareen's old fiancé. She was too busy worrying over her own. She couldn't see any movement in the cabin. She turned to Jackson, who sat in his wheelchair, his walking cane balanced on his knees.

"What injury does Carter have?"

Jackson pursed his lips. He rolled his cane over

his knee as though pushing out the pain of his injury. "He should tell you that himself."

"He tells me everything," said Tilly. "But he never told me about this. Is he dying? Is it cancer?"

"It's not cancer." Jackson rolled the cane back up his thigh.

"Then what?"

Jackson wouldn't meet her gaze. "He should tell you himself."

Tilly didn't need her degree in animal nutrition to know that she was being fed a load of crap. Jackson knew something. They all did. And the fact they wouldn't tell her, let her know that it was bad.

Before Tilly could interrogate the only soldier in the house, his backup arrived. Linc and Wilson came in through the back door. Their faces were stoic, revealing nothing.

"What's wrong?" said Tilly. "Is he okay?"

"He's fine," said Linc. "He's resting now."

"Tilly, where are you going?" said Scout.

"To check on my fiancé."

Tilly was already at the backdoor. Scout slipped her body between Tilly's hand and the knob before Tilly could reach it.

"What?" Tilly didn't bother trying to hide the annoyance in her voice.

Scout had an inch over Tilly. That used to matter to Tilly, adding to Scout's arsenal as an authority figure. Now Tilly was ready to shove her sister aside, extra inch and all.

And just to imagine, she'd been fearful of her sister finding out that she was getting married only an hour ago. Now Tilly didn't care what anyone thought. She should be with Carter. What injury could he possibly have that would make him nearly pass out? She'd known him for two months and never seen any symptoms. Had she?

"If you go, I want you back here by ten," said Scout.

"What?" Tilly repeated. Her annoyance was gone this time. It was replaced with confusion.

"You're not spending the night with that man."

"That man is going to be my husband."

"He's not yet. I won't have any shenanigans going on under this roof. Especially not now with our stepmother breathing down our necks."

"Shenanigans? Who are you? Donna Reed all of a sudden? It's not the first time Carter and I have spent the night together."

"Yeah, but you were watching movies." Scout's gaze narrowed. "You were just watching movies?"

"Saylor and Jeff spent the night together before they got married," said Tilly.

"Yes," agreed Saylor. "But all we did was sleep."

"Look, Carter isn't feeling well. I'm going to go and look after him, which will be a part of our marriage vows."

"Are you really going to marry him?" asked Scout.

That drew Tilly up short. "What are you implying?"

"Just that you have a bad track record with commitment."

The room of opinionated sisters fell silent. The tension grew thick.

"Two months ago, you were going to marry Sergei from the dating app," said Scout, holding up her hand and raising her thumb.

Tilly got a bad feeling in her stomach that it was her thumb that her sister raised. Normally if someone were making a point, they raised their index finger. Because Scout had started with her thumb, it indicated that she had more than one point to make.

"Last week, you swore some guy named David would make the perfect temporary husband. A couple of weeks ago, it was a Sean. Before that—"

"Enough." Tilly drew herself up to her full height to face her sister. Somehow, with the moral high ground, it seemed Scout had a good two inches on her now. "Do you know the only constant with all of those guys? Carter. Every time I went on a date, I always came back and told Carter about it. Or discussed the guy with him before. I realize now that it was his attention that I wanted. Now I have it, and I want to keep it. I've never felt like this before, Scout, and I don't want to lose it."

Scout took a slow inhale as she regarded her. Tilly tilted her chin. She wasn't above bodily removing her sister if it came to that.

"Scout," said Linc, "let your sister go and speak with her fiancé alone."

Linc wasn't a man of many words. He also didn't bother to try and boss Scout around. He seemed more interested in simply watching her go about the day as she took charge of anything and anyone around her. This was the first time Tilly could remember him making a demand of his wife.

"The two of them need to talk," Linc continued, coming closer to his wife. He leaned down and whispered in her ear. "I need you to come remind me of something."

Linc pressed a kiss to her earlobe. Scout's

eyelashes fluttered. With a second kiss, she sighed and melted into her husband's arms.

"Thank you," Tilly mouthed to Linc.

Scout reached out her hand before Tilly could grab the doorknob. "Tilly, just know if you change your mind, it's going to hurt us all."

"Gee sis, thanks for your vote of confidence."

"We're your family. We'll always be here for you. Marriage, despite how our parents did it, should mean forever."

That was just it. Tilly didn't like the idea of a forever without Carter. Scout moved her hand from the door. Tilly turned the knob and dashed out.

"Congratulations, Tilly," Saylor called behind her. The belated sentiment was echoed by her other sisters. Tilly barely paid them any mind. She was more focused on getting to Carter.

CHAPTER TWELVE

Carter heaved a heavy sigh, letting his forehead fall into his hands. The medication was in his system. Like a car that had been running low on gas, now that his tank was refilled, the engine of his heart revved in his ears. His blood rushed through his head, lubricating his thoughts and giving him back his sense of clarity. The heat from all his sensors now firing cooled his skin and calmed his nerves.

All should be right with the world. Except it wasn't. Carter knew the high he felt wasn't about the turn his life had taken with regards to his personal life. His racing heart had nothing to do with the woman who owned it. It was all due to the medication.

Before tonight, he wouldn't have cared where the relief came from, only that it came. He spent so many of his waking hours in pain that any relief was welcome. His movie nights with Tilly had been a source of relief. His helping her with her daily chores around the ranch had offered relief as well. But to do those tasks, to be witty when they watched a film, to remember the details of what they spoke of, Carter needed his daily dose.

Wilson had found Carter's secret stash. But he hadn't found all of it. Carter held a handful of pills in his palm.

He stared down at the pills. He knew he couldn't hold on to the pills if he wanted to hold on to Tilly. It was an easy decision.

Or at least it should have been.

What if Carter couldn't be the man Tilly loved without the pills? She had only ever known him when he was on the medication. Maybe to have her, he needed to have the pills as well?

"Carter?"

Carter shoved his hand behind his back at the sound of Tilly's voice. She stood framed in the doorway, her beautiful face highlighted by the moon. Her blonde strands looked like moonlight. Her bright blue gaze in contrast to the dark sky.

Carter ached to touch her. But he couldn't. His hands were full of pills.

"Are you okay?" Tilly's steps to him were tentative. They had never been before. She'd never hesitated to come up to him, to sit down next to him.

"I'm fine." Carter clenched his fists. The pills in his palms ground against each other. The sound was like fireworks in his head. Could she hear them too?

"Then tell me what's going on?" Tilly closed the distance between them.

Carter reached for her. Then he drew his hands back to his side, his right hand still clenched in a fist with a handful of dirty little secrets inside.

"What injury?" Tilly looked his body up and down, searching for signs of a wound she would never see.

Carter shoved his hands in his pocket, depositing the pills there. When he pulled his hands from his pocket, he could feel a bit of the chalky stains on his palm. He rubbed his hand against his pants leg. Some of the residue stained the fabric. But Tilly wasn't looking down. She was looking him straight in the eye.

"Where are you hurt?" she asked, taking another of those tentative steps toward him. "And why didn't you tell me?"

Carter had never had to explain this to anyone. The guys all got it, and none of them questioned his need for the pain meds. Though he had increasingly felt their concern as the months had gone by.

How to explain this to someone who never had to keep going through the pain and residual effects of combat because their life depended on it?

"I was injured," he began. "Then they put me on medication to help me heal."

There was just an inch between them, but it felt like a gulf. Tilly waited, blue eyes trusting as she looked at him. Carter didn't want the next words out of his mouth to be *I'm a drug addict.*

Because he wasn't a drug addict. This medication was prescribed by the military. It was helping him.

Though he didn't need it anymore. Not now that he had her. He would flush those pills down the toilet and go through withdrawals and what may come.

"I had a bad reaction to the medication," Carter continued. That wasn't a lie. But it did keep the uglier part from her. "There may be a few more bad reactions until it's out of my system."

"Do you need to see a doctor?" She reached out to him, but her fingers only managed to traverse half of the inch between them.

"No." Carter caught her fingers in his hand, bringing them to his heart. The organ leaped at her touch, proving it was Tilly that it beat for and not the meds. "It's just flu-like symptoms. Nothing to worry about, I promise."

"What can I do?" She brought her other palm to his face, cupping his chin. Everything in his mind cleared out, leaving behind only thoughts of her, proving that it wasn't the meds that brought him clarity. It was her.

"Watch *Say Anything* with me."

The concern that had been written all over her features leeched from her face. Carter couldn't bite back his mischievous grin.

"Really? Really, Carter?" Tilly snatched her hands from his chin and chest. She put them both on her hips in the cutest sign of indignation he'd ever seen.

"It would make me feel better," he said.

Carter wrapped his arms around her waist and tugged her to him. She didn't resist. She did pout.

Tilly blew out a sharp breath. "Okay, fine. But the first time I have the flu, we are watching *The Grifters*."

Carter should want to groan at the thought of watching the John Cusack film about con artists. There was hardly a love story in it. It didn't matter.

He had his own real-life love story playing out before him.

"Hey?" he said, resting his forehead against hers.

"Yeah?" she said, wrapping her arms around his neck.

"I'm going to marry you," he whispered.

"I know," she said with a grin.

"You still okay with that?"

"Depends. Can we watch *Con Air* instead of *Say Anything?*"

"Not on your life."

Tilly giggled, and it was the sweetest sound Carter had ever heard. He led her to the couch and then pulled her down with him, tucking her into his chest. Then he grabbed the remote and thumbed through the streaming app until he found *Grosse Point Blank*.

Her sigh of happiness let him know he made the right decision. Besides, he was in the mood to watch a hitman return to his hometown to fight for his true love while leaving a body count along the way.

"What happened to your pants?" Tilly asked, brushing at the white stain on his thigh. "Did you spill something on them?"

"It's fine." Carter grabbed a blanket and tossed it

over both their legs, hiding any trace of the medication. "Hush now, the movie's starting."

CHAPTER THIRTEEN

There was a throbbing in Tilly's skull. The kind where she'd slept wrong all night and would need to down a couple of aspirin alongside a jug of coffee to feel halfway right for the day. The crick in her neck begged her to roll her head and pop some of the tendons.

She didn't. She couldn't. Tilly had no desire to move from the warm, soft spot she was in. In fact, she shifted her body until she was even more dug into the uncomfortable, spine crunching, neck bending position. She inhaled deeply and smelled the sweet citrusy scent of Carter.

Not for the first time, she wondered how such a manly man could smell so delicate and pull it off?

Because Carter did. There were vanilla notes to his scent. A touch of cocoa and a hint of mint. It reminded her of poppy flowers.

There was a patch of them in the northern pasture that grew like weeds. They made sure and kept the horses away from that bit of land as the flowers were dangerous to the animals if consumed in large quantities. But they were still pretty to look at and lovely to smell.

Whenever Tilly went out there, she imagined herself as Dorothy from *The Wizard of Oz* falling to sleep in the poppy field. Instead of a lion, tinman, or scarecrow, she had her very own Prince Charming in her arms. Not even the Wicked Witch could tear her from this dream.

The problem was that her stepmother was trying to rain down on her happily ever after. So Tilly peeled open one eye. When she did, she had not a single regret because the waking world was better than the dream one.

She was lying in Carter's arms. Her head rested against his chest. When she tilted her head to look up at him, her nose brushed the warm flesh of his neck. Even from this angle, Carter Shane was a beautiful man.

His hair was mussed from a night cuddling on the couch. His lips were parted, a slight snore rattling from his nose. It wasn't irritating. It was entirely darling. Just like the man.

Unfortunately, the throbbing in her head was still there. It was actually getting louder and three-dimensional. When Tilly lifted her head from Carter's chest, she realized it wasn't her head that was pounding. It was the door.

"You two had better be decent," called Scout's voice from the other side of the front door.

Both Carter and Tilly groaned, pulling the covers over their head. The sound of the door creaking open was muffled from under the threadbare sheet. The light of the new day shone through. A dark shadow cast over them in the form of Scout, who promptly yanked the sheet from them.

"Good," said Scout. "Still fully dressed."

Tilly and Carter had fallen asleep sometime after the end of *Say Anything* and near the beginning of *Con Air*. Tilly had woken in the middle of the night and retrieved the blanket. She hadn't wanted to wake Carter to move to the bedroom. Besides, they'd fallen asleep many times on this couch. Though last night had felt different.

Last night there had been many stolen kisses between the movie scenes. Last night, they had laced their fingers together with a tightness that had no space for friendship. Last night they had held onto each other with the knowledge that this was how they would spend the rest of their lives together. Today was the first day of the rest of her life with this man. Tilly wanted to get started on forever.

"Scout, go away," Tilly said, curling her fingers into Carter's shirt.

"It's past sun up, and there are still chores to do," said Scout as though she hadn't heard Tilly. "And then we need to figure out how to handle Cruella."

Right. Reality. Tilly wished the credits could roll, and she and Carter could skip to the happily ever after instead of going head to head with the villain of their story. But this was the real world.

"Mareen needs some help with Mr. Tilney. She said he's been acting strange lately."

Tilly loosened her hold on Carter with a sigh. A sick horse was the only thing that would part her from Carter right now. And Mr. Tilney was one of her favorites.

"The guys are replacing the fences in the northern pasture," Scout continued.

"I'll be there in a second," said Carter. He rocked to lift his body, but he slumped back. When he readied himself to try again, Tilly pressed him down.

"You're not going anywhere today," she said. "I don't want another relapse."

She expected a chiding smile. Instead, something dark and defiant crossed his features. In an instant, it was gone.

"I'm fine," he said with a grin that didn't light his eyes like normal.

"Yes, you are," Tilly said, letting her appreciative gaze skate over his disheveled form.

Carter's brittle grin widened into a solid smirk. The light in his eyes became a spotlight that nearly blinded her with his feelings for her. He reached for her, cupping her face in his warm palm.

Except his palm wasn't warm. It was cold and clammy. Tilly pressed the back of her hand to his forehead. He wasn't hot, but he was a few degrees above cool.

"I'm fine," he repeated.

"And you're going to stay that way," she said. "At least wash-up and have some breakfast first, okay."

"Is this how our marriage is going to go? You bossing me around?"

"Did you really imagine there was any other way?"

Carter chuckled as he pulled her to him. He brushed a kiss over her mouth. His lips were the perfect temperature. Aside from that, they tasted sweet. Vanilla, mint, and a hint of chocolate. She felt like she was being pulled back under, like when she lay in the poppy fields and she was all too happy to-

"Okay, okay," Scout barked. "Enough of that. We have to keep this ranch going, and then we still have to save it. Work to do, people. Work to do."

Her older sister marched out of the cabin, leaving the two of them there. At least there was blessed silence again.

Tilly stood, brushing the wrinkles out of her clothing. It was a losing battle. Carter had seen her rumpled before. The way he was looking at her now made her certain he wanted to rumple her a bit more.

He made to stand. But once again, he wobbled. He reached for the side of the couch for support and closed his eyes as though the world were spinning.

"What is it?" asked Tilly.

He tried to smile in the way he did when he wanted to brush something off. But the smile turned to a wince. "Dizziness. It's one of the symptoms."

Tilly ran a hand across his brow. Carter turned his face into her palm and let out a long sigh.

"That is the best medicine," he whispered against her fingers. He turned his head until he met her eyes. "Are you freaked out? Changing your mind?"

"I promised in sickness and health." Tilly wrapped her arms around his neck.

"We haven't actually said our vows yet." Carter stood. His legs were sturdy now, and he didn't wobble as he held onto her.

"I vow it now."

A beep sounded from the table. They both looked over to see Tilly's phone on the surface. It lit up with a text message from the MeetCute dating app. It was the guy she'd been planning to see tonight.

Tilly grabbed the phone. With a few taps of the keys, she deleted the app. When she was done, she held the face of the phone up to Carter.

"Now, you're stuck with me," she said.

"That makes me the luckiest man in the world."

Carter set the phone aside and held her tighter. Without any warning, his lips crashed down on hers. It was now Tilly who felt dizzy and unsteady. She leaned into him for support, and he gave it.

That's how she knew that the two of them would

get through any of it, through all of it. She trusted Carter with her heart, her body, and her soul. He'd never pretended to be something that he wasn't. Which was perfect, because she loved the man that he was.

CHAPTER FOURTEEN

Carter made his way to the northern pasture. He was feeling on top of the world since leaving Tilly. The nagging withdrawal symptoms would be nothing so long as he had her kisses, her touches, her voice whispering in his ear that she would be with him for the rest of his days.

He felt like Lloyd Dobler sitting next to Diane Court on the plane at the end of *Say Anything*. Any minute now, he would hear the ding announcing he could take his safety belt off and move around the plane. Because everything in his life was turning out fine. The turbulence of the past was behind him. There would be smooth sailing from here on out.

The northern pasture was large, but the guys weren't hard to find. Their voices boomed in the morning air like a bugle announcing the command to charge.

Carter pressed his fingertips against his temples before joining the fray. With a few circular rubs, he managed to wrangle the burgeoning headache into submission. The turmoil that the pills had caused was a distant, weak memory. One he was able to smooth away with just a few rubs of his fingers.

"What are you doing up?”

Carter opened his eyes. It took a couple of seconds for his vision to come into focus, and Wilson's large frame came into view. "Scout said you were out here. I'm here to help."

"I think you should take it easy today, buddy."

"I said I'm fine," Carter snapped.

All chatter stopped. All eyes were on him. His friends' faces were carefully blank. That's what bothered Carter the most.

He couldn't hide from his brothers. Each and every one of them knew what he was going through. It might have been easier if he'd seen judgment in their gazes. But not a single one of them judged. Their blank faces waited for his cues, letting him know that they would follow his lead on this road to recovery.

Fentanyl addiction wasn't deadly. It was just

going to be a miserable few days. But Carter wasn't miserable. He was happy. Why couldn't they see that?

His head began to pound. When he lifted his hand to rub out the pressure, the world tilted off its axis. He was toppling over. Somehow he didn't hit the ground.

"Easy there. We got you."

Carter wasn't sure which of his friends said those words. He wasn't sure whose hands were around him. What he did know was that though he loved each and every one of these men as his brothers, he didn't like them seeing him in this vulnerable state.

They were soldiers. They were strong men. Showcasing any of their pain could be deadly. It could get them all killed on the battlefield.

But they weren't on the battlefield anymore. They were on a ranch. Making a border of wooded fencing. Not to keep enemies out, but to keep the gentle horses who roamed this lands inside.

Suddenly Carter felt nauseous. His body itched everywhere like a thousand ants were crawling on him. He just needed a moment of relief. One pill would do it.

His heels itched to about-face and go back to the cabin, back to where he'd hid those last few pills.

He'd intended to throw them in the trash after Tilly left this morning. But then he reasoned that keeping the pills and not using them would prove him stronger.

And now he was in a moment of weakness.

"I'm sorry," Carter whispered.

"You're good," said Jeff, in his calm voice. "You're standing on your own two feet."

And he was. Carter stood center in the circle of his brothers. They were all at a distance where they could reach out to him if he faltered.

The throb in his head had silenced. The blur was gone from his vision. The fog cleared from his mind. All was right with the world.

"It passed," said Linc.

"So, get your lazy butt to work," said Wilson, in his deep, gruff voice.

Carter huffed a short laugh through his gritted teeth. And just like that, they were all fine. He knew his buddies wouldn't let him fail. He also knew they wouldn't let him slip backward.

He was fine.

He had this.

Carter moved slowly and carefully. The dizziness kept creeping back, but not so much that he could hold it at bay with a shake of his head. He noted that the guys gave him the light end of the work. He decided not to complain. He was taking the first steps toward getting clean. He couldn't be expected to run headlong into the action. This was a process, and he'd work the steps.

The sound of a branch breaking behind him made his heart skip a beat. All of the men in his unit were in front of him. That meant an enemy was approaching from behind.

Carter reached for his gun. It wasn't at his side where he normally kept it. He was unarmed, and the enemy was at his back.

Down on the ground was a hammer. He scooped it up and spun to face his attacker.

A dark-skinned man came into the clearing on a horse. There was no fear in the old man's eyes. The horse was another matter.

The beast reared. The old man held fast, leaning into the horse's neck. Once all four of the horse's feet were back on the ground, the man expertly soothed the horse.

Truman came up around Carter. He moved slowly, holding his hands in full view. Carter heaved a breath and lowered his hands. Truman grabbed his arm and took the hammer from him. Then he laid a hand on Carter's shoulder and forced Carter to look in his eyes.

Carter took a few deep breaths, letting reality wash over him in slow waves. He'd been pulled back into battle. It had been a long time since he'd had a PTSD episode. The fentanyl had kept most of those emotions at bay. Without the drug in his system, his entire being was vulnerable to attacks from all fronts.

"Sorry, sir," Carter said to Father Matthews who had gotten his horse under control and was now towering over him.

Father Matthews' gaze raked over Carter. It felt like the old soldier was seeing into Carter's bruised and battered soul. That penetrating gaze was also seeing inside Carter's veins where the last vestiges of the opioid were slowly making their retreat and realizing there would be no reinforcements.

Father Matthews dismounted. He handed the reins of his horse to Truman, then turned to Carter. "Walk with me."

Carter followed the man's orders. He followed behind the old man whose strides were long and measured, like the commanding officer that he was. Once they were at a distance from the others, Father Matthews turned to face him.

"It's a cool day," said Father Matthews. "But you're sweating like it's a hundred degrees."

Carter didn't need to look down to see the pit stains on his shirt. He felt like his entire body had been submerged under water and he'd come out dripping.

"Your pupils are small," Father Matthews continued. "And you slurred your words back there."

He had? Carter hadn't noticed anything amiss with his speech.

"I know opioid withdrawal when I see it," said the old soldier. "You tell Tilly?"

The shame was bitter on Carter's tongue. He wanted to stand at attention with a straight back, but he felt so weary. "No sir, not in so many words."

Father Matthews's gaze was hard. Carter felt his resolve weakening. His entire body was threatening to shake like a petulant child until he got his fix. The tantrum would just have to come. He wasn't going back.

"I quit. I'm going clean. The guys have my back. She has other things to worry about. I don't want to worry her with this."

"You're going to marry this woman? And you're already keeping secrets from her?"

Carter pursed his lips. It wasn't a secret if it was

no longer a factor. Carter was going to stay clean, he was going to marry Tilly, and they would keep the ranch from Catherine.

"Judge Blair gave me a call," said Father Matthews. "He wants me to come in and talk about the marriages and the will."

As if this day couldn't get any worse.

CHAPTER FIFTEEN

"Thanks, Mr. Pete," Tilly called as the trailer pulled off. "Say hi to your wife for me!"

Mr. Pete honked in acknowledgment as he ambled down the road. Tilly turned her attention to the hay he had delivered. Normally, she'd take the tractor out and make the hay for the ranch. But there had been an accident a couple of weeks ago, and the vehicle had been put to rest for nearly decapitating Mareen.

So delivery it was. But she still needed to mix some of her special blends into the bales. She had a legume blend of alfalfa which was higher in proteins and calcium for the older horses. There was a

Kentucky bluegrass blend for one of the horses who was still suffering from colic.

Off in the distance, Saylor and Brig worked with a new horse that had been dropped off a couple days ago. Like most of the horses here at Silver Star, the newly named Elton was a former racehorse who had outlived his usefulness to his owners. Those losers looked at Elton as though he was washed up. Little did they know that here on this ranch, the horse was about to begin living his best life.

Scout sat on the porch with binders and a calculator spread out around her. Unlike all of her younger sisters, Scout hadn't gone to college. There had never been time. Instead, she'd gotten on-the-job training and did a couple of courses online. Scout always had a singular mind about what she was meant to do, and that was to run this ranch.

Scout picked up a post-it note. The singular concentration leached from her face, and she smiled. No doubt the note was from Linc, who had a habit of leaving the sticky scraps around for her to find. Tilly had blushed at a couple of notes she accidentally found. Now everyone averted their gazes when they came across any of the adhesive, square reminders.

In the distance, Tilly saw Mareen. She was

dressed in a pair of jeans and flannel. It was so unlike the high society miss that always came to the ranch in delicate fabrics and heels. Now Mareen was happy to get out in the dirt and make a mess of her clothing.

There was a smile on Mareen's face as she tilted her head to the sunlight. In her hands was a lead as she walked with a horse. From its coat, it looked like Mr. Tilney. Tilney was a docile and gentle creature. So when he reared on Mareen, Tilly rushed to her sister.

Tilly knew that Mareen could handle a horse. The woman had won medals in dressage for years. It was Mr. Tilney that had Tilly's attention. Mareen had the horse under control before Tilly reached them.

"I might be a little out of practice." Mareen looked off toward the house. But Scout had left the porch, likely following the directive on the Post-It and searching for her husband. Mareen sighed with what sounded like relief.

Tilly knew that Scout and Mareen were still getting their footing in their relationship. For so long, there had been a wedge between the two sisters. That wedge had been Mareen's mother, who

was now inserting herself into all of their rela-
tionships.

"You're doing great," said Tilly. She gave Mareen's
arm a quick rub before her attention turned to the
horse.

"I'm pretty useless here," said Mareen. "All I know
how to do is teach a horse to dance, and I'm pretty
rusty at that."

Mr. Tilney pawed at the ground. He yanked at
the lead as though agitated. His breaths came out in
fast spurts as though he'd just been galloping.

"Did you ride him?" Tilly asked.

"No, we were just walking back from the north
pasture."

"You're always such a gentleman, Mr. Tilney.
What's got into you?" Tilly ran her hand over his
side. She could feel the horse's heartbeat racing.

Mr. Tilney backed away from her, flattening his
ears. In any horse, it was a sure sign of aggression.
In this horse, it was entirely out of character.

"You said you took him to the north pasture?"

Mareen nodded. "I noticed Wickham and Heath-
cliff constantly running him off his food. I figured
he could have a few mornings of eating in peace."

The horse let out another huff of air. On his
breath, Tilly smelled the sweet scent of flowers. Not

just the airy perfume of any flower. She smelled hints of vanilla, citrus, and cocoa.

"Oh," Tilly sighed. "That's why you're behaving this way."

"Why?" asked Mareen. "What did I do wrong now?"

"He's been eating poppy flowers."

The plant contained opiates and could act on horses the same way that it acted on humans, making them feel sedate, lethargic, and dazed. Or conversely giving them a sense of euphoria that made their hearts race. The animals normally stayed away from the bitter-tasting plant, but if that was all they had available, they'd eat it.

Mareen's shoulders deflated. She looked crestfallen as Tilly explained the situation.

"So," Mareen sighed, "in short, I screwed up."

"You didn't screw up. You were trying to help."

"You mean like when I asked my fiancé to buy this place, and he brought my mother who figured out what was going on with the will and is now actively trying to prove all of our marriages are a fraud?"

"That's not your fault," Tilly insisted. "None of this is your fault. None of this is any of our faults. We are not our parents. We're certainly not going to make any of their mistakes by hiding emotions, not being honest, and hurting the people we claim to love."

As if she'd called out to him, Carter came out of the woods toward them. He was flanked on either side by the rest of the guys. But all Tilly could see was her guy.

"We're going to fight for this place," said Tilly. "No matter what your mother does, I think both of our futures look bright."

Wilson jogged up to them. He came to stand before his wife and swept her off her feet. Only to put her down a second later and tilt her chin. "Why are there smudges of dirt all over you? Did you fall?"

Mareen pinched her lips together, but she couldn't hide the smile there. Wilson was overprotective. And who could blame him when Mareen had almost died three different ways on the day he'd met her.

Wilson took Mr. Tilney's lead with one hand while he held onto his wife with the other. He led them both toward the stables and disappeared inside. When Tilly looked up, she and Carter were alone.

"We need to talk," said Carter.

Tilly waited for her heart to drop. Those were

not the best words to hear in a new relationship. She'd said them herself with the intent of cutting all ties to guys she'd been dating. But everything in her heart told her that Carter wasn't dumping her.

He reached out a hand to her, and she felt his fingers tremble. He blew out a huff of breath. She noted the normal vanilla and citrus scent of him was fading. Probably due to the excessive amount of sweat collecting on his shirt.

Tilly wanted to rail at him. Hadn't she told him to take it easy today? He was still getting over his injury. Though he looked perfectly fine, better than fine. Aside from the sweat. And the trembling of his hands. And his pupils looked very dilated. He reminded Tilly of Mr. Tilney's behavior. Perhaps Carter needed a change in his diet, too.

"What do you want to talk about?" she asked Carter.

"It'll keep," he said. His gaze was not on her. It was over her shoulder. "We have another problem."

Tilly turned to see a sleek car pull up to the ranch house. When the car came to a stop, she saw Judge Blair step out of the driver's side. He rounded the car and handed out Catherine, who wore a grin that would've scared Maleficent.

CHAPTER SIXTEEN

arter wrapped his hand around Tilly's and squeezed. To those assembled, they presented a united front. He needed to feel her solidarity, but he also needed to disguise the trembling of his body.

Sweat beaded on his forehead. It pooled under his armpits. That he could excuse from working out of doors all morning. The blurry vision and headache he couldn't explain. Luckily, no one could see those symptoms. Still, he felt that all eyes were on him.

The living room of the main house was packed with bodies. On a normal day with the six soldiers and five Silver girls, it was a tight fit. This afternoon they had three other guests added to the fray.

Catherine sneered at the glass of lemonade her daughter set in front of her. The older woman wrinkled her nose as though the glass were dirty or the contents were poisonous. Likely, she thought both instances were the case.

The two men who were guests happily gulped down the offered drinks. Father Matthews, who was a regular guest, emptied his glass and unabashedly held it out for more. Mareen filled it, offering the man a wane smile. The old man ran a gnarled hand over hers, causing Mareen's smile to increase.

Judge Blair took a polite sip. His lips turned up in appreciation, and he took a few more sips before setting the glass down.

"I believe you all know why we're here," said the judge. "Serious accusations have been leveled against you young ladies."

All eyes went to the cause of those accusations. Catherine sat stiffly in her chair. Perched as though she believed the fabric would stain her expensive dress.

"I've determined to speak with you in your home instead of in my courtroom out of respect for your father."

"What exactly are the allegations?" asked Linc. He stood behind Scout, a hand around her waist.

Everyone present knew that her husband's hand was the only thing restraining Scout at the moment.

"Marriage fraud," said the judge.

"Isn't that often to do with immigration?" asked Tilly. "One party marrying to get a green card."

Her sisters' gazes all settled on her. As did the soldiers'. The judge's and Father Matthews's too. But not Catherine's. She brushed an imaginary piece of lint from her immaculate skirt.

"What?" Tilly said to everyone gaping at her. "We watched the movie *Green Card* a couple weeks ago."

Carter remembered that night. Tilly had fallen asleep against his shoulder. He'd sat and gazed down at her slumbering form for the second half of the movie before carrying her in his arms, tucking her into bed, and leaving. But some of the movie penetrated through his brain.

"We're all American citizens," he said. "Half of us have served this country with honor. The Silvers are a military family who has paid the ultimate sacrifice."

The judge shifted uncomfortably in his seat at the mention of the general's passing. It was easy to believe the two men had been friends. They were of the same generation and appeared to have the same family values. And each man had had his ear tugged by a woman who didn't think twice about twisting the world to suit her needs.

"All of these marriages are a sham," said Catherine. "Each and every one of you married under false pretenses with the intent to keep me out of my dear late husband's home."

It would've been impossible to hear a pen drop in the room. The intake of sharp breaths would've deafened the impact of the metal clattering to the floor. Not even a hammer falling could be heard during the indignant gasps of the Silver girls.

"Your *dear* husband?" said Mareen. She'd taken a step in front of Scout. But Wilson tugged her back into his arms.

"Abe's will states that the property will come to me unless all of his daughters marry before his deadline," Catherine went on. "That's clearly a ridiculous notion; the girls all getting married. So it stands to reason he wanted the property to come to me."

Carter looked up at the sound of a scuffle. Linc now had both arms around Scout. He turned her body so that her face was buried against his chest.

"I'm fine," Scout hissed. But when she turned her head, she shot Catherine a murderous gaze. Luckily, her husband didn't loosen his hold on her.

"Haran," said Judge Blair, turning to Father Matthews. "You're the most familiar with this matter since I believe you were in possession of Abe's will."

Father Matthews looked around the room. His gentle gaze taking in each man and woman in turn. When his gaze came to Tilly and Carter, there was a slight crinkle in his eyes as they narrowed on Carter.

"Yes." Father Matthews nodded. "Abe said the girls would inherit the ranch equally after they all married."

"Then soon after, these soldiers showed up," said Catherine. "They'd been in service to Abe all these years, but this was the first time they deigned to visit."

"We were a little busy protecting this country," said Wilson, his arm around Mareen.

"And now you're aiming to steal from the great man who gave your life purpose," said Catherine. "My daughter had been engaged for a year when you turned her head with your lies."

"What lies?" said Wilson. "That I love her and will give my life to protect hers." Wilson gazed down at Mareen with a love so bright that it hurt to look at.

Catherine was undeterred. She turned her

venom on Scout and Linc. "Scout married this man within a week of meeting him."

"Because she's stubborn," said Linc. "It took that long to convince her she was in love with me. I knew on the first day."

The animosity that had been aimed at Catherine leached out of Scout's blue eyes when she turned to look up at her husband.

"Saylor left a relationship of five years to marry an invalid," said Catherine.

"I left an abusive relationship to go into the arms of a man who lifted me up," said Saylor. Her normally pleasant features were screwed into distaste as she shook her head at her stepmother.

"And they gave the child to an old man," said Catherine, turning her ire to Jackson and Brig.

Jackson lifted a brow. He was seated in a chair on the opposite side of the room. His walking cane was leaned against his injured knee. He didn't bother to speak. Instead, he tilted his head to look up at Brig.

Brig shook her head sadly as she regarded her stepmother. "Despite what you think, our father did care about you."

Now the pen could've fallen with a resounding crack of a hammer in the quiet of the room. Mouths hung open with no sound coming out. A few hands flew to chests as though to hush racing heartbeats.

"We care about you," Brig continued. "We could probably even love you. If you let us."

There was a bit of rustling. As though no one was certain of those statements. But neither were they ready to deny them outright.

Catherine's face turned so still her features looked like glass. She reminded Carter of a mannequin in a department store window. An expressionless lump of plastic with a beautiful garment. That was until her gaze turned from Brig and landed on him and Tilly.

"You're running out of time," said Catherine, her voice as cold as her gaze. "I'm assuming that's why you went to the courthouse."

"Going to the courthouse was impulsive," said Carter. "I've been prone to do things without thinking them through in the past. But not anymore."

His voice was steady even as he felt tremors running through his arms and hot and cold across his shoulders. His head pounded in his skull, but he held onto the one thing that mattered to him; Tilly. Her hand was still in his, lending him all the strength he would need to get through this.

Carter's gaze found Father Matthews. Carter felt the man saw straight into his soul. That was good. Because Carter needed the man to know that he was worthy of Tilly.

As though his prayers had been both heard and answered, Father Matthews gave a slight nod. It was all the approval Carter needed.

"We were being selfish the other day," Carter said, turning to Tilly and taking both of her hands in his. "Family is the most important thing in this world. When I promise to honor and protect, to obey and cherish, to have and to hold this woman for every day of my life, I'll do it with our entire family as witnesses."

"With all your family here, why not do it now?"

That hadn't been Scout's commanding voice. It hadn't been a directive from Linc. It came from Judge Blair.

"I don't know exactly what's in that will," said the judge. "What I can see is that there's clearly no fraud going on here. Just young love. Impetuous, a bit impatient. But love, nonetheless."

"You're making a mistake," said Catherine. Finally, her ice features cracked to reveal anger and indignation. "They'll all divorce after they get the deed."

"There will be no divorces here," said Linc. "We're building something. Why not be a part of it? You'll be a grandma someday soon."

Apparently, Linc didn't notice the murmur of *retreat* that came from the girls. Or the hand waving to get down that came from his own wife. The Silver girls all moved a step closer to him as though to block the incoming missile.

Catherine looked murderous. She stood, giving everyone, including her daughter, a once-over that left them all feeling dirty. "Cameron," she hissed at the judge, "take me home."

"It looks like I have a ceremony to perform, Catherine," said the judge. Like Linc, he didn't realize the minefield he was treading on.

The look Catherine gave Judge Blair would melt a glacier. The judge actually cringed. To prove he had a good sense of judgment, the man rose from his chair and offered Catherine his arm.

"It's fine," said Father Matthews. "I'll take it from here."

The judge looked saddened. Sad because he would miss the vows? Or sad because he'd have to be confined with Catherine in that car on the drive out? Whichever it was, Carter didn't care.

His heart was pounding with happiness. His

head was throbbing with joy. His hands were trembling with the knowledge that he would be able to hold Tilly Silver to him for the rest of his days.

He knew these symptoms of the withdrawal wouldn't last long. He knew he wouldn't need any more pills to get through the day. Nothing was worth losing this woman. And he'd tell her what he'd been through, what he was going through.

Now clearly wasn't the time. He made a vow that he would. She'd already promised him in sickness and health. So, he'd tell her right after their vows.

CHAPTER SEVENTEEN

illy held Carter's hand in hers. He'd been shaking since they'd come into the house. She grinned to know that he was more over-come with emotions than her.

"Dearly beloved," intoned Father Matthews's deep voice. "We are gathered here today to witness the joining of this man and this woman."

Now it was Tilly's hands that were shaking. She bounced on her toes, shifting her weight from one foot to the other. Carter pulled her closer until her hands rested on his heart. Through his shirt, she felt the organ beating wildly. It matched the rhythm of her own racing heart.

Neither of them ran for the door, intent on escaping their future. Instead, they held onto one another until the trembling ceased and their hearts slowed down and came into synch. This was where they belonged, together.

Looking down at her, Carter blinked a couple of times as though she wasn't in focus. Tilly could understand. There were tears in her own eyes. She kept waiting for the feeling that this wasn't right, that there was something more, somewhere something greener. Looking into his green gaze, she didn't want to be anywhere else.

"In this union, the two of you will have to push forward through the times that make you want to withdraw and turn back."

Carter lifted his gaze from Tilly and focused on Father Matthew. Tilly watched as his green eyes adjusted and became clear. With a slight gulp, Carter nodded once at Father Matthews, who then turned to Tilly.

"Trust that your love is stronger, despite the odds you will face. Love each other through the dark moments, which will threaten your wellbeing. Have faith that you can recover through any fall."

It felt like Father Matthews was giving a sermon. Which Tilly would've appreciated at another time and place. But this was her wedding day. She wanted to skip to the good parts.

"You will be inextricably intertwined. You will be family."

She and Carter already were both those things. Even now, his fingers were laced with hers. Though his were trembling again, and sweat covered his brow.

Tilly squeezed his hands tightly, trying to let him know that she was here for him. That she was his. And he was hers. That this was right. That this was forever.

"I Artillery Silver, take thee, Carter Shane to be my wedded husband, to have and to hold from this day forward, for better, for worse, for richer, for poorer, in sickness and in health, to love and to cherish, till death do us part."

Carter closed his eyes and let out a sigh. A tear formed at the corner of his right eye. Tilly unlaced her fingers from his just in time to catch it. When he opened his eyes, they shone with a love so bright her knees felt weak.

"I Carter Shane, take thee, Artillery Silver to be my wedded wife, to have and to hold from this day forward, for better, for worse, for richer, for poorer, in..."

He coughed at this next part. Tilly's hand was still on his face. She cupped his cheek, letting him know with her touch that she was here for him, would always be.

"In sickness and in health," he continued, with a renewed strength in his voice. "To love and to cherish, till death do us part."

Tilly tilted her head to seal that deal with a kiss. Before her lips touched his, a throat cleared.

"We haven't gotten to that part yet," said Father Matthews.

"I'm pretty sure it's the next part," said Tilly.

The old man smiled at her. Tilly tried to hold on to her patience, but it was a losing battle.

"You let me know when you get there," she said. "I'm way ahead of you."

And with that, she claimed her prize. Carter chuckled against her lips, but he accepted her kiss. They might not have gotten here the conventional way, but they were here. They were together. And that's the way it would be for the rest of their lives.

"I now pronounce you man and wife. You may now kiss the bride."

Carter swayed a little as he ended the kiss. Instead of letting her go, he pulled her to him as though she was his anchor. When he opened his eyes, his green gaze was steady, as was his large body. His trembling had stopped. His skin was no longer clammy with sweat.

"I love you," he whispered before he captured her lips again.

Tilly wasn't able to respond with words. She was able to respond with her mouth. She used her lips to tell him that her whole heart, her entire body, all of her soul was his.

Carter's breath was shuddery as he broke the kiss. Tilly opened her eyes slowly. Her gaze was hazy. Looking across the room, she thought she was seeing double. Though she'd never be caught dead in khakis and hiking boots.

"Gunny?"

Tilly broke from her husband and peered around his shoulder. Sure enough, her twin stood in the entryway to the parlor. Gunnery Silver had a duffle bag slung over her shoulder as she regarded the scene with quizzical interest.

Tilly went to her twin and wrapped her up in her arms. Gunny smelled like she hadn't showered in a week, along with a hint of dark roast coffee. Tilly inhaled deeply. She might have just given herself to a man, but she had missed this part of herself. With her twin in her arms, Tilly felt whole.

"You're married," said Gunny.

Tilly followed her sister's gaze to Carter, her husband. "I am."

"That's Carter?" asked Gunny.

"Hi," said Carter with a wave.

Gunny waved back before turning her attention to her twin. "Wasn't I supposed to marry him?"

Oh. Right. That had been the plan.

"Well..." Tilly began and stopped. "Technically, you were supposed to marry Jackson."

"And which one is Jackson?" asked Gunny.

"He's mine," said Brig, taking a seat on Jackson's lap.

Gunny looked around the room at her sisters. "I've been on a plane for the better part of two days to get here because you all said I had to come home and get married. And now that I get here, there's no one for me to marry?"

With that, Tilly saw Truman slip out the back door. Father Matthews chuckled. All the sisters launched themselves at Gunny in a hearty Silver family welcome.

They were all here. They were all together. Now they just had to figure out how to keep it that way.

CHAPTER EIGHTEEN

"What are we going to do about Gunny?" Carter asked as he and Tilly made their way to the cottage.

He held her hand in his. As he rubbed his thumb back and forth over her knuckles, he noted the absence of a ring there. He'd have to remedy that oversight soon. He wanted everyone in the whole world to know that this woman was his.

"We'll figure something out," Tilly said. "Who knows? Maybe she'll be interested in MomApproved?"

Carter chuckled. Had that disastrous date only been yesterday? Yes, just twenty-four hours ago, and he'd been sitting by watching as the woman he loved sat across from a man who would never deserve her. And now, here he was, standing beside her as her husband.

The world was a strange place. It didn't matter how crazy things got. He could weather anything with Tilly beside him. The shakes had calmed the moment she'd made her vows. Alongside the sweating and his racing heart. The only thing he couldn't control was her Wicked Stepmother's aim to take the ranch from them.

"We don't have much time left," Carter said.

"You don't think Truman will come around to the idea of marrying Gunny?"

"Your twin is an animal rights activist and anti-gun protestor."

"She's not anti-gun. She knows how to use one. She just doesn't believe in the Second Amendment."

"You do know that Truman is a trained sniper who wants back in the military?"

"Well, yeah. But opposites have been known to attract."

"Not if one is in the North Pole and the other is on Mars."

They came to the door of Tilly's cottage. Carter supposed it was both of theirs now. This is the place where their friendship had blossomed. This is the place where their married life would begin. He was ready to take this first step toward the rest of their lives. But when he opened the door. Tilly waited outside.

"What?" he asked. Was she already having cold feet about their marriage?

"I'm your new bride," she said. "You need to carry me over the threshold."

"Right," he said but hesitated.

"Unless..." Tilly reached a tentative hand out to him. "Are you still feeling ill?"

The withdrawal symptoms had loosened their grip on him. Carter knew that wouldn't last. It was still going to be a rough couple of days before he got all of the poison out of his body. Another side effect of the opioids was that it was a high chance he wouldn't be able to perform as a husband should on this important night. Might as well set that expectation now and then come clean with the rest.

"Yes, I am still feeling ill." Carter took her hands in his. "That's something I want to talk to you about. Come on inside."

He gave her a tug. They walked across the threshold of the cottage, hand in hand.

"There's something I didn't tell you," he said.

Tilly tensed. Carter could feel protective walls erecting around her. They were the barriers she put up between herself and the other men she'd gone out with on first dates. The boundaries she would erect to ensure that no foundation could be set between them.

"No," Carter said the word forcefully. "Don't do that."

He didn't have to clarify what he meant. They knew each other too well. There had never been walls between them. There never had been any reason for them. Tilly took a deep breath, and Carter felt the boundaries crumbling around them.

"Tilly, I've never lied to you. But there is something that I neglected to tell you about myself."

He saw the struggle on her face. She wanted to put something between them. Instead of a mental brick barrier, she grabbed for a pillow from the couch where they sat most nights watching old movies.

Carter placed a hand on the pillow she held against her chest. "It's something personal. We weren't together, so I didn't think you needed to know it and—"

"Stop stalling, please." The quiver of her lip

nearly did him in. "The more you do, the worse I imagine it is."

"It was bad. But it's not a factor any longer."

"Carter!" She tossed the pillow at him.

Carter caught the fluffy missive and set it back on the couch. "I had a fentanyl addiction."

The only hint that she'd heard him was a minute twitch of her brows.

"Have," he corrected himself. "I have a fentanyl addiction."

"Fentanyl? That's an opioid?"

Carter nodded.

"Like heroin?"

"No. Not heroine. I didn't get drugs off the street. They were prescribed to me by the military for pain management."

"Because you were injured."

Carter inhaled. "I was. It healed. But the pills... I developed an addiction. I began to need them to function."

Tilly looked at him as though seeing him anew. "The smell."

"What smell?"

"You. Your smell. Vanilla and citrus with a hint of cocoa. You smell like poppies, which is where opium comes from in nature."

Carter didn't answer. Trust the nutritionist would figure it out with the help of a plant.

"The twitching and trembling," she continued. "The sweating and headaches. Those are all symptoms of withdrawal. How did I not see that?"

"I'm sorry," he said. "For all of it. Especially for not telling you."

"I wish you had," she snapped.

Carter snatched the pillow away before she could use it as a weapon again.

"I would've supported you." She jabbed a finger at his chest. "I was your friend before I was anything else."

"I didn't think I had a problem." Carter took that finger and wrapped it in his hand. "I thought I had it all under control."

"What changed?"

"You. I wanted you more than I wanted the pills. So I gave them up."

"For me?" Tilly sighed and pressed her palm against his chest.

"I'd do anything for you. I want to be the man you need, the man you deserve. That man is not a drug addict. So no more pills, I swear."

"You're going through withdrawals now? Is it dangerous?"

"It's going to be uncomfortable. But it's not dangerous, not life-threatening."

"Okay," she said after a long pause.

"Okay?" Carter asked. "I was expecting a big blowup. More than a pillow grenade and a finger poke. You hate lies. Including ones of omission."

"That was your one pass." She poked him in the chest with her finger. "It'll have to last a lifetime."

"I'll never keep anything from you again."

"You better not, or—"

She picked up a pillow and aimed it for his chest. Carter pulled her to him and kissed her soundly. The pillow fell to the floor with an inaudible thud.

"So, I know we can't sleep together because of your condition," she said. "But we can still *sleep* together, right?"

"Yes."

As though he was letting her be anywhere without him again. Carter guided Tilly to the bedroom. The bed with her comforter was made up with military precision. His things were tucked neatly in corners. They'd have to expand if they were going to live here together. But all that would wait. All he needed was a good night's sleep with the woman he loved tucked securely in his arms. Then he'd wake up and conquer the world for her.

That thought dulled any effects of the withdrawal. In fact, he couldn't feel a single symptom. His head was clear. His heart beat slow and steady. He was no longer sweating, though he could use a shower to wipe away the residual effects.

When Tilly came out of the bathroom, he was surprised to find her in the same messy state as when she'd went in. He wondered if she needed a night shirt. The thought of her in one of his t-shirts made all the symptoms come back, but not as a result of the withdrawals. These were all due to desire. Maybe he could perform his husbandly duties after all?

When Tilly opened her hand, palm up, all his desires turned cold. In her hand, Carter saw three white pills. The reserves he'd sworn he wouldn't use.

"You said you got rid of these," Tilly said.

"I did… Those were just… I wasn't going to take them."

Carter heard the flimsiness of his argument. In real-time, he saw the protective walls erecting around his wife, the ones she used when she saw that her dates were liars who had misrepresented themselves.

"Tilly…" He reached out to her, but even though she was so close, she was beyond his touch.

She set the pills on the counter. The small white shapes merged in his eyes to resemble a white flag being thrown down. If only he were here to save himself. But she'd turned her back on him, was headed for the door.

CHAPTER NINETEEN

*H*e'd lied to her. And not a bald-faced lie. It was worse because he'd hidden the truth until the last possible second, revealing it only when he was caught in the web he'd spun.

Tilly couldn't stand looking at Carter's profile any longer. She could barely recognize the man that had been her friend for the last couple of months. She definitely couldn't see the man who had become her husband.

She turned on her heel and ran. She'd expected Carter to reach out and grab her, to haul her back to him, to wrap her up in his arms and tell her it had all been a mistake.

He did none of those things. He let her go.

So that he could stay with his drugs. Clearly, they

were more important than she was. So important that he'd lied to her about them.

The cool evening air whipped strands of hair about her face. Tilly brushed her locks aside, but they refused to be captive. Her hands fell to her sides, and she looked about the ranch, unsure where to go.

She didn't want to go into the house. Everyone was still up celebrating her union with Carter and likely visiting with Gunny. If she walked through the door, even with a fake smile plastered on her face, her twin would know something was wrong.

Tilly couldn't talk about it. Not with her sister. The only person she did want to confide in about her heartbreak was the one who'd broken the organ.

Her feet took her to the stables. Inside, the horses were settling down for the night. Mr. Tilney put his head over his stall.

There was a bit of slobber at the horse's mouth. His breaths came out raspy. His large eyes drooped with lethargy. The poor animal was still suffering the effects of his accidental poppy consumption.

"You'll be fine once it's out of your system," Tilly said, giving the horse a soothing pat. "We'll take care of you."

She could take care of Mr. Tilney because the

horse wanted to be taken care of. If he'd had another choice, Mr. Tilney would not have eaten that bitter-tasting plant. Unlike Carter, who had other choices and nearly a dozen hands that would offer help. But instead, he'd chosen to lie.

Mr. Tilney whined. He gave a shake of his head and backed away from Tilly. Belatedly, she realized her comforting pats had turned to a rougher grip.

"Sorry, buddy. I'm not fit for company right now."

Tilly didn't want to wreck another horse's slumber. She didn't want to talk to her family. She definitely didn't want to see her husband right now. What she needed was anonymity and a drink. There was only one place to get that.

She headed to the driveway, found her car, and climbed in. Pulling out onto the road, she headed into town. As she drove down the long and winding road, Tilly pressed her temple with one hand. She felt something grainy against her forehead. When she looked at her palm, she saw that there was still residue from Carter's pills there.

How had she not seen this? How had she not known that the man she was falling in love with had an addiction?

She knew how. It was because Carter had been

hiding it from her. Just like the men who put up misleading details on their dating profile.

Her stomach twisted in knots at the realization. She'd trusted Carter. She'd trusted him completely, blindly.

The fluorescent lights of the bar didn't help to clear her vision. It just made things a bit bleary. The bar was at the edge of the town square. Down the street, Tilly could see the bell tower over the courthouse.

Had it just been one day ago that she and Carter had left the restaurant, grabbed an ice cream, and then headed up the steps to the courthouse to be married. All the while, he'd been lying to her.

Tilly climbed out of the car and headed into the bar. She wasn't much of a drinker, but she needed something in her system. If not to help her think clearly, then to help her stop thinking entirely.

"What's a newlywed doing at a bar on her wedding night?"

Tilly had only just taken a seat at the bar. She hadn't even placed her order yet. So she knew she wasn't drunk. Still, she didn't trust what her eyes told her she was seeing.

Catherine stood next to her. She looked down at the empty barstool beside Tilly. With a look of utter distaste on her lovely face, she pinched the edges of a napkin and wiped the seat of the barstool off. Frowning at the smudges that stubbornly remained, she sat perched at the edge of the seat.

It took Tilly a few more seconds to find her voice. "What are you doing in here?"

"I asked first." When Tilly didn't answer, Catherine went on. "I was leaving the courthouse after Judge Blair dropped me at my car when I saw you come in here. Without your husband."

Tilly looked down into the drink the bartender sat in front of her. She didn't want to talk to her wicked stepmother. This would just be more fodder for her to try and use against them. But Tilly's marriage was already over before it began, so Catherine had won.

CHAPTER TWENTY

$\mathcal{C}$arter didn't chase after Tilly. Not because he didn't want to. He physically couldn't. His body was not cooperating with him.

He felt hot and cold. Dizzy and nauseous. All at the same time.

He barely made it to the bathroom before giving up his lunch. His head swam as he praised the porcelain gods. The bile didn't leave his throat, not even after he managed to wash his mouth out. The bitter taste of his lies of omission clung to his tongue.

If only Carter told Tilly what he was going through early on in their friendship. But he hadn't even had the courage to tell the men in his unit. The only reason they knew was because they had seen it or experienced it themselves.

Carter was the weak one. He was the one who had grown dependent on the medication. He'd used it as a crutch long after he was healed. And look at what those pills had done; they had broken him.

The woman of his dreams had slipped through his fingers because he hadn't been able to let go of the pain meds. No, scratch that -the drugs.

The fentanyl had stopped being medicinal a long time ago. They were drugs, and he was an addict. He'd been more devoted to the drugs than he was to himself, to his friends, and to the woman he loved.

Carter would need to seek forgiveness from all wronged parties. Starting with himself. He had lost control of himself. He recognized that now. He also recognized that it would be a fight to regain mastery over himself.

Despite the fact that he knew he didn't want the pills any longer, he had to finally admit the power they'd had over him. His friends had seen that when he couldn't. He owed them an apology at the least, a debt of gratitude at the most.

Carter knew he could get to work on making amends with himself and his friends immediately. It was his wife's forgiveness that would be the hardest.

He'd broken Tilly's cardinal rule; no lying or omissions. He knew that about her, and he'd done it, anyway.

Carter felt wretched. He felt untethered to the world. His body started to shake and tremble. He felt hot and cold at the same time. And tired. Oh, so tired. He knew only one thing would take this pain away.

The pills sat where Tilly had left them. They were like white pearls that would ease his suffering, help him think clearly, make everything feel better.

Carter picked one up. He studied the white tablet. He expected the pill to burn his fingers. But it was cool to the touch, almost an inviting feeling. So familiar.

There was no judgment from the pill. All it wanted to offer him was relief. It was a door, an escape. He just needed to walk through. And by walking through, he'd simply need to put it in his mouth and swallow.

Carter had lost Tilly. She wasn't here now. She likely wouldn't be back until tomorrow if she came back to him at all.

She wouldn't know if he took it. It would be his only comfort. His consolation prize for trying to do the right thing and failing.

Only he didn't want a consolation prize. Carter wanted Tilly. He wanted his wife. These pills were standing in the way of him getting her back.

They were standing in the way of him getting himself back. Carter wanted both of those things equally. But he couldn't have one without the other.

He was not this man. He was not beholden to this drug. But the truth was, the drugs still had a hold on him.

He was strong. But this tiny tablet had an edge on him, an edge that could bring him to his knees. He finally had to admit it. He couldn't do this alone. He needed help.

There was a knock at the door. When Carter called out, the door to the cabin opened. On the threshold stood Tilly. She was bathed in moonlight. She looked tired and haggard. There wasn't love in her gaze. There was suspicion.

With an ache that tore through his heart, Carter realized the worst possible outcome. He'd already lost her. She'd closed herself off to him, just like she'd done with the guys from the dating apps when she was done with them. After she realized that they'd lied or misrepresented themselves.

There had to be someway back into her heart. Carter had never felt this way about anyone. He wasn't about to let her go. He looked at her again, ready to beg and plead. Until he realized...

"You're not Tilly."

"I saw her leave," said Gunny. "It felt like something was wrong. It's the whole twin connection thing. What happened?"

CHAPTER TWENTY-ONE

"He lied to me," said Tilly.

"So soon?" Catherine turned her nose up at the glass of wine that was sat before her on the bar. "And I thought Abe had the world record on that."

Tilly held her own shot glass in her hand. The tumbler was full. Though inside, her gut twisted with acid and fire. She ached with need, but she knew the alcohol wouldn't quench her thirst. So she turned her attention to her stepmother.

"Why do you think my father lied to you?"

"He said he loved me."

Tilly waited. But it appeared that was the beginning and the end of Catherine's accusation. "My father did love you."

Catherine shoved the wine glass away with a scoff. A few droplets spilled over the top of the glass. The white wine splattered onto the wood surface of the bar. But the instant they hit, they dried without leaving a trace.

"My father didn't always keep his word," said Tilly. "Not because he didn't want to. Because he had a habit of over-committing himself."

"He shouldn't have married me if he was still in love with that woman." Catherine grabbed the wineglass and took a gulp.

"He told us that he loved you."

"If he loved me, then he wouldn't have divorced me," Catherine took another gulp. Her eyes were vacant as she gazed out the window.

"*You* divorced *him*."

"Because he loved that woman." Catherine slammed her empty wineglass down on the bar top.

"Yes, he did. He loved Sarah. And he loved my birth mother. And he loved you. A man can love more than one woman in his lifetime. The man had six daughters."

A myriad of emotions skittered over Catherine's features. Confusion, anger, doubt, hope. Not one emotion stayed longer than a full second. It was as though she didn't believe that all those statements could be true at the same time.

Abe had loved each of his wives. Of that Tilly was sure. Her father had failed a lot in his personal endeavors with the women in his life. He'd made promises that he wasn't able to keep. He'd broken his word countless times. But he'd never once done it maliciously. He'd tried his best. But his best wasn't always good enough.

"So, your man is in love with another woman?"

It took Tilly a few seconds to break out of her silent reverie over her father's failings. She blinked at Catherine, repeating her question over again in her head. Was Carter in love with another woman? Tilly knew that answer without a doubt.

"No," Tilly said. She knew she was the only one in Carter's heart.

"Is it a financial thing that broke you up?"

"No."

And they weren't exactly broken up. Were they? This was a fight. A big one because he'd lied to her. He'd said he'd quit, and she found evidence to the contrary.

"A communication thing?" asked Catherine. "He doesn't talk to you and tell you his feelings?"

"We talk about everything." Everything except his addiction.

I didn't think I had a problem. I thought I had it all under control.

Carter should've told her what he was going through. She would've helped him. She didn't have any experience with drug addiction. She knew it had to be hard. Something someone shouldn't do alone.

But she'd left Carter alone when he was clearly struggling.

"Those are the top three reasons for marital trouble," Catherine was saying. "What else could it be."

"He has a… a problem."

Catherine cocked her head one way and then the other. Then she grimaced. "Oh. I see."

She did?

"That's why you're at a bar on your wedding night. Bad luck on you."

"No, not that."

Well, yes, *that*. But *that* wasn't the point.

Tilly had fallen in love with Carter before she'd ever kissed him. She loved him for his wit and his attentiveness. She loved that he could finish her sentences and even begin her thoughts. She loved the way his body curled around hers when they sat next to each other. She loved the sound of his voice, the whisper of his breath, the way he looked at her like she was the only person in the world who understood him. She loved that no one else in the world understood her the way he did.

"Well, whatever it is, best you learn now there's no such thing as true love or happily ever afters," said Catherine. "I tried to teach my daughter that. That soldier will break her heart one day, and she'll come crying back to me."

The warm and fuzzy feelings in Tilly's heart had migrated down into her gut and soothed it. She felt herself heal from the inside out with just the thought of Carter. But her ears stung at Catherine's words.

Tilly looked at her stepmother. Catherine had tried to get Mareen to believe something that simply wasn't true. And while Mareen had believed it, it had hurt her.

I didn't think I had a problem. I thought I had it all under control.

Carter's words rang in Tilly's mind. She could tell that he believed what he'd said. But he'd been wrong. He'd been hurting for months, and she hadn't known it, hadn't seen it. He was hurting even worse now. And she'd abandoned him.

"It would seem I'm the only mother you have left," Catherine was saying. "So let me give you some advice."

Tilly was sure that she didn't want to hear Catherine's advice. Advice that there was no such thing as true love. Tilly knew that was false because she'd felt a connection to Carter the first time she'd met him. It hadn't presented itself as love, but now she recognized it clearly. She loved him, and he loved her right back. And that was never going away.

"Divorce is an ugly affair," said Catherine. "So, stay with him."

Tilly was surprised at her stepmother's words. She'd expected Catherine to tell her to annul the marriage and take him for everything he had—which Tilly knew wasn't much—except those few VHS tapes, which she kinda wanted. Maybe Catherine had grown? Maybe she could step in and finally be the mother they all needed?

"Stay with him and make him suffer for every ounce of pain he brought on you."

Tilly reared back at Catherine's words. She waited for the wicked grin on her stepmother's face to turn her heart cold. She waited for the cruel glint in Catherine's eyes to make her gut twist again. But Tilly's lie radar was back in working order, and she smelled a rat.

"I don't believe you," Tilly said.

Catherine shrugged with a nonchalance that also tickled Tilly's radar. The older woman's shoulders were too rigid. Her half-smile too bland.

"No, I mean, I don't believe you are this person. You work too hard to be cold and unfeeling. I see the strain on you."

"Not possible," Catherine sniffed. "I have an excellent plastic surgeon."

"Mareen loves you. We could all love you if you let us. We could be your family if you just come home with us."

Catherine might want to get a new surgeon because there was a crease that formed at the corner of each of her eyes. But it was straightened in a blink. "Go back and live in your fairytale, little girl. There may be five of you married, but your twin sister isn't even back in the country. And unless she brings someone with her and gets married by next weekend, you won't make that deadline, and the ranch will be mine."

With that, Catherine got up with all the grace of

a queen. Heels clacking against the sticky linoleum, she stormed out of the bar.

Tilly couldn't spare her much more emotion. Catherine had made her choice. But Tilly had also made her choice, and she needed to get back to him.

CHAPTER TWENTY-TWO

Carter stood in the crowded parlor of the main house for the second time tonight. He was sweating even more than when he said his vows to Tilly. His fingers trembled without his wife by his side. But if he had any hope of saving his marriage, if he had any hope of saving himself, he had to go through with this.

"I've been keeping a secret," he began. "I had... *have* an addiction."

The Silver women gasped softly at the news. There was a collective sigh of relief from the President's Men. They weren't surprised at this admission. They all knew. The relief was likely that Carter was finally owning up to it.

"I was prescribed a pain killer after my injuries in

the blast," Carter continued. They all knew what blast he meant. He didn't have to elaborate.

"Is it fentanyl?" asked Brig. "I've been reading about that particular medication. The military prescribes it to many soldiers for pain management."

"Fentanyl?" said Scout. "Isn't that an opioid?"

"Yes, it is," said Carter. "In small doses, if you follow the directions, it's helpful to ease the pain of injuries. But if you abuse it, it can become an addiction."

"You abused it?" asked Saylor, her voice full of concern and empathy.

"I did," Carter admitted. "For months now. But recently, I've been trying to get clean."

"He gave us his last prescription," said Linc.

"I did," Carter admitted. "But…"

"Let me guess," said Wilson. "You had a few pills left."

Carter nodded.

"Tilly found them?" said Gunny.

It was hard for Carter to look at his wife's twin. He would never confuse the two women. Tilly's blue eyes were soft and full of humor. Gunny's were filled with hard judgment. Instead of looking into those judgmental blues, he focused on Gunny's shoulder as he nodded.

"That's why she left." It wasn't a question. Gunny stated the words as the facts they were. "You never told her before tonight?"

Carter shook his head.

"She's going to have a hard time forgiving you," said Scout. "Tilly hates liars."

"I'll face those consequences and spend the rest of my life earning back her trust. But first, I have to get well."

Carter opened his hands and showed the pills in his palm. They were in a plastic baggie so that the white powder couldn't rub off and onto his sweaty palms. The contact would've been the same as a hit, and he was done pulling his punches.

"I'm struggling," he continued. "I'm sure if I keep trying to do it on my own, I'll keep struggling, and then I'll fail."

"You're not on your own," said Saylor, getting up and taking the pills from him. "We're all here for you."

"We're your family," said Scout. "We're not going to let you fail."

Four Silver sisters surrounded Carter. Gunny remained on the outskirts, as though she was still unsure of him. That was fine. He had time to win her over. First, he had to win his wife back.

In the meantime, he leaned on the rest of the Silver sisters' strength. It was almost comical. He was a big, tough soldier. Relying on these women's courage, stability, and unconditional love made Carter feel like he could move a mountain with them behind him.

"And don't worry," said Brig. "Tilly will forgive you in time."

"She already has forgiven him."

They all turned to the front door to see Tilly. Her blue eyes looked heavy, as though she'd been crying. There was no humor there because Carter had turned their happy little romcom into a near tragedy.

Carter wanted to run to her. To scoop her in his arms. To set her in front of a television and play a stream of John Cusack comedies. But he wasn't sure he had the right any longer.

The door shut with a snick behind Tilly. And then she was running to him. She wrapped her arms tightly around him. The impact of having her back in his arms nearly knocked Carter over. He used the remainder of his strength to hold them both steady.

"I'm sorry," he said.

"I'm sorry," she said at the same time.

"I should've told you."

"I should've known."

Carter pulled away to peer down into her eyes. "How could you have known? I hid it from you. I hid it from all of you. I didn't want you to see it. I didn't want you to see me as weak. I wanted to be strong for you."

Tilly pressed kisses to his forehead, each of his eyelids, and finally his mouth. Carter felt soothed by her touch. He felt strengthened by the love she was showing him. But he needed to get it all out so that there were no more gaps between them.

"I don't have any more secrets," said Carter. "I will never leave anything out or hide anything from you ever again."

"I believe you."

Something in Carter's chest caused him to choke. He hadn't realized until now that that was his greatest fear. But he hadn't lost Tilly's trust. Those three little words let him know that they would weather this storm.

"I realize that you meant well, Carter," she said. "You over-committed, and you couldn't deliver on your promise to yourself, to your friends, and to me. But I know you always had the best of intentions."

"I do."

"I believe you," she said again.

Those three little words hit him harder than her saying, *I love you.*

"Tell me what I need to do to help you beat this?" she said.

"Hold my hand," he said. "Stand by me and never leave."

"Done."

"And, I hear romcoms are great therapy for recovering addicts."

Tilly pulled away from him, rolling her eyes. "Don't even—"

"I'm sure a *Say Anything* marathon will be just the thing I need."

"This marriage is doomed," Tilly groaned, but she didn't let go of his hand.

Carter laughed as he pulled his wife to him and kissed her. His world might still be off balance. His body might still be in withdrawal. He might still be craving the unnatural comfort the pills could bring to him. But nothing would ever have a stronger hold on him than the love of this woman.

EPILOGUE

Truman Bates sunk into the quiet of his surroundings. Even the insects seemed to hush as he laid his form against the cool earth. The four legged mammals made no sound either. The metal resting against his shoulder proved that he was the biggest, baddest predator out in these woods today.

There were no claws at the ends of his sure hands. No deadly antlers protruded from the cap covering his dark hair. He was even clean-shaven, not possessing the funk that would ward off any oncoming foe. It was the metal behemoth that kept all others at bay.

However, Truman's finger was not on the trigger

of his rifle. It was on the microscopic lens that doubled as his eyes. He rotated the scope using the grooves on the wheel. All of his focus was on his target. The exercise right now was training his eyes to find the details in plain sight of the scope.

With his vision magnified, Truman could see the details that even an owl couldn't pick out. The turn of the blade of grass in the light breeze. The fall of a leaf as its weight got too heavy for the tree limb. The movement of a pebble as an insect carved a path in new growth.

Nature continued its business in quiet activity. This was how Truman had learned most of his training as a sniper for the US Military. Snipers were masters of hiding in plain sight. They excelled at watching over, or even under, both a target they aimed to take out as well as the person whose back they were tasked with protecting. A sniper's ability to become one with their environment trained them to spot enemies and to take out threats without being detected by man, beast, or even owl.

There were no owls high up in trees today. No snakes slithering through the grasses. Only a bull's eye placed a thousand meters away. It was a little over half a mile. On his best day, he had managed twelve hundred meters. He was hoping his better days were ahead of him. For now, he needed to manage this distance.

With his eye in the scope, Truman fingered the trigger. When he was ready, he pulled his index finger back. The zip of the bullet whizzing through the air hit his ears as the kickback of gun hit his shoulder.

Truman grunted, tamping down as much of the pain as he could. It still hurt. The injury may have shouted, but so did the target. Truman had managed to hit the bull's eye.

He couldn't hear the thud of the impact. But he could see it. A perfect black hole in the center of the yellow paper.

Silence was all that cheered on his victory. Until Truman let out a low sigh, that turned to a groan. The groan became a grunt as he rolled onto his back.

Now that the tension was released, all he felt was the recoil that had hit his injured shoulder. Truman's calculations had been perfect. He'd accounted for everything thing but that.

There was nothing wrong with his aim. The only problem rested tireless in his shoulder where he could no longer lift his rifle without pain. Right now the ground was taking on the weight of his weapon.

Unfortunately, the job of a sniper didn't always call for him to lay in wait with a surface under him to take the weight of his weapon. If he couldn't lift the rifle in protection of anyone in his unit, then he was as good as dead. Which was how he felt at this moment while his shoulder throbbed at the blow the rifle had dealt it.

Instead of letting the rifle go, Truman clung to it. For so many years it had been his constant companion. Never letting him down, until that fateful day when he could no longer carry it.

The sound of gunfire. Of his brothers' shouts. Of women screaming. Of the blast that stole the general's last commands. Those sounds played in repeat inside Truman's once quiet head. So, when the sounds of twigs breaking and footsteps approaching reached him in the present moment, it was too late for him to react.

Someone was coming. It was clear to him that that someone wasn't a soldier. Each of the President's Men knew he was shooting out here. They knew he was trying to recapture his precision, his strength. They knew he didn't want company as he tried to dig himself out of this particular hole.

Because they all knew that, they would announce their presence by calling out to him. Which meant that whoever was coming wasn't one of his fellow soldiers. Whoever was coming was coming in hot.

Truman reached for his weapon. He rolled to his side, wrapping his arms around it. Then she rolled onto his back with the rifle in toe.

Too bad his grunt of pain was just as loud as the encroaching enemy. Truman grimaced as his shoulder protested the weight of the gun. It mutinied when he ordered the muscles to arrange themselves in the position he needed to hold the weapon in order to defend himself. He managed to rest the stock of the rifle against the ground, giving him leverage to get in position when a form came out of the bushes.

Wild blonde hair flew into view. Followed by blue eyes blazing so bright, they were all that would be seen before the storm swept in.

It was Tilly. What was she doing out here? Shouldn't she be holed up with Carter, her knew hubby?

But no, this wasn't Tilly. Tilly wore pretty sundresses and make up. Which was why she was perfect for Truman's best friend who was fastidious when it came to his dress and appearance.

This Tilly imposter wore ill-fitting cargo pants, combat boots, and a rainbow t-shirt with animals frolicking underneath the rays. There wasn't an ounce of makeup to mask her irate features.

"Gunnery?" Truman asked, naming Tilly's twin sister.

In answer Gunnery kicked the rifle out his hand. Had his shoulder been what it was, the move would've never worked. But as it was, the gun clattered out of his hands and onto the ground as he muttered a curse of discomfort and incredulity.

Truman had just been ungunned by a slip of a girl. Well, she was a Silver. The daughter of a General who took no prisoners. So he could always claim that as his excuse if the rest of the guys, or even her older sister Scout, ever found out.

"What do you think you're doing," Gunny hissed.

Gunny and Truman are the last two holdouts to meet the General's deadline.
They're gonna get together.
But not without an epic war of wills!
And the real question is, will they get down the aisle in time?

You don't want to miss the epic conclusion of The Silver Star Ranch Romances with His Pledge to Hold.

183

Shanae Johnson was raised by Saturday Morning cartoons and After School Specials. She still doesn't understand why there isn't a life lesson that ties the issues of the day together just before bedtime. While she's still waiting for the meaning of it all, she writes stories to try and figure it all out. Her books are wholesome and sweet, but her are heroes are hot and heroines are full of sass!

And by the way, the E elongates the A. So it's pronounced Shan-aaaaaaaa. Perfect for a hero to call out across the moors, or up to a balcony, or to blare outside her window on a boombox. If you hear him calling her name, please send him her way!

You can sign up for Shanae's Reader Group and receive a FREE NOVELLA in this world at

http://bit.ly/ShanaeJohnsonReaders

Also By Shanae Johnson

The Silver Star Ranch Romances

His Pledge to Honor

His Pledge to Cherish

His Pledge to Protect

His Pledge to Obey

His Pledge to Have

His Pledge to Hold

The Rangers of Purple Heart

The Rancher takes his Convenient Bride

The Rancher takes his Best Friend's Sister

The Rancher takes his Runaway Bride

The Rancher takes his Star Crossed Love

The Rancher takes his Love at First Sight

The Rancher takes his Last Chance at Love

The Brides of Purple Heart

On His Bended Knee

Hand Over His Heart

Offering His Arm

His Permanent Scar

Having His Back

In Over His Head

Always On His Mind

Every Step He Takes

In His Good Hands

Light Up His Life

Strength to Stand

The Rebel Royals series

The King and the Kindergarten Teacher

The Prince and the Pie Maker

The Duke and the DJ

The Marquis and the Magician's Assistant

The Princess and the Principal

www.ingramcontent.com/pod-product-compliance
Lightning Source LLC
Chambersburg PA
CBHW050339160726
48002CB00001B/380

Falenderim

Falenderoj zonjën Lola Çomo për ndihmën e saj në përshtatjen e dialogëve në dialektin elbasanas. Lola u frymëzua nga "Outlander" e Diana Gabaldon, tani një serial televiziv në Netflix. Dialekti skocez i personazheve, i thurur me mjeshtëri në veprën letrare në tërësi, ishte një vlerë e shtuar për "Outlander". Besoj se "elbasançja" e disa personazheve e ka bërë më origjinal romanin "Grimcat".

P.I.Kapllani
1/18/2025,
Toronto

Parathënie

Vangjush Saro
Shënime për romanin 'Grimcat'
të shkrimtarit Përparim Kapllani

"Grimcat" është një nga romanet e shkrimtarit Përparim Kapllani, i cili jeton në Kanada dhe në dekadën e fundit ka rënë në sy për prozën e tij realiste, me frymë jetësore dhe të zhveshur nga manierat, aq në 'modë' sot. "Grimcat" është një faqe gri e së kaluarës së Shqipërisë nën diktaturë, një 'dramë' personazhet e së cilës heqin shumë, vuajnë pareshtur, sikurse edhe ropaten e shpresojnë për ndonjë ditë më të mirë.

Libri është njëlloj ditari i një kohe të vrazhdë. Megjithëse heraherës leximi nuk është aq i këndshëm - edhe për shkak të mjediseve e ngjarjeve të rënda - mendoj se lexuesi krijon një panoramë të rendit në fjalë, për të mos thënë që arrin t'i shohë ngjarjet e rrëfyera në libër sikur një 'film'. Heroi i romanit, Çimi, një fëmijë i vuajtur, i ndjeshëm, zemërhapur, ndonjëherë na duket si një 'ciceron' i asaj kohe të vështirë, 'vizaton' skena e ngjarje që zbulojnë një jetë në tonet më të errëta, madje e brengosin lexuesin dhe kjo flet për anët më bindëse të prozës së autorit. Në libër, janë sjellë me shumë sinqeritet: Historia e atit të djalit, si e shumë shqiptarëve që studjuan në ish-Bashkimin

Sovjetik dhe u lidhën me vajza ruse, vuajtjet e tij në spital, përpjekjet për të mbijetuar, shpresa se do mund të takojë sërish fëmijët e tij dhe pastaj... humbjet raskapitëse: vdekja e tij dhe e Alketës, motrës së heroit. Këto ngjarje e ndjesi i japin të kuptojë lexuesit se autori dhe heroi i librit të tij, i kanë 'skanuar' mirë ato dekada të vështira, të rënda. Por lënda letrare nuk mbahet pezull e ndonjë fiksimi a maniere; pjesë integrale e rrëfimit, është përpëlitja e njerëzve për të jetuar, durimi dhe mundi i tyre për t'u kapur në atë pak shanse të jetës - bie fjala, Çimi përpiqet të hyjë në punë, më pas të shkojë në një shkollë ushtarake -duke treguar se personazheve u duhej të luftonin e të besonin se mund të kish një të nesërme disi më ndryshe. Më duket pozitive gjithashtu, pse jo edhe mjaft realiste, ajo që autori sjell në roman edhe personazhe të cilët i përkisnin anës së 'pushtetit' ose ishin afër tij - si zysha që e ndihmon djalin ose mjeku i ri, Arbeni - duke mos i lënë të gjitha episodet në errësirën dhe shtypjen e kohës. Mendoj se nga pikëpamja e kompozimit, romani ndërtohet në dy pista kryesore: mbështetet në dinamikën e ngjarjeve të ditës, por ndihmohet edhe nga digresionet; (jeta e Isait në Rusi, problemet shëndetësore të tij dhe sjellja brutale me të shoqen, meditimet për Eseninin dhe poezitë e tij, etj.) Në të njëjtën kohë, si një 'pistë' e tretë shfaqet sfondi i ngjarjeve politike: më pare, teksa prishja e marrëdhënieve mes shteteve, BS dhe Shqipëria në këtë rast, merrte përpara fatet e njerëzve; dhe pastaj varfëria ekstreme në vendin e vogël nën diktaturë. Në roman ka tablo realiste, të shkruara me frymëzim - edhe pse ndonjëherë zgjaten shumë - ka skena dhe episode që e sjellin të gjallë jetën e atyre dekadave. Ka një kompleks ndijimesh, kujtimesh dhe aktesh që tregojnë shumë. Një aso është episodi ku fëmijët luajnë luftash: Ilirët dhe Romakët. Vende-vende nuk mungojnë as skenat lirike, që fatalisht kanë të bëjnë me dy *personazhet kryesore e në vuajtje: dashuria e Isait me Svjetllanën dhe pastaj miqësia aq e çiltër e heroit kryesor, Çimit, me shoqen e vet Amlën. Të bën përshtypje kujdesi i autorit për të ndërtuar një karakter të mirë, të dhënë pas së bukurës, historisë, librave, sikundër është ky djalë i vogël, i rritur para kohe, që megjithë hallet e skajshme, është një meditues model, gjen hapësirë të mendojë për familjen, për të ardhmen apo edhe të admirojë pamjet më mbresëlënëse të qytetit të vet, Elbasanit:*

"E tërhiqnin më shumë rrugicat e ngushta dhe sidomos lagjia "Kala", rrugët e vjetra me kalldrëm." Mjafton kaq për të treguar shije të qendrueshme dhe dashuri për traditën, në çka qyteti dhe jeta nxiren për një moment nga përshkrimet 'danteske', siç edhe cilësohen; (shtëpia tejet modeste e personazheve, spitali si mos më keq, rëndomtësia e lagjes "Vullnetari" apo mjedise të tjera të pista e shumë larg një jete normale). Romani 'Grimcat' është një arritje e rëndësishme për autorin dhe, njëherësh, kontribut në Letërsinë Shqipe të pas viteve '90.

I.

Pallati i Peshkut

Ende pa zbardhur dita, Çimi-një vogëlush 11-vjeçar me flokët si gjemba iriqi dhe hundën majuce si spec, zbriti me vrap shkallët e "Pallatit të Peshkut" për të zënë rradhë para të vetmes çezmë, që ndodhej në oborr. Të Mëdhenjtë thonin se çezmën e zinte shpesh Kuçedra, një kafshë mitologjike me shtatë kokë, e cila e përpinte të gjithë ujin në barkun e saj prej përbindëshi. Të paktën kështu tregonin ata dhe Të Vegjëlit i besonin këto histori plotësisht, pasi nuk kishte sesi të shpjegohej ndryshe. Kuçedra ishte aq e etur, saqë shpesh nuk linte as edhe një pikëz ujë.

Këmbët desh iu morën nëpër shkallë dhe meçja për pak sa nuk i ra nga dora, ndërsa bidoni prej kauçuku i rrëshqiti, duke fluturuar poshtë me oshëtimë dhe e ndali turravrapin poshtë dritares së Danës, një plake ezmere, shtatshkurtër, të mbuluar nga rrudhat e që jetonte në katin e parë.

Gjithë ai mundim i kishte shkuar kot. Para tij tashmë ishin vënë në rradhë dhjetë gra dhe shtatë burra, të gjithë të ngarkuar sekush me bidonë, shishe, madje edhe kazanë të mëdhenj.

"Pallati i Peshkut" ishte një ndërtesë dykatëshe me tulla të dala boje, që shkërmoqeshin sapo t'i prekje me dorë dhe e kishte marrë atë emër nga një dyqan mish-peshku që ndodhej në katin e parë. Ngrehina Danteske fillimisht kishte shërbyer si hotel beqarësh, por me kalimin e kohës vendin e tyre e kishin zënë familjet në nevojë. Në të jetonin 18 familje në apartamente njëdhomëshe, të ndara nga njëra-tjetra me mure të hollë kallamash. Në krah të kundërt të çezmës, ngjitur me murin ndarës të shtëpive përdhese, ndodheshin pesë nevojtore, dy nga të cilat ishin bllokuar dhe kutërbonin një erë të rëndë, që të kallte krupën. Moria e mizave bënte kërdinë, megjithëse banorët përpiqeshin t'i mbanin pastër, duke i larë dhe dezinfektuar sa herë që mundeshin. Ca miza të stërmëdha me këmbë si të oktapodëve zhuzhonin mbi kokat e tyre. Duhej të bëje kujdes se po të të pickonin ato, nuk të iknin shenjat për të gjithë javën. Në qoshkëzat e hirnosura të çatisë së banjove zinin fole edhe grerëzat, të cilat bëheshin një tmerr i vërtetë jo vetëm për fëmijët, por edhe për kalimtarët e rastit. Sapo mbushnin ujë, gratë fillonin të zjenin rrobat disa hapa më tutje, të cilat pasi i lanin, i shpëlanin e i shtrydhnin fort, i ndernin në telat e varur para dritareve, por edhe në oborr, ndanë murit anësor të ndërtesës. Në katin e parë kishte edhe një magazinë, nga e cila vinin si vizitorë minj veshllapushë e të murrmë, që me qimet e tyre të kreshpëruara, trembnin kush t'u dilte para. Një mace e madhe dilte ndonjëherë nga dy shtëpitë private dhe bënte sikur ndiqte minjtë bebe. Në fakt lozte me to, pa mundur të frikësonte babaminjtë që ndiqnin të hirnosur atë valle vdekjeje.

Blerësit vinin në "Pallatin e Peshkut" pothuajse nga e gjithë zona përreth Namazgjasë dhe pjesëve të tjera të qytetit. Megjithëse prisnin me orë të tëra, disa prej tyre ktheheshin duarthatë në shtëpi, pasi banakët zbrazeshin shumë shpejt. Kishte nga ata që e humbnin durimin dhe, në vend që të qëndronin në këmbë të ngjeshur pas njëri-tjetrit, linin një copë gur apo letër. Kur ktheheshin, rradha u ishte zënë e si përfundim fillonin e grindeshin me njëri tjetrin, se kush kishte qenë i pari. Shpesh prindërit nuk kishin se çfarë të sillnin në shtëpi e shumica e fëmijëve shiheshin me bukën të lyer me vaj dhe kripë apo me një shtresë të hollë salceje. Buka me sheqer dhe vaj kikiriku ishte një lloj luksi i paparë, gjë që vihej re në fytyrat triumfuese të fëmijëve gazmorë, që i kapërcenin kafshatat me krenari para bashkëmoshatarëve të tyre.

Një rradhë tjetër akoma më e gjatë se dy të parat, ishte ajo para dyqanit të vajgurit, që ndodhej pas shkollës "Thoma Kalefi", përballë një pallati pesëkatësh. Pothuajse i gjithë qyteti e gdhinte në rradhë në pika të ndryshme të tij dhe për prodhime të ndryshme, që përpiheshin sa hap e mbyll sytë: kishte rradhë për qumësht, rradhë për kos, rradhë për vajguri, rradhë për sheqer, për këmbë lopësh a derri, për mish, për plënca dhe zorrë, për peshk, për vaj, madje edhe për bukë. Në ndryshim nga të gjitha rradhët, rradha për ujë, mbahej në të gjithë qytetin dhe dy herë në ditë: një herë në pikë të mëngjesit dhe një herë në mbrëmje, para se qyteti të binte në gjumë.

Më në fund rradha e Çimit erdhi! Futi njërin nga bidonat nën rrjedhën magjiplote të çezmës e u zhvesh. Trupi iu drodh si purtekë, ndërsa flokët iu shndërruan në gjemba. Vari peshqirin, kanatjeren dhe bluzën në njërin nga telat e rrobave ndanë murit dhe vuri duart përtokë. Shtrëngoi dhëmbët dhe futi kurrizin nën rrjedhën e ujit. Mbylli sytë, si për të duruar disi të ftohtit që tashmë i kishte hyrë në palcë dhe filloi të numërojë me zë të lartë. Një, dy, tre, katër, pesëmbëdhjetë... Uji iu fut në brekë dhe të ftohtit tashmë po e bënte të dridhej të tërin. Nxorri kurrizin që andej dhe u hodh disa herë përpjetë. Mori peshqirin dhe fërkoi trupin aq fort, sa lëkura iu skuq e tëra. Veshi me nxitim kanatjeren dhe bluzën, duke fërgëlluar i gjithi. Aq pak sekonda mjaftonin për ta kalitur si Romakët dikur! Mund të qëndronte edhe më shumë, por tashmë dikush po priste në rradhë. Njerëzit nuk kishin ujë për të pirë, ndërsa ai e kishte mendjen për t'u stërvitur. Po sikur dikush t'i thoshte mamit pastaj?

"Po çar ban, o Çimi, se do ftofesh!" Dana, e mbledhur sa një grusht nga të ftohtët, sapo kishte dalë nga shtëpia për të mbushur ujë. Gishti i saj tregues iu tund para hundës, sikur donte t'i thoshte se nuk ishte mirë të sillej në atë mënyrë, kur njerëzit nuk kishin as për të pirë.

"Po jo, me nan Dana, s'më gjen gja mu! Romakët... laheshin... kshu... mjes për mjes!" Që nga ajo ditë që e kishte lexuar këtë detaj nga jeta e romakëve të lashtë, Çimi bënte pikërisht këtë gjë: mbante kurrizin nën ujin e çezmës, gjersa i erreshin sytë.

Dana tundi kokën dhe nduku faqet e vyshkura. Çimi rrëmbeu dy bidonat në dorën e djathtë dhe meçen në të majtën, duke u përpjekur të mbante drejtpeshimin. Gati gjysma e shkallëve ishin të thyera. Nuk duhej të derdhte asnjë pikë ujë, pasi dikush mund të rrëshqiste dhe të rrëzohej. Me shpirt ndër dhëmbë dhe duke gulçuar sa të mundte, i hodhi këmbët me terezi, pra duke u matur mirë. Nëse nuk bënte kujdes, mund të thyente kokën. Më në fund arriti në majë të shkallëve, aty ku ishte një hapësirë në formën e një ballkoni dhe nga ku shiheshin shtëpitë përballë. Një man i madh dhe hijerëndë kishte varur degët e mbushura me sythe mbi banjot e pallatit.

Në verë manat binin gjithandej dhe kishin një shije aq të ëmbël e ishin aq të butë, saqë të shkriheshin në gojë. Kot që t'i kujtonte ato fruta magjike, kur donte edhe katër muaj që të vinte vera. U fut në korridorin e gjatë dhe të errët, duke kërcëllitur dhëmbët. Llampat ishin gati të gjitha të djegura dhe në korridor ishte pothuajse errësirë, përveç një drite të zbehtë që vinte nga një dritare në fund. Ngadalësoi hapat nga frika se mos përplasej me ndonjë nga furnellat, të cilat familjarët i linin pranë dyerve, ndërsa në fyt ndjeu një erë të rëndë të vajgurit të djegur. Dikush sapo kishte fikur furnellën dhe era e saj mbytëse të kallte krupën. Sakaq kishte mbërritur në apartamentin e vet njëdhomësh dhe shtyu derën fort. Njerku kishte ikur në punë në ndërmarrjen e ndërtimit qysh në pesë të mëngjesit, ndërsa nëna, megjithëse në muajin e gjashtë të shtatzanisë, ishte zgjuar tashmë dhe po ndihmonte Platorin-vëllain tre vjet më të vogël, që të vishte një triko leshi. Sytë i shkëlqenin nga kurioziteti dhe ishte aq i hedhur, sa nuk linte dy gurë bashkë. Gjithmonë në lëvizje, Platorit i pëlqente të eksploronte botën, pavarësisht nëse ishte duke lozur me fëmijët e tjerë në oborrin e përparmë të Pallatit të Peshkut apo në shtëpi. E qeshura ngjitëse dhe entuziazmi i pakufi e bënin të ndihej i lumtur për të qenë pranë dhe natyra e tij miqësore i tërhiqte të tjerët lehtësisht. Kur nëna ndjeu erën mbytëse të fitilave të djegur, hapi njërën nga dy dritaret me shpejtësi. Ajri i ftohtë i dimrit e bëri Çimin të dridhej edhe më shumë, por të paktën kolla iu qetësua disi. Pastaj bebi që do të lindte pas tre muajsh, kishte nevojë për ajër të pastër apo jo?! Oh, sa do të kishte dëshirë që mami të sillte në jetë një motër! Nuk do të kishte gjë më të bukur në botë. Do ta donte si dritën e diellit. Do të kujdesej për të si për gjënë më të shtrenjtë. Dhe të jetuarit vetëm në një dhomë, nuk do të ishte më shqetësim. Berti dhe Xhilda-çifti që jetonte përballë tyre, kishin marrë një apartament të ri dhe do të iknin nga Pallati i Peshkut. Drejtori i Strehimit në Këshillin e Qytetit kishte thënë se shteti do t'ua jepte dhomën e tyre si shtesë. Kështu që strehimi nuk do të ishte më problem. Por këto probleme i dinin më mirë Të Mëdhenjtë. Rëndësi për të si i Vogël ishte që të bëhej sa më parë me motër.

Futi dorën nën rripin e pantallonave dhe ndjeu se brekët i ishin lagur. I gjithë perimetri i pantallonave përreth mesit ishte bërë ujë.

"Po ç'je bërë kështu, Çimi? Prapë ke futur kurrizin në ujë?"

"Po", -tha shkurt Çimi.

"Po njerëzit nuk kanë për të pirë dhe ti shkon e lahesh me ujë të ftohtë në mes të dimrit?"

"Po nuk kishte njeri n'rradh, o ma!" u shfajësua Çimi!

"Mos e bëj më, se është turp! Mos u bëj si ajo kuçedra e përrallave që zinte pusin dhe nuk linte të gjithë fshatin të pinte ujë…"

"Mirë, mirë! Nuk e baj ma!"

"Tani vishu, se t'u bë vonë për shkollë! Merr edhe Platorin për në kopësht!"

Çimi tundi kokën nga e majta në të djathtë në shenjë pohimi dhe i shkeli syrin çapkënçe të vëllait. Edhe dhjetë minuta dhe fiks në orën shtatë e gjysëm binte zilja e shkollës. Mbajti këmbët para pasqyrës së thyer të dollapit dhe i hodhi një sy trupit të vet ende të mbuluar nga bulëzat e ujit. Ishte shtatmesatar, me lëkurën të përskuqur vende-vende dhe flokët sterr të zinj të kreshpëruar përpjetë. Veshi kanatieren, këmishën e bardhë dhe të hekurosur, që nëna ia kishte lënë të varur në dollapin e vetëm dykanatësh dhe lidhi përreth qafës shaminë e kuqe të pionerit. Rrëmbeu nga karrigia xhakoventon blu që i kishte blerë teta Xhozi për ditëlindje dhe me çantën e shkollës në sqetull, doli jashtë. Platori puthi të ëmën në faqe dhe nxitoi hapat pas të vëllait më të madh.

Çimi çakërroi sytë në korridor. Gjënë më të fundit që do të dëshironte në ato çaste ishte që të përplasej me ndonjë furnellë. Hajde të dëgjoje klithmat e të zotit të furnellës pastaj! Muret e ndërtesës ishin të ndërtuara me kallama dhe për këtë arsye, me pak mundim, mund të dëgjoje të gjitha bisedat. Pak nga frika se mos përplasej dhe pak më shumë se po digjej nga kureshtja, eci në majë të gishtave, si një hije. Vuri gishtin në buzë, duke ia bërë "shshsht" të vëllait, që të mos bënte zhurmë. Platori ju bind, duke ndenjur sus si një kone e vogël.

Dy dyer më tutje ishin dy dhomat e familjes pesë anëtarëshe të Met ezmerit, babai i të cilit Toma, ishte memec dhe punonte në fabrikën e çimentos.

"Are, uk, do iksh në shko.. ti? Të vojti vo...!" Zëri bubullues i Tomës dukej sikur do ta rrëzonte derën përtokë, ndërsa qortonte me sa kishte në kokë, djalin e madh, Metin!

Një derë më tutje në të majtë, e kishte dhomën një çift rreth të dyzetave pa fëmijë. I zoti i dhomës, Taulanti, ishte vëlla me Skënderin, i cili banonte një derë më tutje. Skënderi ishte më i shkurtër se Nadireja dhe së bashku kishin tre djem: Rizain, Petritin dhe Bukuroshin. Nadireja ishte përsëri shtatzanë dhe, sipas thashethemeve që qarkullonin lart e poshtë, ia kishte premtuar fëmijën për adoptim të vëllait të burrit, Taulantit. Nuk kishte rëndësi nëse do të ishte djalë apo vajzë, ai fëmijë do t'i përkiste atyre, sapo Nadireja ta nxirrte në jetë. Pikërisht për shkak të këtyre thashethemeve të çuditshme, Çimi mbajti frymën dhe ngjeshi veshin pas derës së shtëpisë së Nadiresë.

Gjithmonë i kishte bërë përshtypje ajo familje, kjo edhe për atë arsye se rrallë gjeje ndonjëherë ndonjë familje, ku burri të ishte një kokë më i shkurtër se bashkëshortja. Në fillim dëgjoi një të qarë burri, si me gulçima. Çimi asnjëherë nuk kishte parë ndonjëherë ndonjë burrë të qante. Uli dorezën ngadalë, aq ngadalë, sa të mos bënte as zhurmën më të vogël dhe e shtyu derën me shumë kujdes, aq sa të fuste paksa kokën. Shqeu sytë dhe goja ju hap nga habia. Skënderi ishte ulur në divan dhe po lexonte një letër me zërin që i dridhej.

"Babi i dashur! M'kan met edhe njimedhit muj që t'maroj ushtrin! E di që të ka marr malli, por ti mos u murzit!..." Letra kishte ardhur nga djali i madh Rizai, ushtar në kufi me Greqinë. Skënderi vazhdonte të lexonte me zë të lartë, duke u ndërprerë herë pas here nga gulçet e ngashërimit. Çimi tërhoqi përsëri derën me kujdes dhe bëri më tutje.

Në hyrje të shkallëve, në të djathtë, jetonte një familje vllehe: Miri me të dy prindërit e tij, Vangjën dhe Filipin. Vladimiri ishte i gjatë gati 2 metra, por kishte një të metë shumë të madhe: bënte shurrën kur flinte. Për këtë arsye dhoma e tyre vinte era shurrë. Çimi kapi hundën me dorë dhe doli në ballkonin e vetëm të shkallëve. Që aty shiheshin përsëri ato tre shtëpi përdhese me oborr. I njëjti man i madh me trupin e vet kockor, dukej sikur mezi priste gjersa të vinte vera e të mbushej përsëri nga manat e zinj dhe të ëmbël. Syri i kapi Kacamiun, miun më të madh të lagjes. Ndryshe nga herët e tjera ajo krijesë e pistë po i dukej e dashur dhe miqësore. Kacamiu thinjosh kishte varur veshët dhe ishte ulur galiç në skajin më të largët të oborrit.

"Çimi, çfarë bën? Të vajti vonë për shkollë!" tha Kacamiu dhe sakaq nxorri majën e gjuhës e lëpiu mustaqet e gjata.

Çimi po bënte çudi, sesi njëri nga minjtë më të moshuar të pallatit të kishte lënë depon e tij të pëlqyer e të kishte ardhur gjer aty.

"E di, e di! Po ti, si ka munci, që flet? S'e ke ba asiher!" Tha Çimi dhe përpëliti kapakët e syve, i mrekulluar nga ajo që po shihte. Vërtet Kacamiu fliste si një njeri i zakonshëm? Madje kishte ardhur atë mëngjes dhe e kishte përshëndetur? Çfarë mrekullie kishte ndodhur që edhe kafshët kishin filluar të flisnin? E përshëndeti me dorë dhe doli në rrugë.

"Lali, m'prit ne mu!" u ankua Platori dhe ndërkohë nxitoi hapat e vegjël. Çimi ndali këmbët dhe priti me padurim që vëllai të afrohej edhe më e ta kapte prej dore. Pak metra më tutje shkolla gumëzhinte nga zërat gazmorë të fëmijëve.

II.

Makina e elektroshokut

"**S**iemens AG, Convulsator!" Isai lexoi me zë të lartë markën e aparatit të elektroshokut, një kutie të verdhë me dorezë, nga e cila zgjateshin dy elektroda si tentakula mizore oktapodi. Shigjeta në dritaren e xhamtë të vatmetrit tregonte ende zero. Një buton jeshil poshtë dritares i kujtoi syrin e vetëm të djallit. Kishte kaq shumë dëshirë ta nguliste në mendje edhe detajin më të parëndësishëm, saqë zgurdulloi sytë, por ankthi nuk e linte të përqëndrohej. Zëri i tingëlloi në vesh më shumë si një thirrje për protestë. E kishin sjellë përsëri në dhomën e elektroshokut, ku po i nënshtrohej një terapie intensive me goditje të impulseve elektrike në tru. Këtë herë në dhomë kishte ardhur doktor Xhindi, emri dhe hija e rëndë e të cilit i ngjalli një frikë kapitulluese. Isai po vriste mendjen, nëse "Xhindi" ishte mbiemri i vërtetë i doktorit famëkeq.

Dy infermierë e mbajtën nga krahët dhe e tërhoqën pothuajse zvarrë drejt krevatit portativ të mbuluar me një çarçaf të bardhë. I kishin veshur një palë pizhama me kuadrate ngjyrë kafe, ndërsa në këmbët e zbathura kishte një palë shapka të shqyera. Shtrëngoi fort dhëmbët që të mos i dilte asnjë klithmë apo pasthirrmë sado e vogël që të ishte. Sa më shumë panik që të shprehte, aq më e gjatë do të ishte goditja elektrike. Sikur të mos mjaftonte kjo, sytë e doktorit sikur po e shponin tejpërtej, duke ia shtuar edhe më shumë frikën. E vërejti me kujdes. Doktori Xhindi duhej të ishte rreth të pesëdhjetave. Kishte një trup mesatar dhe flokë të zinj që kishin filluar t'i thinjeshin. Frymëmarrja sikur i ishte rënduar disi nga ai stërmundim fizik për ta kontrolluar të sëmurin. Përreth qafës kishte të varur aparatin e stetoskopit. Këpucët prej lëkure, dukej se sapo i kishte lyer, pasi i shkëlqenin nën dritën e diellit, që kishte nxjerrë kryet paksa në dritare. Këmisha e bardhë borë dhe faqet e rruara taze, të jepnin përshtypjen se doktori i kushtonte shumë rëndësi higjienës personale dhe pamjes së jashtme, përkundër gjendjes së mjerueshme të spitalit.

"Jaka e këmishës është e bardhë borë. Këpucët e doktorit xixëllojnë si pasqyrë!" Çuditërisht kishte folur sërisht me zë. Rrotulloi sytë naivë përreth dhomës.

Këtë herë doktorit i pëlqeu ai pohim i beftë i të sëmurit në sy të kolegëve të tjerë. Iu duk sikur ja përkëdheli disi sedrën e sëmurë prej egoisti. Dy infermierët mezi e mbajtën të qeshurën nën buzë, por doktori bëri sikur nuk i vuri re. Duhej të përqendrohej tek i sëmuri dhe të mbaronte punë sa më shpejt që të ishte e mundur.

"Hape gojën!" i thirri fort.

Zëri i metaltë i doktorit e mpiu Isain krejtësisht. Njëri nga infermierët, me mustaqet e prera spic, i ngjeshi në gojë një top fashoje të mbledhur shuk, e cila gati sa nuk i ngeci në fyt dhe po i vinte për të vjellë. Nuk kundërshtoi si herët e tjera. Ajo masë e butë fashosh do t'i mbronte dhëmbët, kur i gjithë trupi do t'i nënshtrohej goditjeve elektrike. Mustaqespici kishte një vështrim të vëngërt dhe te mprehtë. Po e vëzhgonte çdo lëvizje të të sëmurit, sikur do ta hante të gjallë. Duhej të ishte rreth të tridhjetave dhe me një shtat mbimesatar. Flokët i kishte të prera shumë shkurt, ndërsa nga pas e kishte të rruar gjer në çaçkë të kokës, stil alla komunist, si ushtarët e kazermave. Infermieri tjetër ishte disi më i moshuar. Rrinte paksa i gërmuqur dhe pa qejf, sikur e kishin sjellë aty me zor. Kapsalliste sytë nga pagjumësia. Ndoshta po punonte jashtë orarit dhe dukej se mezi priste që të dilte prej aty. Flokët ngjyrë gështenjë i kishte të pakrehur, me ca grimca zbokthi që zbardhnin tek-tuk.

Doktor Xhindi ia vuri elektrodat në kokë presë së vet, që nuk kishte se nga lëvizte më dhe shtypi me gishtin tregues butonin jeshil. Rrotulloi ngadalë dorezën e vatmetrit. Me një ndenjë vetëkënaqësie të dukshme ne fytyrë kontrolloi parametrat. Nëpër trupin e pacientit do të kalonin mbi dy mijë valë elektrike për 50 sekonda! Lloji i impulsit duhej të ishte ¼ e dallgëve sinus dhe me një frekuencë 50HZ. Impulsi duhej të zgjaste jo më shumë se 5 mS dhe duhej të përsëritej pas 15mS interval.

"Tani do të shohim, nëse do të jesh në gjendje të flasësh përsëri me zë të lartë," ironizoi doktori dhe ngërdheshi fytyrën me qesëndi.

I sëmuri u përpoq të hapte kapakët e syve, por ato ishin bërë të rënda plumb. Pamja iu mjegullua aq shumë, saqë krijoi përshtypjen e rreme, sikur ishte brenda kabinës së një avioni udhëtarësh që po fluturonte mes reve. Lëvizi trupin që të ngrihej nga shtrati dhe të vazhdonte të regjistronte gjithçka në kujtesën e tij të lodhur, por fashat e kishin shtrënguar fort nga të gjitha anët! E ndjeu veten peshk të alivanosur në rrjetën e peshkatarëve. Me sytë gjysëm të hapur dalloi fytyrën e doktorit, e cila i ishte avitur aq pranë, saqë dukej sikur do t'i numëronte poret e lëkurës. Fytyra e doktorit ishte e mbuluar nga një tis i hollë djerse, ndërsa poshtë kapakëve të syve i dalloheshin dy rrathë të mëdhenj e të zinj. Trupi filloi t'i shkundej vrullshëm nga konvulsionet elektrike. Hapi duart në të dy anët e krevatit, që të mbahej diku, pasi po i mirreshin mendtë, por fashat nuk e linin. Ndjeu t'i dhimbnin kockat. Tavani mori përsëri formën e një kabine avioni. Ishte me të vërtetë në avion, duke fluturuar për diku? Ja retë e bardha që dukeshin nga dritarja e vogël në krah. Ishte një dritare apo thjesht një vegim?! Ku po shkonte vallë?

"Si të quajnë ty? Si ta thonë emrin?" e pyeti doktori, ndërsa njëri nga infermierët, ai me flokët ngjyrëkafe, i hoqi topin e fashos nga goja. Fashot kishin marrë ngjyrën e gjakut. Zgurdulloi sytë me habi, duke parë përreth, si për të kërkuar ndihmë nga dikush. Përse vallë doktori duhej t'ia bënte një pyetje të tille prej idioti? A nuk e kishte kartelën e të sëmurit para syve? Mos ndoshta dëshironte t'i vinte në provë edhe atë pakëz kujtesë që i kishte mbetur? Vërtet si quhej? Nga kishte ardhur dhe pse gjendej aty?! Mblodhi supet në shenjë pasigurie.

"Quhem Isa Vishanji!" Fjalët i dolën nga goja të shkëputura, sikur po jepte shpirt.

"Hëhë! Kujtesën e paske të fortë. Të shohim sesa do të mbash mend pasi të dalësh prej këtej," u ngërdhesh doktori dhe ia bëri me shenjë infermierit me flokë ngjyrë kafe, që të vijonte punën. Infermieri pa ngurruar fare, i ngjeshi në gojë një top fashoje tjetër. Pasi u sigurua se pacienti nuk kishte asnjë mundësi që të kundërshtonte, doktor Xhindi rrotulloi përsëri dorezën e vatmetrit. Impulset elektrike filluan ta godisnin të sëmurin njëherësh në tëmtha. Imazhet iu rrokullisën e iu palosën me njëra-tjetrën. Mendja po i vinte vërdallë. U kap fort pas hekurave të krevatit, si për të kërkuar shpëtim. Vetëtimat filluan të çajnë qiellin e errët të natës. Në veshë i gjëmuan bubullimat e stuhisë që po afrohej. Pa trupin e vet të lodhur të rrëshqiste nëpër një labirinth llamarine e të zhdukej pa gjurmë në një vrimë të zezë në hapësirë. Impulset elektrike po e masakronin pa mëshirë në çdo qelizë të trurit. Masa e trurit po dallgëzonte nën kafkë, e cila filloi të ziente si një tenxhere me presion. Shtresa e kraniumit gati sa nuk po pëlciste nga shtypja e madhe që po ndjente nga të gjitha anët. Befas qielli u hap dhe për çudi pa veten qindra kilometra larg prej andej.

NGRITI JAKËN E PALLTOS ushtarake për t'u mbrojtur disi nga ajri i ftohtë. Picërroi sytë me padurim në thellësi të parkut Marsovo Polje. Svjetllana Konstandinova nuk po dukej gjëkundi. Bëri disa ecejake rreth Vechniy Ogon-it, (Вечный огонь), flakadanit të ndezur për nder të Heronjve të Rusisë, por ora kishte ngecur në vend. Sa ditë dhe netë kishin kaluar bashkë në këtë park nën dritën e hënës! Kurrë nuk e kishte menduar se do të vinte një ditë që t'i thonin njëri-tjetrit "lamtumirë". Ndjeu dhimbje për atë qytet të madh e të lashtë, të emërtuar rishtazi "Leningrad". Ato gjuhë të holla flakësh nuk po arrinin t'i ngrohnin dot shpirtin e mbushur përplot me dashuri dhe mall për Svjetllana Konstandinovan.

Eci më tutje dhe këmbët e mbajtën para një tabele, ku ishte shkruar historia e parkut. Në fillim ishte çuditur se pse parku quhej "Fusha e Marsit", ndonëse nuk kishte asnjë lidhje me planetin Mars. Më vonë kishte mësuar se ai park i magjishëm e kishte marrë emrin nga Perëndia Romake e Luftës! Aty ishin organizuar të gjitha paradat ushtarake të ushtrisë Ruse. Dikur ai park i themeluar që në fund të viteve 1900 e kishte patur emrin "Livadhi i Madh".

"Isa!" Ndjeu një zë femëror ta thërriste në emër. Svjetllana po vinte me hap të ngadaltë dhe krejtësisht e shkujdesur. Flokët e lidhur gërshet i dukeshin më të praruar nën rrezet e forta të diellit. Kishte një trup mesatar dhe bel të hollë, ndërsa sytë e kaltër i rrezatonin vetëm ëmbëlsi. As që e kishte menduar ndonjëherë më parë ndarjen me Svjetllanën. Kishin tre vjet që dashuroheshin, që nga ajo ditë kur i kërkoi të kërcenin bashkë në një mbrëmje të Akademisë Ushtarake Detare të Saint Petersburgut. Svjetllana i hodhi krahët rreth qafës dhe e shtrëngoi fort, sikur të mos e kishte parë për një kohë të gjatë. Ndoshta e ndjente që diçka e rëndë dhe e madhe kishte ndodhur. Kishin vetëm pesë ditë që nuk ishin takuar, por atij i dukej sikur kishte kaluar një shekull.

"мой друг" ('I dashuri im'), çfarë ka ndodhur? Pse je kaq i mërzitur?"

"Sot kishim një takim me atasheun tonë ushtarak…"

"Edhe…?"

"Ka ardhur një urdhër nga Shqipëria që të gjithë studentët shqiptarë të lënë studimet dhe të kthehen urgjentisht në atdhe!" I ktheu menjëherë shpinën për të fshehur disi dridhjen e zërit. Nuk ishte mirë të tregonte dobësi para një vajze. Shqiptarët nuk derdhin lotë para femrave dhe këtë fakt ai e kishte ngulitur në mendje shumë mirë. Kapërceu lëmshin që iu mblodh në fyt dhe iu kthye përballë. E pa me ngulm në sy, sikur donte të depërtonte thellë qenies së saj të brishtë.

"Ti, çfarë do të bësh?" Zëri i saj doli i dobët, gati si një pëshpërimë gjethesh.

"Më duhet të kthehem!" Iu duk sikur atë çast një dorë e padukshme po i shkulte zemrën. "Mund të vish edhe ti me mua, nëse do," shtoi, si për ta zbutur gjendjen. Zëri i doli i mekët, sikur po mbytej. Ndoshta ishte shumë ajo që po kërkonte nga Svjetllana. Ishte thjesht një aludim, një fjalë e mirë sa për të larë gojën. Si vajzë oficeri ajo e kishte më të vështirë se ai, që të braktiste gjithçka e të vinte për të jetuar në një vend të vogël dhe tashmë "armik" si Shqipëria.

"Qëndro ti këtu! Nuk kam mbaruar shkollën akoma dhe pasdite jam në punë. Po të qëndrosh ti këtu, babai do të të ndihmojë të gjesh një vend të mirë në ushtri." Svjetllana po e shikonte me ngulm. "Këtu do të kesh të ardhme!"

Përfytyroi arratisjen nga konvikti dhe ikjen me një taksi të rastit në apartamentin e saj. Do të shkëputej përfundimisht nga babai, vëllai dhe tri motrat që e prisnin në shtëpi. Nuk do të kishte më asnjë mundësi, që të vinte një tufë me lule në varrin e nënës, atje në Vishanjin e largët. Shokët e shkollës do ta tregonin me gisht si armik të popullit. Po vetë gjenerali Konstandinov-babai i saj, vërtet do ta pranonte një veprim të tillë? Ai ishte ushtarak karriere dhe natyrisht që nuk do të kishte ndonjë simpati për dezertorët. Megjithëse do t'i pëlqente fakti që Svjetllana ia kishte mbushur mendjen të fejuarit të saj shqiptar që të qëndronte në Rusi, thellë në shpirt gjenerali do ta përçmonte për veprimin që kishte bërë. Nga ana tjetër, nëse vendoste të kthehej në Shqipëri, kishte shumë mundësi që ta humbiste përgjithmonë Svjetllanën, sytë e saj të bukur dhe atë kurm të ngrohtë. Mjaftonte të ndante *mendjen dhe të thoshte "po" e gjithçka do të merrte një drejtim krejt tjetër, të paparashikuar. U drodh i gjithi, sikur ta kishin zënë ethet. As që e imagjinonte dot të qëndronte aty, duke flakur tej uniformën e ushtarakut. Kjo do të cilësohej si dezertim nga Ushtria dhe atij padyshim që do t'i vihej damka e tradhtarit. Me imagjinatën e ndezur rikrijoi atë moment, kur do të zhvishej e flakte tej uniformën ushtarake. Në fillim do të fuste në valixhe kapelen, pastaj xhaketën dhe pantallonat. Krejtësisht lakuriq, në rroba civile, vetja do t'i dukej një njeri pa vlerë dhe pa dinjitet. Atdheu apo Svjetllana? Svjetllana apo Atdheu? Oh, sa do të kishte dëshirë që t'i kishte përjetësisht të dyja dhe të mos humbiste asnjërën. Shqipëriza e vogël dhe Svjetllana e kishin secila nga një qoshe në zemrën e vet. Hapi krahët, ashtu si skifteri mbi prenë e vet. E shtrëngoi fort si i marrë dhe e puthi disa herë në ato buzë të rrumbullakëta e të kuqe, pa kuptuar se lotët kishin filluar t'i rridhnin në faqe instinktivisht.*

"Eja ti me mua, Svjetllana! Të lutem, eja vetëm si vizitore. Nuk ka pse të martohesh me mua. Rri ca ditë në shtëpinë time në Shqipëri. Po nuk të pëlqeu, ik!" Nuk e kuptoi as vetë, sesi i erdhi ai propozim i beftë, por që në momentin që ia tha, e kuptoi se ishte një gjë e kotë që t'i kërkonte t'i hynte një aventure të tillë për të vizituar Shqipërinë. Nuk kishte kohë për vendime të përkohshme. Mund të dilnin njëqind pengesa nga më të paimagjinueshmet. Svjetllana duhej ta ndante mendjen e të merrte një vendim të prerë: ose të vinte përfundimisht, ose të rrinte përgjithmonë aty, në Saint Petersburg. Svjetllana duhej të zgjidhte ndërmjet të dashurit të saj dhe Rusisë. Oh zot! Përse vallë ndarja duhej të vinte nga një arsye e tillë? Mund të kishte ndonjë arsye më të bindshme, përshembull vdekja. Mund të bëheshin shkak për ndarje dhjetra yçkla të tjera, por jo grindjet politike ndërmjet

dy shteteve. E ç'lidhje kishte Svjetllana me idetë revizioniste të Hrushovit? Ç'punë kishte ai vetë me qëndrimin aventuresk të Enver Hoxhës për t'u hequr më stalinist se vetë Rusët?! E gjithë ajo gjendje i tingëllonte krejtësisht absurde dhe e gënjeshtërt. Të gjitha ato ëndrra që kishin ndërtuar bashkë, tashmë po shembeshin me një të rënë të një shkopi magjik. Që nga ajo ditë që e kishte parë për herë të parë, kurrë nuk e kishte menduar se do të ndahej nga ajo. Kjo botë që kishin ndërtuar ishte një kështjellë mbi grimcat e rërës dhe prandaj po u shkërrmoqej parasysh.

"Nuk di se çfarë të them. Kur bëhet nisja për në Shqipëri?"

"Na kanë dhënë ultimatum që të ikim të gjithë brenda një jave! Atasheu ynë u shpall 'non grata.'" Ia shtrëngoi dorën e vogël dhe të brishtë, sikur donte të merrte pak ngrohtësi nga zjarri i saj i brendshëm. Svjetllana fshehu kokën në gjoksin e tij të bëshëm dhe qau në heshtje. Më në fund e kishte kuptuar se Isai nuk mund të qëndronte aty dhe të mos i bindej urdhërit për t'u kthyer në atdhe.

"Përse u dashka të bëjmë zgjedhje të tilla kaq të vështira? Përse?!" Fjalët e Svjetllanës i vinin si të përgjysmuara në vesh.

"Do të të shkruaj letra përditë. Gjithçka do të jetë kalimtare. Mbase ka qenë thjesht një keqkuptim dhe ata lart do të merren vesh një ditë!"

"Nuk më besohet! Konflikti mund të zgjasë me vite të tëra!" Svjetllana fshiu lotët me shami të qëndisur në cepat nga vetë ajo, të cilën e nxorri nga çanta e dorës dhe e futi prapë në të me delikatesë. "Eja të shkojmë te restoranti ynë i preferuar në 'Moroshka për Pushkinin.' Mund të jetë hera e fundit."

Isai i hodhi krahun rreth qafës dhe të dy të përqafuar morën rrugën në këmbë për në restorantin me emrin e poetit të shquar rus, që për fat ishte vetëm 200 metra larg nga parku. Svjetllana nuk ia lëshoi për asnjë çast dorën, gjersa mbërritën në restorant.

Sa netë romantike kishin kaluar aty, të ulur në karriget me ato forma të çuditshme! Hyrja ishte disi e fshehur nga sytë e kalimtarëve të rastit, duke e bërë një qoshkëz të parapëlqyer për dashnorët. Ngjitur me lumin Moika, "Moroshka për Pushkinin" e kishte marrë atë emër "Luleshtrydhe për Pushkinin", pasi poeti i madh kur ishte gjallë, sillte luleshtrydhe me vete pikërisht aty, në atë restorant. U futën në katin e nëndheshëm dhe menjëherë zunë vend në tavolinën e tyre të parapëlqyer. Nën tingujt e muzikës dhe shijes së verës, Isai po uronte në heshtje që ato çaste të zgjasnin në përjetësi. Svjetllana e pezmatuar treti shikimin nga dritarja dhe qëndroi gjer në fund si në gjemba, gjersa mbaruan dhe dolën jashtë. Para se të ndaheshin, e përqafoi fort dhe e puthi me afsh në buzë. Kishte një parandjenjë që nuk do të shiheshin më.

"Kur bëhet nisja?"

"Të Hënën. Do të vijë një autobuz para derës së akademisë dhe do të na marrë për të na dërguar drejt e në aeroport."

"Do të vij të të përcjell. Mbase të mbushet mendja gjer atëherë që të rrish këtu," shtoi ajo me gjysëm zëri.

Isai e përqafoi sërisht. Ajo buzëqeshje e ëmbël e mbështolli të gjithin, sikur donte t'ia hiqte me magji trishtimin që e kishte zënë. As që donte ta mendonte ndarjen nga Svjetllana, veç luti zotin, që ajo të vinte edhe njëherë të vetme në stacionin e autobuzit, kur të nisej për në aeroport. Ndoshta do të ishte Svjetllana ajo që do të ndërronte mendje dhe të vinte me të në minutën e fundit.

"A do të vish për fundjavë të ndahesh me prindërit e mi?" Shikimi i saj lutës iu ngul thellë në shpirt. Svjetllana po mendonte të njëjtën gjë. Një takim me babain e saj, gjeneralin Ivan Konstandinov, mund të ndryshonte për mirë a për keq rrjedhën e ngjarjeve. Nuk ishte hera e parë që kishte qenë në shtëpinë e saj. Më mirë të ikte pa u takuar me askënd, sesa të përballej me Ivanin e tmerrshëm, gjeneralin Konstandinov. Kujtoi ato netë të gjata në dimrin e ftohtë të Saint Petersburgut dhe fytyrën e kuqerremtë, gati të egër të gjeneralit, që në kushte të tjera mund të ishte bërë vjehrri i vet. Do të tingëllonte e pasjellshme të mos shkonte dhe të përshëndetej jo vetëm me gjeneralin, por edhe me nënën e Svjetllanës, Mira! Një ndjesi turpi dhe zori i skuqi fytyrën.

"Kam frikë se jo," tha shkurt, me zemër të thyer.

Ende pa mbaruar fjalën, Svjetllana i ktheu krahët dhe mbuloi sytë me duar, sikur nuk donte të besonte se çfarë kishte ndodhur atë çast. Eci disa hapa, por këmbët nuk e mbajtën. U ul ne gjunjë dhe shpërtheu në dënesë. Supet e vegjël filluan t'i dridheshin. Isai zgjati dorën që ta ngushëllonte. Molllëzat e gishtave prekën supin e saj të brishtë. Vetëm një sekondë, se pastaj Svjetllana ia shtyu tutje me inat dhe dëshpërim. Zgjati dorën përsëri, por nuk guxoi ta prekte.

III.

Akupara

Isai ende ndjehej i trullosur dhe i vinte tmerrësisht gjumë. Më në fund e kishin sjellë në dhomën e vet, ku ndodheshin edhe pesë të sëmurë të tjerë. Më i moshuari prej tyre, një malësor rreth të gjashtëdhjetave, flinte me gojën e hapur, nga ku i dukeshin dhëmbët e nxirë dhe të krimbur. Një gërhimë e rëndë gati sa nuk tundte muret. I sëmuri ngjitur pranë tij ishte një djalë rreth të njëzetave. Kokën e kishte të qethur tullë dhe trupin të hollë si gjethe. Bënte ecejake përmes shtretërve, duke kënduar me zë të ulët. Fytyra i shkëlqente nga një dritë e magjishme kënaqësie, që dukej sikur i vinte nga një botë krejtësisht e panjohur, që nuk kishte asnjë lidhje me mjedisin në të cilin ndodhej. Pacienti i tretë ishte një burrë rreth të tridhjetave, krejtësisht i parruar dhe i pistë. Ishte mbledhur kutullaç mbi shtrat dhe shtrëngonte nënkrejsën në gjoks me krahët e dobët. Krah derës në të majtë rrinte një burrë rreth të dyzeatve. Shpesh krruante kokën dhe me thonjtë e gjatë dhe të nxirë përpiqej të kapte morrat në flokët e trashur nga yndyra dhe pisllëku. Fytyrën e kishte të mbuluar nga puçrat, disa nga të cilat kishin filluar të qelbëzoheshin.

Isai ndjeu dhjetëra gjilpëra të holla ta çponin në të gjithë trupin. Kishte alergji ngjitëse, sa herë që sytë i ndeshnin në diçka të pështirë. Vuri duart në dy anët e krevatit prej hekuri dhe mblodhi forcat që të ngrihej. Krisja e thatë e sustës së ndryshkur i çpoi veshët. Ndjeu një dëshirë të papërmbajtur që të dilte prej andej një orë e më parë. Veshi shapkat dhe tërhoqi këmbët ngadalë. Edhe zinxhirë të kishte të lidhura në kyçe, kockat nuk do t'i dhimbnin aq shumë.

Hekurat e dritares i jepnin dhomës pamjen e një kafazi të kopshtit zoologjik. Mjekët nuk parashikonin dot se çfarë mund të bënin pacientët në gjendje depresioni. Shpesh mjaft prej tyre gjendeshin në një situatë aq të mjerë, saqë tentonin vetëvrasjen. Dhoma e shtrimit gjendej në katin e parë dhe dritarja shikonte në krahun e prapëm të spitalit, nga ku dukej oborri, si në pëllëmbë të dorës.

Muri rrethues ishte i ndërtuar me tulla, të cilave u kishte dalë boja e gëlqeres dhe ishin plasaritur vende vende nga agjentët atmosferikë, por ishte i lartë mbi tre metra. Hera e fundit kur ishte lyer, mund të kishte qenë dita e inaugurimit të spitalit, afro njëzet vjet të shkuara. Rrëzë murit ishin vendosur stola të stërgjatë, mbi të cilët ishin ulur disa nga pacientët. Secili prej tyre dukej sikur ishte zhytur në botën e vet, me vështrimet e humbura në hapësirë dhe duart e kryqëzuara mbi gjunjë. Nga dhjetë paciente të mbledhur në qoshen verilindore të oborrit, vetëm njëri kishte veshur një palë shapka të shqyera. Te tjerët ishin zbathur. Shputat dhe mollëzat e gishtave të këmbëve u kishin formuar një shollë të zezë dhe të ashpër. Të gjithë ishin të parruajtur dhe të palarë prej javësh. Uniformat që mbanin veshur ishin të grisura dhe vetëm emrin kishin të tillë, pasi ishin një kombinim xhaketë-pantallona gjithëfarësoj.

Një pacient me flokë ngjyrë kafe që ishte ulur këmbëkryq në mes të oborrit, kishte veshur një xhaketë pizhamash me vija ngjyrë kafe dhe të bardha, por pantallonat i kishte ngjyrë blu. Një pacient ezmer pinte duhan, i ulur këmbë përmbi këmbë në një stol, disi më i shkëputur nga të tjerët. Ky kishte veshur një palë pantallona blu të errët. Tre të tjerë ishin krejtësisht pa pantallona dhe xhaketat e zbërdhylura mezi u mbulonin organet gjenitale.

Për dallim me dhomën e tejmbushur nga kutërbimi mbytës i trupave të të sëmurëve, oborri jepte ndjesinë e lirisë. Rrezet e diellit ngrohnin lumturisht njësoj atë grumbull shpirtrash dhe ajri i pastër u freskonte mushkëritë. Ndërsa po bëhej gati të largohej nga dritarja, syri i zuri diçka të rrumbullakët dhe të murrme që po dilte nga një e çarë horizontale në mur. Zgurdulloi sytë për të parë më mirë. Gjallesa kishte formën e një guri petashuq, që kishte ngecur mes tullave e përpiqej të lëvizte. Kokën e kishte në formën e kokës së gjarpërit, që hynte e dilte nga një guackë e murrme me kuadrate të verdhë. Isai nënqeshi me ngazëllim dhe nxitoi hapat.

"Qenka një breshkë! Për atë zot, qenka një breshkë!" Klithi me zë.

Nuk e mbante mend, se kur ishte hera e fundit që kishte parë ndonjë mace apo qen, por një breshkë në oborr as që e kishte imagjinuar kurrë. Ishte njësoj sikur të shihje ndonjë alienth të ardhur nga kozmosi në një minianije guackore. Në qoshet dhe korridorët e spitalit syri i kishte kapur minj të vegjël, por ato kafshë të hirta veçse ia shtonin zymtësinë e shpirtit dhe nuk i ngjallnin kurrfarë kënaqësie. Breshka si gjallesë ishte ndryshe dhe nuk kishte asnjë të krahasuar me minjtë e pistë. Breshkën mund ta mbaje në dorë dhe mund të mos ndoteshe. Ajo kafshë e heshtur dhe paqësore i solli në mendje kujtimet e fëmijërisë. Gjyshja njëherë i kishte treguar se ushtarët italianë kur kishin pushtuar fshatin, nuk kishin lënë breshkë pa kapur, të cilat i zjenin dhe më pas i gatuanin, gjë që binte ndesh me zakonet e fshatarëve vendas, të cilët i preknin breshkat vetëm kur donin të loznin me to. Sapo doli në oborr, dielli i paradites i vrau sytë. Me qepallat gjysëm të mbyllura, pa parë majtas a djathas, Isai e mbajti frymën ndanë murit, aty ku breshka kishte ngecur, duke dhënë e marrë me këmbët e përparme, por pa mundur që të shtyhej përpara. E tërhoqi ngadalë, duke u munduar që faqet anësore të vrimës të mos e gërvishtnin kafshën e gjorë. E mori në duar dhe me gjunjët mbështetur në tokë, vazhdonte ta shikonte si gjënë më të rrallë në botë. Kur po bëhej gati të ngrihej, ndjeu dikë ta kapte si me darë nga supi. Një burrë shtatlartë dhe me flokët e zinj të lëpirë pas kokës gati sa nuk i zuri dhe atë copë diell që shndriste mbi oborr. Burri ishte veshur me uniformën e infermierit dhe po i tundte gishtin në shenjë kërcënimi. Ishte Fatmiri, infermieri i turnit. Ndjeu dëshpërim në zemër dhe duart po i dridheshin. Ishte e çuditshme që infermieri më i dhunshëm i spitalit t'i shfaqej parasysh pikërisht në atë moment. Të sëmurët e tjerë ishin bërë kureshtarë dhe po ndiqnin atë skenë që dukej si e sajuar në çast.

"Sille këtu!"

Zëri i vrazhdë i infermierit i përshkoi trupin. Një drithërimë frike e kaploi nga koka tek këmbët. Hodhi sytë nga të sëmurët e tjerë, si për të marrë miratim, por pamja e tyre edhe më kërcënuese e meku të tërin. Një pacient vetëm me një xhaketë hedhur supeve dhe pothuajse lakuriq nga brezi e poshtë u afrua ngadalë, duke thithur vrullshëm një bisht cigareje.

"Breshkën e qujn Akupara! Pse na e merr Akuparën, or burrë? A e di ti që në mitologjinë indiane Akupara man botën n'kurriz?"

Trupi gërdallë iu shkund nga një e kollitur e fortë. Qëroi gurmazin me sa fuqi kishte dhe pështyu para këmbëve të infermierit.

"Bëj kështu siç them unë," iu hakërrua infermier Fatmiri, pa ia hequr sytë Isait, që ende ishte në mëdyshje me breshkën në duar. Zëri i infermierit tingëlloi më frikësues se normalisht. Mustaqet spic sikur iu holluan edhe më nën hundën e gjatë dhe të hollë si teh shpate. Këtë herë Fatmiri nuk kishte kamzhik me vete, as edhe shkopin prej druri, me të cilin eglendisej në të shumtën e kohës.

"A e di si quhet latinisht kjo breshkë? "Testudinata"! Breshkat janë gjallesat ma t'hershme në Tokë. Janë shfaq qysh para 250 milionë vitesh. Ka mbi 300 lloje sysh, por kjo a e llojit 'caretta'!" tha me të shpejtë i sëmuri gjysëm lakuriq. Atij ia kishin vënë nofkën "mësuesi". Para se të shtrohej në spital, kishte punuar si mësues biologjie në gjimnaz.

"Mjaft!" Fatmiri i tundi gishtin tregues në fytyrë dhe në çast u kthye nga Isai. Ia rrëmbeu breshkën nga duart dhe i hodhi një vështrim të egër nga koka te këmbët, sikur do ta përpinte të gjallë. Të sëmurët e tjerë u ngritën nga stolat ngadalë, duke e vënë në mes. Infermier Fatmiri çau me bërryla rrethin dhe u fut në ndërtesën e spitalit. Të sëmurët mbetën të shastisur në mes të oborrit, pa ditur se çfarë të bënin. "Mësuesi" dukej më i revoltuari nga të gjithë. Ngriti dorën hollake drejt kupës së qiellit, sikur po kërkonte ndihmë nga ndonjë fuqi e mbinatyrshme. Të sëmurët e tjerë u ngjanin më shumë hijeve, pasi as nuk flisnin dhe as bënin ndonjë gjest. Thjesht prisnin si spektatorë të durueshëm se çfarë do të ndodhte.

"Na e arrestun 'Akuparën' për agjitacion dhe propagandë!" deklaroi me ton solemn "Mësuesi". Sytë e picërruar nga qielli befas u kthyen nga Isai, që tashmë ishte bërë sa një grusht njeriu nga frika e ndonjë hakmarrjeje të mundshme prej të sëmurëve të tjerë. "Nuk do ta lëmë me kaq! Të gjithë të kërkojmë lirinë e Akuparas!" Zëri i "Mësuesit" ishte aq urdhërues, sa njëri nga pacientët filloi të mërmëriste "Akupara". Fillimisht zëri i doli i dobët, por shumë shpejt atij iu bashkuan zëra të tjerë. Në fillim një pacient, pastaj tre dhe në pak sekonda në oborr po dëgjohej një kor prej nëntë vetësh.

"A...KU..PA..RA!" "A..KU..PA..RA!" Britmat e pacientëve në oborr tërhoqën vëmendjen e të sëmurëve të tjerë, që filluan të nxirrnin kokat në kangjellat e kryqëzuara. Isait po i merreshin mendtë nga ajo galeri fytyrash të përçudnuara. Ngriti jakën e xhaketës për t'u mbuluar disi, por në çast u kujtua se ai gjest naiv ishte krejtësisht i kotë. Iu duk vetja si një struc që po fuste kokën në rërë. Eci mbrapsht, për t'u shkëputur disi nga pacientët në oborr. "Mësuesi" e dalloi me bisht të syrit, por ende nuk po kuptonte gjë. Isai ngriu në vend, duke pritur se çfarë do të ndodhte. Një lëvizje e gabuar mund t'i kushtonte shumë shtrenjë. "Mësuesi" u kthye paksa nga ai dhe vazhdoi të bërtiste "Akupara" me duart e ngritura drejt qiellit. Isai pëshpëriti diçka nëpër dhëmbë, duke u shtirur që po i bashkohej edhe ai asaj proteste naive dhe boshe. "Mësuesi" i kënaqur që Isai po i bashkohej korit, u kthye nga pacientët e tjerë. Isai bëri edhe një hap prapa, duke dalë më në fund jashtë rrethit të hekurt. Nxitoi hapat, ndërsa fryma iu mor nga ankthi dhe frika. Po sikur ta pikasnin në moment dhe t'i vërsuleshin papritur? Nga sulmi i nëntë njerëzve të shfytyruar askush nuk do të kishte shpresë shpëtimi.

Nuk ka ushtri më të fortë në botë sesa turma e uritur, kishte thënë Napoleon Bonaparti. Ishte vetëm pak metra larg nga dera e pasme e oborrit. U dha këmbëve me sa fuqi kishte, por "Mësuesi" tashmë e kishte pikasur dhe e ndoqi nga pas, por pa arritur të futej brenda. Isai i vuri llozin derës dhe u mbështet pas saj me kurriz. Mori frymë me gojë për të qetësuar disi frymëmarrjen. Ajo kryengritje e çuditshme ishte përhapur si rrufe në të gjithë spitalin. Infermierët e turnit vraponin nëpër korridore, me sytë dhe veshët nga dhomat, nga ku mund të dilnin të sëmurët e tjerë. Disa prej të sëmurëve kishin dalë jashtë kontrollit dhe goditnin me ç'të mundnin, çka u dilte përpara. Turma e të sëmurëve po e qëllonte derën me një nga stolat e oborrit. Isain nuk e mbajtën më gjunjët dhe ra përmbys mbi dyshemenë e korridorit. U tërhoq zvarrë, duke u përpjekur të largohej disi nga "mësuesi" pas të cilit po hynin me vrull pacientët e tjerë. "Mësuesi" përplasi disa herë një karrige druri pas murit anësor, gjersa karrigia u bë copë-copë. Pa ia hequr sytë presë së vet, shkuli njërën nga këmbët e drunjta e filloi të thyente xhamat e dritares më të afërt.

Doktor Arbeni doli nga zyra, e cila ndodhej disa metra më tutje dhe u përpoq ta qetësonte, por "mësuesi" nuk u zmbraps. Thërrmijat e xhamave filluan të binin mbi dysheme. Isai u tërhoq rrëshqanthi në drejtim të doktorit. Nëse doktor Arbeni do të arrinte ta ndalonte "Mësuesin", atëherë mund të kishte shpresë shpëtimi. Një cifël xhami i hyri në thembër, duke e shpuar keqazi. Mbylli sytë nga dhembja dhe u përpoq të mblidhte veten. Currilat e gjakut filluan të skuqnin dyshemenë.

Akili e kishte pikën e dobët në thembër. Për shkak të thembrës, ra Troja!

"Mësuesi" ndaloi një çast dhe me sytë e errur nga tërbimi u kthye nga ai. Isai u tërhoq sërisht mbrapsht me duart e mbështetura në dysheme. Grimcat e xhamave të thyer i shpuan pëllëmbët e duarve. "Mësuesi" qëlloi fort me këmbën e karriges në drejtim të Isait, por nuk arriti ta prekte. Tërhoqi vrikthi këmbën e djathtë dhe vazhdoi të zvarritej mbrapsht me kurriz nga dyshemeja, por nuk arriti t' i shpëtonte goditjes së rradhës. Këmba e karriges e goditi fort në kofshën e djathtë dhe përpak sa nuk i krisi kockën. Iu errën sytë nga dhembja dhe klithi me sa fuqi kishte. "Mësuesi" u mat ta godiste përsëri, kur një dorë e fuqishme e mbërtheu nga supi dhe e tërhoqi pas.

"Isa! Futu në zyrën time. Rri aty gjersa të qetësohet gjendja!" Arbeni e shtyu lehtazi drejt zyrës së vet, e cila ishte lënë gjysëm e hapur. I befasuar nga mirësia e tij, Isai ende po ngurronte të hynte. Doktori e kishte thirrur me emrin "Isa". Mbylli sytë, në një përpjekje të strërmundimshme për të mbledhur veten. Shqiptimi i atij emri të shkurtër me tri gërma i shkaktoi të rrënqethura në trup. Padyshim që doktori dinte se çfarë bënte dhe nuk e kishte ngatërruar me dikë tjetër. Arbeni ishte një burrë rreth të tridhjetave me shtat mesatar. Flokët i kishte bjond dhe sytë blu dhe atij ia kishin vënë nofkën "gjermani". "Gjermani" ishte i qetë dhe shumë i rregullt me pacientët. Ishte nga të rrallët, të cilit të sëmurët i bindeshin si me magji. Seç kishte diçka mistike dhe paqësore në të gjithë qenien e tij, që të bënte menjëherë për vete. Kishte mbaruar specializimin në Kinë para një viti dhe e kishin sjellë aty. Sa herë që kishte trazira të dhunshme në spital, doktor Arbeni do të hynte në mes të turmës së tërbuar pa ia bërë syri tërt. Qetësia e tij ishte pushtuese dhe i detyronte pacientët e irrituar të heshtnin.

"Hidhe poshtë copën e drurit!"

"Ai dorëzoi Akuparan! Dum Akuparën!" "Mësuesi" e ndali disi revanshin, por ende mbante këmbën e karriges me të dyja duart.

"Do ta gjej unë Akuparën! Të jap fjalën e burrit! Tani, hidhe copën e drurit dhe ik në dhomën tënde."

"Qentë kanë pamje periferike ma të mirë se qeniet njerëzore." Mësuesi i dikurshëm i biologjisë e harroi Akuparan dhe filloi të zbrazë tërë njohuritë e veta rreth kafshëvë. Doktor Arbeni mori frymë i lehtësuar dhe buzëqeshi lehtë.

"E saktë!" tha shkurt dhe duatrokiti me sa i hanin duart. "Mësuesi" ndjeu një lloj krenarie të gjithëpushtetshme ta pushtonte të gjithin. Vlerësimi që po i bënte doktori e bëri të humbte përqëndrimin. Këmba e karriges i ra nga dora, ndërsa zëri i mori një ton normal sikur të mos kishte ndodhur asgjë.

"Milingona nin nji lëvizje 5 centimetra thellë dhe mund të shofë dritën e polarizume."

"Oh, sinqerisht nuk e dija! Nga i ke marrë vesh të gjitha këto?"

"Kam qenë msues biologjie! Bletët punëtore janë të pajisme me nji unazë të oksidit të hekurit, për të dallu fushat magnetike."

"Aha, shumë interesante!" Doktori Arbeni i ra lehtazi me majën e këpucës këmbës së karriges, e cila u rrokullis nja dy metra më tutje nga vendi ku ndodhej mësuesi. Dukej se më në fund ishte jashtë rrezikut për jetën.

"Flutura ka qime te krahët, për të ni nryshimin e presionit të ajrit."

"Vërtet?"

"Po, po! Dhe kameleoni mund t'i luaj kokordhokët në mënyrë krejtsisht të pavarur, si dhe mund të shofë në dy drejtime të nryshme në nji kohë. Brumbulli dallon nji lëvizje 2000 herë ma të vogël në diametër se atomi i hidrogjenit. Syni i shqiponjës asht 35 mm në diametër, nërsa syni i njeriut vetëm 24 mm. Elefanti mund ta ngjoj nji tingull na 1 deri në 20000 HZ, ndërsa ne njerzit, s'mun të ngjojm dot infratingujt. Miza ka në secilin sy 2999 lente. Mos vallë jam akrep që duhet t'vras veten, i rrethum nga zjarri?"

"Jo, ti nuk je akrep!"

"Akrepat kanë 12 sy, nrsa merimangat kanë 8 lente. Po shkoj të kërkoj infermier Fatmirin. Ai e mori "Akuparan!""

"Mësuesi" bëri prapakthehu dhe u turr në drejtimin e kundërt për të gjetur infermier Fatmirin që nuk dukej gjëkundi. Doktor Arbeni psherëtiu disi i lehtësuar dhe futi dorën në xhepin e përpares. Nxorri që andej një bllok të ri shënimesh me shkronja kineze sipër dhe një stilolaps fringo dhe ia dha.

"Merre. Shkruaj ndonjë gjë, që të mos mërzitesh," tha doktor Arbeni dhe nxitoi hapat në drejtim të një grupi pacientësh që po jepnin e merrnin me një tavolinë në hollin kryesor. Mjaft prej tyre e kishte harruar Akuparën dhe po shkallmonin bustin e Enver Hoxhës.

IV.

Një vizitë e papritur

Sapo kishte mbaruar ora e Frëngjishtes dhe mësuese Dafina i bëri me shenjë Çimit që të priste pak. Vogëlushi hodhi çantën e shkollës në kurriz dhe i skuqur nga turpi, po vriste mendjen se çfarë gabimi kishte bërë atë ditë, që mësuesja kujdestare nuk po e linte të ikte. Mësuesja fshiu dërrasën e zezë dhe me një buzëqeshje të ëmbël në fytyrë u përkul paksa në drejtim të tij, sikur do t'i bënte ndonjë pyetje tepër sekret.

"Çimi! Ash mami n'shpi?" Zëri i saj i butë ishte shumë më i ulët, gati si një fëshfërimë gjethesh dhe tingëllonte shumë miqësor, si asnjëherë tjetër.

"Po, n'shpi ash!" u përgjigj, pa e ngritur kokën.

"Thuji, se do vimë mas i çike t'urojm ditlindjen. U bafsh 100 vjeç!" Mësuesja ia ngriti njërën nga cullufet rebele që i kishin rënë mbi ballë dhe e puthi lehtazi në faqe. Çimi u skuq edhe më në fytyrë dhe ia mbathi nga aty me sa i hanin këmbët, për të shpëtuar nga ajo ndjenjë zori që e kishte kapluar. Atë mëngjes nëna i kishte dhënë një qese me karamele, të cilat i kishte shpërndarë, sapo kishte ardhur në klasë. Iu duk çudi e madhe që mësuesja kujdestare kishte vendosur t'i bënte një vizitë në dhomën ku jetonin katër vetë: ai, vëllai tre vjet më i vogël-Platori, njerku që e kishte emrin "Hamdi" dhe e ëma. Në atë dhomë nuk kishe ku merrje frymë e jo më të prisje siç duhej miqtë dhe vizitorët e rrallë. Vrapoi mespërmes oborrit të shkollës, kaloi rrugën e asfaltuar dhe sakaq u gjend në oborrrin e pallatit. Me një frymë arriti tek shkallët, të cilat i kapërceu dyengatre dhe u fut në korridorin e errët. Era e furnellave i shpoi hundët. U kollit fort dhe hyri me të shpejtë brenda. Nëna po paloste rrobat e lara dhe të hekurosura dhe as që ia vuri veshin të birit, që hyri gjithë vrull në shtëpi.

"Ma, po vijnë msuset për ditlindje!" Zëri ju drodh nga emocionet dhe mezi po merrte frymë nga të vrapuarit. Mbajti këmbët para të ëmës, e cila u skuq e tëra nga turpi dhe zori. Nëna u zu aq ngushtë, saqë nuk dinte se çfarë të bënte, vetëm sa fshiu duart me nxitim në përparësen e bardhë. Dhoma e vetme ishte rregulluar si asnjëherë tjetër. Gjithçka shkëlqente nga pastërtia, ndërsa në tavolinën e bukës ishte vendosur një tufë me lule. Përreth ishin vendosur katër karriget prej druri, enkas për vizitorët që mund të vinin në shtëpi. Ndoshta ishte në dijeni për vizitën që do të bënin mësueset e shkollës dhe vetëm sa qeshi gjithë gëzim.

"Le të vijnë," tha shkurt dhe hapi derën.

ÇIMIT ATË DITË NJË fytyrë i ikte dhe një tjetër i vinte. Më mirë do të ishte të gjente ndonjë skutë ku të fshihej. Po sikur ndonjë mi të hynte nga korridori dhe të nxirrte kokën e vet kureshtare gjatë kohës që aty do të ishin mësueset? Oh, nuk do të kishte turp më të madh. Megjithëse Hamdiu kishte vënë çarqe minjsh gjithandej, popullata e tyre heroike shtohej papushim. Si për të larguar disi mendimet e këqija, Çimi vrapoi gjer në fillim të korridorit, aty ku gjendej një dritare e madhe me kanate të prishura dhe pa xhama, e cila fatmirësisht ndodhej pikërisht përballë shkollës. Ja ku po vinin mësueset, duke folur më njëra-tjetrën. Filloi të dridhej nga emocionet. Kishte edhe pak minuta që të merrej vesh me Kacamiun, me më të moshuarin e të gjithë minjve. Nëse nuk donte të fëlliqej, që të mos shihte asnjë turi miu, duhej të merrej vesh me Kacamiun. Vetëm ai mund ta bindte atë turmë rebele, që të fshihej ku të mundej. Vuri dy gishtat në gojë dhe vërshëlleu fort. Hodhi sytë përreth, por Kacamiu nuk po dukej gjëkundi. Fërshëlleu përsëri. Sekondat po kalonin njëenganjë. Ndjeu zemrën t'i rrihte fort. Ku dreqin ishte futur vallë? Ishte gati të hiqte dorë nga ajo ide e marrëzishme kur befas dalloi turirin e tij të murrëtyer pas një furnelle. Kacamiu kishte ngritur veshët përpjetë. Megjithëse ishte pothuajse errësirë, Kacamiu i druhej edhe hijes së vet. Jeta e kishte mësuar se duhej të qëndronte sa më larg njerëzve nëse donte të jetonte gjatë dhe pa kokëçarje.

Kacamiu ishte më i madhi jo vetëm nga përmasat, por edhe nga mosha dhe urtësia. Me trupin e tij të gjatë e të stërvitur nga vite të tëra arratisjesh, me qimet e hirta, me veshët gjithnjë ngritur, gati të kapnin edhe zhurmën më të vogël, Kacamiu ngjallte respekt e frikë njëkohësisht. Sytë e tij të vegjël, por të mprehtë, ishin gjithnjë në kërkim. Kacamiu kishte parë minj të zhdukeshin pa gjurmë, kish dëgjuar britmat e grave dhe vajzave që pastronin shtëpitë dhe mezi u kishte shpëtuar grackave të panumërta. Prandaj, çdo hap i tij ishte i matur, çdo vendim i tij i menduar gjatë.

Në lagjen e Namazgjasë, Kacamiu ishte pa dyshim mbreti. Asnjë mi nuk guxonte të vepronte pa marrë më parë miratim e tij. Një fjalë e vetme e Kacamiut mjaftonte për t'i futur të gjithë në strofulla, për të ndalur gjuetinë apo për të lënë mënjanë ndonjë plan grabitjeje që mund të ishte në zhvillim e sipër.

Vetëm një urdhër nga Kacamiu mund ta shpëtonte Çimin nga prania e padëshirueshme e ndonjë miu në mes të festës. Prandaj e kërkonte me dëshpërim dhe përulësi. Vërshëlleu fort përsëri. Pa ndihmën e mbretit të minjve, gjithçka mund të shkonte shumë keq. Kur më në fund dalloi atë siluetë të njohur pas një furnelle, me veshët përpjetë dhe sytë zhbirilues, Çimi e kuptoi më në fund që kishte shpëtuar. Sepse vetëm Kacamiu mund ta ndalte një turmë rebele minjsh. Dhe në atë moment, në heshtjen e errët, nën dritën e zbehtë të korridorit, ky mbret pa fron mund të kishte pushtet më shumë se kushdo tjetër në atë botë të nëndheshme.

"Kacamiu... Kacamiu, je aty?" i pëshpëriti Çimi me zërin e dridhshëm dhe i zverdhur në fytyrë. Befas dalloi turirin e tij të stërzgjatur përtej furnellës. "Sa mirë që erdhe! Ku ishe?! Kam pesë minuta që po t'kërkoj! Nuk kam ma koh'!

"Qetsohu, mor çun! Ule zanin, se po na nigjon gjith lagja!"

"Po vijn msuset për vizit. Kam frik se po shofin nonji nga ju dhe kam për t'u flliq."

"Po pun e madhe se po na pan. Ça t'keqe ka ktu?"

"Si s'ka! Do thon që nuk ka pastërti."

"Do thush ti, që jemi t'pist ne? Or mik, dum t'jetojm edhe ne. Si do e majm frymën?"

"Mir, mir! Leni llafet! Nuk ka koh me u zan. A ma ban nji ner?"

"Ça neri do, se nuk po t'marr vesh?"

"Shih si ban sikur nuk merr vesh! Banu thirrje shokve t'tu që t'mos dalin kto dy or, gjersa t'maroj vizita."

"Dy or, e? Do majm barkun me dor dy or rresht? Po kalamajt e vegjël që pillen çdo tre-katër jav? T'i lejm me north? Masanej, nuk asht aq e leht me majt nji ushtri napar vrima me zor."

"Nuk t'kam kërku asiher nonji ner. Kjo asht hera e par. Asht ma mir edhe për ju. Sa ma pak t'ju shofin, aq ma mir asht ene për ju. Msuset jan t'rrezikshme. Mun ta bajn problem."

"Ku pysim ne nga msuset e tuja? Un kujtova se ti ishe burr i fort!"

"Ma ban dot kët ner apo jo? Po e bane, do t'sjell nji cop t'madhe djath kaçkavalli."

"Djath kaçkavalli, e? Po ti qeke për t'u ngrit n'krah, mor çun!"

"Domethan, do e bash?' pyeti Çimi me mosbesim.

"Do e baj, the? Me i kam cinglli!"

"Rrofsh!"

Kacamiu u kthye nga turma imagjinare që ishte fshehur në të gjitha vrimat e mundshme të ndërtesës së vjetër dhe shkundi me madhështi mustaqet e gjata. Mjaftuan ato pak sekonda që Kacamiu të kthehej nga Çimi dhe të tundte me krenari bishtin e gjatë dhe të pistë.

"Maroi ne kjo pun!"

"Kaq ishte? Si ka munci? A mund t'më thush, pse të nigjojn vetëm ty? Ti je... çfarë je ti për ata?"

"Jam ma i vjetri ktu. Kam kalu tri lagje, kam shpëtu nga tri mace dhe kam jetu në frigorifer për nji muaj të tan. Nuk më duhen llafe që të më nigjojn. Mjafton të shkun mustaqet dhe të gjith rrijn sus."

"Ti je nji hero i vërtet! Mos them që je mret!"

"Mret nuk jam, po aty afër!"

"Falemnerit, o mreti i madh i minjve! Ti je ma i miri që njof!"

"Mos harro copën e djathit! Kur do ma sjellësh?"

"Ta sjell për tre or ktu mrapa furnellës."

"N'rregull!" psherëtiu Kacamiu dhe u zhduk në errësirë.

Çimi u ngrit edhe pak në majë të gishtave, që të shikonte më mirë dhe të mos i shpëtonte asgjë nga ajo pamje jo e zakontë që nga dritarja e vetme e korridorit. Mësuese Vilma kishte veshur një pardesy të hollë në ngjyrë të zezë, e cila e tregonte më shumë elegante sesa ishte. Sytë e saj të kaltër gjithmonë e kishin bërë për vete. Zëri i saj i ëmbël mbartte vetëm ngrohtësi.

Mësuese Nertila vinte pak si e shkurtër dhe xhaketa blu ia nxirrte më në pah format e trupit. E shëndoshë dhe me një vështrim të vëngërt, ajo mësuese i ngjallte një lloj ndrojtjeje të përzier me frikë. Ndoshta edhe lënda e aritmetikës që ajo jepte e bënte mësuese Nertilën më pak tërheqëse se të gjitha mësueset e tjera. U kapërdi me padurim dhe u kthye në apartamentin njëdhomësh, ku po priste nëna.

"Ma, mrritën!" tha me një frymë. Manushaqja nxitoi t'u dilte përpara në krye të shkallëve kryesore të pallatit, megjithëse shtatzënë. Platori ju qep të ëmës nga pas, një hap prapa. Ja ku mbërritën të trija mësueset, disi të druajtura dhe të hutuara nga ajo mizeri që po shikonin përreth. Mësuese Dafina kishte si gjithnjë një buzëqeshje gazmore dhe flokët kaçurrela që i binin mbi ballë i lëshonin mbi fytyrë një hije të praruar. Dafina jepte lëndën e frëngjishtes, të cilën Çimi e kishte orën e tij më të dashur. Do të ishte gjëja më e bukur në botë, nëse në klasë do të mësohej vetëm frëngjisht. Në frëngjisht Çimi i kishte të gjitha notat dhjeta dhe mësuese Dafina nuk linte rast pa e vënë Çimin të recitonte në frëngjisht para të gjithë klasës. Mësuese Dafina e tërhoqi Çimin nga dora dhe e puthi në të dyja faqet e trëndafilta. Në duar mbante një libër me përmbledhje të krijimtarisë së Migjenit, të firmosur nga të trija ato e të lidhur me fjongo të kuqe.

"Kjo dhuratë është për ty," i tha shkurt ajo dhe ndoqi të zonjën e shtëpisë nga pas.

Dhoma ishte shumë e ngushtë, por Çimit ajo dhuratë e veçantë ia tërhoqi menjëherë vëmendjen. Shfletoi me nxitim faqet e para.

"Kafshatë që s'kapërdihet asht, or vlla, mjerimi, /kafshatë që të mbetë në fyt edhe të ze trishtimi/kur shef ftyra të zbeta edhe sy të jeshilta/që të shikojnë si hije dhe shtrijnë duert e mpita/edhe ashtu të shtrime mbrapa teje mbesin/të tanë jetën e vet derisa të vdesin. /E mbi ta n'ajri, si në qesëndi, /therin qiellën kryqat e minaret e ngurta, /profetënt dhe shejtënt në fushqeta të shumngjyrta shkëlqejnë. /E mjerimi mirfilli ndien tradhti."

U zhyt menjëherë në faqet e atij libri, ndërsa Manushaqja filloi t'u rrëfejë gjer në detaje mësueseve sesi kishin përfunduar aty. Uli zërin, duke u munduar disi që ai rrëfim të mos dëgjohej nga i biri, që me librin para syve, kishte ngritur veshët përpjetë si një maçok çamarok.

"Sa mirë bëtë që erdhët! Nuk di si t'jua shpërblej." E zonja e kotecit, (kështu e quante nëna dhomën ku kishin përfunduar, sa herë që ankohej për gjendjen në të cilën ndodheshin), e mbuluar nga një ngjyrë purpuri, nuk po gjente dot fjalë për t'u uruar mirëseardhjen.

"Shpërblimin e kemi marrë na Çimi. Ashtë djalë i shkëlqyshëm", tha mësuese Vilma. "Më vjen keq që keni përfundu në kët dhomë, pas gjithë atyne peripecish."

"Eh, çtë bësh, i ka jeta këto!" shfryu Manushaqja dhe përnjëherësh iu mbushën sytë me lotë. Manushaqja qante për hiçgjë dhe lotët i kishte gati për t'i derdhur në çdo çast.

"Po ku mson Çimi ktu? Ju nuk keni ven as me marr frymë!" u çudit Vilma.

"Ja ashtu, keq e keq!" psherëtiu ajo.

Vilma hodhi vështrimin e saj pyetës nga koleget për të marrë aprovimin e tyre dhe, ende pa marrë ndonjë reagim, u kthye nga e zonja e shtëpisë.

"A e di çfarë? Që nesër e tutje Çimi le të msojë në Laboratorin e Biologjisë." Nxorri një çelës nga xhepi i pardesysë dhe ia la në dorë Manushaqes. "Na, merre dhe maje kët çelës, gjersa Çimi të mbarojë shkollën."

Manushaqja shtangu disi, por ashtu gjysëm me turp e mori çelësin në dorë dhe nuk dinte se çfarë të thoshte. Zëri iu mek dhe mjekrra iu drodh nga një ngashërim që sa vinte e rritej.

"Ma ke bërë aq shumë qejfin, sa nuk di se çfarë të them. Të kam motër dhe kaluar motrës." Iu afrua Vilmës dhe e përqafoi fort. E mbajti për sekonda të tëra në krahët e saj pa thënë as edhe një fjalë të vetme.

"Po si ndodhi që përfunut kshu?" pyeti Vilma me sytë e hapur nga kërshëria. Dukej sikur ajo po ia ushqente atë ndjenjë të fshehtë të zonjës së shtëpisë, që edhe pa atë ngushëllim, ishte gati të rrëfente ngjarjen më të hidhur të jetës me të gjitha detajet. Manushaqja aq donte, një gërvishtje në plagë nga dikush që kishte dëshirë të dëgjonte, se pastaj nuk do të pushonte së rrëfyeri historinë e saj.

"Ishim ulur rreth tavolinës dhe po hanim bukë: unë, Isai, Çimi që atëherë ishte 7 vjeç dhe djali tjetër Platori-katër vjeç. Ishte qetësi e plotë dhe pas një dite të lodhshme pune, po prisja të mbaronim darkën e të binim të flinim. Papritur im shoq përplasi tenxheren në mur dhe u ankua se gjella nuk kishte kripë. Mori thikën e bukës në duar e ma vuri në fyt. Më zuri një frikë e tmerrshme dhe nga ankthi për jetën e shtyva fort me duar, dhe vrapova drejt ballkonit. Ktheva kokën për një të qindtën e sekondës dhe pashë nga dy djemtë e vegjël. Çfarë do të bëhej me ta vallë? Po sikur Isai të tërbohej më keq dhe të godiste fëmijët? Atë çast urova me gjithë shpirt se asgjë e keqe nuk do të ndodhte dhe se e gjithë vëmendja e tij ishte drejtuar tek unë. Po të rrija aty dhe të theresha me thikë, do të ishte më keq akoma për të gjithë ne. Hodha sytë rrotull. Jashtë ishte shumë errët. Duhej të ishte ora tetë e darkës. Në palcën e dimrit erret qysh në orën pesë. Në kupë të qiellit shkëlqenin vetëm një grusht me yje, ndërsa Hëna nuk dukej gjëkundi. Fatmirësisht vinte gjer aty një dritë e zbehtë nga llampa e korridorit në katin e dytë. Një mendje më thoshte të hidhesha e të vritesha. Më mirë të vdisja duke u hedhur, sesa nga një thikë. Sytë më kapën fytyrat e frikësuara të atyre engjëjve të vegjël dhe ndërrova mendje. Dikush duhej të kujdesej për ata fëmijë. Më mirë të shpëtoja e të kthehesha t'i merrja. Ballkoni ishte shumë afër me shkallët kryesore të ndërtesës trekatëshe. U kapa fort pas murit anësor e zgjata këmbën. Gishtat e zbathur prekën paksa sipërfaqen e ashpër të betonit. I lashë duart të lira dhe kërceva tek shkallët. Nuk mbajta dot ekuilibrin dhe u rrëzova në vendrrotullimin që të çonte në katin e dytë. Ndjeva një dhimbje të fortë në kupë të gjurit, por arrita të çohem në këmbë. Aty e kuptova se kisha shpëtuar, por ankthi nuk po më linte të qetë. Një mendje më thoshte të trokisja në derën e komshiut ngjitur, por ishte shumë vonë dhe kisha frikë se nuk do të ma hapte derën. Zbrita shkallët dhe vrapova me sa fuqi kisha drejt stacionit më të afërt të policisë. Atje bëra padinë dhe në shtëpi nuk u ktheva më. Policia vajti që atë natë në shtëpi dhe e dërgoi Isain drejt e në spital, ndërsa të dy fëmijët u bashkuan me mua. Nuk kishte gëzim më të madh, kur vura re se Isai nuk u kishte prekur as një fije floku. Nuk u besoja dot syve dhe i mbulova me të puthura. Fatmirësisht që atë natë fjetëm në shtëpinë e një kushëriri të parë që banonte në një pallat afër stadiumit. Atje ndenjëm disa ditë, gjersa i dërgova fëmijët në Berat, tek njerëzit e mi. Kaluan disa muaj dhe tre vëllezërit më kërkuan që të martohesha përsëri, përndryshe duhej të kthehesha në shtëpinë e prindërve të mi. Ashtu bëra dhe bashkë me Hamdiun përfunduam këtu në këtë pallat beqarësh, në pritje për të marrë zgjerim. U bënë plot tre vjet, por zgjerim nuk ka. Ndërsa hallet shtohen. Hamdiu është me cen në biografi! Njerku i tij ka qenë korier me Ballin në kohën e luftës. Shikoni si vijnë punët: fëmijët e mi vuajnë për faj të njerkut, njerku i të cilit kur ishte i ri, kishte qenë korier me Ballin Kombëtar! Hapu dhe të futem, thuaj!" Manushaqja mbushi sytë me lotë. Duart e holla i dridheshin nga një rrënqethje e brendshme që sa vinte e shtohej.

Mësuese Vilma ia mori duart në duart e saj e filloi t'ia përkëdhelë, për ta qetësuar disi.

"Çimi ash shum i vëmenshëm dhe i kap shpejt gjanat," tha ajo, në një përpjekje të mundimshme që t'ia hiqte mendjen nga kujtimet e zymta asaj gruaje të re që nuk i kishte mbushur ende të tridhjetat. Manushaqja u çel disi në fytyrë, por nuk dinte se çfarë të thoshte. Fjalët asnjëherë nuk gjendeshin, atëherë kur i kërkonte me ngulm. Gjatë muajve të fundit kishte përjetuar vetëm dëshpërim e zhgënjim.

"Zoti jua bëftë sa më mirë e paçi vetëm gëzime e lumturi në familjet tuaja!"

"Mos ki merak për asi gja. Do të kujdesemi si për çunin tonë! Asht çun i squt. Ka për t'hec shum në jetë." Mësuese Vilma hodhi një vështrim nga Çimi dhe i përkëdheli kokën gjithë dashuri. Çimi u skuq disi dhe uli kokën i ndrojtur.

"Nuk di si t'ua shpërblej! Më bëhet qejfi sa më s'ka." Në zërin e Manushaqes ndihej një lloj gëzimi.

"M'thuj për çdo gja që të kesh nevoj!" Ngulmimi i mësuese Vilmës për t'ia hequr mendjen nga peripecitë e jetës, ishte aq prekës dhe i ngrohtë, sa Manushaqja nuk duroi dot dhe e përqafoi fort.

"M'u thaftë goja dhe mua! Ngela duke u rrëfyer këto fatkeqësi."

"Qofshin të shkuara! Ke dy djem si drita, këtë duhet të mendosh!"

"Së shpejti do të kem tre. Me barkun tek goja!"

"Po si do t'ia bësh, moj korbë?"

"Si të gjithë të tjerët. Na kanë dhënë një fjalë që kur të lirohet dhoma përballë, do të na e japin neve!"

"Po shumë mirë. Sa për Çimin, kur t'maroj shkollën, do t'i them tim shoqi t'i gjej nonji shkollë të mirë. Nuk do ta lejm me kaq. Ti e di që burrin e kam nën kryetar në Komitet Ekzekutiv!"

"E di, si nuk e di! Burri juaj ka qenë në një klasë dhe në një bankë me Isain. Ju falenderoj shumë! Nuk di si t'ua shpërblej." Manushaqja shpërtheu në lotë, por jo si herët e tjera. Këtë herë ishin lotë gëzimi dhe lumturie, që dikush po rrezatonte ngrohtësi njerëzore.

Mësueset dolën nga apartamenti njëdhomësh, duke lënë pas një ndjesi sigurie dhe shprese. Manushaqja i përcolli gjer jashtë në oborrin e pallatit, ku biseda vazhdoi e gjallë njësoj si më parë. Çimi i ndoqi me sy gjer në portën e madhe të oborrit dhe u përpoq të deshifronte që andej gjestet me duar të nënës. Kur nëna prekte papritmas flokët e saj të gjatë dhe sterr të zes, druhej për diçka. Ose ndjente një farë zori apo turpi për atë që dëgjonte. Hamendësimet e tij nuk zgjatën shumë, pasi nëna u kthye shpejt dhe nuk i la të mendohej gjatë. Një ngjyrë e kuqe i kishte mbuluar fytyrën dhe dukej paksa e inatosur. Kur zemërohej nëna, Çimi kërkonte vrimë ku të futej. Sa herë që bënte ndonjë gabim të rëndë, nëna do ta kafshonte në krah ose do ta pickonte.

"Kur është hera e fundit që e ke takuar *Të Çmendurin?*" pyeti, pa e parë të birin drejt e në sy siç ndodhte rëndom, kur e qortonte për diçka. U fut e para në dhomë, pa pritur përgjigjen e të birit. "*I Çmenduri*" ishte epiteti, me të cilin nëna thërriste babain. Sa herë që e dëgjonte nënën ta thërriste babain ashtu, ndjente një ligështi dhe dhimbje në zemër, por nuk kishte as forcë e as mundësi që ta kundërshtonte nënën. Fundja, a nuk ishte thjesht një sëmundje si të gjitha të tjerat? A do të ishte babai më shumë i pranueshëm dhe i respektueshëm, nëse do të vuante, përshembull, nga zemra? Po si t'ia thoshte nënës të gjitha këto?

"Nuk e di! Mase para gjasht mujsh?" Çimi nuk e mbante mend saktësisht ditën se kur e kishte parë babain për herë të fundit. Dinte që ai ishte shtruar në spital dhe kaq.

"Të djelën do të shkojë hallë Nirvana atje."

"Do të dalë babi nga spitali?"

"Ndoshta pas disa javësh. Kështu i kishte thënë hallë Nirvana mësuese Vilmës." Një psherëtimë e lehtë i shpëtoi nga buzët që po i dridheshin. Fjalët i dolën si të gjymtuara që nga thellësia e shpirtit. Nuk do të dëshironte që të shprehte asnjë keqardhje, gëzim apo mëshirë për ish-bashkëshortin në sy të Çimit, por ajo psherëtimë dhimbjeje e kishte tradhtuar. "Meqë halla jote do të shkojë për ta marrë, mund të shkosh edhe ti me Platorin!"

"Sa mirë! Do të dalë babi nga spitali! Si andërr m'duket ajo ditë, kur të dali prej anej." Çimi hodhi vështrimin nga dritarja, andej ku zgjatoheshin të ngrysura selvijat e Namazgjasë. Dukej sikur u lutej atyre pemëve të stërgjata, që ashtu gjysëm të vdekura, dukeshin edhe më të vetmuara. Manushaqja e përqafoi të birin pa thënë as edhe një fjalë të vetme. Këtë herë fytyra e saj u bë lulëkuq nga turpi dhe zori. Sa herë që do të vinte biseda tek AI, Manushaqja nuk do të ndjehej mirë. Atë pasdite nuk kishte sesi të ndodhte ndryshe.

Çimi nuk u çudit nga ftohtësia e nënës. Njëherë kur ishte në bulevard me nënën, në krahun tjetër të rrugës kishte parë babain. Oh, sa kishte dëshirë që nëna të ngrinte kokën dhe ta përshëndeste Atë, që ashtu i vrerosur priste në anën tjetër të rrugës, por më kot. Ja, si tani i erdhi ai çast parasysh.

"Ja *i çmenduri*!" pëshpëriti ajo nën zë. "Shshsht, mos e kthe kokën!" Nëna ia shtrëngoi dorën fort, që të vazhdonte rrugën dhe të mos shikonte në krahun nga po ecte AI. E skuqur gjer në rrëzë të veshëve, nëna dukej sikur nxitonte që të ikte sa më parë që andej. Çimi u përpoq ta largojë mendjen nga ato kujtime që nuk po e linin të qetë.

"Kur do vij halla?"

"Të djelën në mëngjes, pra! Nuk më besohet që ka takuar mësueset e tua! Shtriga!" Nëna psherëtiu thellë, si për të larguar disi mllefin që i ishte krijuar nga ish-kunata, e cila nuk linte rast pa folur keq për nusen që kishte ikur me të dy djemtë dhe kishte braktisur vëllain e saj. "Të keqen mami ty! Ja kështu vazhdo. Të bëhesh shembullor në shkollë. Jam shumë krenare me ty!" Manushaqja e përqafoi fort të birin dhe e mbajti për disa çaste në gjirin e saj, sikur të kishte muaj pa e parë. U pezmatua në fytyrë dhe sytë iu mbushën me lotë. Nuk para kishte qejf që të dy djemtë të shkonin në spital me Nirvanën. Ish-kunata nuk ia falte që Manushaqja ishte ndarë nga i vëllai i saj Isai dhe të gjithë fajin për divorcin ia hidhte nuses së re. Për këtë arsye dukej sikur gjithçka, çdo kujtim të së kaluarës, donte që ta fshinte. Të shkëpuste çdo lloj kontakti me cilindo që i sillte ato grimca të trishta. Këtë herë ishin mësueset në mes dhe nuk kishte se çfarë të bënte. Kishte dhënë me mëdyshje pëlqimin që të dy djemtë të ishin aty atë ditë, kur babai të dilte nga ai spital i mallkuar.

V.

Letra në sirtar

Blloku i shënimeve kishte kapakë të fortë të veshur me lëkurë ngjyrëkafe. Në kapakun e përparëm ishte vizatuar flamuri kinez me një yll të madh në ngjyrë të verdhë dhe katër të tjerë më të vegjël, poshtë të cilëve ishin shkruar tre hieroglife, që në shqip kishin kuptimin "bllok shënimesh". Një lidhëze mëndafshi në ngjyrë kafe ndante faqet plot shkëlqim e bardhësi verbuese. Isai e goditi kapakun me majën e thojit, ndërsa trupi iu drodh nga një ngazëllim i beftë. Kur ishte hera e fundit qe kishte marrë një dhuratë kaq të çmuar? Nxorri nga xhepi stilolapsin dhe e rrotulloi nëpër gishta. Mund të shkruante në ngjyrë të zezë, blu, jeshile apo të kuqe. Me sytë e fantazisë përfytyroi fjalët e pathëna që i zjenin brenda qenies prej kaq kohësh. Tërhoqi tavolinën e punës së doktorit dhe e mbështeti pas derës. Në pak sekonda dikush rrotulloi dorezën. Isai u mbështet pas tavolinës me të dyja duart, por personi që po rrotullonte bravën e derës, filloi ta godiste me grushta. U dëgjuan disa zëra që jepnin e merrnin me njëri-tjetrin. Sytë iu errën nga sforcimi i tepërt, por goditjet e turmës nuk zgjatën më. Psherëtiu i lehtësuar dhe hodhi sytë përreth. Ndaloi para

një pasqyre në formën e zemrës që ishte varur në mur. Vetja ju
duk plotësisht i dërrmuar dhe i vrarë shpirtërisht. Nuk ishin
më ata flokë sterr të zinj si nata. Thinja të panumërta i kishin
mbirë në tëmthat e fryrë. Ngjyrën e syve e kishte të kuqerremtë
nga pagjumësia. Fërkoi sytë dhe bëri disa hapa nëpër dhomë.
Në një cep të dhomës ishte një dollap, ku rrinin varur disa
përparëse të bardha dhe të hekurosura. Në një kabinet ishin
vendosur kartelat mjekësore të të sëmurëve sipas renditjes
alfabetike. U shtri në krevatin portativ, por gjumi nuk po e
zinte. Tëhoqi karrigen e drunjtë pas tavolinës dhe mori sërisht
në duar bllokun e shënimeve. Sa kohë kishin kaluar që nga
ajo ditë, kur kishte prekur një stilolaps me dorë? Ai bllok
shënimesh po i dukej si një diamant i çmuar. Jashtë zyrës së
doktor Arbenit zërat sikur filluan të rralloheshin. Hodhi fjalët
e para ashtu krejt instiktivisht.

E SHTUNË 7 SHKURT 1976!

Ishte vërtet e Shtunë në atë muaj shkurti të vitit 1976?
Fatmirësisht blloku i shënimeve kishte edhe një kalendar në
faqet e fundit. E shfletoi në ethe dhe lexoi historikun në rusisht.
Kalendari ishte në tre gjuhë: në kinezçe, në anglisht dhe në
rusisht. Ajo ditë i përkiste shenjës së Akuariumit. Shkroi me
nxitim:

E dashur Svjetllana! Nuk e di nëse një ditë do të jesh në
gjendje të kuptosh se sa kam vuajtur. Para dy javësh më kuruan
me makinën e elektroshokut, por unë po përpiqem ta harroj
dhimbjen e me shpirt të uroj nga zemra të gjitha të mirat e kësaj
bote. Paç vetëm gëzime në jetë e qofsh gjithnjë ajo që kam njohur

dikur: një zonjë e vërtetë dhe e bukur. Nuk e di nëse kjo letër do të mbërrijë ndonjë ditë atje në Saint Petersburgun e largët, por shpresoj se me ndihmën e Zotit, do t'i lexosh këto fjalë që po shkruaj sonte me kaq nxitim. Atë ditë kur të prita në stacionin e autobuzit dhe më pas në aeroport, shpresoja se do të shfaqeshe nga çasti në çast dhe do të vije me mua. Fati i keq e deshi që të ndahemi dhe unë të sëmuresha e të përfundoja këtu në këtë spital.

Ditët ngrysen shumë ngadalë dhe netët nuk bëjnë shumë dallim nga njëra tjetra. Shikoj muret dhe nuk më bëhet për asgjë. Më mungon kaq shumë ti, princesha ime e vogël. Në ëndërr më dalin buzët e tua të rrumbullakëta dhë sytë e kaltër të mbushur me vetëtima. Nuk e di pse sot, kur njëri nga doktorët më dhuroi një bllok shënimesh, më vajti mendja pikërisht tek ty! Ndoshta, sepse kësaj terapie shoku nuk i kam besë. Ti as që nuk e di se ku jetoj. Ndoshta më ke harruar dhe është normale që të më harrosh. Jeta vazhdon, e dashur, por thellë në shpirt shpresoj që në çaste vetmie, të të shfaqem unë, pa e patur idenë se ku kam përfunduar e çfarë bëj.

Në fakt nuk jam i lejuar të bëj dot shumë gjëra. Natë e ditë kuvendoj me muret. Për shëtitje jashtë spitalit nuk na lënë, ndërsa dritaret i kemi me hekura! I vetmi njeri që më kupton është Arbeni, doktori i turnit të mbrëmjes. Ai ma dha bllokun e shënimeve dhe një stilolaps si dhuratë për sjellje të mirë. Edhe sikur këto letra të mos mbërrijnë asnjëherë tek ty, kam përshtypjen se këto shënime do të më forcojnë kujtesën. Në këto faqe do të hedh grimcat e ditës për të mos harruar. Këtë bllok do ta marr gjithnjë me vete. Madje edhe kur të fle, do ta mbaj të fshehur poshtë nënkrejsës.

E dashur Svjetllana!

Para se të hyja në dhomën e elektroshokut, rrufita një supë të shpifur që më ngeci në fyt. Në mëngjes hëngra bukë me çaj dhe djathtë. Çaji ishte i klorinuar, ndërsa djathi kaçkavall vinte erë të qelbur, që mezi e durova. Nuk duhej të qahesha, pasi kishte edhe më keq. Brenda mureve të këtij spitali nuk ka shtet në kuptimin e mirë të fjalës. Unë do ta quaja "Zoo park!" Në këtë kopësht zoologjik ku jemi mbledhur ne, kafshët-njerëz, nuk ekziston respekti për Njeriun. Xhungla është në mes dhe katër muret e bardhë anash! Kur na vënë në rresht në fiskulturën e mëngjesit nuk na drejtohen me emra, por me numra. Unë jam numri 12! Në shumicën e rasteve ata më thërrasin "Numri 12". Ndërsa të gjithë ne kemi një emër të përbashkët: "Kafshët!" Nuk e kuptoj se si një qenie njerëzore, t'i drejtohet po një qenieje tjetër njerëzore me atë emër: "Kafshë!" Kur m'u drejtuan në fillim me atë nofkë, ndjeva një lloj poshtërimi, që nuk e kisha provuar asnjëherë në jetën time. Më vonë u mësova dhe përpiqesha të justifikoja rrethanat në të cilat ndodhesha. Fundja kafshët nuk i bëjnë keq askujt. Më mirë të më thërrasin "kafshë", sesa të jem "njeri" njësoj si ata, që vrasin përditë njerëz! Para një ore më ndoqën disa "paciente" të tjerë dhe për pak më rrahën. Njëri përdori këmbën e një tavoline të prishur dhe u përpoq të më godiste, por shpëtova paq.

U përpoqa të mbrohesha me sa mundesha dhe për fat ishte po doktor Arbeni që ndërhyri dhe sonte më la të flija në zyrën e vet. Shpesh përpiqem të kuptoj se nga u vjen gjithë ai tërbim i çmendur. I bëj pyetje vetes, se si është e mundur që ka kaq njerëz të këqinj? Mezi marr frymë dhe më dhemb kurrizi. Çfarë është tani? Ah, po! Eshtë mbrëmje vonë. Bën shumë ftohtë. Kam një therje të fortë në krahun e djathtë. Kam frikë se do të vdes pa të të parë, Svjetllana!

Ndërsa po përpiqej të vazhdonte fillin e mendimeve, dikush trokiti në derë. Fillimisht lehtazi, më pas me grushta. Fiku dritën dhe mbajti frymën. Duhej të ishte përsëri "Mësuesi" që ishte vënë në kërkim të atyre që kishin arrestuar Akuparan. Mbylli kapakët e syve të rënduar nga lodhja, por imazhi i Svjetllanës nuk po e linte të qetë. Pëshpëriti me buzët e thara vargun e parë të poezisë që e kishte kaq kohë në mendje. U rrënqeth nga koka tek këmbët. Një ide e guximshme e mbushi të tërin me një lloj energjie të mbinatyrshme. Duhej që të ikte prej andej nga sytë këmbët, por ishte krejtësisht e pamundur. Shtrëngoi fort penën me gishtat që i dridheshin dhe shkruajti vargjet e para të një poezie që po i lindte në shpirt fluturimthi.

"ME PENËN TIME/
    Do të shpoj natën e zezë të Kremlinit!"
Mbylli sytë që të përqëndrohej disi, por një goditje e fortë në derë e tromaksi të tërin. Këtë herë kanatat e saj nuk mbajtën më. Menteshat krejtësisht të ndryshkura dolën nga vendi dhe dera ra në dysheme. Një grumbull prej pesëmbëdhjetë të sëmurësh të prirur nga "Mësuesi" hynë gjithë vrull në zyrën e doktor Arbenit. Të armatosur me shufra hekuri dhe shkopinj druri ju vërsulën të vetmit njeri që kishin para syve.

Isai futi me ngut bllokun e shënimeve në xhep dhe u zmbraps gjithë frikë. Syri nuk i kapi asnjë cep se ku mund të fuste kokën. Ndoshta në dollapin e rrobave, ku varnin uniformat mjekët? Eci mbrapsht me shpejtësi, duke mbrojtur me sa mundej fytyrën. Arriti të futej në dollap, por të sëmurët i dhanë një të shtyrë dhe e rrëzuan dollapin përmbys në dysheme. Shkopinjtë dhe shufrat e hekurit tashmë binin pa pushim mbi dollap. Atëherë kur i kishte humbur të gjitha shpresat, dëgjoi një zë të njohur.

"Mjaft! Pushoni! Ikni që andej!" Doktor Arbeni ishte shfaqur aty pikërisht atëherë kur duhej më shumë. Edhe pak sekonda të ishte vonuar, do të kishte përfunduar nën mëshirën e asaj turme të furishme.

Goditjet filluan të rralloheshin si me magji, gjersa ra një qetësi e plotë. Isai ende mbante sytë mbyllur, i mbledhur kutullaç në dollap. Kur dikush e ktheu dollapin me hyrjen nga lart, drita e llampës i vrau sytë. Një dorë miqësore i ishte zgjatur për ndihmë. Hodhi sytë përreth gjithë frikë. "Mësuesi" ishte zmbrapsur disi dhe ende po e vëzhgonte me një shikim të vëngër, i gatshëm të hidhej në sulm sërisht. Të sëmurët e tjerë, si një tufë zombish ecnin mbrapsht, ende të pasigurt nëse duhej që të lëviznin prej andej. Kur "Mësuesi" u largua nga pragu i derës, kthyen kurrizin dhe ndoqën me nge të parin e tyre.

Dëgjoi psherëtimën e lehtësuar të doktor Arbenit!

"Shpëtove paq, or mik!" tha dokori dhe e tërhoqi me forcë që të ngrihej. Po i dridheshin leqet e këmbëve dhe gjunjët nuk po e mbanin më. U ngrit me mundim të madh, duke rënkuar. Megjithëse i dhimbnin kockat, ndjeu lehtësi në shpirt. Për herë të parë pas kaq kohësh po i lindte një fije shprese. Mbase ishte ende në kohë të dilte gjallë prej andej. Të ikte nga sytë këmbët. Po si të ikte vallë, kur spitali ishte nën kontrollin e rreptë të mjekëve dhe infermierëve? Ndoshta një kërkesë e zakonshme ndonjë mjeku si Arbeni do të bënte më shumë punë, sesa një tentativë për arratisje.

"Doktor, a mund të më nxjerrësh që këtej? Kam frikë se do të më vrasin!" Padashur e kishte kapur doktorin nga krahët. I tërhoqi duart menjëherë mbrapsht, por pa ia hequr sytë përgjërues. Doktor Arbeni ishte nga të rrallët që e kuptonte gjendjen e tij. A ishte e mundur vallë të dilte prej andej?

"Do të flas me drejtorin. Mbase të dërgojnë në shtëpi për disa muaj."

"Më fal, nuk të dëgjova mirë!"

"Kam teorinë time për terapinë që duhet ndjekur në këtë spital. Terapia e shokut nuk është më e mira e mundshme. Drejtori më ka kërkuar në takim urgjent!" tha shkurt Arbeni, këtë herë me zë më të lartë dhe duke shkoqitur fjalët.

Isai ndjeu një lehtësi në shpirt. Doktor Arbeni bënte dallim nga të gjithë mjekët e tjerë. Megjithëtë po i dukej gati e pamundur që të ndodhte një gjë e tillë. Vetja ju duk sikur ishte në delir e më keq akoma: po përjetonte halucinacionin e rradhës.

"Nuk e di, sesi do të ta shpërbleja, doktor!" Zëri iu mbyt nga emocionet dhe po i dukej sikur po shikonte një ëndërr të bukur. Vërtet mund të shkonte për disa muaj në shtëpi?!

"Asgjë nuk është e sigurt, por se flas me të, nuk humbasim asgjë. Tani eja të të çoj në dhomën e urgjencës. Po të rrjedh gjak nga koka dhe mund të kesh ndonjë hemorragji." Doktori i futi krahun dhe të dy së bashku dolën në korridorin kryesor. Gjithandej nëpër spital dukej sikur sapo kishte përfunduar stuhia: copa karrigesh të thyera, grimca xhamash dhe zërat e egërsuar të të sëmurëve që sa vinin e rralloheshin. Doktori gati e tërhoqi zvarrë, pasi këmba e djathtë nuk po i bindej. Që të arrinin gjer në dhomën e emergjencës, duhej të përshkonin të gjithë korridorin nga e djathta në të majtë. Tek-tuk hasnin në vështrimin e egërsuar të ndonjë të sëmuri, që ende vërdallosej nëpër korridor.

VI.

Kështjella

Oborri i pallatit kishte një portë kryesore dykanatëshe, e cila ishte vetëm pak metra përballë shkollës tetë-vjeçare. Porta e oborrit ngjante më shumë me atë të një kështjelle, e cila gati sa nuk rrëzohej përtokë nga goditjet e fëmijëve. Atë mbrëmje, ashtu siç ndodhte shpesh në fundjavë, ushtarët "Ilirë" po e mbronin portën nga brenda, ndërsa ata "Romakë" po e godisnin nga jashtë me çfarë t'u vinte për duarsh. Komandant Çimi ishte skuqur i gjithi në fytyrë dhe dihaste me zor nga stërmundimi i madh. "Romakët" ishin dyfish në numër, ndërsa "Ilirët" bëheshin a nuk bëheshin nja dhjetë vetë, të cilët jetonin në "Pallatin e Peshkut" dhe shtëpitë përreth.

"Mështetni kurrizin mas portës dhe mos luni prej anej. Ne pak! Ne pak!" Çimi përpiqej t'u jepte zemër dhe si një mbret i vërtetë jepte shembullin i pari sesi mbrohej pragu i shtëpisë. Ndryshe nga herët e tjera, atë ditë secili kishte shpatën e vet. Ristelat ishin marrë nga arkat e domateve dhe me ato kishin bërë shpatat prej druri, ndërsa për mburojë kishin marrë kapakët e kazanëve të plehrave, të cilat do t'i kthenin në vend sapo të mbaronte lufta. Vajzat kishin këputur degët e mimozave dhe me to kishin krijuar kurorën e mbretëreshës. Vajzat ishin gjithsej katër: Amla, Lidra, Erëza dhe Zajmina. Nga djemtë në luftë kishin ardhur Çimi, Met ezmeri, Ver Çami, Miri Gjatovini, Roshi Pikaloshi dhe Platori. "Armiqtë" udhëhiqeshin nga Gëzimi, që ishte në një klasë me Amlën dhe Çimin dhe që banonte në një nga shtëpitë përdhese, në hyrje të rrugicës, që të çonte në shkollën e muzikës. Porta ngjasonte me një njeri të gjallë, që dukej sikur nga çasti në çast do të jepte shpirt. Djemtë dhe vajzat kishin zgjedhur për mbretëreshë Amlën, një vajzë me flokë te zes, sytë me bisht dhe lëkurën borë të bardhë. Amla ishte vajza e mësuese Vilmës dhe vetëm ky fakt i jepte asaj një status të veçantë. Jo vetëm kaq. Në një konkurs të fshehtë bukurie, ajo ishte zgjedhur si vajza më e bukur e shkollës dhe i kishte të gjitha notat dhjeta. Për të gjitha këto arsye asaj i ishte dhënë roli i mbretëreshës.

U duk sikur "Romakët" u lodhën shpejt dhe filluan t'i rrallonin goditjet në portë. Vajzat vazhdonin t'u sillnin shishe me ujë ushtarëve të lodhur, të cilët për asnjë çast nuk largoheshin nga "pozicionet" që kishin zënë. Muzgu ra dhe "Romakët" të ardhur nga pjesë të tjera të lagjes filluan të tërhiqen. Pikërisht atëherë, Çimi ngriti shpatën e drunjtë lart dhe i ftoi ushtarët e vet të dilnin jashtë kështjellës.

"Hapni portën! Të hidhemi në sulm! Përpara!" Kanatet e portës u hapën dhe "Ilirët" pa e zgjatur u hodhën në kundërsulm. Shpatat e drunjta filluan të kryqëzoheshin, ndërsa klithmat e ushtarëve armiq mbushën terrin e natës që po afrohej. Romakët të shumtë në numër i rrethuan Ilirët dhe arritën të kapin mbretëreshën Amla rob. Të gjithë ushtarët Ilirë ishin rrëzuar përdhe të "vdekur", ndërsa Çimi ende rezistonte i rrethuar nga të gjitha anët. Gëzimi, si komandant i Romakëve, ngriti lart shpatën dhe i rrëmbyer nga deliri thirri fort!

"Të ftoj në dyluftim! Unë ne Ti: ballëpërballë! Kush fiton, merr mretneshën Amla me vete," tha Gëzimi dhe u bëri me shenjë ushtarëve të tjerë të largoheshin. Sakaq Romakët e tjerë u larguan, duke i futur Gëzimin dhe Çimin në mes.

Çimi shtrëngoi fort shpatën me të dyja duart, sikur të donte të merrte fuqi prej saj. Nuk do ta lejonte kurrsesi që Amla të binte në duart e armikut. U përkul disi përpara dhe e pa kundërshtarin në sy. Gëzimi u turr i pari dhe i dha një goditje të drejtpërdrejtë, por Çimi kërceu majtas, duke e shmangur plotësisht. Gëzimi e goditi përsëri, këtë herë, sikur donte ta priste në mes, por sakaq shpata i shpëtoi nga duart, duke i fluturuar disa metra larg turmës së grumbulluar. Çimi mori frymë i lehtësuar dhe eci drejt tij me shpatën në duar. A ishte e drejtë të vazhdonte dyluftimin me kundërshtarin e paarmatosur apo duhej ta hidhte shpatën tutje e të vazhdonte luftën? Hodhi sytë nga Amla, sikur donte te kërkonte miratimin e saj. Dy ushtarë Romakë e mbanin fort nga krahët, ndërsa ajo e tmerruar nuk ia ndante sytë. Më mirë do të ishte t'i jepte një goditje përfundimtare e të gjithë të shkonin në shtëpi, por jo! Ilirët ishin njerëz të drejtë, trima dhe bujarë. Kurrë nuk bënin hile në luftë! Hodhi shpatën e vet përtokë dhe përveshi mëngët. Ushtarët Ilirë që bënin si të vdekur klithën nga habia. Erëza klithi "mos", ndërsa Romakët shpërthyen në brohoritje. Gëzimi u afrua dhe e qëlloi me një të majtë të shpejtë me grusht në stomak. Çimit iu errën sytë, por nuk e bëri veten. Shtrëngoi fort dhëmbët dhe e qëlloi me nje breshëri grushtash ku të mundte. Një grusht e kapi m'u në hundë dhe Gëzimi sakaq ra i përgjakur mbi asfalt. Çimi iu hodh sipër dhe ia vuri duart në fyt, por Gëzimi u mblodh kutullaç dhe me dorën lart bëri shenjë që dyluftimi të mbaronte.

"Mjaft! Mjaft! Fitove!"

Çimi u ngrit në këmbë dhe i zgjati dorën. Ushtarët Romakë të zhgënjyer filluan të tërhiqeshin. Kur nuk kishte mbetur më këmbë "Romaku" përreth, "Ilirët" u mblodhën rreth mbretit, duke shtyrë njëri-tjetrin. E ngritën komandantin në krahë dhe gjithë ngazëllim brohoritën me sa kishin në kokë. Kur turma u qetësua disi, Çimi çau rrugën me kujdes mespërmes fëmijëve dhe pasi arriti para Amlës u ul në gjunjë para saj me një pamje solemne në fytyrë. Me zërin që i dridhej nga ngazëllimi mbajti fjalimin e rradhës.

"Mretnesha Amla! Kështjella meti e paprekun. Ushtarët Romakë u kthyn nga kishin ardh."

Priti në gjunjë, gjersa "mbretëresha" të fliste. Zemra po i rrihte fort nga ajo fitore e paparashikuar. Kurrë nuk do të lejonte që e zgjedhura e tij e zemrës të binte në duart e armikut.

"Ju lumtë, o ushtarë të Ilirisë. Me kcoj trimash, Iliria kurr s'do vdesi!" Zëri i ëmbël i Amlës e bëri edhe më gazmore festën që sapo kishte filluar. Fëmijët shpërthyen në "urra" dhe pas pak minutash u shpërndanë, për të shkuar gjithsecili në shtëpinë e vet.

Amla ende qëndronte aty e ngurrosur para mbretit të saj, që dukej sikur kishte lëshuar rrënjë dhe nuk donte të ikte prej andej. Çimi dukej sikur donte të thoshte diçka, por u tërhoq menjëherë sikur të kishte bërë ndonjë faj. Kishte aq shumë dëshirë që ta puthte në faqe, por një zë i brendshëm i thoshte se ishte shumë shpejt. Po sikur Amla të zemërohej e të mos i fliste më kurrë?

"Çimi, sa kohë keni që rrini në Pallatin e Peshkut" e pyeti Amla.

"Kemi tre vjet!"

"Po Hamdiu, babi jot asht?"

"Jo, ai ashtë njerku!" "Njerku" apo "Baba", për Çimin nuk kishte asnjë ndryshim. Si tani e mbante mend atë ditë, kur nëna e solli Hamdiun për herë të parë në shtëpi, tre muaj mbasi ishte ndarë nga babai. Nëna e kishte pyetur nëse do ta thërrisnin "xhaxhi" apo "babi". Ai kishte qenë shtatë vjeç dhe Platori katër. Kishte ndjerë aq shumë keqardhje në ato momente, kur kishte parë fytyrën e pafajshme të vëllait të vogël, saqë e kishte dhënë përgjigjen pa u menduar fare: "babi". Për moshën që kishte Amla nuk duhej të bënte asi pyetjesh. U ndje disi në siklet, megjithëse kishte aq shumë dëshirë të fliste me të.

"Po babi jot i vërtetë ku asht?" pyeti përsëri Amla.

"Babi..., babi im ashtë i smun dhe asht shtru në spital."

"Na çar asht i smun?" këmbënguli Amla.

"Ka nji smunje të ran, që nuk di si ta shpjegoj. Nuk man men ne flet kot."

"Sa kohë ka n'spital?"

"Ka disa muj... Ohu, po ti pse pyt?"

"Kot!"

"Po iki unë! Shifemi nesër në shkoll."

"Mirë!" Fytyra e Amlës ndriste nga një ndjenjë e veçantë. Oh, sa kishte dëshirë të rrinte edhe disa minuta me të, por Meti i fërshëlleu në rrëzë të veshit, duke i kujtuar se tashmë ishte bërë shumë vonë e të gjithë duhej të ktheheshin në shtëpitë e tyre. Po sikur ta puthte Amlën tani, kur të gjithë po shpërndaheshin dhe askush nuk e kishte mendjen tek ata të dy? Ky ishte rasti më i mirë për t'i shprehur dashurinë, pasi nuk do të kishte më mundësi për çaste të tjera. Sa më shumë ta mendonte si veprim, aq më të rëndë do ta kishte. Nesër do të ishte shumë vonë. Mbylli sytë dhe e puthi lehtë në faqe. Fytyra e Amlës ishte ndezur e tëra nga emocionet e sikur kishte marrë pakëz vegim nga hëna që sapo kishte nxjerrë vetullën e saj të artë.

"Natnemir, Amla!" Ktheu kurrizin menjëherë, duke patur frikë se mos ndoshta ai moment magjik mund të prishej. E kishte puthur vërtet apo ishte imagjinata e tij e ndezur, që po e krijonte atë çast aq shumë të dëshiruar? U kthye përsëri nga ajo për t'u siguruar që vërtet kishte ndodhur diçka.

"Natnemir!" tha Amla, e skuqur lehtazi.

"Mos i thuj njeriu!" i pëshpëriti në vesh me ndrojtje, sikur të kishte frikë, se tashmë ajo puthje e beftë ishte pikasur nga të gjithë banorët e pallatit dhe rrethinat përreth.

"Jo, nuk i them!" tha Amla dhe nxitoi hapat. Çimi e ndoqi me sy, gjersa Alma doli nga oborri dhe mori rrugën kryesore për në pallatin e saj pas shkollës. Zemra filloi t'i rrihte me forcë. Një ndjenjë e fortë dhe e ëmbël e bëri të dridhej. Të mëdhenjtë nuk duhej të mendonin se ata të vegjëlit nuk kishin ndjenja dhe se nuk dinin se ç'ishte dashuria. Amla ishte vajza më e bukur e shkollës. Ajo i kishte të gjitha nota dhjeta dhe për këtë arsye duhej të ishte më e zgjuara nga të gjitha vajzat e tjera. Kishte një farë ndrojtjeje, se mos mësuese Vilmës nuk do t'i pëlqente që vajza e saj të lidhej me ndonjë djalë që në atë moshë, por Çimi as që donte ta çonte në mendje një gjë të tillë. E kishte ndarë mendjen, që do të martohej me të dhe asnjë tjetër.

VII.

Doktor Xhindi

Për fatin e mirë të të gjithëve, askush nuk kishte vdekur. Pasi e kishin nxjerrë mirë dufin e grumbulluar prej shumë kohësh, të sëmurët ishin kthyer në dhomat e tyre, sikur të mos kishte ndodhur asgjë. Këta njerëz të shfytyruar më shumë ngjanin me bishat e plagosura, që në ato momente qetësie po lëpinin plagët e marra nëpër trup. Infermierët të shtuar në numër hynin e dilnin nëpër dhoma, duke vëzhguar gjithë frikë, të gatshëm për të ndërhyrë në rast nevoje. Në ajër ende ndihej frika se dhuna mund të shpërthente nga çasti në çast.

Arbeni trokiti lehtazi në derë. Ky takim jashtë rradhe e kishte shqetësuar disi. Ndoshta afria me të sëmurin Isa Vishanji e kishte futur në telashe të paparashikuara. Nuk ishte çudi që drejtori mund ta pushonte nga puna me ndonjë arsye të kotë. Zakonisht mbledhjet bëheshin njëherë në javë dhe rrallë ndodhte që në zyrë të thirrej dikush jashtë mbledhjes rutinë, pikërisht të Hënën në mëngjes.

"Hyrë!" u dëgjua një zë i mbytur dhe Arbeni i djegur nga kureshtja, shtyu menjëherë derën. Drejtor Xhindi i bërë sa një grusht pas tavolinës së punës po shkruante diçka në një bllok shënimesh. I bëri shenjë me kokë që të ulej në njërën nga dy kolltuqet përballë dhe vazhdoi të shkruante në bllok. Vështrimi i vëngërt i Enver Hoxhës, që nga portreti i varur në mur, dukej sikur po ia rëndonte disi gjendjen shpirtërore. Arbeni bënte çudi sesi ishte e mundur vallë, që një mjek në një pozitë aq të lartë në spital, të mbartte një nofkë të tillë aq të dyshimtë si Xhindi, të cilën për ironi të fatit, ia kishte ngjitur njëri nga mjekët psikiatër i pushuar kohë më parë ndoshta për atë arsye. Mbiemri i tij i vërtetë ishte Malindi, por ngaqë bëhej xhind, sa herë që ndodhte ndonjë rrëmujë, ia kishin ngjitur "Xhindi".

"Mirëdita!" e përshëndeti nëpër dhëmbë Arbeni me gjysëm zëri, por drejtori rrinte i zhytur në shkresurinat e veta, sikur në zyrë të mos kishte njeri tjetër përveç atij. Arbeni u ndje si në gjemba, por nuk e dha veten. Drejtori ngriti syzet me skelet të trashë me majën e thojit dhe i hodhi një vështrim mospërfillës nga koka tek këmbët. Pa e ftuar të ulej, drejtor Malindi ngriti lart gishtin tregues.

"Çfarë ishte gjithë ajo rrëmujë që ndodhi?"

Ajo pyetje e beftë dhe me ton të vrazhdë tingëllonte paksa e rëndë, pothuajse si një akuzë e drejtpërdrejtë bërë pikërisht atij, që ishte munduar me aq shpirt për ta qetësuar turmën. Ishte vetëm merita e tij dhe e askujt tjetër, që askush nuk kishte mbetur i vrarë. Të paktën, këtë mendim kishte krijuar për veten me ndërhyrjen që kishte bërë. Drejtori patjetër që duhej të ishte në dijeni të ngjarjes gjer në detajet më të parëndësishme dhe nuk kishte nevojë ta dëgjonte edhe njëherë nga goja e tij. Po i dukej si një ofendim që të jepte një përgjigje, qoftë edhe të kotë.

"Besoj se nuk ka nevojë ta dëgjoni nga unë, se çfarë ndodhi, shoku drejtor!" Zëri i doli i ashpër, si për ta paralajmëruar se çfarëdo paragjykim nga ana e drejtorit, nuk do të pritej aspak mirë.

"Desha të di opinionin tuaj si mjek. Ju ishit gjatë të gjithë kohës aty, apo jo?"

"Po"

"Si filloi rrëmuja?"

"Nga një motiv banal dhe i kotë! Për një breshkë që infermier Fatmiri ua mori të sëmurëve dhe donte ta nxirrte përjashta!"

"Kam një raport të hollësishëm se çfarë ka ndodhur, por ju si mjek nuk duhej ta kishin lejuar që gjendja të dilte jashtë kontrollit."

"U përpoqa shoku drejtor, por ishte e pamundur. Mendoj se, gjithsesi shpëtuam jetë njerëzish. I sëmuri Isa Vishanji është jashtë rrezikut për jetën."

"Aha," e ndërpreu drejtori dhe ia nguli sytë, sikur donte të deshifronte se çfarë mendonte në atë çast mjeku i ri, që sapo kishte ardhur nga specializimi në Kinë. "Meqë ra fjala, çfarë mendimi keni për këtë të sëmurë, që sapo përmendët? Si mund të shmangim ndonjë revoltë tjetër të dhunshme?"

"Isai ishte krejtësisht i pafajshëm dhe nuk kishte asnjë gisht në këtë mes. Mbase do të ishte më mirë, që të lihej i lirë, jashtë mureve të spitalit për nja gjashtë muaj. Nëse gjendja e tij përkeqësohet, mund ta sjellim përsëri këtu." Arbeni kujtoi në çast, se ndoshta ai mendim i sinqertë dhe i drejtpërdrejtë mund të keqkuptohej.

"Mendoni se duke e lënë të lirë, mund të përmirësohet?"

"Ky i sëmurë flet normalisht, vepron normalisht, madje edhe shkruan. Jeta me njerëz normalë përreth mund ta shërojë plotësisht!" këmbënguli Arbeni. Një dritë shprese i ndriçoi sytë. Ndoshta kishte gabuar në gjykim, kur e kishte paragjykuar atë njeri, pikërisht nga ajo nofkë e çuditshme që i kishin vënë kolegët e tjerë. Drejtori mbështeti kokën mbi të dyja duart, por nuk po gjente qetësi. Futi gishtat leshtorë në rrëzë të qafës dhe kapi si me pinca damarët. U lehtësua disi dhe u shtriq në kolltuk. Ai mendim i mjekut të ri po e ngacmonte dhe nuk po e linte të qetë.

"A keni ndonjë lidhje familjare me këtë të sëmurë?"

Arbeni ngriti supet me habi, pa ditur se çfarë përgjigje t'i jepte. Kishte një lidhje krejtësisht njerëzore dhe aq. Ndjente një farë afrimiteti dhe keqardhjeje për atë të sëmurë dhe aq. Po si mund t'ia shpjegonte një burokrati të gjitha këto?!

"Asnjë lidhje, shoku drejtor! U nisa thjesht nga vëzhgimet e mia personale, kur dhashë atë mendim."

Doktor Xhindi u kthye nga ai dhe e pa drejt e në sy, me një çehre tallëse në fytyrë.

"E di që nuk e keq? Me një gur vrasim dy zogj: qetësojmë gjendjen dhe i japim një shans të artë shkrimtarit për t'u shkëputur nga këtu. Kështu mendoni ju?" Doktor Xhindi u ngrit në këmbë dhe, pa pritur ndonjë përgjigje, iu avit dritares. Qielli i vrenjtur nga retë që sa vinin e dendësoheshin, sikur ia shtonte dozën e zemërimit dhe të humorit të zi.

"Kam mendimin tim për trajtimin e të sëmurëve. Disa nga pacientët mund të kenë më shumë shanse për t'u përmirësuar jashtë mureve të spitalit!"

"Nuk ka rëndësi se çfarë mendon ti. Këto që thua ti janë gjepura! A e di ti, që ky pacient flet kundër qeverisë, sa herë që kthehet në gjendje normale? Ai duhet të trajtohet vazhdimisht me elektroshok, që të harrojë se çfarë thotë."

"Shoku drejtor! Të sëmurët nuk duhet të mbajnë përgjegjësi për ato që thonë dhe bëjnë! Unë mendoj..."

"A e dini ju që disa nga armiqtë e klasës kanë kërkuar të strehohen në këtë spital, si e si që t'i shpëtojnë burgut?"

"Sigurisht që e di! Dhe nuk mendoj se janë armiq të klasës, por thjesht viktima. Ju nuk po thoni që Isai është njëri nga "armiqtë" dhe duhet dënuar?"

"Nuk po them këtë! Ne jemi mjekë në rradhë të parë. Nuk jemi oficerë burgu!"

"Ndoshta për këtë duhet lënë i lirë!"

"Aha! Të sëmurët të dalin jashtë, ndërsa normalët të strehohen këtu, nga frika e sigurimit! Paradoks!"

"Nuk është keq ta provojmë. Ky i sëmurë mund të përmirësohet!"

Drejtori u ul në karrigen e tij dhe tundi kokën në shenjë kundërshtimi. Nëse do të ishte dikush që duhej të fajësohej për trazirat, duhej të ishte pikërisht Isai dhe për këtë gjë duhej bërë e kundërta. Lirimi nga spitali do të shihej si një lloj shpërblimi nga ata Lart! Dylbitë ushtarake të Partisë vëzhgonin gjithçka.

"Të vazhdojë trajtimi me elektroshok! Kthim mbrapa nuk ka! Mund të shkoni!" Ia bëri me dorë të largohej dhe i hodhi nga sytë protreti i Enver Hoxhës i varur në mur. Dukej sikur Udhëheqësi i lavdishëm sapo ishte lumturuar nga ai vendim i rëndësishëm.

"Shoku drejtor, mendojeni edhe njëherë, para se të merrni ndonjë vendim."

"Nuk kam se çfarë të mendoj!"

"Këtij të sëmuri iu rrezikua jeta seriozisht! Nëse nuk do të kisha ndërhyrë në kohë, sot mund të ishte i vdekur. Nuk ka asnjë garanci se nuk do të sulmohet përsëri. Nuk e di nëse do t'i drejtoheni gjykatës për ta mbajtur këtë pacient më shumë se tre muaj. Ky afat ka kaluar tashmë! Ai nuk përbën asnjë rrezik për njerëzit përreth. Krahasuar me të sëmurët e tjerë, mund të thosha se është krejtësisht normal."

Doktor Xhindi goditi lehtazi me laps xhamin që mbulonte tavolinën i kapur në befasi nga argumenti ligjor i mjekut të ri. Që të zgjatej koha e shtrimit të pacientit patjetër që duhej një vendim gjykate. Në fund të fundit, një pacient më pak do të thoshte më pak kosto për buxhetin e spitalit. Ndoshta, kushedi, rifutja në shoqëri mund të ndikonte për mirë në shëndetin e të sëmurit. Tashmë kishte kaluar pothuajse një vit që Isai trajtohej në spital. Ngriti duart lart, sikur të kishte ngritur flamurin e bardhë.

"Mirë, do të shohim mundësinë që ta nxjerrim nga muaji i ardhshëm!" tha me një lloj pezmi, por dukej se Arbeni nuk e priste atë përgjigje, pasi nuk po lëvizte nga vendi. "Besoj se u morëm vesh! Do të shohim mundësinë që të dalë nga spitali pas disa javësh."

"Shoku drejtor, koha nuk pret as edhe një ditë të vetme. Duhet të dalë menjëherë nga spitali, pa humbur as edhe një minutë. Nëse do t'i ndodhë ndonjë gjë, do të jeni ju, që do të mbani përgjegjësi pastaj," shfryu. Ende nuk mund ta besonte se përpjekjet e tij kishin marrë fund.

Drejtori fërkoi fytyrën me të dyja duart, si për të larguar atë ndjesi sikleti dhe turpi që i kish përskuqur fytyrën. Ky mjek i ri po e vinte në pozitë të vështirë. Vërtet, po sikur ndonjëri nga të sëmurët të mos e kishte harruar Isain dhe ta sulmonte përsëri? Mos ndoshta vërtet ekzistonte mundësia që gjërat të viheshin përfundimisht nën kontroll?! Po atje jashtë, a kishte siguri për jetën e Isait?!

"A mban përgjegjësi ti si mjek për jetën e këtij të sëmuri?" Zëri i doli i dobët, gati si justifikim.

"Askush nuk mund t'i shpëtojë përgjegjësisë. Besoj se firma ime duhet të jetë mëse e mjaftueshme, shoku drejtor!"

"E hedh apo nuk e hedh firmën, kjo në terren nuk ndryshon asgjë. Megjithëkëtë, mendimin tënd po e marr parasysh, por nuk mund ta nxjerrim në këtë gjendje që është. I sëmuri ka marrë plagë të rënda në kokë e në trup. I duhen të paktën disa javë që të marrë veten." Zëri i doli i mbytur dhe i zvargur. Ia shtyu dosjen mjekësore në tavolinë dhe fërkoi tëmthat për të larguar mendimet e zymta.

"Disa javë?!"

"Nuk është fundi i botës! Ndërrojini dhomën! Dërgojeni në ndonjë kat tjetër. Nuk mund t'ia dorëzojmë të afërmve në këtë gjendje. Këto javë le të mbahet nën mbikqyrjen tonë në një dhomë të veçantë, larg syve të të sëmurëve të tjerë."

"Ky është fundi i botës. Imagjinoni shoku drejtor, se çfarë mund të thotë Partia, nëse njëri nga pacientët vdes në këtë mënyrë, qoftë ky edhe Isa Vishanji! Ju sapo keni dhënë urdhër që ai të dënohet me vdekje." Arbeni mori dosjen nga tavolina, e vuri nën sqetull me shpejtësi dhe u bë gati të dilte, pothuajse i nxirë në fytyrë.

"Kështu mendoni ju?

"Nuk ka si të jetë ndryshe!"

"Nëse e ke fjalën për ndonjë nga të sëmurët apo një grusht të sëmurësh që e kanë kërcënuar atë ditë, kjo nuk do të thotë se do të ndodhë përsëri. Të sëmurët psikikë nuk janë të vetëdijshëm për veprimet që bëjnë. Të siguroj që nuk mbajnë mend asgjë se çfarë ndodhi. Le të qëndrojë edhe disa javë në spital, jo më shumë!" Doktori Xhindi këmbënguli në të vetën e shfryu i lehtësuar, sikur të kishte hequr nga kurrizi një barrë të rëndë.

Arbeni u kap në befasi nga ai argument i papeshuar mirë i drejtorit. U mat të thoshte diçka, por ndërroi mendje. Ndoshta drejtori kishte të drejtë, por kjo pritej për t'u parë. Disa javë! Tundi kokën me mëdyshje, mërmëriti diçka nëpër dhëmbë dhe tërhoqi derën pas vetes. Fytyra i qeshi nga një rrezatim i beftë.

VIII.
Ora e Frëngjishtes

Që nga ajo ditë, kur kishin fituar luftën kundër "Romakëve", Amla kishte filluar ta shihte me sy tjetër. Lajmi për dyluftimin me Gëzimin kishte marrë dhenë dhe gati të gjithë fëmijët e lagjes përshkruanin gjer në detaje atë që kishte ndodhur. Dukej se Çimi ishte bërë heroi i ditës. Amla ulej gjithmonë në bankën e parë, ndërsa Çimi ulej në bankën e fundit, në rreshtin ngjitur me dritaret dhe pikërisht ai kënd që nga pika me e largët e klasës, i jepte mundësinë që asgjë të mos i shpëtonte vështrimit të tij të kujdesshëm. Ende pa filluar ora e frëngjishtes, Amla ktheu kokën pas dhe i nguli sytë e saj plot shkëlqim. Gërshetat e gjatë dukej sikur e bënin edhe më tërheqëse fytyrën e saj borë të bardhë të mbuluar me dritë. Shkruajti emrin e saj në fletore me gërma të mëdha: AMLA! Sa emër i bukur dhe sa shqip, por dhe me plot kuptim! Oh, sa do të kishte dëshirë që atë emër t'ia vinte motrës, kur të vinte në jetë! Natyrisht, nëse vërtet natyra dhe fati do ta lejonte që të bëhej me motër dhe nëse Hamdiu dhe mami do të bënin marrëveshje, që pikërisht ai t'i vinte emrin motrës. Ehuuuu! Kishte kohë edhe dy-tre muaj. Tani duhej të vizatonte sytë e

Amlës, ata sy me bisht që dukej sikur ishin krijuar si për të shpërndarë magji dhe mister. Ishte e çuditshme, që mendonte kaq shumë për të. Madje i vinte edhe turp nga vetja, që e mendonte një gjë të tillë. Pas asaj puthjeje të lehtë në faqe, kishte përshtypjen se bota do të përmbysej dhe Amla nuk do t'i fliste më kurrë, por fatmirësisht asgjë nuk kishte ndryshuar. Përkundrazi, Amla ishte bërë më e afrueshme dhe miqësore. Megjithëse ora e frëngjishtes filloi, Amla kthente kokën herë pas here me lezet, duke e parë me bisht të syrit. Si zakonisht, edhe këtë herë mësuese Dafina nuk harroi ta thërriste Çimin para të gjithë klasës.

"Çimi, dil këtu përpara dhe na recito vjershën e Viktor Hygoit për pranverën. Dua që të gjithë ju ta dëgjoni me kujdes dhe të merrni shembull nga ai." Mësuese Dafina duatrokiti vetë e para dhe pas saj e gjithë klasa.

Çimit i ishin skuqur edhe më shumë veshët nga ato fjalë aq inkurajuese, të cilat mësuese Dafina i derdhte pa kursim, sa herë që i jepej mundësia. Eci si mbi gjemba drejt dërrasës së zezë dhe u kthye me fytyrë nga klasa. Zemra po i rrihte me forcë nga zori dhe turpi se ndoshta nuk do të ishte në gjendje ta recitonte me atë zë të ëmbël dhe melodioz poezinë për pranverën. Amla kishte kryqëzuar krahët dhe nuk po ja ndante sytë. Klasa dukej sikur kishte mbajtur frymën dhe po priste me ankth recitimin e tij të magjishëm. Atë vjershë e kishte mësuar përmendësh dhe e kishte recituar kushedi sesa herë, madje edhe me sy të mbyllur. Hodhi vështrimin në thellësi, mbi kokat e bashkëmoshatarëve të vet dhe e mbajti në një pikë imagjinare në hapësirë. Klasa u bë e padukshme dhe para tij tashmë shfaqej një pyll me pemë shtatlarta, kurorat e të cilave tundeshin nën vallen e erës. Më tutje një livadh i mbuluar nga lulet shumëngjyrëshe, dukej sikur po e ftonte në gjirin e vet. Ngriti duart lart dhe e la zërin t'i dalë nga kraharori.

"Printemps"

"Voici donc les longs jours, lumière, amour, délire!
Voici le printemps! Mars, avril au doux sourire,
Mai fleuri, juin brûlant, tous les beaux mois amis!
Les peupliers, au bord des fleuves endormis,
Se courbent mollement comme de grandes palmes;
L'oiseau palpite au fond des bois tièdes et calmes;
Il semble que tout rit, et que les arbres verts
Sont joyeux d'être ensemble et se disent des vers.
Le jour naît couronné d'une aube fraîche et tendre ;
Le soir est plein d'amour; la nuit, on croit entendre,
A travers l'ombre immense et sous le ciel béni,
Quelque chose d'heureux chanter dans l'infini."

("Ja pra ditët e gjata, drita, dashuria, përçartja!
Ja pranvera! Marsi, Prilli me buzëqeshjen e tij të ëmbël,
Maji që lulëzon, Qershori që digjet, të gjithë muajt e bukur miqësorë!
Plepat, në brigjet e lumenjve të fjetur,
Përkulen butësisht si palma të mëdha;
Zogu fluturon thellë në pyjet e ngrohta dhe të qeta;
Duket sikur gjithçka po qesh dhe se pemët e gjelbra
Janë të gëzuara që janë bashkë dhe i thonë vargje njëra-tjetrës.
Dita lind e kurorëzuar me një agim të freskët dhe të butë;
Mbrëmja është plot dashuri; natën, mendon se dëgjon,
Përmes hijeve të pafundme dhe nën qiellin e bekuar,
Diçka të lumtur që këndon në pafundësi.")

Sapo mbaroi së recituari, pamja iu kthjellua dhe më në fund e pa veten përsëri në klasë. Dukej se ajo poezi i kishte elektrizuar të gjithë. Shokët shpërthyen në duartrokitje, njësoj sikur të kishin marrë pjesë në një shfaqje të vërtetë.

"Të lumtë, Çimi! Shkëlqyeshëm. Mund të ulesh. Tani rradhën e ka..." Mësuese Dafina i drejtoi gishtin Gëzimit, që u duk se u kap në befasi pasi u nxi në fytyrë.

Çimi u ul në bankën e vet në rreshtin e fundit dhe me bisht të syrit pa përsëri nga Amla. Buzëqeshja e saj e ëmbël, sikur e çliroi nga ai makth që e kishte zënë.

"J'aurais préféré ne jamais t'avoir vu,"- (*Do të doja mos të të kisha parë kurrë*,) i pëshpëriti nga cepi i largët i klasës.

IX.

Breshka shpallet në kërkim

Arbeni fërkoi tëmthat fort dhe mori frymë thellë, si për t'u çliruar nga ajo barrë e rëndë që i kishte rënë mbi supe. Për një breshkë që infermier Fatmiri ua mori të sëmurëve ishte bërë gjithë ajo rrëmujë në përmasat e një kryengritjeje. Përveç dëmeve materiale të shkaktuara, ishin rrezikuar edhe jetë njerëzish. Kishte vetëm një mënyrë për të kthyer besimin e të sëmurëve: të mendonin të paktën njëherë si ata. Nëse vërtet donte që të mos kishte më trazira në spital, duhej të gjendej patjetër breshka dhe t'i kthehej "Mësuesit". Të ishte kaq e thjeshtë zgjidhja vallë? Vërtet që në spital nuk lejoheshin kafshë të asnjë lloji, as mace, as qen, as gardalina, as pëllumba; por kjo shkelje e vogël e ligjit do të ndikonte sadopak në uljen e tensioneve, që edhe ashtu ishin shumë të larta. Minjtë hynin pa leje, po ashtu edhe pëllumbat, por askush prej tyre nuk mbahej peng nga të sëmurët. "Mësuesi" dhe aq më pak të sëmurët e tjerë nuk do të kishin më arsye që të sulmonin fizikisht Isain. Po sikur infermier Fatmiri të mos pranonte të bashkëpunonte dhe përkundrazi ta akuzonte se nuk po zbatonte rregulloren e spitalit? Duhej të gjente diçka kompromentuese, që ta detyronte Fatmirin të pranonte. Mbylli sytë dhe u mundua të përqëndrohej. Sa herë që mbyllte sytë, i dukej sikur shikonte më qartë. Tërhoqi derën e zyrës dhe doli në korridor. Dhoma e infermierëve nuk ishte shumë larg prej aty. Atë ditë Fatmiri nuk punonte dhe ishte rasti më i mirë për t'i kontrolluar vendin ku vishte uniformën. Nga dera gjysëm e hapur doli një infermiere, një vajzë e re, e cila kishte filluar punë para disa ditësh. E përshëndeti nxitimthi dhe priti gjersa ajo të largohej. Në dhomën e Infermierëve nuk kishte më njeri. Hodhi sytë rretheperqark për të parë se ku i linin infermierët rrobat. Mbajti frymën para një dollapi të madh dhe hapi të dyja kanatet. Në njërin raft lexoi emrin e Fatmirit. E tërhoqi me nxitim, ndërsa zemra filloi t'i rrihte me forcë. Hapi rrobat e palosura njëenganjë dhe mbajti frymën. Nuk u besoi dot syve. Poshtë pantallonave të palosura ishte një kamzhik me lëkurë të zezë. Shkopi ishte i hollë dhe i lëmueshëm. E futi poshtë bluzës dhe doli jashtë.

ARBENI NGRITI TELEFONIN dhe formoi numrin.

"Alo, doktor Arbeni jam. A ka mundësi të njoftoni infermier Fatmirin ju lutem? Po! Të vijë urgjentisht në zyrë!" Uli receptorin dhe mbështeti kurrizin e lodhur në shpinën e karriges. Kishte pritur gati 24 orë, gjer sa të gdhinte dita e nesërme, por ato pak minuta po i dukeshin shumë të gjata. Gjatë të gjithë natës e kishte munduar ajo ide e çuditshme se rikthimi i Akuparës do të përmbyste situatën. Fundja çfarë do të humbiste po të provonte të bënte një gjest alogjik, si ai i të menduarit njësoj si ata? Ishte një lloj eksperimenti apo jo?!

Nuk ishte hera e parë që infermier Fatmiri acaronte të sëmurët me qëndrimin e tij. Një bisedë vetëm për vetëm me të, nuk do t'i bënte keq askujt. Si nuk i kishte vajtur mendja më parë që ta bënte një gjë të tillë? Fundja e kishte për detyrë që të fliste me punonjësit e tjerë, sa herë që ta shihte të arsyeshme.

Fatmiri hyri brenda dhe me një vështrim triumfatori ndali këmbët në mes të zyrës. Dukej se as që e kishte idenë se për çfarë ishte thirrur. Doktor Arbeni ishte nga më të rinjtë në spital ndërsa Fatmiri kishte më shumë vjet aty.

"Mirëdita, doktor!"

Seç kishte një lloj ngërdheshjeje në fytyrën e infermierit më të rreptë të spitalit. Diçka si kryeneçësi dhe arrogancë. Ishte po ai me këpucët plot shkëlqim dhe mustaqet e prera spic. Flokët i kishte lyer me llak dhe të ngjeshura pas kokës. Fatmiri ishte shtatlartë dhe trupin e mbante gjithnjë drejt. Atë mëngjes i mungonte diçka e rëndësishme, të cilën e mbante shpesh në duar. Kamzhiku!

"Mirëdita!" ia ktheu me gjysëm zëri dhe u ngrit nga karrigia. "Të kam thirrur për breshkën!"

"Për breshkën?" Sytë e Fatmirit u hapën, sikur të kishte dëgjuar çudinë e shekullit. "Cilën breshkë?" Në tonin e zërit ndjehej një farë ironie dhe sarkazme.

"Për atë që u more të sëmurëve. Pse pyet? Ke parë ndonjë breshkë tjetër?"

"Jo, por bëj çudi se për çfarë të duhet!"

"Duhet t'ua kthejmë të sëmurëve."

"Doktor, më falni, por kjo kërkesë më duket absurde. Në spital nuk lejohen kafshët. Kjo është thyerje e ligjit. Ju e dini shumë mirë."

"Kështu si të them unë! Urgjentisht ta gjesh dhe të ma sjellësh këtu në zyrë!"

"Kjo nuk ka as logjikë! Ata janë të çmendur. Nuk mund të plotësojmë kërkesa të tilla."

"Nuk mund të lejoj që për një motiv kaq banal të ketë përsëri trazira. Aq më tepër të vihet në rrezik jeta e ndonjë të sëmuri."

"Vërtet mendoni, se me gjetjen e breshkës, do të ulni gjakrat?"

"Po! Dhe mos guxoni të më përmendni ligjin, pikërisht ju që e shkelni me të dyja këmbët. Nuk besoj se do të dëshironit që të dërgoja ndonjë raport lart!

"Për çfarë?"

"Ju e dini shumë mirë për "çfarë". Ku e ke "kamzhikun", me të cilin rreh të sëmurët? Ligji nuk thotë se ndonjë punonjës i spitalit duhet të dhunojë fizikisht të sëmurët. Apo jo, infermier Fatmiri?" Doktor Arbeni i erdhi pranë.

"Nuk e kuptoj për çfarë kamzhiku e keni fjalën, shoku doktor!" Fatmirit i kaluan mornica në trup, por nuk e dha veten. Mbajti të njëjtën ngërdheshje në fytyrë, si një maskë plastike.

Arbeni iu afrua tavolinës së zyrës dhe hapi sirtarin. Nxorri kamzhikun prej andej dhe e tundi lart.

"Për këtë e kam fjalën! Ju abuzoni fizikisht me të sëmurët dhe kjo është ligjërisht e dënueshme. Nëse nuk e gjen breshkën, do të përfundosh në burg."

"Kamzhikun e mbaj vetëm për vetëmbrojtje! Nuk ke prova që e përdor për të dhunuar të sëmurët."

"Atëherë mund të shkosh! Këtë kamzhik do ta dërgoj si provë gjer në drejtori. Nuk besoj se atje do ta shohin si mjet vetëmbrojtjeje."

Fatmiri tundi kokën në shenjë mohimi dhe uli sytë përdhe. Donte ta kundërshtonte, por nuk po gjente dot fjalët. Kjo kërkesë jo vetëm që i dukej absurde dhe e kotë, por dhe pa kuptim. Vërtet doktori mendonte se plotësimi i një kërkese kaq naive do të sillte paqen aq shumë të dëshiruar në spital? Ishte njësoj sikur vullnetarisht të lozin rolin e të sëmurit edhe vetë ata, personeli i kualifikuar mjekësor.

"E kuptoj se çfarë mund të të vijë në mendje, por ne nuk jemi policë. Ne duhet të tregojmë anën tonë njerëzore e jo të sillemi më keq se kafshët. Madje mendoj se kafshët ofendohen po të fillojmë të thërrasim njëri-tjetrin me emrin e tyre. Të jesh i sëmurë mendor është njësoj si të jesh i sëmurë nga zemra. Të gjithë të sëmurët duhet të trajtohen njëlloj: me dashuri dhe profesionalizëm!"

"Dakord! Do të mundohem ta gjej. Të lutem, mos thuaj asgjë atje lart. Do ta gjej breshkën me çdo kusht."

"Ku e hodhe?"

"E kam lënë jashtë gardhit rrethues të spitalit, nga prapa."

"Shpresoj ta gjesh sa më parë që të jetë e mundur. Tani dil nga zyra. Ke afat vetëm sot."

"Si urdhëron, shoku doktor!" Dukej sikur nuk ishte më ai Fatmiri i parë, por dikush, që sapo kishte marrë një lajmërim vdekjeje.

Arbeni mori frymë i lehtësuar dhe për herë të parë pas gjithë atyre trazirave, ndjeu një lehtësi në shpirt.

X.

Shtrigë Nirvana

Të dy vogëlushët ecën ngadalë përmes oborrit të Pallatit të Peshkut, me sytë e ndrojtur në drejtim të hallë Nirvanës, asaj gruaje të çuditshme të cilën nëna e thërriste "shtrigë". Hamdiu u çapit pa qejf pas tyre, krejtësisht i zhytur në mendime të zymta. Halla nuk duroi dot më, por u turr në drejtim të tyre me krahët hapur. Sytë ju mbushën me lotë, teksa puthi Platorin në të dyja faqet.

"Të keqen halla ty, sa i mir që je! Po si e ka harru hallën tate ti? Nuk ke ardhë asnjiher që ta shofësh?" Pllaq! Plluq! Kaluan disa sekonda, gjersa Halla u ngop së puthuri të dy bijtë e të vëllait dhe e hutuar, ia hodhi sytë Hamdiut, që priste në heshtje me cigaren në dorë. E pyeti ashtu nëpër dhëmbë "si jeni ju" dhe i përqafoi edhe njëherë të dy fëmijët fort me krahët që i dridheshin nga ngashërimi.

Halla ishte një grua e mbajtur rreth të dyzetave, me flokë të kuqerremtë dhe fytyrë të bardhë e të rrumbullakët, ku binte në sy një nishan në faqen e djathtë. Për dallim nga emërtimi që i kishte gjetur e ëma, Çimi nuk gjente dot asnjë tipar në fytyrën e saj, që mund t'i kujtonte ato shtrigat tradicionale të përrallave. Ishte paksa kuqalashe dhe sytë i mbusheshin përherë me lotë, sa herë që shihte ata të dy. Halla kishte edhe një vëlla tjetër, Bardhylin, që kishte edhe ai dy fëmijë, një vajzë dhe një djalë, por dy djemtë e Isait kishin një vend të veçantë në zemrën e saj. E skuqur në fytyrë Halla, nuk pushonte së ndukuri nga faqet vogëlushët, që atë ditë ishin veshur si asnjëherë tjetër me pantallona të zeza e të hekurosura dhe me këmishat borë të bardha.

"Maroni punë dhe silli prapë kalamajtë sonte në darkë, se nesër kanë shkollë!" tha Hamdiu dhe, si për të hequr bezdinë që po i shkaktonte ai takim me ish-kunatën e gruas, thithi edhe njëherë cigaren e dredhur vetë dhe e hodhi bishtin e zbërdhylët në tokë. E shtypi me thembrën e këmbës fort, si për të marrë hak ndaj një diçkaje të padukshme që po e mundonte pa masë dhe lëpiu buzët e thara. Mollëzat e gishtave i ishin zverdhur nga nikotina, por atij aq i bënte. Duhani i grirë, i blerë në tregun e fshatarëve, ishte ilaçi i tij i parapëlqyer. Tymi i atij duhani, të prodhuar pas asnjë lloj kimikati, sikur e dërgonte në një botë tjetër, pa telashe dhe kokëçarje.

"Mos ki marak! Sa të marojmë, do të kthehemi menjiherë ktu." Nirvanës një fytyrë i ikte dhe një tjetër i vinte. I hodhi edhe një vështrim të vëngërt, sikur donte ta hante të gjallë dhe tërhoqi nga duart të dy djemtë e vegjël që kishin mbetur si të ngrirë. "Ashtë në terezi ky?" dukej sikur thoshte. "Fëmijëve u del i ati nga spitali, nërsa ky i kërkon me vrap në shpi!"

I hipën autobuzit të Banesave dhe pas disa ndalesave të shkurtëra zbritën në stacionin pranë kinemasë "Vullnetari". Nga aty Spitali Psikiatrik mbante jo më shumë se gjysëm ore në këmbë. Ajo ndërtesë tre katëshe në ngjyrë blu të çelët binte në sy që larg dhe të ngjallte në zemër vetëm trishtim. Çimi kishte ndjesinë sikur po i merrej fryma dhe i lindi dëshira që të ikte sa më parë prej andej. Teksa u afrua edhe më, për çudinë e tij dalloi edhe një kat tjetër gjysëm të nëndheshëm. Të gjitha dritaret pa përjashtim ishin të mbrojtura me shufra hekuri, siç dukej për të parandaluar të sëmurët nga ndonjë tentativë për vetëvrasje. Në një nga dritaret e katit të tretë, vihej re një i sëmurë, i cili i kishte vënë të dyja gjunjët mbi parvaz e shikonte me kërshëri ata vizitorë të rastit që prisnin të takonin të dashurit e tyre. Një i sëmurë tjetër nja dy dritare më tutje, kishte mbështetur kurrizin pas murit anësor, pa shikuar asgjëkundi, sikur nuk i interesonte agjë nga ajo ditë e zhurmshme dhe e mbushur plot diell.

Hyrja kryesore e spitalit ishte e ruajtur nga një derë me shufra hekuri ngjitur me postbllokun, ku bënte shërbimin infermieri roje. Halla dhe të dy djemtë u ulën në një stol aty pranë, disa metra më tutje nga porta kryesore dhe pritën që të vinte babai, por ai nuk po dukej gjëkundi. Çimi filloi të shqetësohej disi dhe si për t'u eglendisur hodhi sytë përreth. Grimca të vogla të kujtesës i sollën parasysh ato mbrëmje të vona të natës, kur babai e mbante në prehër dhe i recitonte poezi. Zëri i tij i ngrohtë mbushte dhomën e ftohtë, në të cilën xixëllonte flaka e dobët e qiririt. Në atë kohë binin shpesh alarmet dhe popullsia civile ishte udhëzuar të fikte dritat dhe të mbyllej në shtëpi. Në raste të tjera, banorët duhej të vraponin për në vendstrehimet e nëndheshme, në pritje të bombardimeve imagjinare nga armiqtë imperialisto-revizionistë. "O malet e Shqipërisë/dhe ju o lisat e gjatë/fushat e gjera me lule/që ju kam ndërmend ditë dhe natë," recitonin të dy vargjet e Naimit. Kur sirenat e alarmeve pushonin dhe dritat ndizeshin përsëri, ato çaste poetike shuheshin si me magji.

"Hallë Nirvana, pse po vonohet babi?" Zëri i hollë i Platorit e shkundi nga ajo vorbullë kujtimesh.

"Nuk e di, të keqen halla! Mos u murzit! Hajde ktu te prehri i hallës, që të mos lodhesh! Ja, pothujse ka ardhë!" Platori nuk e zgjati dhe hop kërceu në prehërin e hallës. E ulur në stol, halla bënte herë pas here fresk me një dorashkë trengjyrëshe, të kuqe, të zezë dhe të verdhë.

Çimin sikur nuk po e mërziste dhe aq ajo vonesë e babait. Si tani i kujtohej ajo mbrëmje e vonë, kur përpak desh e pësoi nga oreksi dhe pangopësia. Nëna kishte skuqur një tavë me petulla dhe e kishte lënë sipër dollapit që të ftohej. Çimit nuk i durohej dhe ato minuta i dukeshin si orë pambarim. Kur u sigurua se nuk po e shihte njeri, vuri dy stola sipër njëri- tjetrit dhe u përpoq që të fuste duart në tavë. Në atë çast i rrëshqiti këmba dhe u rrëzua, duke përplasur kokën në dysheme. Befas ndjeu një dhimbje të tmerrshme sipër syrit të djathtë. Vuri gishtat gjithë frikë mbi të çarën e shkaktuar nga një cep i mprehtë i karriges, por shkulma e gjakut nuk pushonte së rrjedhuri. Pak nga dhimbja e pak nga frika Çimi filloi të bërtiste, gjersa aty erdhën me një frymë nga dhoma tjetër të dy prindërit. Babain e zuri menjëherë paniku dhe, pa humbur as edhe një minutë kohë, e rrëmbeu mbi supet e tij dhe e çoi drejt e në ambulancën e lagjes, që nuk ishte as një stacion autobuzi larg. Lagja "Vullnetari" ishte e zhytur e gjitha në qetësi. Babai vraponte me Çimin e gjakosur në kurriz dhe vazhdimisht i fliste, që t'i jepte zemër. Trupi i tundej dhe shkundej nën ritmin e hapave të shpejtuar, ndërsa sytë i ndiqnin pikat e gjakut që binin mbi trotuar.

"Mos ki frikë, të keqen babi! Bëhu burrë i fortë! Ja edhe pak, erdhëm!" përsëriste ai. Infermieri ia qepi atypëraty, sapo mbërritën në infermierinë e lagjes. Çuditërisht si tani i kujtohej, teksa rënkonte, ndërsa mjeku ia qepte vetullën e djathtë, e cila ishte çarë mespërmes. Babai ishte aty në këmbë pranë tij, duke i dhënë zemër.

ÇIMI BËRI NJË ECEJAKE përreth stolit ku ishte ulur halla, me sytë nga hyrja kryesore e spitalit. Befas u skuq në fytyrë, kur kujtoi atë mëngjes të ftohtë prilli afro tre vite më parë.

ÇIMI U RROTULLUA ME dëshpërim në krevat dhe hodhi sytë nga dritarja. Yjet kishin filluar të zbeheshin e rralloheshin. Gjinkallat ende këndonin në kor, por jo më me atë vrullin e mbrëmjes. Kur do të gdhihej vallë? Edhe sa orë duhej të priste gjersa të vinte agimi? Puliti sytë dhe me imagjinatën e ndezur u përpoq të krijonte edhe një herë imazhin e asaj torte të madhe shumëngjyrëshe me pesë kokërra qershije sipër, që e kishte parë në ëmbëltoren e lagjes. Kremi i bardhë dhe copëzat kafe të errët të çokollatës, sikur ia shtonin edhe më shumë dëshirën për ta patur në duart e veta një herë e përgjithmonë. Më mirë mos ta kishte parë kurrë atë mollë të ndaluar! Mbrëmë i kishte thënë babait se kishte parë një tortë të madhe në shitoren e lagjes, teksa ishin ulur të katër rreth tavolinës për të ngrënë darkën, por babai as që ia kishte vënë veshin. Tani e dinte ai se çfarë duhej të bënte. Ja, edhe pak! Sa të gdhihej dhe atje do ta mbante frymën. E si mund të hiqte dorë nga një mrekulli e tillë? Nga ai krem aq i

butë dhe i ëmbël? Nga thelpinjtë e arrave që shponin aty këtu koren e çokollatës? Jeta është e shkurtër dhe duhet të shijohet. Të mos e provonte atë tortë, mos ta kishte të gjithën në duart e veta, do të ishte padrejtësia më e madhe në jetë. Kur të ndalojnë për diçka, sikur të shtojnë më shumë dëshirën për ta patur. Nuk është se kishte ditëlindjen, por kjo nuk ishte arsye e mjaftueshme për të mos e patur. Ohu, kush priste ditëlindjen edhe tre muaj! Tortën donte ta kishte tani para sysh. Ajo ëmbëlsirë ishte gjëja më e bukur në botë, që i dilte përnatë në ëndërr. Do të ishte krim dhe mëkat, fatkeqësi po të mos e prekte atë tortë me mollëzat e gishtave ose të paktën t'i merrte erë.

U çua nga krevati, duke parë përreth me kujdes. Ora ishte pesë e mëngjesit. Zemërthyer u kthye mbrapsht sërisht në majat e gishtave, me sytë nga Platori që flinte në krevatin tek në krahun e majtë të dhomës. Po ta dëgjonte vëllai i vogël, i gjithë plani hidhej në erë. Ia qepi sytë tavanit për ta larguar disi atë imazh, por ishte e pamundur. Torta merrte më shumë ngjyra e më shumë shkëlqim. Sikur zmadhohej e rrotullohej në dhomën e errët, si një anije e vogël kozmike që po mbërrinte nga hapësira. Ja ai, vetë, teksa dilte nga torta me një pirun të artë dhe i mbuluar i gjithi nga kremi i bardhë.

Ndërsa përpëlitej në krahët e imagjinatës, Çimi u kujtua se duhej të hidhej në veprim. Më mirë të dilte nga shtëpia sa pa u zgjuar askush, por më parë duhet të gjente paratë. Në njërën nga karriget pranë tavolinës së bukës ishte varur xhaketa e babait. Çimi eci në majë të gishtave, duke u munduar që të mos bënte as zhurmën më të vogël. Hodhi njëherë sytë nga dhoma ku ende flinin babai dhe nëna. Dukej se prindërit ishin zhytur në gjumë të thellë. Futi ngadalë dorën në xhepin e xhaketës së babait dhe nxorri prej andej kuletën. Ishte një kuletë prej lëkure ngjyrë kafe me disa xhepa, në njërën nga të cilat babai kishte futur fotografinë e dy djemve. Syri i zuri një kartmonedhë 250 lekëshe të vjetër, të cilën e bëri shuk dhe e futi me shpejtësi në xhep. Përreth nuk pipëtinte as edhe miza. Rrotulloi çelësin në bravën e derës së jashtme. U dëgjua një kërcitje e thatë, aq sa për të zgjuar dikë në dhomën tjetër. Kafshoi buzën dhe gjithë frikë ktheu kokën pas. Asnjë lëvizje. Veshi këpucët dhe ashtu siç ishte me pantallona të shkurtra dhe në një këmishë të hollë në ngjyrë blu, ia krisi vrapit poshtë shkallëve. Zemra filloi t'i rrihte fort nga emocionet. Po sikur babai të zgjohej dhe ta kapte mat? As që nuk duhej ta çonte në mendje një gjë të tillë! Nxitoi edhe më shumë hapat: një, dy tre. Tashmë po vraponte me të gjitha fuqitë. Fryma po i merrej, ndërsa faqet i ishin skuqur nga ajri i ftohtë. Ja më në fund ëmbëltorja dhe torta e stërmadhe në vitrinë. Embëltorja hapej që në orën tetë të mëngjesit dhe akrepi shënonte tetë e pesë minuta. Brenda nuk kishte xhan xhin njeri, përveçse shitësit, një burri babaxhan me fytyrë të rrumbullakët. Kartmonedhën e kishte ende shuk në grusht.

"Dua të ble atë tortën aty!' tregoi me gisht, gjithë padurim, por shitësi nuk lëvizi nga vendi. Sytë e tij shikonin diku, përtej shpatullave të tij të vogla. Ktheu kokën. Pas tij qëndronte një shtatmesatar i veshur në pizhama, me flokët e zinj dhe të harlisur, e fytyrën të bërë flakë të kuqe nga një zemërim i brendshëm që sa vinte dhe i rritej. Zgurdulloi sytë, duke mos e besuar atë skenë, që nuk do të dëshironte ta shihte as në ëndrrën më të keqe. Ishte babai! Siç dukej, e kishte pikasur dhe e kishte ndjekur nga pas, pa u ndier fare. Babai nuk e zgjati më, por ia kërciti me një flakërimë të shpejtë në fytyrë dhe me dorën tjetër i tërhoqi krahun. Ja mori kartmonedhën nga dora, mërmëriti një "më fal" shitësit nëpër dhëmbë dhe ju drejtua të birit.

"Ec në shtëpi!" Fjalët e babait tingëlluan të vrazhda dhe të rënda, si një urdhër lufte. Çimi i skuqur gjer në rrënjët e flokëve uli sytë dhe doli si pulë e lagur nga ëmbëltorja. Seç ndodhi më pas, nuk mbante mend asgjë, por ajo skenë turpi do t'i mbetej në kujtesë për gjatë të gjithë jetës së vet.

U DËGJUA NJË ZHURMË kuzhinetash të ndryshkura, që po klithnin me mërzi. Zhurma e tyre çjerrëse gati sa nuk i çau timpanët e veshëve. Prej andej ja ku doli babai: Këmbëzbathur, i veshur me pizhama me kuadrate ngjyrëkafe. Atë të djelë qershori dielli shkëlqente me të gjithë madhështinë e vet. Isai shtrëngoi fort kapakët e syve për t'u mbrojtur disi nga ai rrezatim verbues. Të qenit gjatë të gjithë kohës brenda e kishte shndërruar në një lloj qenieje të qullët e të flashkët që gjente qetësi vetëm në errësirë. Por ja ku kishte ardhur ai çast aq i shumëpritur, që të dilte prej andej, sikur të mos kishte ndodhur asgjë. Nuk po i besohej se vërtet ishte jashtë mureve. Nirvana dhe të dy djemtë vrapuan menjëherë drejt tij, kush e kush ta përqafonte i pari. Platori ndenji disi më i ndrojtur nga i vëllai i tij më i madh dhe mbajti sytë përdhe.

"Përqafoje babin!" gati sa nuk i klithi Nirvana, por Platori u step disi, duke qëndruar dy hapa më larg, sikur të kishte frikë se mos babai nuk do ta njihte. Nirvana ngulmoi në të vetën dhe e tërhoqi prej dore gati me forcë. Platori çapiti me ndrojtje hapat në drejtim të tij dhe pa u menduar shumë ju hodh në qafë.

Isai gjer në atë çast kishte qëndruar i gërmuqur dhe i bërë sa një grusht, i zhytur thellë në mendime të zymta, por ai përqafim i beftë sikur e zgjoi nga ajo gjendje e mjerueshme. Sytë i qeshën nga një ngazëllim i brendshëm që sa vinte dhe rritej. I parruar prej kohësh dhe me flokët që sapo kishin filluar të thinjeshin, Isai nuk bënte ndonjë dallim të madh nga të sëmurët e tjerë. Të njëjtat pizhama të zbërdhylëta që të ngjallnin vetëm zymtësi dhe dhimbje. Platori mbylli sytë dhe ia mbështeti kokën në gjoks. Isai e përqafoi të birin, ndërsa trupi filloi t'i dridhej nga emocionet. Ishte gati të shpërthente në të qara, por e mbajti veten. Ç'ishte kjo mrekulli që po ndodhte? Si ishte e mundur që kishte dhe çaste kaq të mrekullueshme në jetë? Pas gjithë atyre katrahurave që kishin ndodhur, ai takim po i dukej si diçka jashtëtokësore, një ëndërr nga e cila nuk donte të zgjohej kurrë.

Nirvana kishte marrë me vete dy qeska plastmasi të mbushura plot: njërën të mbushur me ushqime dhe tjetrën me rroba të lara dhe të hekurosura.

"Isa! Të keqen motra! Tek kjo qese ke disa mathje dhe kanatiere të pastra. Tek kjo tjetra të kam fut nja dy bugaçe, pak byrek dhe nji komposto pjeshke. Ulu pak tek ky stoli ktu që të të laj kamët!"

Isai nuk bëri zë. Ishte përhumbur në mendime aq thellë, sikur Nirvana të mos i kishte folur kurrë. Mjaftoi që e motra ta tërhiqte paksa për krahu dhe Isai çapiti këmbët në drejtim të stolit më të afërt. Sapo u ul aty, Nirvana nxori nga qesja e ushqimeve një shishe plastike të mbushur me ujë dhe filloi t'i lajë këmbët. Thonjtë e zinj nga këllira të kallnin krupën, por Nirvana nuk jepej, duke ia fërkuar me shkumën e sapunit papushim. Fytyra iu skuq dhe balli iu mbulua nga bulëza të panumërta djerse, por dukej sikur zgjyra nuk donte të jepej. U kthye nga Çimi me një dritë shprese në fytyrë.

"Të keqen halla, shko tek ajo çezma atje dhe mushe kët shishen me uj!" Fryma po i merrej dhe dukej sikur një makth nuk po e linte të qetë. Çimi nuk e bëri fjalën dy, por ia dha vrapit me shishen në dorë. Atë copë rrugë të shkurtër gjer te çezma, e bëri edhe dy herë të tjera, gjersa më në fund këmbët e të atit shkëlqenin si bora.

"Tani haje këtë copën e byrekut. E kam ba me gjizë dhe me spinaq. Kushedi sesa kohë ke që je pa hangr." Nirvana ofshani dhe ia mbajti copën e byrekut para hundës, gjersa më në fund Isai e mori dhe filloi ta hante me një uri të atillë, sikur të kishte një javë pa ngrënë. E kullufiti në copa të mëdha aq shpejt sa njëra nga kafshatat i ngeci në fyt dhe iu morr fryma. Fytyra iu nxi e filloi të kollitej. Nirvana e goditi fort në kurriz dhe i afroi shishen e ujit në buzë. "Na, pije se përpak desh na u mbyte!"

Supa e pështirosur e spitalit e kishte bërë punën e vet. Isai gurgulliti shishen e ujit në gurmazin e tharë, fshiu buzët e plasaritura me kurrizin e dorës dhe pa me endje nga fëmijët.

"Ba, kur do dalësh nga spitali? Eja me ne sot!" pyeti Platori dhe, pa pritur përgjigjen e të atit, i ngjeshi turirin në prehër. Isai vazhdonte të rrinte i përhumbur në mendimet e veta pa ditur se çfarë përgjigje t'i jepte të birit. Ishte aq shumë i zhytur në botën e vet, sa kishte përshtypjen se brenda vetes i kishte ndodhur një dyzim shpirtëror. Ishte edhe nuk ishte aty.

"Babi do të dalë shumë shpejt që knej, por jo sot!" Zëri i hallë Nirvanës tingëlloi i pasigurt, i hollë, i dhimbshëm.

"Pse jo sot?" Çimi i qëndroi në krah të vëllait dhe e pa më mosbesim.

"Kështu tha njani nga mjekët. Ka nevojë edhe për ca ilaçe të tjera!" Nirvana psherëtiu lehtë. "Do të vijmë prapë, kur të bahet ma mirë." E përqafoi Isain fort dhe ktheu kokën mënjanë për të fshehur disi lotët që po i rridhnin.

Ato pak minuta në spital kishin kaluar aq shpejt, sikur të mos kishte ndodhur asgjë. Të dy djemtë e përqafuan fort babain dhe e ndoqën me sy, gjersa Isai kaloi portën e madhe të hyrjes.

XI.

Mea Culpa

Isai vuri bërrylat mbi parvazin e dritares dhe treti vështrimin jashtë. Një re e bardhë në formën e një barke të vogël sapo kishte nisur udhëtimin e saj që nga maja e Krastës. Në të djathtë, një shtëllungë gjigande pluhuri rrinte pezull mbi kombinatin metalurgjik "Çeliku i Partisë". Çfarë kishte shpërthyer këtë rradhë? Sa vetë ishin djegur për së gjalli nga llava e çelikut? Largoi menjëherë vështrimin prej andej, sikur të kishte frikë nga ato mendime rebeluese që i mbinë padashur. Dhoma në fund të korridorit në katin e tretë nuk dallonte shumë nga dhoma e mëparshme ku kishte kaluar pothuajse të gjithë vitin. Vetëm se kishte tre shtretër gjithsej. Ishte ora 9:00 e mëngjesit, por dy të sëmurët e tjerë ende po flinin. Si i kishte thënë doktori? "Edhe dy javë dhe do të dalësh nga spitali". Po kush priste edhe dy javë aty, mes atyre katër mureve të lagësht që të ngjallnin vetëm trishtim?! Megjithëse kishte qëndruar aty gjatë të gjithë kësaj kohe, ato dy javë më shumë në spital po i rëndonin sikur të ishin plot dy vite të tjera. Ndjeu trishtimin t'ia mbështillte zemrën si asnjëherë më parë. Nuk i rrihej brenda, megjithëse trupi ende i dhimbte nga goditjet që kishte marrë. Hapi derën dhe doli jashtë në korridor. Doktori Arbeni e kishte porositur që të bënte kujdes dhe të mos binte në sy të të sëmurëve të tjerë. Mbështeti ballin mbi xhamin e dritares për të parë më mirë poshtë, në oborrin e pasëm të spitalit. Rrezet e diellit dukej sikur jepnin pakëz shpresë për ata shpirtra të plagosur, që ashtu të mbledhur kutullaç, sikur i gëzoheshin qetësisht natyrës.

Ende nuk po arrinte të kuptonte sesi ishte e mundur që kishte ndodhur e gjithë ajo rrëmujë në spital. Përkundër të gjitha paralajmërimeve të doktorëve dhe infermierëve, përkundër gjithë frikës, ndrojtjes dhe panikut që e kishte kapluar gjatë të gjitha atyre ditëve, këmbët filluan të zbrisnin shkallët. Ngadalë! Pothuajse në mënyrë krejtësisht të pavetëdijshme, si një hije e tejdukshme, pa mish, lëkurë dhe kocka. Thellë në shpirt sikur e ndjente se ai shfrim energjish nga të sëmurët disa ditë më parë, nuk kishte të bënte pikërisht me vetë atë. Duhej të kishte qenë thjesht një rastësi që ishte gjendur në mes asaj rrëmuje. Por ndërsa përpiqej të qetësonte veten, aq më shumë ndjente nevojën për një arsyetim të shpejtë nga dikush, nëse me të vërtetë nuk kishte diçka nga Lart në këtë mes. Ndërsa hidhte hapat ngadalë, kishte ndjesinë se rrjedha e turbullt e lumit do ta merrte me vete përsëri dhe nuk do ta linte të kalonte në bregun tjetër. Pse gjithë ai shfrim energjish i kotë dhe a do të shmangej e gjitha kjo nëse nuk do të ishte përfshirë në atë histori idioteske me ...breshkën? Gjithçka që kishte ndodhur i kishte kaluar kufijtë e absurdit. Doktor Arbeni e kishte paralajmëruar që të shmangte sa më shumë kontaktet me të sëmurët e tjerë.

Zbriti shkallët dhe u drejtua për nga dera që të çonte në oborr. Papritur ndjeu dikë t'i vinte dorën në sup. Ndjeu të rrënqethura në trup dhe frikën ta kaplonte të gjithin. Ktheu kokën ngadalë. Ishte pikërisht ai të cilit i druhej, "Mësuesi". Për dallim nga hera e fundit, këtë herë "mësuesi" dukej krejtësisht i qetë. Në fytyrë i lexohej ndjesia e fajit.

"Mësuesi" ishte një burrë shtatlartë rreth të dyzetave. Ruante ende formën e mirë fizike, pavarësisht nga të qënit për një kohë të gjatë në spital. Fytyra i shkëlqente nga pastërtia. Dukej se sapo ishte rruar, pasi pikla të vogla gjaku i dalloheshin nën gushë dhe në mjekër nga prerjet e briskut. Vinte erë sapun dhe për mbi të gjitha, nuk e kishte më atë egërsi jashtënatyrore prej bishe, që vetëm para disa ditësh mund t'ia dalloje në bebet e syve. Të sëmurët mendorë bëheshin njerëz krej tjetër kur ktheheshin në gjendje normale. Megjithëkëtë Isai u bë gati të ikte. Më mirë t'i rrinte sa më larg sherrit, sesa të ndodhej përballë ndonjë situate tjetër, që mund të dilte sërisht jashtë kontrollit. I ktheu kurrizin, por këtë herë "Mësuesi" e kapi nga krahu, duke ia shtrënguar miqësisht.

"Isa, 'Mea Culpa'! M'fal për t'gjitha ato që nodhën."

"Çfarë ndodhi?" Mbajti këmbët, duke u kthyer plotësisht nga ai. Një i sëmurë mendor nuk ishte përgjegjës për veprimet që mund të bënte gjatë krizës mendore. Madje nuk duhej të mbante mend asgjë. Por dukej se rasti i "Mësuesit" bënte dallim nga të gjitha të tjerat. "A mund të më thuash saktësisht se çfarë ndodhi?"

"Ja, pra! Gjithë ajo rrëmujë për nji breshkë! Infermier Fatmiri e gjeti dhe e pruni prap te ne! Hajde ta shofësh." Tha me një ton urdhërues dhe bëri vetë i pari drejt daljes.

Në oborr të sëmurët po i gëzoheshin diellit, secili sipas qejfit të vet. Breshka kishte zënë vend poshtë një stoli, ku ishin ulur dy të sëmurë. "Mësuesi" e mori në duar dhe ia zgjati Isait miqësisht.

"Jo, të falemnderit!"

"Prekja kurrizin, se do të të sjellë fat!", këmbënguli "Mësuesi" në të vetën. Isai zgjati gjithë frikën gishtat që i dridheshin dhe ia preku guackën paksa, duke parë rrethepërqark. Të sëmurët e tjerë as që e kishin mendjen aty. Të zhytur në botët e tyre të mistershme, dukej se u ishin mbytur gjemitë dhe as që u bënte përshtypje së çfarë ndodhte përreth. "Fati dhe rastësia na ka mbledhur këtu. Ndjehem shumë keq dhe sinqerisht po të kërkoj edhe njëherë falje për të gjithë atë tmerr që pe me sy."

"Nuk ka pse të kërkosh falje. Ne jemi të sëmurë, ndaj nuk mund të gjykohemi për veprimet tona. Mund të flasim ndonjë ditë tjetër bashkë. Tani më duhet të iki lart! Të më falësh!"

I lehtësuar disi në shpirt, ende duke i bërë sytë katër, eci mbrapsht disa hapa, pastaj hyri me të shpejtë në ndërtesë. Ktheu kokën për t'u siguruar nëse po e ndiqte ndokush, por gjithçka dukej se i ishte kthyer normalitetit të përkohshëm. Do të duronte edhe ato pak ditë, ashtu me shpirt nëpër dhëmbë, gjersa të zhdukej nga ai vend i mallkuar.

XII.

E dashur!

Kishin kaluar gjashtë javë që nga dita kur mendohej se do të dilte nga spitali dhe ja ku gjendej përsëri në atë burg të bardhë. Trupi i ishte bërë i plogët dhe sytë i mbante gjithnjë të mbyllur. Fantazia e bënte më shpejt efektin e vet. I shikonte më mirë fytyrat e atyre njerëzve të dashur, që tashmë i ishin rrënjosur përjetësisht në kujtesë. Ja Svjetllana, teksa shëtiste nëpër Saint Petersburg, ndësa flokët bjond ia puthte era e lehtë, e brishtë dhe e butë si mëndafsh. Do të bënte mirë t'i shkruante Svjetllanës. Ndoshta ato letra mund të mos përfundonin kurrë në dorën e saj, por të paktën t'i shprehte. Nëse i mbante të burgosura në qenien e vet, do të ndihej më i rënduar shpirtërisht. Mori bllokun e shënimeve dhe hodhi fjalët e para. Sa kohë kishte pa shkruar?! I dukej sikur gishtat i ishin ngurosur dhe nuk i kontrollonte dot më. Mendimi i ishte ngurtësuar dhe fjalët i dilnin të thara e të shpifura. Nuk duhej t'i dorëzohej atmosferës mbytëse të spitalit. Duhej të përpiqej disa herë, pa pushim, gjersa të ishte në gjendje të formonte fjalitë e para. Të dorëzohej ishte më keq se vdekja. Do të ishte më lehtë po të kish humbur njërën këmbë apo dorë. Kur humbte frymëzimin, i dukej sikur kishte ardhur vërtet fundi. Pa krijimin do të kthehej përfundimisht në një objekt më shumë, në një kufomë të harruar në një qoshkëz të spitalit, i papërfillur nga askush. Të shkruante! Kjo ishte sfida: qoftë edhe pakëz fjalë të hedhura kuturu e krejtësisht pa kuptim.

LETRA I – JANAR, VITI Pa Emër.

E dashur Svjetllana,

Janari trokiti si një udhëtar i heshtur dhe i ndrojtur; pa borë në çatitë e qytetit, por me grimca akulli që depërtojnë thellë në shpirt. Hekurat e ftohtë të dritares nuk janë veçse degë të zhveshura të një trungu të vjetër — të tharë, të braktisur. Gjithçka përreth është bërë gur, gjithçka hesht. Edhe fryma ime është bërë e rëndë, si mjegulla që zvarritet mbi rrugët e zbrazëta. Rri i mbështjellë me batanijet e mykura të kohës, ku era e kujtimeve endet si një fantazmë e ngrohtë e harruar diku në fund të një dimri të largët. Dhe përpara syve të mbyllur më del buzëqeshja jote — e lehtë, e çiltër, si një rreze dielli që guxon të puthë tokën e ngrirë. Vetëm ajo më ngroh, vetëm ajo më jep jetë. Në çdo qelizë të qënies sime ndiej një zjarr të vogël që pulson, që nuk shuhet — dhe ai zjarr je ti. Akrepat e orës janë ndalur në ajër, si zogj të ngrirë në fluturim, si fjalë të pathëna që varen pezull në buzë të natës. Koha s'ka më kuptim për mua. Gjithçka ka ngecur në atë çast kur më preke zemrën për herë të fundit me një përqafim të butë, që tani është bërë kujtim i përjetshëm.

Në këtë shkretëtirë të harrimit, ku gjithçka duket e zbehur, ti je ai zjarr i vogël, një dritë që më mban gjallë, një premtim që nuk shuhet kurrë. Zjarri yt më fton të jetoj, edhe kur gjithçka tjetër më fton të harroj.

Letra II – Shkurt, Viti nuk ka rëndësi

Princesha ime e largët,

Shkurti hyri në dhomë pa zhurmë, si një fllad i ftohtë dhe i athët, por nuk më çliroi dot nga kujtimet. Ndjej muret që më aviten çdo ditë më shumë. Sikur janë qenie të gjalla, sikur duan të më gëlltisin. Muret nuk kanë sy, por më shikojnë. Nuk kanë zë, por më flasin me heshtjen e tyre. Dhe në atë çast, kur gjithçka më ngjan si një akullnajë që më përpin ngadalë, ti vjen. Ti, një zog i bardhë, që fluturon mbi çatinë e spitalit si një vegim i dritës, si një ëndërr që s'mund të preket, por që më prek mua. Zëri yt, që e dëgjoj në shpirt, më thërret:

"Mos u dorëzo!"

Dhe unë nuk dorëzohem. Sepse ti je arsyeja ime. Çdo fjalë që ta shkruaj është si një flakadan shprese në errësirë. Ti je muza ime e padukshme. Je shpresa që ngjitet ngadalë si dielli në mëngjesin e një dite që nuk do të jetë më gri. Në çdo germë që të shkruaj, fsheh një pjesë të zemrës time — të paprekshme, por të gjallë. Dhe kështu mbijetoj. Me buzët që pëshpëritin emrin tënd, me sytë që të kërkojnë edhe kur janë mbyllur, me shpirtin që nuk pranon të zhytet në harresë.

Sepse ti më kujton se edhe këtu, në këtë spital të ftohtë dhe të vrazhdë, dashuria gjen mënyra për të jetuar.

LETRA III – MARS, VITI XXX

E dashura ime, Svjetllana,

Marsin këtë vit e njoh vetëm nga kalendari mbi mur. Brenda nuk ka asnjë lule, asnjë gjurmë gjelbërimi, asnjë premtim pranvere. Vetëm një ngjyrë gri më rrethon, si një mjegull e trashë që varet mbi mua, duke më fshehur dritën, duke më ndarë nga gjithçka që më mbante gjallë.

Por ti...

Ti je ajo lule që çel sa herë që buzëqesh. Je ajo pranverë që nuk pyet për stinët, je blerimi që lind nga brenda meje. Ti je pranvera ime, Svjetllana.

E vetmja që më mbin në shpirt kur gjithçka tjetër është zbehur. Si është Shën Petersburgu në mars, vallë? A ka ende akull mbi Neva? A fryn ende ajo erë që mbështjell rrugicat me kujtime?

A të kujtohet kur shkonim në atë kafene të vogël, "Moroshka për Pushkinin"? Aty ku muret ruanin zërin tonë, e gotat qeshjen tënde të kristaltë.

Të kujtohet, ë? Si fshiheshe pas librave dhe më shikoje si pa dashur... dhe unë bëhesha poet pa shkak.

Po gjenerali? Babai yt, Ivan — si është?

Mos vallë ende i rreptë, por me sytë që zbuten kur të sheh ty? E kujtoj fytyrën e tij kur më pa për herë të parë — si një kështjellë që s'do të lejonte askënd brenda, por që më vonë ma hapi një portë të fshehtë, vetëm pse ti ia çele zemrën më parë. Kur mbyll sytë tani, nuk shoh më katër muret që më mbajnë këtu. Ndiej aromën e fushave me bar të njomë, si atë ditë që ecnim të dy mes shiut të lehtë.

Çdo pikë shiu binte si një notë e pastër mbi pentagramin e botës sonë. Ne ishim melodia — një simfoni e heshtur që vetëm ne e dëgjonim.

Por këtu, Svjetllana, nuk bie shi.

Këtu bien vetëm pika loti. Dhe çdo pikë është mallkim.

E megjithatë, unë i mbledh, i lidh njëra pas tjetrës dhe i kthej në këngë. Sepse vetëm në muzikë, vetëm në fjalë të shkruara me shpirt të kam pranë.

Kështu mbijetoj, duke risjellë kujtimet, duke shpresuar kthimin tënd, duke pritur ditën kur aroma e pranverës nuk do jetë thjesht një iluzion, por vetë ti — në prag të derës sime, sërish.

Me një dashuri që nuk zbehet,

I yti,

Isai

DITË TË TJERA I SHFAQEJ ajo vajza 16-vjeçare që u martua me të me mblesëri. Vëllezërit e Manushaqes ishin burra zakoni që mendonin se motra e re nuk duhej mbajtur në asnjë mënyrë në shtëpi. Duhej hequr qafe sa më parë që të ishte e mundur dhe mundësisht të degdisej sa më larg. Burrin ta kishte sa më të madh në moshë dhe të paktën të mos e kishte njohur kurrë më parë. Madje të kishte edhe ndonjë të metë fizike, që t'i bëhej shërbëtore e devotshme gjatë të gjithë jetës së vet. Për të gjitha këto Isai ndjehej me faj. Ishte ai burri i keq, shembulli që nuk duhej marrë dhe për këtë arsye ndihej fajtor gjer në dhimbje, e cila përpak sa nuk ishte kthyer në dashuri.

Letra e parë – Kujtimi

Manushaqe,

Sa herë ngjitem shkallëve të pallatit tim, sytë më mbyllen vetvetiu dhe shoh vegimin tënd. E ndjej çastin kur do të shfaqesh ti, me flokët si nata dhe fytyrën të bardhë si bora. Por ky vegim shuhet sapo ndizet drita e ditës. Mbeten vetëm muret e vranëta, të heshtura, që më shikojnë pa më thënë gjë.

Ah, sa e rëndë është kjo heshtje pa ty... Kur do të mund të takohemi përsëri? Nganjëherë të shoh nga ana tjetër e rrugës dhe kam guximin të të përshëndes. Por tashmë je martuar me dikë tjetër, fëmijët e mi kanë tjetër rrugë, tjetër jetë. Si mund ta duroj këtë, nuk e di.

Letra e dytë – Malli

E dashura ime e dikurshme,

Erdha sërish në dhomë dhe ndjeva mungesën tënde si një thikë që më shpon shpirtin tejpërtej. Nuk më mungon vetëm prania jote, por çdo gjest i vogël që më bënte të ndjehesha gjallë: si hidhje flokët pas shpine, si qeshje pa arsye që ndriçonte gjithçka, mënyra si më shikoje sikur unë të isha gjithë bota jote.

Pa ty, jeta është një udhë pa fund, bosh dhe e ngrirë. Zërat tanë tingëllojnë gjysmë të shurdhët, ajri është gjysmë frymë, dhe çdo rreze drite është disi e zbehtë. E mban mend kur kërcenim bashkë dhe unë të rrotulloja nëpër dhomë? Të mbaja fort në krahë dhe të puthja deri kur dielli i agimit nxirrte vetullën e artë në dritare.

Çdo moment pa ty është një kujtim i zbehtë, çdo hap pa ty më degdis larg. Dhe megjithatë, në heshtjen e dhomës, ndjej ende shpirtrat tanë të bashkuar në një zjarr që kurrë nuk shuhet.

Letra e tretë – Braktisja

Manushaqe,

Ti zgjodhe një rrugë tjetër, dhe unë nuk kam të drejtë të të gjykoj; ndoshta as nuk do të kisha mundur ta mbaja krahun tënd kur errësira të vinte. Por unë, shpirti im, mbeta këtu, i mbyllur në qeli të kujtimeve që s'kanë fund. Çdo natë e ndiej mungesën tënde si një plagë që nuk shërohet; pyes veten: a ndjen edhe ti mungesën time, apo unë jam vetëm një emër që koha e fshiu nga mendja jote? Megjithatë, pavarësisht largësisë, pavarësisht rrugëve të ndara, unë jam babai i fëmijëve të tu. Dhe kjo e vërtetë nuk mund të shuhet, as të harrohet.

Letra e katërt – Vetmia

Manushaqe,

Muret flasin për mua në heshtje, dhe dritaret më shikojnë me sy të ftohtë si akulli. Nuk ka më duar që të më prekin, as buzë që të thonë "mirëmëngjes." Vetmia më rrethon si një varr i gjallë, dhe unë dridhem nën peshën e saj. Por emri yt digjet në gjoksin tim si flakë e ngrohtë, dhe kujtimi yt më mban gjallë, si ajri që nuk mund ta ndalësh. As makina e elektroshokut, as mjekët dhe infermierët, nuk mund të shuajnë imazhin tënd. Ti je këtu, duke marrë frymë në çdo pore të lëkurës sime, duke më mbajtur gjallë edhe kur gjithçka duket e vdekur.

Letra e pestë – Falja

Ndoshta nuk ka faj askush. Ndoshta ishte fati që na ndau, jo dobësia ime, as zgjedhja jote. Të fal për çdo lot që më ke dhënë, ashtu siç shpresoj që edhe ti të më falësh për çdo hidhërim që ndoshta të kam shkaktuar.

Çdo dashuri e madhe lë gjurmë, edhe kur shndërrohet në hi. Ti je plagë dhe dritë njëkohësisht, një kujtim që djeg dhe ngroh në të njëjtën kohë.

Nuk mund të të fajesoj për vendimin tënd për t'u larguar. Ndoshta ishe e frikësuar nga sëmundja ime mendore, ndoshta shqetësoheshe për sigurinë e fëmijëve. Ndoshta, po të isha i sëmurë, nuk do të ishim këtu ku jemi. Por edhe në këtë largësi, të mbaj mend me dashuri, me hidhërim dhe me mirënjohje. Sepse çdo çast me ty ishte një dhuratë që nuk do ta harroj kurrë.

Letra e gjashtë – Përjetësia

Edhe kur trupi im të plaket dhe flokët të më zbardhen krejt, ti do të mbetesh në zemrën time si vajza gjashtëmbëdhjetëvjeçare me fytyrë prej dëbore. Dashuria që të dhashë nuk ka ndryshuar kurrë; ajo mbeti e njëjtë si në fillim, e pastër dhe e pafajshme. Si këngët që nuk humbasin asnjëherë freskinë e tyre, edhe ndjenja ime për ty do të qëndrojë gjithmonë e gjallë, si vetë përjetësia.

XIII.

Alketa

Manushaqja gati sa nuk po jepte shpirt në krevat. Dhimbjet e lindjes i ishin shtuar aq shumë, sa i ishin errur sytë dhe klithte gjer në kupë të qiellit. Në martenitet nuk lejohej askush përveç mamijeve dhe sanitareve dhe në atë gjendje aq të vështirë kishte aq shumë nevojë për një fjalëz të ngrohtë dhe për sytë e ëmbël të të dy fëmijëve të tjerë. Përkundër rregullave të forta në maternitet, mamiet i kishin premtuar se, sapo të lindte, e gjithë familja e saj do t'i gjendej pranë. Ato dhimbje therëse që i errësonin pamjen ishin edhe më të mëdha se dhimbjet që ndjente sa herë që kthehej nga puna e lodhshme në fermë. Mbi tetë orë punë me lopatë dhe kazmë të pestë ditët e javës ishin asgjë krahasuar me atë stërmundim dhe stres që po ndjente, ndërsa po sillte fëmijën e tretë në jetë. Që ditën e parë kur ishin martuar, Hamdiu ia kishte bërë të qartë se donte të kishte një djalë të vetin, pavarësisht se ajo kishte trashëguar dy djem nga martesa e parë. Dhe ja tani kishte ardhur ai çast i shumëpritur që Çimi dhe Platori të bëheshin me vëlla apo motër, siç ta kishte shkruar zoti. Por kishte aq shumë therje në bark, saqë nuk po duronte dot më. Kafshoi batanijen e pambuktë, nguli gishtat mbi dyshek, si një shqiponjë e plagosur, por ajo torturë që po ndjente vetëm sa i shtohej gjithnjë e më tepër.

"Jepi fort! Ma fort! Merr frymë thellë ne shtyj!" Mamia, një grua rreth të dyzetave, e mbajti fort nga këmbët, ndërsa njëra nga sanitaret, një vajzë e re rreth të njëzetave, i vuri një shami të njomë në ballin e mbuluar nga bulëzat e djersës.

Fundi i botës, mbase do të ishte më i parashikueshëm se ai çast. Momenti i sjelljes në jetë të një qenieje të re njerëzore duhej të ishte i ngjashëm me shpërthimet e vullkaneve. Mbylli sytë dhe u mundua të sillte në mendje ato ditë të bukura nga jeta e fëmijërisë në fshatin Remanicë të Beratit, ku kishte lindur dhe kishte ikur prej andej në moshën 16 vjeçare, për t'u martuar me mblesëri me Isain. Ishte vetëm shtatëmbëdhjetë vjeçe, kur kishte lindur Çimin. Tre vjet më pas kishte sjellë në jetë djalin tjetër Platorin. Kishte kaluar kaq shumë kohë të vështira me dy fëmijë të vegjël dhe bashkëshortin e sëmurë, por ruante edhe kujtime të bukura. Kur dilte në rrugë me të djemtë, njerëzit e shikonin me habi, pasi nuk e besonin që të dy djemtë ishin fëmijët e saj. Tashmë, vetëm 27 vjeçare, po sillte në jetë fëmijën e tretë.

Gjysmë në delir, e ndodhur kurrkund dhe askund, iu shfaq vetvetja, një vajzë rreth 10-vjeçare, e hipur në një tavolinë, ndërsa recitonte një poezi që sapo kishte mësuar në shkollën e fshatit. Ja tre vëllezërit, Muharremi, Engjëlli dhe Tomorri, si dhe tri motrat, Gela, Fatimeja dhe Fajreja, duke ndjekur çdo lëvizje të motrës, ndërsa ajo recitonte me shpirt dhe emocion poemën e Naim Frashërit "O Malet e Shqipërisë". Baba Rrapoja, i vjetër dhe i rrudhur si një rrap, fërkonte mustaqet, duke hedhur sytë herë pas here nga e shoqja Tagjibeja, që ashtu e mbledhur sa një grusht, dridhej nga frika se mos ndoshta kishte bërë gabim të rëndë që e kishte lënë vajzën e vogël të kërcente mbi tavolinë dhe të aktronte për të gjithë fshatin.

"Ne içik, ne içik!"

Sytë iu errën edhe më dhe gati sa nuk i ra tavani në kokë. Fytyrat e vëllezërve iu zhdukën si me magji nga kujtesa. U dëgjuan të qarat e para të fëmijës së porsalindur dhe një çlirim i përgjithshëm trupor pas gjithë atij stërmundimi të tmerrshëm.

"Asht gocë! T'ju rrojë!" tha mamia dhe sakaq ia la vogëlushen mbi prehër, të mbështjellë më çarçafë.

Manushaqja nuk i mbajti dot më lotët. Ia preku disin ballin e vockël me buzët e zhuritura dhe mbylli sytë instiktivisht. E këputur plotësisht nga lodhja dhe e mbuluar nga djersët, atë moment kishte dëshirë vetëm të flinte, por zërat e gëzuar të Çimit dhe Platorit, sikur e sollën disi në vete. Hamdiu pas tyre, dukej krejtësisht i përhumbur. Megjithëse nga natyra e mbante veten për burrë me zemër të fortë dhe hije të rëndë, në sy i dalloheshin dy pika loti.

"Asht gocë", përsëriti mamia, këtë herë me zë akoma më të lartë.

"Oh, u bamë me motër! Do t'ia vem emnin "Amla"! Si thu, ma?"

Çimin nuk po e mbante vendi dhe me padurim po priste vendimin e të ëmës.

"Po pse 'Amla'?", pyeti me qesëndi Hamdiu.

Manushaqja qeshi lehtë dhe me sytë ende të perëndueshëm pëshpëriti nja dy fjalë nëpër dhëmbë, sikur por jepte shpirt.

"Amla quajnë komandanten e klasës. Goca më e bukur e shkollës."

"Aha! Hë çapajev që je ti!" u ngërdhesh Hamdiu dhe u kthye nga e shoqja. "Sikur tingëllon paksa e çuditshme! Ma mirë t'ia vem emrin "Alketa", si thu ti?"

"Më mirë të mos flas. Nuk po mbaj anën e askujt!" tha Manushaqja. Çimi, duke parë që e ëma nuk po e ndihmonte, u tërhoq më në fund.

"Po mirë! Edhe 'Alketa' emër i bukur asht," pranoi me gjysëm zëri.

"Me vërte?" shpotiti Hamdiu.

"Me vërte!" përsëriti Çimi me ton mosbesues.

Hamdiu fërkoi mjekrën e parruar me gishtat gungacë. "Asht emën i bukur! Nuk kam se çfarë të them! Ta gzojë!" Ngulmoi Hamdiu.

"Alketa! Alketa! Alketa!" klithi Platori gjithë gëzim e iu turr Hamdiut. "Ma len ta maj edhe unë pak!"

"Vetëm pak, se do të ikim ime! Mami ka nevoj për pushim," tha Hamdiu dhe ia afroi beben e porsalindur me kujdes, por pa ia lëshuar plotësisht.

Manushaqja u përpoq të kuptonte se cilat ishin ndjenjat e vërteta të të shoqit pas lindjes së vajzës...Ndjehej që në ajër, se Hamdiu nuk ishte fort në qejf. Nëse fëmija i tij i parë do të ishte djalë, nuk do të kishte gëzim më të madh në jetën e vet. Në fshatin e tij, në Polis Gurëshpatë të Librazhdit, por edhe në shumë zona të Shqipërisë, lindja e një djali në shtëpi përshëndetej me batare pushkësh. Shpesh herë si me shaka, në orët e vona të natës, Hamdiu ia kishte bërë të qartë se nuk do të hiqte dorë së provuari, gjersa të vinte në jetë biri i tij prej gjaku dhe mishi. Nëse fëmija i parë do të ishte vajzë dhe fëmija i dytë vajzë dhe e treta vajzë, dhe e katërta vajzë, përsëri Hamdiu nuk do të hiqte dorë, gjersa të vinte në jetë djali aq shumë i dëshiruar. "Oh, zot! Herë tjetër më jep një djalë," u lut me gjithë shpirt Manushaqja, ndërsa në mendjen e turbulluar i lindnin aq shumë pyetje dyshuese, se përse vërtet Hamdiu e donte trashëgimtarin një djalë të tijin, kur në fakt pretendonte se fëmijët do t'i kishte të gjithë njëlloj. Nëse vërtet fëmijët do të ishin të gjithë njëlloj, atëherë nuk ishte nevoja për një djalë "të tijin", pasi i kishte dy djem që i kishte sjellë gruaja!! Shtrëngoi kapakët e syve fort, duke u munduar të shkundej disi nga ato hije dyshimi.

"Ma në fund u bana me motër!" Zëri i Çimit, ai zë aq i ëmbël dhe fëminor, sikur ia solli përsëri atë ndjesi të ëmbël në shpirt. Një gjë ishte e sigurt: fëmijët nuk do të bënin dallim në mes tyre. Ia nguli sytë gjithë çudi asaj krijese që sapo kishte mbërritur në këtë botë, ende pa e kuptuar se ishte vërtetë në realitet apo po shihte një tjetër ëndërr të bukur.

XIV.

Kalendari

Shëmbëlltyra e Svjetllanës arratisej për në skajin më të largët të fantazisë dhe mendjes dhe vendin e saj e zinte një qenie tjetër po aq e dashur, por e ndryshme në llojin e vet. Duhej të shkruante disa këshilla për djalin e madh Çimin. T'i skiconte që tani për secilin muaj. Dymbëdhjetë muaj –dymbëdhjetë letra, një kalendar letrash në vend të fotografive. Viti nuk kishte rëndësi, pasi muajt dhe stinët ishin po ata. Do të ishte sikur i shkruante edhe përtej Vdekjes. Prej Andej në Botën e Këtejme. T'i shkruante paraprakisht, të gjitha me një frymë. Nuk po linte dot pasuri, por të paktën t'i linte djalit një pasuri ndryshe, që as nuk shitej dhe as nuk blihej. Që kishte vlerë më shumë se të gjitha thesaret e botës të marra së bashku. T'i hidhte si skica e t'i zhvillonte më pas. Ndoshta do të ishte në gjendje t'i zgjeronte më shumë, atëherë kur fantazia t'i kishte shëruar krahët e saj të plagosur.

Letra I – Urtësia (Janar)

I dashur biri im, Çimi,

Po të shkruaj me mall e dashuri, me fjalë që dua t'i mbash afër zemrës, si qirinj që ndriçojnë edhe në errësirën më të thellë.

Këto nuk janë vetëm këshilla, por grimca të vogla dashurie, që dua të t'i lë trashëgim për çdo hap të jetës tënde.

Mos harro të jesh gjithnjë i urtë, biri im.

Mos u bëj si rrufeja që shkrep e shkon, duke djegur ç'të gjejë përpara. Drita që ndriçon më gjatë nuk është ajo që verbon, por ajo që ngroh ngadalë.

Kot nuk kanë thënë të vjetrit tanë: "Uthulla e fortë prish enën e vet." Mos lejo që nxehtësia e momentit të të prishë shpirtin e bukur që ke. Ruaje qetësinë si një pasuri të rrallë.

Urtësia, biri im, është si një lis i gjatë, me rrënjë të shpërndara thellë në tokë, që nuk dridhet nga erërat, as nuk thyhet nga stuhitë. Ai rri i palëkundur, dhe të gjithë gjejnë strehë nën hijen e tij. Edhe ti, bëhu ashtu — një njeri që njerëzit ndihen mirë pranë tij, sepse është i qetë, i drejtë, i fortë në shpirt.

Nëse njerëzit të flasin fjalë të hidhura — dhe jeta, herët a vonë, do të të përballë me to — mos ua kthe me të njëjtën monedhë.

Përgjigju me heshtje, ose me një buzëqeshje të lehtë, që flet më shumë se njëqind fjalë.

Fjalët e liga shuhen nga mendja e urtë si gurët që bien në një ujë të thellë dhe zhduken pa gjurmë.

Njeriu i urtë fiton edhe mbi armiqtë, sepse ai nuk lufton me urrejtje, por me mençuri.

Thonë që një qingj i urtë ka dy nëna, por unë besoj se ai ka edhe tri, ndoshta edhe më shumë. Sepse njerëzit e mirë, të butë e të dashur, prekin zemrat e të gjithëve dhe të gjithë duan t'i kenë afër, t'i mbrojnë, t'i duan, t'i ushqejnë me mirësi.

Ti, biri im, je pikërisht një i tillë.

Prandaj të dua shumë dhe dua që të ecësh në jetë me kokën lart, por me zemrën pranë tokës, pranë njerëzve, pranë dashurisë.

Mbaje fjalën time në mendje, por mbi të gjitha, mbaje zemrën tënde të pastër, sepse ajo do të të udhëheqë kur rrugët bëhen të mjegullta.

Me përqafimin më të ngrohtë që një baba mund të japë,

Isai

Letra II – Mësimi (Shkurt)

Biri im i dashur, Çimi,

Sot dua të të flas për mësimin — jo si një detyrim që ta vë mbi supe, por si një dritë që dua ta ndez brenda teje.

Mëso shumë, biri im! Mëso pa pushim, mëso siç thith frymë qenia jote.

Jo për të mbushur kokën me fjalë të zbrazëta, por për të ndriçuar zemrën.

Mos e lër librin të pluhuroset në ndonjë qoshe harrese. Mos e lër të mbyllet si një dritare që nuk hapet kurrë. Libri është një mik që nuk lodhet së foluri, një shok që nuk të zhgënjen, një udhërrëfyes që të çon në vende ku këmbët nuk të mbërrijnë dot, një dritë që ndriçon edhe netët më të errëta.

Ai nuk të tradhton kurrë.

Kur gjithçka tjetër në jetë mund të lëkundet — njerëzit, ndjenjat, rrethanat — libri mbetet aty, i heshtur por i gjallë, i gatshëm të flasë sapo ta prekësh.

Mëso, biri im, sepse sa më shumë të lexosh, aq më shumë do ta kuptosh botën rreth teje — me gjithë bukuritë dhe padrejtësitë e saj — por më e rëndësishmja, do të fillosh të kuptosh vetveten.

Pa mësim, njeriu mbetet si një pemë pa rrënjë — mund të rritet pak mbi sipërfaqe, por bie në stuhinë e parë.

Dija të jep rrënjë. Të jep forcë. Të jep dinjitet.

Ajo është e vetmja pasuri që nuk të vidhet, që nuk digjet, që nuk ndryshket.

Ajo është busulla jote kur humbet rrugën, mburoja jote kur bota bëhet e padrejtë.

Mos e shih librin vetëm si fletë të shkruara. Brenda tij jetojnë njerëz, histori, mendime, pyetje dhe përgjigje që s'kanë nevojë për pasaportë.

Kur lexon, ti takon njerëz që kanë vdekur shekuj më parë, por që flasin me ty si të ishin ulur përballë në një kafe të heshtur.

Kur lexon, ti sheh përtej asaj që sytë shohin. Sheh atë që është thellë – nën sipërfaqe – dhe kjo është ajo që të bën të urtë.

Mos harro, biri im:

Në një botë që shpesh të ngatërron drejtësinë me forcën,

Në një botë që mund të të gjykojë për atë që dukesh,

Dija do të të gjykojë për atë që je.

Dhe ajo gjykon drejt.

Shumë do të thonë se për të fituar në jetë, duhet të jesh i fortë.

Por unë të them:

Libri është arma më e fortë.

Armë pa gjak, pa dhimbje, por me forcë që shemb muret e paditurisë dhe ndan dritën nga errësira.

Është e vetmja armë legale, që nuk të bën armiq, por të afron me njerëzit.

Mëso, biri im. Mëso çdo ditë; e kam si një lutje të brendshme.

Jo për të marrë nota të mira, por për të ndërtuar një Njeri të Ri.

Sepse dijetari i vërtetë nuk është ai që mburret me sa di, por ai që e përdor diturinë për të qenë njeri.

Dhe kur të rritesh, kur të ecësh më tej në jetë, kur të jesh vetë në udhëkryq,

kujto këtë letër, dhe kujto që një libër, një fjali, një ide – mund të jetë harta jote për të dalë nga errësira.

Me dashurinë më të madhe që një prind mund të ketë,

nga kjo anë e jetës ose nga përtej saj,

Isai.

Letra III – Ndershmëria (Mars)

Çimi,

Në jetë do të përballesh me shumë zgjedhje e do të të tundohet shpirti nga gjëra që duken të vogla por që peshojnë shumë. E prandaj po të shkruaj këtë letër – që ta mbash si një gur të çmuar në gji, një kujtim dhe një udhërrëfyes që të ndihmon të zgjedhësh rrugën e drejtë, edhe kur ajo duket më e gjatë. Nuk ka pasuri më të madhe në këtë botë se një zemër e ndershme. Mund të kesh xhepat bosh, por nëse ke ndërgjegjen e pastër, do të flesh qetë si një mbret. Ndërsa pasuria që vjen përmes rrugëve të shtrembra, e ngre si shtëpi rëre — të shembet me erën e parë, dhe ta ndot shpirtin më shumë se çdo baltë.

Ndershmëria ta bën jetën të lehtë — si të ecësh zbathur mbi bar të butë, në një mëngjes pranvere. Nuk të gërvisht shpirti, nuk të kafshon ndërgjegjja. Pa të, çdo hap është i vështirë, si të ecësh mbi gjemba të mprehtë. E çdo gjemb është një gënjeshtër, një fshehje, një zhgënjim që lë plagë.

E mban mend atë ditë, kur ishe i vogël?

Kur more një 250 lekësh të vjetër nga xhaketa ime, në heshtje, dhe u arratise si një njeri i vogël me një mision të ëmbël — për të blerë një tortë që e doje shumë. E bërë me gjithë zemër, por pa leje.

Një gjest i pahijshëm, por njerëzor. E unë, kur e kuptova, nuk u mërzita se more paratë, por nga hija që ai veprim hodhi mbi sytë e tu të sinqertë.

Ajo shpullë që të dhashë me dashuri, jo për të të lënduar, por për të të zgjuar,

— dua të mos e harrosh kurrë.

Jo si dhimbje, por si kufirin ku për herë të parë ndjeve dallimin mes të drejtës dhe të gabuarës.

Ishte një shpullë që nuk la shenjë në faqe, por dua të ketë lënë një kujtim të qartë në zemër. Që atë ditë, e pashë tek ti një ndryshim. Një ndriçim të ri në sy. Një vetëdije të vogël që nisi të rritej me ty.

Dhe tani, kur më sheh në sy dhe më flet me ndershmëri, ndiej se ajo shpullë s'ishte dënim, por një mbrojtje – një përqafim në formë tjetër.

Në jetë do të joshesh shumë herë të marrësh nga të tjerët pa leje, të thuash një të pavërtetë për të shpëtuar veten, të shmangësh përgjegjësinë. Por çdo herë që ndodh kjo, kujto se e vërteta që përballon sot është më e lehtë sesa gënjeshtra që do të të rëndojë nesër.

Mos harro kurrë, biri im:
Është më mirë të jetosh një jetë të thjeshtë dhe të drejtë,
sesa të jetosh në luks me një ndërgjegje që të kafshon çdo natë.

Boll të jesh i ndershëm — e të jesh vetvetja — dhe do ta shohësh se edhe bota të kthen të njëjtën ndershmëri në forma që as nuk i pret.

Me gjithë dashurinë që mund të bartë kjo zemër e lodhur,
dhe me gjithë shpresën që ke për të qenë një burrë i drejtë,
I yti, gjithmonë..

Letra IV – Për Nënën (Prill)

Biri im,

Respektoje gjithnjë nënën tënde. Nëna është si dielli: edhe kur fshihet pas reve, përsëri ngroh tokën. Mos e urre kurrë. Kujdesu për të, sepse një ditë do ta kuptosh se zemra e saj është gjithmonë e lidhur me ty.

Nëntë muaj në barkun e saj janë kohë mëse e mjaftueshme për t'i dhënë të drejtën legjitime e të qenit Krijuese e Botës. Babai ka vendin e vet, por jo aq sa nëna.

Manushaqja vërtet u nda nga unë, por mos e bëj me faj. Ishte vetëm gjashtëmbëdhjetë vjeçe kur u martua me mua, dhe atëherë martesat bëheshin me mblesëri. Por edhe vendimet e gabuara kanë anët e tyre të mira. Fryt i asaj martese je ti, bashkë me Platorin. Dy djem si dy pëllumba, si dy rreze drite të zemrës sime.

Letra V – Për Vëllain (Maj)

Çimi,

Platori është gjaku yt, gjysma e shpirtit tënd. Ji dritë për të, që edhe ai të bëhet dritë pas teje. Nëse ti ecën me urtësi, me dituri e me nder, ai do të ndjekë hapat e tu si hija që ndjek trupin në mesditë.

Mos e lër vetëm, mos e lëndo kurrë. Vëllai është krah i djathtë, është mburoja jote dhe nënkrejsa ku do të mbështetesh në ditë të vështira. Ai është tre vjet më i vogël se ti, por në zemrën e tij ti je mali ku ai kërkon mbështetje.

Kujtoje gjithnjë: siç do të jesh ti, ashtu do të bëhet edhe ai. Bëhu shembull që ai të ndjekë, udhërrëfyes që ai të mos humbasë kurrë në jetë.

Letra VI – Shpresa (Qershor)

Biri im,

Shpresa është si pranvera: vjen edhe pas dimrit më të gjatë. Edhe kur jeta të duket e padrejtë, mos e humb kurrë shpresën. Mbaje gjithmonë një dritë të vogël brenda vetes, sepse edhe një qiri i vetëm mund të ndriçojë një shtëpi të tërë të errët.

Ti linde në muajin qershor, muaj i veçantë, që mban shenjën e gaforres. Kjo shenjë është ujore dhe udhëhiqet nga Hëna. Motoja e saj është: Unë ndjej. Dhe ti je vërtet i tillë: me zemër të butë, i përkushtuar ndaj shtëpisë e familjes, i ndjeshëm deri në thellësi, me një imagjinatë të bujshme që shpesh mund të të bëjë të dukesh i mbyllur në botën tënde.

Mos harro se pikat e tua të forta janë qëndrueshmëria, besnikëria dhe dashuria pa kushte që di të japësh. Po, do të kesh edhe dobësitë e tua – humor të ndryshueshëm, ndonjëherë pasiguri, herë pesimizëm. Por dije se këto nuk janë mallkim, janë thjesht prova që të mësojnë të bëhesh më i fortë. Ngjyra jote është vjollca, ngjyra e shpirtit të thellë. Lulet e tua janë orkideja dhe trëndafilat e bardhë, si shenja e pastërtisë dhe e bukurisë së fshehtë. Ditët me fat janë e hëna dhe e enjtja, ndërsa numrat e tu fatlumë janë 2, 3, 15 dhe 20. Përdori këto dhurata si kujtesë: ti je i lindur për të ndjerë, për të dashur, për të krijuar, për të mbrojtur. Shkëlqe në profesionin që të do zemra, qoftë art, shkrim, mësim, apo çdo udhë që ta ndriçon Hëna. Mos harro: shpresa dhe ndjenja janë busulla jote. Nëse i ndjek me zemër të pastër, nuk do të humbasësh kurrë rrugën.

Letra VII – Jeta (Korrik)

Çimi,

Jeta është si lumi: rrjedh pa pushim, herë me dallgë të ashpra, herë me qetësi. Nganjëherë do të të përplasë në shkëmbinj, nganjëherë do të të mbajë butë mbi valë. Mos ki frikë prej saj. Mëso të notosh në çdo lumë, pa pritur që rrjedha të jetë gjithmonë e lehtë. Jeta ka kuptim, kur nuk të mungon guximi për të ecur përpara edhe kur lumi të tërheq poshtë.

Në muajin korrik ka lindur Platori. Ai është si vetë zjarri i verës: dëshiron të jetë në qendër të vëmendjes, në krye të aksionit. E do jetën, fëmijët, pushtetin. Është autoritar, por edhe shpirtgjerë e elegant. Pëlqen të admirohet, bie lehtë në komplimente, e ndonjëherë di të jetë kokëfortë e krenar. Me kalimin e viteve, zjarri i tij shuhet pak e nga pak, por brenda tij gjithmonë rri ndezur një shkëndijë.

Shenja e tij është Luani, i udhëhequr nga Dielli. Motoja e tij është: Unë dua. Dhe vërtet, dëshira është forca që e shtyn përpara.

Ngjyra e tij është ari, lulja e diellit, perla Carneliane-simbol i vitalitetit dhe kurajos. Dita e tij është e diela, dita e dritës. Numrat e fatit: 1, 3, 10, 19. Pikat e forta: krijues, i pasionuar, bujar, me zemër të ngrohtë. Dobësitë: arroganca, kokëfortësia, egoja që ndonjëherë e bën të verbër. Platorit i pëlqen teatri, pushimet, gjërat e bukura, argëtimi me miqtë. Nuk e duron të injorohet, as të mos trajtohet si mbret në oborrin e vet.

Mbaje afër, biri im. Ashtu si lumi ka nevojë për brigje që ta drejtojnë, edhe Platori ka nevojë për dashurinë e vëllait që t'ia zbusë zjarrin. Ti je lumi, ai është flaka; bashkë qofshi!

Letra VIII – Varfëria (Gusht)

Biri im i dashur,

Kjo është letra ime për muajin Gusht.

Mos u turpëro kurrë nga varfëria, sepse ajo nuk është njollë, por një provë e shpirtit. Pasuria e vërtetë nuk qëndron në ar e argjend, por në mendje të kthjellët dhe në shpirt të ndershëm. Kush është i ditur e i drejtë, s'mund të poshtërohet as nga më i pasuri i botës.

Edhe një copë bukë e thatë, kur është e fituar me djersë, ka shije më të ëmbël se çdo darkë e begatë. Mund ta lysh me pak vaj, me kripë a me sheqer të tretur në ujë, dhe përsëri ajo do të të ngopë më shumë se tryezat mbretërore, sepse nuk ia ke shtrirë dorën askujt.

Është më mirë të jesh i varfër dhe të flesh me zemër të qetë, sesa i pasur e të tretesh në ankth. Mos harro, biri im: makutëria ka shembur mbretëri dhe ka përmbysur perandori.

Letra IX – Sëmundja (Shtator)

Çimi,

E ndiej se sëmundja më ka lidhur këmbë e duar. Ka ditë kur nuk jam më unë, kur shpirti më tretet si mjegull dhe trupi më dridhet i pafuqishëm. Por dua që ti të mos kesh kurrë frikë nga e liga. Trupi është i përkohshëm dhe i brishtë, por shpirti është i pavdekshëm dhe i fortë.

Ruaje mendjen tënde, bir, si pasurinë më të çmuar. Mbaje të kthjellët, mos e lër kurrë errësirën të hyjë brenda saj. Sëmundja mendore është plagë e rëndë — më e rëndë dhe më e paragjykuar se kanceri apo sëmundjet e zemrës. Ata që vuajnë prej saj, vuajnë dyfish: nga dhembja e brendshme dhe nga gjykimi i botës. Por në të vërtetë, ata meritojnë të njëjtin mjekim, të njëjtën dashuri, të njëjtin kujdes nga shteti e nga shoqëria.

Mos i shto dhimbje kurrkujt, Çimi. Kurrë mos bullizo të sëmurin mendor. Madje, mos bullizo askënd në këtë jetë. Sepse pas çdo njeriu ka një histori të fshehtë që ti nuk e di.

Dhe mos harro kurrë: babai yt është njëri prej tyre.

Letra X – Dashuria (Tetor)

Biri im,

Një ditë do të dashurosh. Mbaje dashurinë të pastër dhe të sinqertë; mos e njollos me fjalë të kota apo gënjeshtra. Gruaja që të do me shpirt është pasuria më e madhe që mund të kesh. Mos bëj si unë... mos e humb atë që të rreh zemrën. Dashuria e vërtetë është flakë që ngroh, jo zjarr që djeg.

Dëshiroj të dish se poetët më të mëdhenj të botës kanë folur për dashurinë, secili me mënyrën e vet:

Sapho, nga lashtësia greke, thoshte se dashuria është forcë që shkund edhe zemrat më të forta.

Dante Alighieri e ngriti dashurinë e Beatrices deri në qiell, duke treguar se ajo mund të të ngrejë lart shpirtin.

Shakespeare na la sonete ku dashuria është më e fortë se koha.

Rumi e pa dashurinë si dritë hyjnore që bashkon njeriun me gjithçka rreth tij.

Pablo Neruda ndezi pasionin e zjarrtë, shpesh të përzier me mall dhe dhimbje, por gjithmonë të bukur.

Mëso prej tyre, biri im. Dashuria është frymë dhe jetë. Nëse e gjen, ruaje si thesar të shenjtë. Dhe kur zemra të të rrahë fort, mos u frikëso; ajo të tregon rrugën drejt asaj që vërtet ia vlen.

Letra XI – Drita (Nëntor)

Çimi,

Biri im i dashur,

Kërko gjithmonë dritën. Edhe kur errësira duket e thellë, syri i shpirtit mund ta gjejë. Drita është e vërteta, është mirësia, është ajo që të mban në rrugën e drejtë. Nëse ndjek dritën, nuk humbet kurrë. Ji si qiri që digjet për të ndriçuar të tjerët.

Spektri i dritës është i përbërë nga ngjyrat e ylberit: e kuqe, portokalli, e verdhë, jeshile, blu, indigo dhe vjollcë. Çdo ngjyrë ka bukurinë dhe rëndësinë e vet – ashtu si çdo virtyt dhe cilësi e zemrës sonë ka vendin e vet. Të jesh i ndershëm, i guximshëm, i sjellshëm dhe i mençur është si të jesh një nga ato ngjyra që bashkë krijojnë dritën e plotë.

Mos harro kurrë, biri im, drita nuk është vetëm ajo që shikon me sy, por ajo që ndjen me shpirt. Mbaje të fortë, shpërndaje tek të tjerët, dhe bota rreth teje do të bëhet më e ndritshme.

Me dashuri,

Letra XII – Liria (Dhjetor)

Biri im i dashur,

Liria është dhurata më e çmuar. Edhe nën diktaturë, edhe brenda mureve të një spitali psikiatrik, ekziston një liri që askush nuk mund ta marrë: liria e mendjes, e shpirtit, e zemrës. Ajo është si një flakë e vogël brenda një dhome të errët – ndriçon gjithmonë, edhe kur gjithçka tjetër duket e shuar.

Mos u bëj rob i frikës, gënjeshtrës apo padrejtësisë. Mbaje mendjen tënde të pastër dhe fjalën tënde të vërtetë, sepse këto janë krahët që të mbajnë lart, pavarësisht nga zinxhirët.

Edhe kur unë të mos jem, ti je i lirë të ngjitesh mbi çdo pengesë, të bëhesh më i mirë se unë dhe të ruash këtë dhuratë që askush nuk mund ta marrë: lirinë tënde të brendshme.

Babai yt,

Isai

XV.

Kuçedra me shtatë kokë

Isai përqafoi fort të dy djemtë dhe përshëndeti me kokë doktor Arbenin, që kishte dalë ta përcillte. I dukej ende e pabesueshme, që pas një viti të tërë në spital, më në fund ishte i lirë të shkonte në shtëpi. Ishte pothuajse drekë, por çuditërisht atë të Shtunë nuk kishte shumë familjarë që prisnin. Bënte freskët, megjithëse dielli shkëlqente me të gjithë madhështinë e vet. Era e mimozave kishte mbushur rrugën e sikur donte të kujtonte vizitorët e rastit se pranvera sapo kishte trokitur me gishtat e saj të brishtë.

"Faleminderit për gjithshka, shoku doktor! Nuk di si të ta shpërblej për të gjithë ato të mira që ke bërë." Zëri iu mek disi dhe sytë iu mbuluan nga një tis i hollë lotësh. I kishin ngelur në mendje ato çaste, kur për pak sa nuk kishte humbur jetën, por doktor Arbeni e kishte marrë nga thonjtë e vdekjes dhe e kishte strehuar në zyrën e tij. I shtrëngoi dorën fort doktorit dhe me dëshpërim u përpoq të gjente fjalët më të mira për t'ia thënë në shenjë mirënjohjeje të thellë, por truri i ishte mjegulluar nga ai turbullim ndjenjash. Fjalët asnjëherë nuk gjendeshin, atëherë kur duheshin thënë.

"Nuk ka asgjë! E kemi për detyrë! Më bëhet qejfi që ndjehesh mirë dhe t'ja kaloni sa më mirë," tha Arbeni dhe u kthye nga Nirvana, që priste disa hapa më tutje. "Për çdo gjë që të keni nevojë, ju lutem mos ngurroni. Do t'ju përgjigjemi sa më parë që të jetë e mundur. Gjithë të mirat!" I dha dorën Nirvanës që priste dy hapa me tutje, kapi për faqesh Çimin dhe Platorin, që ende rrinin si të ngurosur pranë Isait dhe nxitoi hapat për në portën e hyrjes.

Isai e ndoqi me sy, gjersa doktor Arbeni u fut në ndërtesën e spitalit dhe gjithë gëzim iu hodh Nirvanës në qafë. Nga të trija motrat, Nirvana ishte më e vogla dhe më e dashura. Ishte pikërisht ajo që i kishte ndenjur pranë gjatë të gjithë jetës së vet dhe kishte bërë aq shumë sakrifica. Nirvana i shplante rrobat e i kishte ardhur çdo javë në spital dhe ja tani, gjendej përsëri aty. Në momentin e duhur, në vendin e duhur.

"Ku do të shkojmë sot?"

"Sot do të shkojmë nga shpia ime. Nesër, me kismet shkojmë nga shpia jote. Si thu?" pyeti Nirvana, thjesht për respekt, pasi në mendjen e saj e kishte vendosur gjithshka dhe nuk kishte sesi të ndodhte ndryshe. Në shtëpi prisnin burri i saj Abedini, dy djemtë Veri dhe Kastri, dy vajzat Bleona dhe Arjola.

"Patjetër!" tha Isai dhe pa mëdyshje u kthye nga djemtë. "Do të shkojmë nga halla sot apo jo?"

"Pooo!" Djemtë pohuan me kokë dhe të kapur përdore ndoqën hallën nga pas.

Rrugës kryesore të qytetit, ndonjë që e njihte Isain, ngrinte dorën grusht për ta përshëndetur, ashtu siç përshëndeteshin me njëri tjetrin të gjithë komunistët. Megjithëse kishte qenë i shtruar për një kohë të gjatë në spital, Isain nuk e kishin harruar shokët e fëmijërisë. Ish nxënësi i dikurshëm, mbajtësi i medaljes së artë dhe ish-studenti që kishte studiuar në Bashkimin Sovjetik, kishte lënë gjithmonë përshtypje të mira tek bashkëkombësit e vet. I veshur në kostumin blu të larë dhe të hekurosur nga Nirvana, Isai dukej një njeri krejt tjetër, si ndonjë zyrtar i lartë i Partisë dhe jo si një ish i sëmurë, që sapo kishte lënë derën e spitalit.

Apartamenti i Nirvanës ishte në krahun lindor të qytetit, pak metra larg nga varrezat e Dëshmorëve, në një nga pallatet tre katëshe të ndërtuara jo shumë larg nga stadiumi i futbollit. Ende pa u hapur dera, u ndje era e tavës së kosit dhe e ballakumeve, të cilat hallë Nirvana i kishte përgatitur për merak, para se të shkonte për në spital. Abedini, një burrë babaxhan me vetulla të trasha dhe trup të bëshëm, hapi krahët dhe e përqafoi Isain fort, sikur ta kishte vëllanë e vet, pa harruar të dy djemtë e vegjël, të cilëve u dhuroi nga një të puthur në faqe. Megjithëse drekë, dukej se dita do të ishte tejet e gjatë, me një tavolinë të mbushur plot dhe me bisedat pa mbarim. Nuk u mor vesh, sesi erdhi nata dhe sesi arriti ta mbulojë me krahët e saj magjikë të gjithë qytetin.

Kur nata përfundimisht ra, duke lëshuar gjithandej mëndafshin e saj të errët, Nirvana i mori të dy djemtë për dore dhe i futi në dhomën e gjumit.

"Sonte do të flini këtu, në kto dy divanet përballë me njani-tjetrin. Nesër në mjes do t' ju çojë babi në shpi tek Namazgjaja, që të baheni gati për shkollë."

"Shkolla fillon të Hanën. Du të shkoj tek shpia e babit, te Banesat." Platori shtrembëroi turinjtë në shenjë pakënaqësie dhe mosaprovimi të thellë. Nirvanës iu thye zemra e ashtu me lotë në sy, nxitoi ta përqafonte edhe njëherë nipçen e vogël.

"Si të dush ti, të keqen halla! Nesër që ashtë e Dil, do të shkoni tek Banesat. Aty do të rrimë pak dhe do t'u çojmë tek shpia tjetër te Pallati i Peshkut. Të Hanën keni shkollë!" Nirvana rrokjezoi fjalët njëenganjë, duke u siguruar që më në fund Platori e kishte kuptuar.

"Po pse 'pak'? Du që të rrijmë gjithë ditën!"

"Herë tjetër! I kemi dhanë fjalën mamit tat, që të dilën duhet të jesh herët në shpi."

Platori rrudhi turinjtë dhe u struk pas të vëllait, si për ta ngacmuar që të thoshte edhe ai diçka.

"Oh sa mirë! Do të shkojmë tek shpia e babit. Sa qejf! Herën e funit që isha atje, babi më dha nji pjatë plot me mjaltë," tha Çimi dhe lëpiu buzët.

"Edhe nesër do të hamë mjaltë. Ehu, sa herë do të shkojmë tek shtëpia te Banesat ne! Nuk do të jetë hera e funit."

Platori u hodh përpjetë nga gëzimi dhe u turr të përqafojë hallën me krahët e tij të brishtë. "Hallë Nirvana, do të shkomë gjithato herë! Tani pse nuk na tregon atë përrallën me kuçedrën?"

"Cin prrallë, të keqen halla?"

"Atë të plakës dhe kuçedrës me shtatë kokë."

"Aha! Po si jo, moj zemër! Ja, të vijë halla aty afër teje dhe ta tregoj."

Sakaq Nirvana u ul mbi krevat mes dy nipçeve dhe filloi të rrëfejë me zërin e saj të ëmbël.

FSHATI REMANICË E KISHTE marrë atë emën nga nji remë, që kalonte në të hyme të fshatit. I ngulitun në rranzë të

Shpiragut, Remanica mlidhte në qillin e saj të errët re të mdha shiu. Gjatë dimnit rema fryhej dhe bymehej aq shumë sa merrte përpara rranjë pemësh dhe jetë njerzish, por gjatë verës thahej e përhumej, duke u shnrru thjesht në nji vijë uji. Megjithse lumi Osum nuk ishte shumë larg prej aty, ndoshta nji orë në kamë, puset kishin fillu me u zbraz dhe çezma e florinjtë ku laheshin zanat, nuk po nxirrte as edhe nji pikëz uji. Toka ishte tha e rrudh gjithanej, si një gru plakë, që gati sa nuk po jepte shpirt e të jepte përshtypjen se gjenej në grahmat e funit. Aso kohe ishin hap llafe që ujin e kishte zaptu Kuçedra me shtatë kokë dhe fshatarët e gjorë po vdisnin nga etja dhe uria. Pemët ishin zhvesh nga gjethet në atë vjeshtë të përhershme dhe pamarim. Pulat nuk kakarisnin ma e zogjtë kishin marrë arratinë për në vene të largëta dhe të begata.

Ashtu si çdo mjes, edhe atë ditë e zonja e shpisë Tagjibeja, rrotulloi çikrikun dhe msholi kovën e lidhun me litar në pusin e thellë dhe të zi. Priti disa sekonta, uli edhe kokën për të majt vesh, nëse po dëgjohej ndonji llokoçitje uji, por asgja. Me gishtat që i dridheshin filloi të tërhiqte litarin ngadalë, shumë ngadalë, nga frika se mos po i derdhte edhe ato pakëz pika uji. Kur kova u njit lart, me dëshpërim vuri se kova ishte bosh. Nuku faqet me dur dhe ngriti kokën lart. Dilli digjte si saç dhe për çudi në qiell nuk shifej asnji shtëllungë reje. Ndërsa po bahej gati të ikte, nga lartësia e qillit zbriti furishëm nji monstër me shtatë kokë, dhe me krahët gjigandë të mbulum me luspa si ato të peshqve. Kokat në nji rreth gjeometrik të saktë, villnin zjarr njana pas tjetrës, në krahun e akrepave të orës. Kur gjuhët e zjarrit zhdukeshin nga koka e parë, koka e dytë hapte nofullat e saj të lemerishme dhe fillonte të villte flakë edhe tym me sa të mundte dhe nga të katër anët. Sapo mbaronte së vjellmi koka e dytë, fillonte e treta, duke u zgjat dhe u zmadhu aq shumë, saqë dukej sikur do pullciste nga çasti në çast. Koka e katërt zgurdullonte sytë lemerishëm dhe ngaqë nuk dinte se çarë të bante kafshonte kokën e pestë. E pesta i kthehej me dhamët e saj të mprehtë, duke e kafshu miqësisht në qafë, pa i shkaktu nonji plagë të randë. E gjashta dhe e shtata thjesht prisnin në heshtje, me sytë dhe veshët nga koka e parë.

Fillimisht Tagjibesë iu prenë kamët dhe iu morr fryma, por kur nxehtësia dhe gjuhët e flakëve i përzhitën ftyrën, atëherë e mblodhi veten dhe u përpoq të ikte nga sytë kamët. Kuçedra me hapat e saj galopantë filloi ta ndjekë nga pas, duke u tall. Zani i Kuçedrës ma shumë i ngjante nji bubullime që zbriste hovshëm nga malet.

"Ky ashtë fundi! O zot, më jep forcë, që të shpëtoj nga kjo krijesë e shumtut, "tha Tagjibeja.

FËMIJËT I KISHTE ZËNË gjumi. Nirvana buzëqeshi ëmbël dhe i mbuloi me jorgan. Djemtë e të vëllait dukeshin si dy engjëj me flatra, që sapo kishin nisur të fluturonin në botën ëndrrave. Ishte nata e parë me babain pas kaq shumë muajsh ndarjeje dhe dita kishte qenë tejet e ngjeshur. Tërhoqi derën e dhomës së gjumit dhe vuri gishtin në buzë, si për t'i thënë Isait, që të mbante qetësi.

XVI.

Muret

I sai rrotulloi çelësin në bravën e ngurosur dhe shtyu derën ngadalë. Një e rrënqethur malli e përshkoi të gjithin, teksa hodhi vështrimin përreth. Megjithëse kishte gati një vit që kishte qenë i mbyllur në spital, shtëpia vinte erë sapun dhe shkëlqente nga pastërtia. Nirvana shkonte të paktën njëherë në javë në shtëpinë e të vëllait për të fshirë pluhurat dhe për t'u siguruar që gjithçka ishte në rregull. Nirvana kishte larë edhe njëherë të gjitha pjatat dhe kishte blerë gjërat më të domosdoshme, pa harruar edhe një kavanoz me mjaltë. Kur u ulën përreth tavolinës, Isai i vuri secilit nga një pjatë të vogël me mjaltë. Gjithçka ishte si më parë: krevati dopio në dhomën e gjumit, soba e vogël prej druri, bilbioteka e mbushur me libra të shkruar në rusisht dhe shqip, madje edhe lodrat e Platorit. Aty mungonte vetëm nëna, zëri i saj i ëmbël që mbushte gjithë shtëpinë. Dukej sikur apartamenti ishte sërisht bosh pa nënën e dashur. Çimi hapi njërin nga sirtarët e bufesë ashtu krejt rastësisht dhe syri i kapi një album të vjetër fotografish. E mori me kërshëri në duar dhe shfletoi faqet e zverdhura nga koha. Disa nga fotografitë ishin prerë përgjysëm me gërshërë. Çimi e merrte me mend se babai kishte bërë ç'ishte e mundur, që nëna të mos ishte në asnjë nga fotografitë. Pavarësisht nga kjo, tek tuk nga ajo kirurgji e kujdesshme, kishin shpëtuar ndonjë copëz fustani, një dorë e bardhë gruaje, apo ndonjë bisht flokësh. A kishte dhimbje më të madhe për një fëmijë, sesa kur shihte dy prindërit e tij të ndarë? Çimi nuk dinte sesi t'i përgjigjej asaj pyetjeje, por vetëm për një gjë ishte i sigurt: Nëse do të martohej, do të përpiqej me çdo kusht që fëmijët e tij të rriteshin të lumtur.

Ato pak minuta në apartamentin e Babait kaluan aq shpejt, saqë Çimit iu duk sikur nuk kishte qenë asnjëherë aty. Kur dolën në qytet, Nirvana e pa të arsyeshme që ta linte të vëllanë vetëm me të dy djemtë e tij e vetë të kthehej në shtëpinë e saj në lagjen "5 Maji".

"Tani po ju lë vetëm, se kam shumë punë për të bërë. Do të takohemi prapë." I puthi të dy djemtë në faqe dhe përqafoi të vëllanë me përmallim.

Çimi shtrëngoi fort dorën e babait dhe i lumtur pa nga Platori, që ia kishte qepur sytë një dyqani lodrash. Do të ishte dhurata më e bukur në botë, nëse babai do t'u blinte një top. Isai dukej sikur po fluturonte nga ai çast magjik. As në ëndrrën më të bukur nuk e kishte imagjinuar një moment të tillë: të shëtiste në qytet me të dy djemtë e vet, sikur të mos kishte ndodhur asgjë. Ditët gri të spitalit ishin davaritur e tretur në kujtesën e tij. Nuk kishte pse të jetonte ende me të shkuarën që kishte lënë pas. Duhej të shijonte atë moment gjer në fund, të shtrëngonte duart e tyre të vockla e t'i hidhte hoopla në ajër. T'i mbante në kraharorin e tij, njësoj si atëherë kur ishin edhe më të vegjël. Pa u zgjatur shumë në atë vorbull ndjenjash e mendimesh të përzjera, e rrëmbeu Platorin në krahët e tij dhe e hodhi disa herë lart.

"Do top futbolli, ti të keqen babi? Ta blej unë!" Pa e bërë fjalën dysh, iu drejtua dyqanit të lodrave pranë kinemasë "Vullnetari" dhe bleu topin më të madh e më me shumë ngjyra që ndodhej në vitrinë. Platori e mori gjithë qejf topin me të dyja duart, me një buzëqeshje të atillë, sikur të kishte marrë dhuratën më të shtrenjtë në botë. E përplasi njëherë mbi asfalt dhe u përpoq ta mbante pakëz, por topi i rrëshqiti, duke përfunduar para një dyqani akulloresh. Çimi vrapoi pas topit, duke mbajtur sytë në akulloret shumëngjyrëshe që ta bënin me sy.

"Në rregull! E mora vesh! Doni akullore!" tha Isai dhe qeshi me gjithë shpirt. Sa pak kërkonin fëmijët për t'u ndjerë të lumtur. Por edhe ai vetë nuk kërkonte asgjë më shumë: disa çaste të tilla normale, ashtu si të gjithë prindërit, kudo që të ndodheshin. Do të blinte tre akullore: një për Platorin, një për Çimin dhe një për vete.

"Unë e du të kuqe!" klithi Platori, sikur ta kishte pickuar ndonjë grenxë dhe zgjati doçkat me padurim drejt banakut. Lëpiu buzët me majën e gjuhës dhe lëshoi disa pasthirrma kënaqësie: "Hm, hm, hm"! Çimi, disi më i përmbajtur zgjati gishtin nga akullorja blu, duke pritur me nge pas kurrizit të të vëllait.

Isai i harruar në ato çaste magjike, po lutej me gjithë shpirt që ajo ditë të zgjaste gjer në pafundësi. Nuk kërkonte as më pak dhe as më shumë, veçse të rrinte me të dy djemtë e tij, ashtu siç do të bënin prindërit e tjerë në të gjithë botën. Ah sa do të kishte dëshirë që fëmijët t'i rriteshin të edukuar, me shkolla të larta dhe me dëshirat të gjitha të realizuara. I vinte mirë që djemtë kishin aq shumë dëshirë të loznin me top, por mirë do të ishte që të merreshin më shumë me libra. U fut i pari në librarinë më të afërt, që ndodhej në qendër të qytetit dhe pa e menduar gjatë iu drejtua Çimit.

"Çfarë libri të pëlqen?" E bëri pyetjen të tillë, duke mos e vënë asnjëherë në mëdyshje, se "librat ishin një gjë e pëlqyer" dhe kjo nuk ishte çështje për diskutim.

Çimi zgjati gishtin në drejtim të banakut të xhamtë, duke i mbajtur sytë në përmbledhjen "Cicërimat në liqenin Tung Pin", (*Tung Pin Hu De Niao Sheng*). Megjithëse nuk i erdhi mirë, që Çimi zgjodhi një libër kinez, Isai ia bleu menjëherë. I përkther rrjedhshëm në gjuhën shqipe dhe i mbushur me ilustrime, libri dukej tërheqës për moshën e tij.

Dita kaloi shumë shpejt, aq më tepër që mendja e tendosur i rrinte gjithnjë aty: si të sillte fëmijët në kohë në shtëpinë e ish-gruas. Megjithëse me një ndjenjë zori dhe sikleti të madh, Isai po digjej nga kërshëria ta takonte Hamdiun-burri me të cilin ishte martuar ish-gruaja e tij dhe të cilin fëmijët e thërrisnin "baba". U përqafua edhe njëherë më të dy djemtë dhe priti gjersa Platori të ngjitej lart e të njoftonte Hamdiun se ai- "babai" biologjik i fëmijëe po e priste poshtë në oborrin e Pallatit.

Isai e dalloi që larg siluetën e atij burri, që pothuajse ishte në të njëjtën moshë me të, me trup mbimesatar dhe flokët ngjyrë kafe të errët. Megjithëse e kishte kapluar një ndjenjë xhelozie e dëshpërimi, pamja e Hamdiut e qetësoi disi. Të jepte përshtypjen e një burri bablok, me një shprehje të butë në fytyrë dhe sytë kafe, që të jepnin siguri. I shtrëngoi dorën miqësisht, atë dorë muratori të vrarë dhe të ashpër dhe sikur zbriti përsëri në tokë, i kthjellët dhe i përzemërt. Fundja

Hamdiu nuk kishte asnjë faj që ishte martuar me ish-gruan e tij dhe që përkujdesej për të dy bijtë e vet, kur duhej të ishte pikërisht ai në vendin e babait dhe të bashkëshortit.

"Si jeni, mirë?" e përshëndeti nëpër dhëmbë, pa kërkuar në fakt ndonjë përgjigje për atë pyetje kortezie. Hamdi pohoi me kokë dhe hyri drejt e në temë.

"Hec kur të dush të takosh kalamajtë! Sa herë që të kesh munsi!"

"Faleminderit!" Isai u lehtësua disi nga gjithë ajo barrë emocionesh dhe i shtrëngoi edhe njëherë duart në shenjë respekti. Të paktën ai burrë i panjohur dukej njeri serioz dhe kishte karakter. Mund të kishte edhe më keq: t'i thoshte që nuk kishte se pse të vinte më aty dhe mundësisht të qëndronte sa më larg nga familja e tij e re, të cilën sapo e kishte krijuar. Personalisht nuk e bënte asfare me faj atë person, kushdo që të ishte ai. Fati e desh që Isai të sëmurej dhe gjithçka të merrte rrokullimën, por në fund të fundit, njerëzit duhej të merreshin vesh me njëri tjetrin, pavarësisht nga e shkuara.

Ktheu krahët dhe nxitoi hapat në krah të selvijave të Namazgjasë, duke hedhur edhe njëherë sytë në katin e dytë dhe pikërisht në dritaren e tretë, aty ku jetonin tashmë të dy vogëlushët e tij dhe nëna e tyre. I sëmbonte në zemër që ishin ndarë ashtu, por atë çast u përpoq të harronte gjithçka dhe të përqëndrohej vetëm në ato grimca të imëta lumturie. Ta harronte që do të jetonte këtej e tutje pa fëmijët e dashur. Le të kapej pas atij fakti, që vetë Hamdiu i kishte thënë të vinte sa herë të donte. Kaq kishte rëndësi. Të tjerat nuk kishin shumë rëndësi. Kështu i pëshpëriste një zë i brendshëm thellë në qenien e vet, ndërsa një zë tjetër kundërshtonte të parin.

"Siç e shikon, gjithçka ka marrë fund! Je braktisur nga të gjithë dhe do të jetosh vetëm si qen. Ke humbur gruan, dy fëmijët, domethënë gjithçka. A ia vlen vërtet të jetosh, tani që je përballur me të vërtetën e ashpër dhe lakuriqe? Nuk ka rëndësi së çfarë bën dhe çfarë mendon, pasi nuk e ke situatën në dorë,"-tha Zëri i Parë.

"Kaloji gjërat me qetësi! Qetësohu dhe mendo me gjak të ftohtë. Shijoji këto pak momente të bukura dhe mundohu t'i shtosh në të ardhmen. Përpiqu të ruash veten dhe mos u konsumo nga mendimet e këqija. Shiko anën e mirë të gjërave: ke dalë më në fund nga spitali. Djemtë të erdhën dhe të takuan. Mund edhe të mos i kishe parë kurrë. E mira nuk ka fund, por edhe e keqja nuk ka fund. Gëzoju ditës dhe asaj që të sjell rasti."

Zëri i Dytë e mbyti Zërin e Parë, ndërsa iu bashkua spontanisht rrymës së njerëzve që kishin dalë për shëtitje në të vetmin bulevard të qytetit. Sa shumë njerëz, një lumë fytyrash të panumërta që përshëndesnin njëri-tjetrin! Ecnin krah për krah burrat me gratë e tyre të dashura, me fëmijët e kapur për dore, ndërsa ai i vetëm si një gur i ngrysur. I përhumbur në mendimet e zymta, as që e vuri re tisin magjik të mbrëmjes teksa hidhej mbi shpatullat e asaj rryme njerëzore. Eci për gati tre orë, gjersa në shëtitore mezi shihej ndonjë kalimtar i rastit dhe kur mbeti plotësisht vetëm, u fut në hyrjen kryesore të Kalasë së qytetit. U çapit në rrugicat e ngushta, gjersa arriti tek "Banesat". Ngjiti shkallët ngadalë gjer në katin e tretë, duke ëndërruar me sytë mbyllur për atë çast jashtëtokësor, kur në derë do t'i shfaqej Manushaqja me ata flokët e saj sterr të zinj dhe fytyrën borë të bardhë. Por ai vegim u tret menjëherë sapo ndezi dritën dhe futin këmbën nrë shtëpi. Përsëri ato mure memecë dhe të ftohtë, që dukej sikur e shikonin me ata sytë e ftohtë dhe të akullt. Mure të lyer me bojë të bardhë, por që e vështronin vëngër dhe për dreq nuk thonin as edhe një fjalë të vetme. Zemra gati sa nuk po i çahej nga dhimbja, kur mendoi se kjo ishte vetëm nata e dytë në shtëpi dhe se ky ishte vetëm fillimi. Sapo e kishte ndjerë në të vërtetë se çdo të thoshte të ishte vetëm për një javë, për dy javë, për një muaj dhe për muaj e vite të tjera me rradhë, që do të vinin dhe ai do të gjendej përsëri aty, i plakur dhe i thinjur, i etur për një buzëqeshje të djemve dhe një prekje femërore të dy grave që kishte dashur në jetë: Svjetllanën që kishte mbetur në Rusi dhe Manushaqen që kishte zgjedhur një jetë tjetër. Çfarë duhej të bënte? Mos ndoshta kaq ishte për të dhe nuk ja vlente të jetonte më?! Kishte frikë se çfarëdo që të bënte, nuk do të ishte në gjendje të ndryshonte atë situatë në të cilën ndodhej. Një pikëllim i madh i rëndoi gur në zemër. Ndoshta do të ishte më mirë të dilte prej aty dhe të bënte një shëtitje në ajër të pastër dhe të harronte disi ato mendime të zymta. Sapo kishte kaluar mesnata dhe akrepat e ngrysur të orës, sikur lëvizën më me vrull, teksa veshi me nxitim pallton dhe hodhi një shall rreth qafës. Një shëtitje në qytetin e boshatisur që sapo kishte rënë në gjumë, mbase ishte zgjidhja më e mirë e mundshme.

NJË JAVË MË PAS. ORA shtatë e mbrëmjes, shëtitorja kryesore e qytetit. Bënte ftohtë dhe njerëzit ishin të paktë në rrugë. Isait iu bë sikur pa Çimin, teksa kishte mbetur si i ngrirë ndanë cepit të ndërtesës së Teatrit të qytetit. Kryqëzoi shikimin me të dhe u mat t'i fliste, por Çimi u kthye mbrapsht dhe iku me vrap. Diçka iu thye në thellësi të shpirtit. Përse djali i tij i madh u shmang në atë mënyrë? Përse iku nga sytë këmbët?

Mos ndoshta Manushaqja i ushqente fëmijët me frikë? I shtynte djemtë që të mos takoheshin me të? Të qenit "I sëmurë mendor" patjetër kishte të ngjitur nga pas etiketën e të qënit "I rrezikshëm" për fëmijët e tij dhe të tjerët. Oh, sa e kishte vrarë ai largim i beftë, sa e kishte dërrmuar shpirtërisht! Ndoshta nuk duhej t'i kushtonte aq shumë rëndësi. Fëmijët do të rriteshin dhe do ta kuptonin se babai ishte "babai" dhe do të duhej e të respektohej njësoj si nëna. Një ditë do ta kuptonin se sëmundja mendore kishte të njëjtin status si sëmundja e zemrës. Se të sëmurët mendorë ishin njësoj si të sëmurët nga stomaku apo mushkëritë. Se nuk kishte asnjë lloj turpi apo aq më keq frike, të ishe biri i një babai të çmendur. Një ditë...! Ndoshta ajo ditë do të ishte e shumë e largët dhe Isai kishte frikë se nuk do të ishte në gjendje të duronte gjer atëherë. Ditët ishin të zbrazëta pa djemtë dhe netët të mërzitshme. Mbase duhej të bënte diçka dhe të mos rrinte duarkryq. Të shkonte atje në shtëpinë e Manushaqes e të fliste me të apo me të shoqin e saj. Nëse ishte e vërtetë, që Manushaqja i ushqente fëmijët me përbuzje ndaj babait të tyre, apo frikë.... Kësaj gjendjeje duhej t'i jepej fund.

KISHTE MË SHUMË SE katër orë që ishte çapitur nëpër rrugët e qytetit, por hijet e atyre mureve memecë dhe të ngrysur, sikur e kishin kapur peng dhe nuk po e linin të shkëputej prej tyre. I dukej vetja si një grenzë e egërsuar e ngecur befasisht në rrjetat e një merimange gjigande. Fytyra i ishte skuqur nga të ftohtët dhe duart po i dridheshin. Ishte ora 4 00 e mëngjesit, por atij nuk i bëhej të kthehej në shtëpi.

Ato mure do t'i zbardhnin dhëmbët prej gëlqereje dhe do të gajaseshin së qeshuri me gjendjen në të cilën ndodhej. Edhe nja dy orë të mira dhe qyteti do të zgjohej. Vërtet ishte i zhytur në trishtim, por ajo englendisje e stërgjatë nëpër natë po e lehtësonte disi. Tek-tuk vinte re pastrueset, që fshihnin rrugët dhe në një farë mënyre ndjente një lloj ngushëllimi. Jeta ishte e vështirë edhe për punëtore si ato, që punonin aq shumë për të nxjerrë bukën e gojës. Përshëndeti njërën prej tyre kalimthi- një grua ezmere rreth të dyzetave. Gruaja as që nuk e vuri re, ndërsa i mëshonte fort një fshese gjigande prej kashte, e rrethuar nga një shtëllungë e madhe tymi. Diku u dëgjua një klithmë e largët gjeli dhe një e lehur qeni akoma më e largët. Kapakët e syve filluan t'i rëndoheshin më në fund dhe dukej sikur muret brenda tij tashmë ishin shembur të gjithë. Edhe pak do të gdhihej.

XVII.

Në krahët e erës

I sai veshi pallton e trashë ngjyrë blu që kishte blerë në Rusi, hodhi shallin e zi dhe të trashë rreth qafës dhe doli jashtë. Kishte ndjesinë se duart e buta të erës do t'i sillnin pranë ato përkëdhelje të munguara nga mijëra kilometra larg. Ku ishte Svjetllana vallë? Ndoshta ende jetonte në Shën Peterburg, atje ku kishte lindur. Patjetër që duhej të ishte martuar. Mund të kishte krijuar familjen e saj dhe ndoshta e kishte harruar përfundimisht. Shpejtoi hapat, me dëshirën për të ikur sa më parë nga lagja "Vullnetari", ajo lagje e ngritur artificialisht, me pallatet pa shije të ngritura me kontribut vullnetar. Ajo lagje sikur i ngjante me një garnizon ushtarak të pashpallur. E tërhiqnin më shumë rrugicat e ngushta dhe sidomos lagja "Kala", rrugët e vjetra me kalldrëm. Ata gurë të punuar nga mjeshtra të mëdhenj i kujtonin babain, që kishte qenë një nga gurëskalitësit më të mirë të Stambollit. Kalaja, ajo fortifikatë ushtarake fushore ishte ndërtuar fare pranë vijës "Egnatia"-arteries gjigande që në kohën e Romës lidhte Lindjen me Perëndimin. Gurët, se pse i ngjanin me koka njerëzish shurdhmemecë, që digjeshin nga dëshira për të treguar historitë e tyre.

Më tutje Kulla e Sahatit tregonte orën një pas mesnate. Gjithmonë e kishte magjepsur kjo ndërtesë trekatëshe, që rrëfimtari Osman Evlia Çelebi e përmendte në shekullin e XVII-të dhe ia përcaktonte vendndodhjen afër Xhamisë së Hyngjarit, mbi portën e Kiblës. Kulla ishte dëshmitari gjigand 19,45 metra e lartë, që ashtu si Guliveri shikonte liliputët, teksa vazhdonin rutinën e tyre të mërzitshme: punë-shtëpi, shtëpi-punë dhe në fundjavë bënin një shëtitje përmes bulevardit të vetëm të qytetit. Akrepat dukeshin të lodhur, si krahët e një njeriu që kishte punuar gjithë ditën e ishte gati të merrte një sy gjumë. Shtyu me forcë deriçkën e metaltë, që ndodhej në anën jugore, me pamjen nga çarshia. U mbajt fort pas parmakëve të drunjtë dhe për pak minuta e pa veten pranë këmbanës gjigande. Iu duk sikur po i merrej fryma dhe zbriti poshtë sa hap e mbyll sytë.

Dimri ende nuk kishte dhënë shpirt. Kurorat e mimozave kundërmonin që larg, duke e bërë edhe më romantike atë natë të vetmuar shkurti. Lajmëtaret e para të pranverës, ato kokrriza të verdha i binin papushim mbi supe, në fytyrë dhe duar. U mori erë thellësisht atyre luleve plot aromë dhe mbylli sytë me përmallim. A nuk ishin këto rruaza magjike simboli më i bukur i një dashurie të fshehtë e sublime, që nuk vdiste kurrë?! Frynte erë dhe bënte pak ftohtë, ndërsa qielli qëndisej tek-tuk nga yje të vetmuar. Këputi një degëz mimoze dhe e thërrmoi me gishtat që i dridheshin. Sa do të kishte dëshirë që t'i dhuronte një tufë më lule nënës së dy djemve të tij, Manushaqes, pavarësisht se ajo e kishte filluar një jetë tjetër. U martua me mblesëri dhe kishte diferencë të madhe moshe me të, por Isai gjithnjë e kishte trajtuar si bashkëmoshatare dhe më shumë si një shoqe të ngushtë. I kujtoheshin ato ditë të bukura të fejesës, kur kishin shkuar së bashku në Vishanj të Skraparit, atje ku pulat hanin gurë. Atje ku fshatarët kishin hapur zemrat dhe dyert dhe e prisnin mikun me çfarë kishte në shtëpi. Atje ku kosi pritej me thikë dhe nuk ngopeshe dot me ajrin e pastër. Kujtonte ato netë, kur e ngrinte nusen në krah e rrotullohej me të nëpër dhomë, gjersa i erreshin sytë. Sa më shumë që i zgjoheshin ato kujtime, aq më shumë ndjehej i trishtuar dhe aq më pranë i afrohej të vërtetës. Ato kokrriza të verdha mimoze që i derdheshin mbi supe, sikur ia nxirrnin parasysh edhe njëherë të vërtetën lakuriqe, se Manushaqen nuk kishte për ta patur më në krahët e tij. Dita kalonte e tensionuar, me frikën se diçka e keqe mund të ndodhte. Jashtë spitalit, dita dhe nata ishin të plota dhe nuk mbaronin kurrë. Dielli i vriste sytë. Ditën njerëzit e shumtë në rrugë sikur e frikësonin. I bëhej sikur e shihnin me mëshirë e njëkohësisht me përbuzje. Të qënurit i sëmurë mendërisht, nuk ishte njësoj si të qënit i sëmurë nga zemra apo kanceri. Njerëzit e zakonshëm sikur kishin frikë dhe ndrojtje e përpiqeshin t'i rrinin sa më larg të sëmurit mendor. Dhe kështu do të ishte përgjithmonë. Ndoshta do të kthehej përsëri në spital dhe ekzistonte mundësia, që mund të mos shërohej kurrë më. Djemtë do të rriteshin pa babain e tyre biologjik dhe për të kjo ishte më e keqja e të gjitha të këqijave. Ai ishte damkosur përfundimisht nga ajo sëmundje e pashërueshme, më e keqja nga të gjitha sëmundjet e tjera të marra së bashku. Më e keqe se kanceri apo sëmundja e zemrës. Të ishe i sëmurë mendor, ishte njësoj si të dënoheshe me përbuzje dhe braktisje. Nëse do të ishte i sëmurë nga kanceri, mbase gjërat do të kishin rrjedhur ndryshe. Mbase

Manushaqja nuk do ta kishte lënë dhe ai do të mund t'i kalonte ditët e fundit të jetës pranë fëmijëve të tij të dashur.

Përse vallë ishte bërë kaq melankolik atë natë shkurti? Po sikur t'i harronte të gjitha e të mos e rëndonte veten aq shumë, por thjesht të shijonte ato çaste në shëtitoren e qytetit? Përse duhej ta rëndonte veten aq shumë për ca gjëra, që nuk i kishte patur asnjëherë në dorë? Nëse do të ishte në gjendje të zgjidhte sëmundjen nga e cila duhej të vuante, ajo do të ishte patjetër-dashuria. Dashuria për gjysmën tjetër të botës-femrën. Si vallë zoti e kishte krijuar atë qenie të butë e të ëmbël? Ata sy plot diell e flokë të derdhur mbi supe si shtëllunga resh? Ato buzë të plota e të rrumbullakta, të lyera me ngjyrën e qershive? Ai bel i hollë dhe trup lastar! Sa i mungonte kurmi i femrës, vithet e plota dhe gjoksi i bëshëm, fustani i derdhur gjer në fund të këmbëve. Zëri i ëmbël, që i çuçuriste në vesh ato dy fjalëza aq të brishta: Të dua! Nga ajo torturë e përditshme duhej të kishte një zgjidhje. Vërtet ishte shumë larg dhe nuk kishte kthim pas, por ai mund të bashkohej me vajzën e ëndrrës, duke fluturuar vetë drejt asaj.

...DUKE FLUTURUAR VETË DREJT ASAJ!

Ai mendim i beftë i futi mornica në të gjithë trupin, por sikur ia hoqi si me magji atë gur të rëndë në zemër. Në një dimension tjetër, mbase do të ishte në gjendje të ishte pranë tyre: si hije, si vision, si mendim. Edhe pak do të agonte. Duhej të gjente një lartësi më të madhe dhe më me pak bujë. Ja, ai pallati pesëkatësh në hyrje të lagjes "Vullnetari" iu duk më i përshtatshëm. Acari i ftohtë i natës iu fut në palcë. Ndoshta nuk ishte thjesht të ftohtët, por edhe frika nga ai vendim i rrufeshëm. Ngjiti shkallët një e nga një, duke u munduar që të mos bënte as zhurmën më të vogël. Banorët e pallatit dhe i gjithë qyteti po bënin gjumin e tretë, ndërsa ai po bëhej gati të flinte gjumin e përjetshëm. Duhej të ngjitej gjer në katin e pestë. Sa më lart të hidhej, aq më e sigurt ishte vdekja. Fryma filloi t'i merrej e këmbët iu mpinë. Ndjeu një zbrazëti në gjoks, si një lloj shkretëtire, që po e përpinte të gjithin. Një zë i brendshëm i thoshte se duhej të mblidhte veten e t'i jepte fund asaj dileme një herë e mirë. Burrat nuk e bëjnë fjalën dysh dhe ai i kishte dhënë fjalën vetes, asaj dhe atyre zërave që nuk e linin të qetë, se sonte ishte nata pa agim. Nata që nuk do të gdhihej kurrë. Nata, kur ai do të mbetej dyzetetre vjeç përjetësisht.

Ktheu edhe njëherë kokën pas nga frika se mos papritur ishte pikasur nga banorët. Mbajti vesh...Dëgjohej vetëm frymëmarrja e tij e rënduar. Vuri duart mbi mbajtësen e shkallëve dhe sakaq u gjend me të dyja këmbët mbi murin anësor. Mbylli sytë dhe e la trupin të binte. Në ato të qindta të sekondës iu bë sikur krahët nuk deshën t'i bindeshin forcës së gravitetit. Ato gjymtyrë të pafuqishme luftuan edhe një herë për herë të fundit me vorbullën e ftohtë të ajrit, pastaj thjesht u lëshuan mbi trupin e plandosur në tokë, të rrethuar nga një pellg gjaku.

XVIII.
Nebula

Trupi i pajetë i një burri rreth të dyzetave ishte gjetur poshtë një pallati pesëkatësh, pak metra nga rruga kryesore, që të çonte në lagjen "Vullnetari". Në vendngjarje kishin mbërritur menjëherë forca të policisë dhe ekspertë të kriminalistikës, që kishin rrethuar vendin dhe po mundoheshin të mblidhnin prova. I pamësuar me ngjarje të tilla, qyteti i vogël i metalurgëve ende nuk e kishte marrë veten dhe hamendësonte lloj lloj teorish. Njëri nga fqinjët kishte dëgjuar një thirrje për ndihmë rreth orës pesë të mëngjesit, duke u gdhirë e Hënë, por nuk kishte dalë nga apartamenti i tij, megjithëse banonte në të njëjtën hyrje ku kishte ndodhur ngjarja. Një tjetër hamendësonte se ndoshta i njëjti banor mund të ishte dorasi i vërtetë. Kishte mundësi që viktima mund të kishte trokitur gabimisht në derën e dikujt dhe banori për hakmarrje mund ta kishte shtyrë nga shkallët. Çfarë mund të kishte ndodhur në të vërtetë? Një teori krejtësisht e paimagjinueshme ishte ajo e vrasjes nga KGB-ja ruse. Përflitej se viktima në momente krize dilte në publik dhe fliste kundër Stalinit. Thashethemexhinjtë e zellshëm harronin se nuk kishte as motiv dhe asnjë mundësi që kjo të ndodhte në të vërtetë. Viktima ishte pothuajse i vrarë edhe ashtu siç ishte, pasi gjatë të gjithë kohës gjendej më shumë në spital sesa jashtë mureve të tij! Të tjerë sugjeronin se ndoshta pas atij krimi makabër ishte ndonjë hajdut ordiner. Nuk përjashtohej mundësia që dikush mund ta kishte grabitur, kur e kishte parë të veshur mirë, me një pallto ruse gjer në fund të këmbëve dhe kaq mjaftonte ta ndiqte atë të panjohur teksa vërdallosej në orët e para të mëngjesit! Fare pak tregoheshin më skeptikë dhe realistë, duke dhënë detaje për shëndetin mendor të viktimës. Ata më së shumti argumentonin se këta lloj pacientësh vuanin nga haluçinacionet dhe përfundonin zakonisht në vetëvrasje, si pasojë e depresionit dhe gjendjes së rënduar shpirtërore në të cilën ndodheshin.

Atë mëngjes Çimi ende po flinte i mbledhur grusht në krevat, kur ndjeu në sup dorën e nënës. Hapi sytë me përtesë dhe para se të bëhej gati të ankohej se pse nëna po e zgjonte aq herët, vuri re se sytë e saj ishin të skuqur dhe të mbushur me lotë. Buzët i dridheshin dhe dukej sikur do të shpërthente në ngashërim. Çimi mbështeti bërrylat mbi krevat dhe i tronditur nga ajo gjendje e rënduar e nënës, nuk dinte se çfarë të thoshte. Larg qoftë nëna mund të kishte marrë ndonjë lajm të keq se gjyshja ishte sëmurë rëndë. Gjyshja ishte njeriu më i dashur në të gjithë botën dhe as që nuk mund ta merrte dot me mend se nuk ndjehej mirë.

"Ma! Çfarë ka nodh? Mos ashtë smun gjyshja? Ka ardh nonji telegram nga Berati?"

Manushaqja mbuloi padashur gojën, sikur të donte të ndalonte ato fjalë të vrazhda dhe të rënda.

"Jo, të keqen mami!"

Çimi hodhi sytë nga Alketa, motra e vogël tre muajshe që ende flinte si engjëll në krevatin e saj.

"Alketa, mirë ashtë?"

"Mirë! Mirë!"

"Po atëherë çarë?"

"Babi yt...është gjetur i vrarë në rrugë!"

"Çarë?"

"E ka gjetur policia sot në mëngjes pranë hyrjes së një pallati."

Çimi u hodh nga krevati dhe fërkoi sytë, për t'u siguruar se po i dëgjonte vërtet ato fjalë apo se ishte ende në gjumë dhe po përjetonte një ëndërr të tmerrshme. Apo ndoshta kishte ndodhur më e keqja: realiteti i hidhur dhe ëndrra e keqe ishin ngjizur dhe bërë një dhe se ai duhej të bëhej burrë e ta përballonte atë lajm të frikshëm.

"Çarë mund të ketë nodh?" Zëri iu mek, para se të artikulonte fjalët. Megjithëse lexonte libra pa mbarim, fantazia e tij e shfrenuar ende nuk kishte arritur gjer aty sa të fantazonte pistën më ordinere.

"Ndoshta i ka rrëshqitur këmba dhe është rrëzuar diku. Vishu të keqen mami dhe shko në shkollë. Atje mund të të vijë hetuesi dhe do të të bëjë disa pyetje."

" 'Hetusi'?" Çimi rrudhi buzët. "Çarë domethanë 'hetus' "?

" 'Hetuesi' është personi që merret me studimin e rrethanave sesi ka ndodhur ngjarja. Ai përpiqet të zbulojë të dhëna rreth krimit e të zbulojë kush e ka kryer krimin."

Çimi tundi kokën i hutuar, i pakënaqur me shpjegimin e nënës. Çfarë do të mësonte hetuesi pikërisht prej tij? Po sikur të ngatërrohej e të jepte ndonjë përgjigje që mund të ngjallte dyshime të kota dhe të panevojshme? Kujtoi atë mbrëmje kur kishte parë babain në rrugë. Për një çast kishte kryqëzuar shikimin me të. Babai e kishte pikasur, por Çimi kishte ikur me vrap që aty. Ndoshta babai ishte fyer dhe rënduar thellë në shpirt, që Çimi ishte frikësuar. Ndoshta ai veprim i kotë dhe i pamenduar e kishte prekur aq shumë babain, sa që kishte kryer vetëvrasjen.

"Çarë pytjesh?"

"Nuk di se çfarë të them! Ndoshta se ku kemi qenë ne gjatë të gjithë kësaj kohe. Me çfarë e kemi ngrënë gjellën dhe kur e kemi ngrënë...Gjëra të tilla. Përshembull, çfarë gjelle hëngre dje?"

"Dje? Gjellë me patate. Po ça lidhje ka kjo me babin?"

"Nuk e di. Tani shko laj sytë dhe bëhu gati për në shkollë. Vish pallton e bardhë, se ta ka larë mami dhe ta ka bërë dritë," tha Manushaqja e ngriti njërin cep të jorganit për të mbuluar Platorin, që ende po flinte. Alketa dukej sikur buzëqeshte, teksa kotej në krevatin e saj.

Në oborrin e shkollës jeta vazhdonte normalisht. Të gjithë nxënësit ishin rreshtuar para hyrjes së shkollës, në pritje për të filluar mësimin. Atë mëngjes Çimit i dukej sikur të gjithë e shihnin në sy dhe po e qortonin që kishte veshur pallton e bardhë prej lëkure. Ja, mësues Rolandi, ai i historisë, sikur po e shikonte vëngër për atë zgjedhje që kishte bërë. Ndoshta ai mëngjes duhej të ishte mëngjes zie dhe ai duhej të kishte veshur diçka të zezë. Por palltoja e bardhë ishte e vetmja pallto e mirë që kishte në shtëpi, ndërsa xhakoventon e kishte të grisur.

U ndje krejtësisht i çliruar, kur Amla i erdhi pranë dhe e përqafoi me aq dhembshuri. Alma nuk e kishte përqafuar asnjëherë më parë dhe ai gjest e preku thellë në zemër. Nuk kishte asnjë dyshim që ajo ishte vërtet një shpirt njeriu. Luftoi me veten për të mbajtur disi lotët dhe u ul në bankën e tij, pa parë as majtas e as djathtas, nga frika se mos sytë i ishin mbushur me lotë. Ai ishte burrë dhe burrat nuk lejoheshin të përloteshin.

Gjatë orës së parë të mësimit i bëhej sikur shokët e klasës e shikonin me çudi, ndryshe nga herët e tjera. Po rrinte si mbi gjemba dhe mendja ku nuk i shkonte, por fatmirësisht nga ajo gjendje e nxori drejtoresha e shkollës, zysh Sanija. I ra derës lehtë dhe njoftoi mësues Rolandin se Çimi duhej të ndërpriste mësimin. Hetuesi sapo kishte mbërritur dhe po e priste në një nga klasat bosh.

HETUESI ISHTE NJË BURRË rreth të tridhjetave me një fytyrë të vëngër që të kallte frikën. Kishte veshur një kostum të zi dhe mbante një kollare në ngjyrë blu të errët. I zgjati dorën sikur të ishte ndonjë burri i madh dhe e ftoi të ulej në karrigen e vendosur përballë tavolinës së mësuesit. Krruajti zërin si për të fituar kohë.

"Më vjen shumë keq për babin tënd dhe ndoshta nuk është koha e përshtatshme për të bërë pyetje të tilla, por nuk do të të mbaj gjatë." Hetuesi i nguli sytë, sikur donte ta shponte tejpërtej. "Si e more vesh për babin, që kishte humbur jetën?"

"Më tha mami, sot në mjes!"

Hetuesi hapi një dosje të zezë që e kishte lënë mbi tavolinë dhe filloi të hedhë shënime.

"Ku ka qenë mami mbrëmë?"

"Në shpi!"

"Po njerku?"

"Në shpi".

"A i ke parë të largohen ndonjëherë gjatë natës së mbrëmshme?"

"Jo. Kam qenë në gjumë"

"Kur ishe hera e fundit që e ke parë babin?"

"Para nji jave."

"Ku e pe?"

"Në bulevard! Ishte darkë dhe e pashë që po shëtiste, por nuk e takova."

"Pse nuk e takove?"

"Ishte larg dhe po ikte."

Hetuesi u ngrit nga tavolina dhe bëri një ecejake nëpër dhomë. Dukej se po gjendej në siklet për pyetjet e përshtatshme që duhej t'i bënte një vogëlushi 11 vjeçar.

"Jemi duke e hetuar çështjen, por gjer tani nuk kemi zbuluar ndonjë gjë të dyshimtë. Ka mundësi që babi yt të ketë vrarë veten."

Përgjersa e thoshte hetuesi, duhej të ishte e vërtetë. Po përse duhej ta vriste veten babai vallë? Herën e fundit, kur kishin dalë në qytet, babai dukej i lumtur. Oh sa do të kishte dëshirë ta zbulonte vetë se kush ishte vrasësi dhe ta sillte para drejtësisë! Ndoshta duhej të vazhdonte ndonjë shkollë për t'u bërë hetues njësoj si ai, që po e merrte në pyetje. A ekzistonte mundësia që vrasësi të shëtiste i qetë në rrugë, sikur të mos kishte ndodhur asgjë? Gjithshka ishte e mundur, përgjersa asgjë nuk ishte provuar faktikisht.

Hetuesi pikasi hijen e dyshimit në fytyrën e trishtuar të djaloshit dhe u mundua ta lehtësonte disi.

"Bisedova me drejtoreshën e shkollës dhe sot mund ta marrësh pushim. Më vjen shumë keq për babin tënd. Gjithsesi do t'u njoftojmë nëse do të ketë ndonjë informacion shtesë. Mund të shkosh!" Hetuesi i shpupuriti flokët dhe i zgjati përsëri dorën, si të ishte bashkëmoshatari i tij. Çimi u çua nga karrigia me një brengë të madhe, që ai takim kishte përfunduar aq shpejt. Kishte patur aq shumë shpresa se diçka do të dilte nga ai takim formal. Befas u dëgjua zilja e shkollës dhe zërat e zhurmshëm të nxënësve që mbushën korridoret.

XIX.
Takimi i fundit

"Trupin e babit e kanë sjellë në shtëpinë e xhaxhait. Atje do të vijnë njerëzit për ngushëllim. Atje do të shkoni edhe ju. Në këtë qeskë kam futur një pako sheqer dhe një pako kafe. Jepja teta Xhozit në dorë. Merri edhe këto dy pako cigare. Do t'ua ndash burrave, kur të vijnë për ngushëllim." Manushaqja ia zgjati qeskën të birit dhe e shtrëngoi fort në krahët e saj. Atë ditë djemtë ishin veshur me rrobat më të mira që kishin: pantallona teritali dhe pulovra të trasha e të ngrohta. Edhe këtë herë, Çimi kishte veshur pallton e bardhë prej lëkure, e cila dukej akoma më e bardhë, pas fërkimit me ujë të ngrohtë e sapun, që i kishte bërë e ëma një orë më parë.

Çimi kapi të vëllanë për dore dhe kaloi përmes rrugës automobilistike ndanë selvijave të Namazgjasë. Atë mëngjes të djele selvijat dukeshin më të zymta, më të thara dhe më shtatlarta. Të ngrysura dhe disi të kërrusura pëshpërisnin me njëra tjetrën ca fjalë ngushëllimi, që i merrte me vete era e Krastës. Zgjatnin krahët e këputur dhe i përqafonin vogëlushët dashurisht.

Çimi nuk kishte parë asnjëherë një njeri të vdekur në jetën e vet dhe për këtë arsye, seç ndjente një lloj frike. Në ëndërr i dilnin lloj lloj fytyrash të heshtura dhe të vrenjtura, që nuk thonin asgjë, por që me sytë e mbyllur, ngjanin më shumë me alienët, që vinin nga pafundësia. Përse vdiste njeriu dhe ku shkonte shpirti pas vdekjes? A do të shndërrohej babai në diçka tjetër: përshembull në një pemë ulliri apo qiparis? Apo ndoshta në një mjegull që davaritej në hapësirë? Gjatë natës së shkuar gjumi i kishte dalë disa herë. Nuk i besohej se babai nuk jetonte më, për aq kohë që nuk e kishte parë ende me sy. Nuk mund ta imagjonte dot, se babai nuk merrte më frymë.

"Lali, ça domethanë, që babi ka vdek?" Zëri i Platorit e shkundi nga ajo gjendje e përhumbur. Nuk e dinte as vetë sesi të përgjigjej, ndërsa u përpoq të përfytyronte diçka.

"Domethanë që babi ka ra në gjumë dhe nuk do të zgjohet ma!"

"Ça domethënë që nuk do të zgjohet ma?"

"Domethanë që ktej e tutje do të rrijë i shtrim dhe me sytë myll."

"Po pse nuk do të zgjohet?"

"Se ashtë shumë i lodh."

"Ma mirë mos ta zgjojmë. Babi ka nevojë të shlodhet."

"Ëhë!" tundi kokën Çimi. Ndjeu një dhimbje të madhe në shpirt, që nuk ishte në gjendje të jepte shpjegimin e duhur. Nuk ishte mirë të gënjente. Mami sa herë i kishte thënë se "gënjeshtra i ka këmbët e shkurtëra." Kur të rritej, Platori do ta kuptonte se çfarë kishte ndodhur, por gjer atëherë nuk donte që ta mbante atë barrë në shpirt. Nuk duhej ta gënjente vëllain e vogël dhe t'i tregonte të vërtetën e madhe dhe lakuriqe se babai nuk do të ishte më. Se babai do të shkonte diku në një vend të largët e të errët, ku mbretëronte vetëm nata. Se në atë vend kishte me qindra e mijëra njerëz të mirë, që rrinin së bashku dhe nuk merrnin frymë. Befas ndaloi këmbët dhe u kthye plotësisht nga ai.

"Tori! Ky lloj gjumi ashtë gjumë nryshe nga ai që bajmë ne çdo natë."

"Po pse nryshe?"

"Nuk di si ta shpjegoj. Ja, kur të mbërrijmë të shpia e xha Agimit dhe teta Xhozit, do ta kuptosh vetë. Në ktë lloj gjumi, njeriu nuk merr frymë dhe trupi fillon t'i prishet. Nëse nonjanin e kap gjumi i vdekjes, atëherë trupin e tij e fusin në dhe."

Platori pohoi me kokë, pa ditur se çfarë të thotë e krejtësisht i hutuar çapiti hapat e vegjël.

"Po ta fusin në tokë, nuk e shohim dot ma babin, apo jo?"

"Jo, sot asht hera e fundit! Tani të nxitojmë, se mos bëhet vonë." Ia shtrëngoi doçkën e vogël të vëllait dhe të dy kaluan në krahun tjetër të rrugës automobilistike, që të çonte për në qendër të qytetit.

TË DY DJEMTË DUKESHIN si të përhumbur në mes atij grumbulli njerëz që prisnin rradhën për të bërë ngushëllim. Në njërën nga dhomat ishin ulur vetëm burrat. Një rradhë karrigesh ishte vendosur përgjatë mureve të dhomës. Çimi e mbante mend që, kur rrinin të dyja familjet bashkë, se ajo dhomë i përkiste familjes së xha Agimit. Dhoma e mesit, ajo përballë derës kryesore, ishte pikërisht dhoma, ku kishin jetuar para se të shkonin në lagjen "Vullnetari". Në atë dhomë prehej babai, në pritje të lamtumirave të fundit nga të afërmit, miqtë dhe shokët. U zgjat në majë të gishtave për të parë më mirë, kur ndjeu në sup një dorë të butë ta prekte lehtazi në sup.

"U të keqen teta Xhozi! Ejani brenda!" Sytë e teta Xhozit ishin skuqur nga të qarët. Flokët sterr të zes ia shtonin më shumë kontrastin me fytyrën borë të bardhë. I puthi të dy vogëlushët dhe befas u habit disi.

"Çfarë ke tek kjo qesja?"

"Dy pako kafe dhe dy pako sheqer. Mami më tha: 'Jepja teta Xhozit në dorë.'" Zëri iu drodh. Ndoshta dhuratat nuk ishin të pranueshme, ngase bëheshin nga nëna. Por dyshimet iu davaritën menjëherë, sapo teta Xhozi e përqafoi sërisht plot dashuri.

"Mirë, silli këtu," Zëri i saj u bë edhe më i ëmbël. Çimi zgjati dorën i lehtësuar, duke u ngushëlluar, që të paktën teta Xhozi nuk po ia kthente mbrapsht. Xhozi ishte kushërira e parë e nënës! Ishin dy kushërira të para që ishin martuar me dy vëllezër! A nuk ishte po ajo grua që i blinte çdo vit të ri ato dhurata aq të bukura? Kurrë nuk do ta harronte atë xhakovento blu që teta Xhozi i kishte blerë për ditëlindje vite më parë. Ishte po kjo teta Xhozi që merrte mishin e saj nga frigoriferi dhe ia jepte fshehurazi nënës sa herë që takoheshin. Një herë xhaxhai e kishte parë dhe jo vetëm që nuk e kishte ndaluar, por e kishte nxitur të merrte më shumë. Mes fëmijëve të të dy vëllezërve nuk bëhej asnjë dallim. Çimi nxorri paketën me cigare nga xhepi dhe ia tregoi tetës si me mëdyshje. Teta u ngrys disi.

"Po cigaret pse i ke sjellë?"

"Do t'ua jap burrave. Kështu më tha mami." Çimi uli kokën si i zënë në faj. Mos vallë kishte bërë gabim që i kishte sjellë?

Tetoja i shpupuriti flokët dhe e shtrëngoi edhe njëherë fort në krahët e saj.

"Mirë, të keqen teta! Je bërë burrë tani. Shko te dhoma e burrave!" Teta Xhozi fshiu me nxitim një pikë loti që i shpëtoi papritur dhe u fut menjëherë në dhomën, ku gratë po qanin me zë. Zërat e tyre dukej sikur bënin bashkë një tufë shpirtërash të thyer.

ÇIMI TËRHOQI PLATORIN prej dore, sikur të kishte frikë se mos i rrëshqiste dhe i humbiste në turmën e njerëzve që sa vinte e dendësohej. Ndjeu një farë zori ta kaplonte të tërin, kur hyri në dhomë dhe filloi t'i japë dorën të gjithë burrave të ulur në karriget e vëna rrethepërqark dhomës së gjumit. Me gishtat që i dridheshin, nxori cigaren e parë dhe ja dha xhaxhait. Xha Agimi, ngaqë nuk e pinte cigaren, e mori si me mëdyshje.

"Nuk e pi duhanin, por do ta marr!" Zëri i përhumbur i xhaxhait, sikur e shkundi disi nga ajo gjendje e rënduar në të cilën kishte rënë. Xha Agimi ishte tre vjet më i vogël se babai. Ishte rreth të dyzetave, me flokët ngjyrë kafe e të dallgëzuara, të krehura me kujdes. Xhaxhai i përqafoi të dy me dashuri, duke i mbajtur për pak sekonda në krahët e vet. Edhe xha Fitimi, burri i hallë Nirvanës nuk e pinte cigaren, por menjëherë e pranoi, duke vënë dorën në zemër. Burrat filluan të tymosnin e pëshpërisnin fjalët më të mira që mund të thuheshin për atë që sapo kish shkuar në botën tjetër.

"Burrë si Isai nuk lind më nëna," tha një plak rreth të tetëdhjetave, me bastunin në mes të këmbëve dhe mustaqet e gjata. Në kokë mbante një qylaf të bardhë borë. Sytë e lëngëzuar i mbante të ngulura në hapësirë e dukej sikur fliste me muret. Të tjerët tundnin kokën në shenjë pohimi e thonin me rradhë shprehjet e mortit.

Ishte shpirt njeriu. Nuk i bënte keq as edhe mizës. Nuk ka burrë nëne si ai. I pashëm, i mençur, dritë iu bëftë shpirti. Fati i keq, por njerëz si ai nuk lindin më. Çfarë t'i bësh, njerëzit e mirë i merr me vete Vdekja. Nuk ka gjë më të keqe: të lësh dy djem pas e të ikësh kaq i ri. Nuk kemi patur njeri më të zgjuar se ai në fis. Fatkeqësi që i ndodhi ajo sëmundje se kushedi se ku do të ishte sot. Sa gjysma e tij t'i bëhen djemtë, lum si ata. Sa herë që vdesin njerëzit, gjithkush përpiqet të thotë fjalë sa më të mira, por Isai i meriton të gjitha. I qetë, i dashur, i pastër, i komunikueshëm, me sqimë. Të marrësh medalje ari në shkollë, nuk i thonë shaka. Shyqyr që la dy djem pas, se do t'i kishte humbur nami dhe nishani. Nganjehërë nuk gjenden kollaj fjalët për këta njerëz kaq të mirë.

Çimit filluan t'i merreshin disi mendtë. Ndjeu një lloj plogështie në trup e i dukej sikur nuk po ngopej me frymë. Të paktën porosinë që i kishte lënë nëna e kishte kryer më në fund. Të dyja paketat e cigareve ua kishte shpërndarë miqve që kishin ardhur për ngushëllim. Megjithëse nuk i kishte mbushur të njëmbëdhjetat, atë ditë vetja i dukej më burrë se kurrë. Një burrë i vërtetë në mes burrave të tjerë. Xhafa, djali i madh i hallë Sadijes, i bëri me shenjë t'i afrohej. Xhafa ishte një burrë rreth të tridhjetave me flokët sterr të zinj dhe kaçurrelë. Ishte piktor dhe punonte në Teatrin e qytetit. Fytyra e tij rrezatonte mirësi dhe një dhimbje të thellë.

"Hajde ta shofësh babin për herë të fundit," tha Xhafa dhe bëri vetë i pari përmes turmës së njerëzve. Çimi e ndoqi i hutuar pas me një farë kërshërie të përzier me frikë. Vërtet ishte hera e fundit dhe nuk do ta shihte babanë as edhe një herë tjetër? Ktheu kokën pas për të parë se ku ishte Platori, por dora e hekurt e Xhafës po e tërhiqte fort përmes turmës. Kishte parë të vdekur edhe më parë, por këtë herë ishte ndryshe. Ja ku ishte babai i shtrirë në arkivol me sytë e mbyllur përjetëisht. Megjithëse e kishin larë ende i dalloheshin në fytyrë njolla gjaku. U përkul ta puthë për herë të fundit. çuditërisht babai atë mëngjes ishte krejtësisht i ftohtë si një copë akulli. Këmbët iu morën dhe për pak sa nuk ra, por Xhafa e mbajti fort nga krahu dhe nuk e la të binte.

Sapo doli disi nga ai grumbull njerëzish, menjëherë dalloi Platorin, që si një zog i vetmuar hidhte sytë kuturu për të gjetur të vëllanë. E kapi për dore dhe e tërhoqi për në oborrin përballë pallatit. Platori nuk fliste as edhe një fjalë të vetme, sikur ta kishte kuptuar se për çfarë bëhej fjalë dhe se në atë moment aq të rëndësishëm të jetës së tyre ishin thënë të gjitha.

Në rrugën automobilistike priste makina e funeraleve dhe një autobus fizarmonikë i Urbanistikës. Kortezhi i shkurtër kaloi përmes qytetit, që kundërmonte nga era e këndshme e mimozave tër porsaçelura. Rruga për te Varrezat zgjati më pak se pritej, me trafikun pothuajse zero dhe njerëzit që në atë orë pasditjeje ishin mbledhur nëpër shtëpitë e tyre. Ishte mesi i shkurtit të vitit 1977. Natyrisht makinat numëroheshin me gishtat e dorës dhe njerëzit përpiqeshin të shikonin hallet e tyre.

XX.

Laboratori i Biologjisë

Mornica të ftohta i përshkuan trupin, megjithëse ende mbante të veshur pallton e bardhë prej lëkure. Një ndjenjë padurimi e angushtie e bëri të ngrihej nga karrigia dhe t'i afrohej dritares. Në katin e pestë të pallatit e kishte shtëpinë Amla. Sa herë i kishte hedhur sytë në atë dritare, pas perdeve të së cilës shfaqej nganjëherë ajo fytyrë engjëllore, që e linte pa gjumë. Do të ishte gjëja më e bukur në botë, nëse një ditë Amla do të bëhej shoqja e jetës. Mrekullitë prandaj quhen të tilla, sepse rrallëherë ndodhin. Po sikur mësuese Vilma ta kishte marrë vesh për atë zënkën që kishte ndodhur para pak ditësh? Më shumë do t'i vinte turp për atë puthje të lehtë në faqe. Ende nuk i besohej se ajo puthje e pafajshme kishte ndodhur vërtet apo ishte fantazia e tij e shfrenuar. Hodhi përsëri sytë nga dritarja, por Alma nuk po dukej gjëkundi. Ku të ishte vallë? Sa mirë do të ishte të vinte edhe ajo aty në laborator dhe të mësonin së bashku! Laboratori atë pasdite vonë i ngjante më shumë me një dhomë të madhe të mbushur plot me fantazma.

Në shpirt i peshonte një gur i rëndë. Vdekja e babait e kishte pikëlluar aq shumë, saqë ajo ndjenjë e ëmbël për Amlën iu tret me magji. Vuri majën e hundës në njërën nga xhamat e kabineteve dhe pa me kërshëri një embrion njerëzor të mbyllur në një epruvetë të madhe. Embrioni e kishte penisin sa një majë thoji dhe sytë plotësisht të mbyllur. I mbledhur sa një grusht, embrioni i shkaktoi sërisht drithërima. Nëse do të mbijetonte, ndoshta ai embrion do të ishte bërë burrë dhe madje mund të kishte krijuar familje. Më tutje syri i kapi një epruvetë tjetër me mbishkrimin: "Kujdes! Rrezik Vdekje". Poshtë shënimit ishte vizatuar një kafkë njeriu me dy kocka këmbësh anash.

A kishte jeta kuptim pa babain? Përse duhej të jetonte, kur babai kishte ikur nga kjo botë në moshë aq të re? Çfarë kuptimi kishte të merrte frymë? Lotët i rrodhën çurkë në faqe dhe buzët iu drodhën nga ngashërimi. Hapi kanatin e xhamtë dhe nxorri prej andej njërin nga kavanozët me etiketën paralajmëruese. Mbushi dorën me kokrrat e bardha dhe kapërdiu njërën ngadalë. Me sytë mbyllur, i zhytur në një qetësi të mistershme, priti të ndodhte diçka e madhe dhe e frikshme. Diçka, të cilën nuk e kishte provuar asnjëherë në jetën e vet. Sekondat e para kaluan, por për çudinë e tij asgjë nuk po ndodhte. Futi në gojë një tjetër kokërr të bardhë me një vijë në mes. E përtypi me neveri, njësoj sikur të shijonte ndonjë jashtëqitje njerëzore. Priti t'i pushonte menjëherë zemra, por rrahja e saj vazhdonte të ishte normale, ashtu si një orë tavoline e kurdisur mirë: tik-tok, tik-tok, tik-tok. Siç dukej, ilaçi nuk po bënte asnjë efekt. Ndoshta ishte pluhur i rëndomtë pa asnjë lloj efekti. Ndoshta duhej të kishte ndonjë epruvetë tjetër me helm akoma më vdekjeprurës. Nuk duhej të humbte shpresën, thjesht duhej ta kërkonte dhe të mbaronte punë.

Ja, edhe pak dhe do të bashkohej përfundimisht me babain, atje ku bota kishte rënë përjetësisht në qetësi. Ja ku ishte një enë tjetër me të njëjtën emblemë dhe me të njëjtin mbishkrim: "Kujdes! Rrezik Vdekje!" Hapi enën e dytë, që ishte disi më e vogël dhe me kapak ngjyrë gri. Kokrrat ishin disi më të vogla dhe me një vijë në mes. E mbushi gojën plot dhe u përtyp. Sytë iu errën dhe për pak i erdhi për të vjellë. E gëlltiti masën e qullët të kokrrave helmatitëse dhe priti që zemra t'i pushonte, por në fakt nuk po ndodhte asgjë. U turr drejt kabinetit përbri dhe me gojën ende plot, kërkoi për ndonjë enë tjetër me helm. Ja ku ishte një kavanoz më i vogël nga dy të tjerët dhe po me të njëjtin mbishkrim. E rrëmbeu me shpejtësi dhe e ngriti lart, sikur të kishte një gotë uji. E hapi dhe e zbrazi të gjithin në gojë e filloi të përtypej aq shumë, saqë po i kërcisnin dhëmbët. Ndjeu të njëjtën shije të hidhur. U palos më dysh nga neveria dhe e nxorri të gjithë atë masë të qullët, por ende i vinte për të vjellë. Trupi iu drodh dhe këmbët i ndjeu të dobëta. Karriget, tavolinat, madje edhe tri dritaret e mëdha të laboratorit iu sollën vërdallë. Mbështeti duart në karrigen më të afërt, por gjunjët nuk e mbajtën më. Tëmthat iu rënduan dhe damarët iu frynë nga rritja e presionit të gjakut. Ra përsëri, këtë herë me hundë në dysheme. Një vijë e hollë gjaku iu vizatua në fytyrë. Këmba e djathtë iu pengua në një karrige, e cila fluturoi mbi rreshtin e mesit të tavolinave dhe u përplas në mur. Një tavolinë u ngjesh me një tjetër, duke shkaktuar një zhurmë të çjerrë. U përpoq të ngrihej sërisht, duke u mbështetur fort me të dyja duart në dyshemenë e ftohtë, por ishte e pamundur.

NJË TUFË BARDHOSHE resh e kishte mbuluar të gjithë hapësirën përreth. Çimi nuk po kuptonte se çfarë kishte ndodhur

në të vërtetë dhe si ishte e mundur që të ecte mbi to. Zgjati duart për t'i shtrydhur me sa fuqi kishte, por ai veprim naiv e i kotë thjesht e bëri për të qeshur. Eci me hapa të shpejtë, i çuditur me atë gjendje të re në të cilën ndodhej. Duhej të ishte ëndërr, se nuk kishte e mundur që të ecte mes tyre. Nuk kishte kaluar shumë kohë, kur retë u davaritën dhe para syve iu shfaq një pyll i vogël ndanë një liqeni të qetë, që merrte frymë shumë ngadalë, i përkëdhelur nga gishtat delikatë të erës. Pylli sa vinte dhe i dendësohej para syve, me gjithë përpjekjet e stërmundimshme, që të çante mes shkurreve dhe degëve të trasha e të arrinte sa më parë buzë liqenit. I çjerrë, i gjakosur e duke dihatur me zor kërkoi me ngulm babain. Ku ishte vallë? Pse nuk dukej asgjëkundi? A ishte tashmë në botën e përtejme? Përgjersa kishte kaluar kufirin mes dy botëve, babai duhej të ishte aty, i fshehur gjëkundi pas ndonjë gëmushe apo ulur në ndonjë gur, duke shkruar poezi. Përse kishte kaq shumë vetmi dhe era ishte aq e ftohtë?

Një tufë pulëbardhash fluturuan buzë bregut, duke rrahur pammbarimisht krahët e bardhë. Rëra e butë dhe e shkrifët, iu shkërmoq në këmbët e zbathura, ndërsa gjethet e pemëve i folën me zërat e tyre meliodiozë. Atëherë kur i kishte humbur të gjitha shpresat një shëmbëlltyrë njerëzore qëndroi mbi horizont. Dy palë sy të errët të ngarkuar me shi, dy vija resh si vetulla të ngritura në habi dhe një buzëqeshje pranvere. Shëmbëlltyra i pëshpëriti diçka të ëmbël, si një farë urimi thellësisht të përzemërt, që të flinte sadopakëz e të kthehej andej nga kishte ardhur. Në atë realitet nuk ekzistonte asgjë dhe se babain nuk do ta takonte më kurrë. Babai i kishte thënë Shëmbëlltyrës që Biri t'i rikthehej dritës e ta jetonte jetën gjer në sekondën e fundit. Se ai akt vetëflijimi nuk kishte asnjë kuptim. Nuk do të shikonte aty poshtë asgjë, pas nuk kishte asgjë për të parë.

"Kthehu!" tha Shëmbëlltyra, me zërin e vet prej ere. Nuk e kuptoi se ç'ishte: një rrymë ajri apo një re e dalldisur, që kishte marrë arratinë? Universi po përpiqej t'i fliste. "Kthehu!" thanë dallgët që filluan të ashpërsoheshin e përplaseshin më me furi në bregun e ashpër të thepisur. "Kthehu!" thanë vetëtimat, teksa kryqëzuan shpatat.

ÇIMI E NDJEU KOKËN të rënduar si asnjëherë tjetër. U ngrit përgjysëm nga dyshemeja dhe bëri çudi sesa kohë kishte kaluar pa ndjenja. Ndjeu një lehtësi në shpirt, që ishte gjallë, pavarësisht nga përpjekjet e stërmundimshme për të vdekur. Ose nuk kishte ardhur rradha e tij, ose helmet do të kishin patur ndonjë afat skadence. Ashtu në gjysëm errësirë mori një leckë dhe pak ujë e pastroi dyshemenë. Nuk duhej ta merrte vesh askush se çfarë kishte tentuar të bënte. Mbylli derën e laboratorit me çelës dhe nxitoi hapat.

Jashtë pothuajse ishte errur fare. Shkolla "Thoma Kalefi" në atë mbrëmje të vonë, sikur i ngjallte një lloj frike. Diku u dëgjua një sirenë e largët, nga ato që përdornin makinat e policisë dhe patkonjtë e një kali që çapiste i lodhur në rrugën kryesore. Karrocieri e fshikulloi fort me kamzhik, pa ia hedhur aspak sytë Çimit që kishte mbetur i shtangur në Portën e Madhe të Oborrit, për të kuptuar disi, nëse vërtet ishte gjallë apo kishte kaluar në botën e përtejme. Kali ishte shumë i lodhur, gati i këputur në mes, me brinjët që i numëroheshin me gishtat e dorës, pothuajse kockë e lëkurë, njësoj si Rocinante i Saavedras në romanin "Don Quixote".

Konturet e ngrëna të selvijave të Namazgjasë sikur mbanin mbi supe një grusht me yje. Selvijat seç pëshpërisnin ca sekrete mes tyre e dukej sikur e kishin vënë në mes Çimin e po i bënin magji. Shpejtoi hapat, si për të shpëtuar nga dalldia e tyre e marrë, duke e mbajtur frymën drejt e në oborr. Në dhomën e katit të parë të Pallatit nuk kishte drita. Dana duhej të kishte rënë për të fjetur, pasi zgjohej herët e pastronte rrugët e qytetit. Ngjiti shkallët e betonta të pallatit duke iu marrë fryma. Duhej të ishte ora dhjetë e mbrëmjes dhe në shtëpi do të ishin shqetësuar shumë. Në korridorin e gjatë zverdhte një llampë lakuriqe, e cila lëkundej nga era që frynte përmes xhamave të thyera të dritares. Dikush sapo kishte fikur një furnellë vajguri, që i çpoi hundët. Ende po trokitur, dera u hap dhe në prag të saj u shfaq nëna. Hamdiu kishte rënë në gjumë në krevatin dopio. Alketa guguriste si një pëllumbeshë në krevatin e saj të vockël, me një buzëqeshje nanuritëse në fytyrë. Platori lozte me një makinë lodër i ulur përgjysëm në krevatin tek, aty ku flinin të dy bashkë, njëri nga këmbët dhe tjetri nga koka. Çimi ende nuk mund të arrinte të kuptonte sesi mund të jetonin pesë vetë në një dhomë për vite me rradhë. Ishin bërë afro 4 vjet, që kur u futën në Pallatin e Peshkut. Tashmë ishte shtuar një anëtar i ri i familjes dhe nevojitej një dhomë tjetër. Manushaqja dhe Hamdiu kishin bërë kërkesë për zgjerim në bashkinë e qytetit, por letra e tyre kishte përfunduar në koshin e plehrave. Edhe sa kohë do të jetonin ashtu në atë hapësirë aq të ngushtë, ku nuk kishe të hidhje as kokrrën e mollës?!

"Hë mor bir, u bëmë merak! Pse u vonove kaq shumë?"

"Kisha shumë msime për të ba!"

Manushaqja i mori çantën e librave nga duart dhe e vari pas derës.

"Po pse je verdhur kaq shumë në fytyrë? Mos nuk je mirë?"

"Jo, nuk kam gja! Jam pak i lodh!"

"Ulu të hash bukë!"

Gjella e ngrohë me patate sikur ia ndezi oreksin me magji. Sapo futi kafshitën e parë në gojë, Hamdiu u çua përgjysëm në shtrat me sytë mbyllur, pasi nuk e duronte dritën e llampës. Dhoma u tund nga kolla e thatë që i shkaktohej nga duhani i fortë dhe rakia, të cilën nuk e hiqte asnjëherë nga dora.

"Hë, pse u vonove?" Sytë e vëngërt të Hamdiut nuk kishin nevojë të shoqëroheshin me fjalë, pasi me atë vështrim të egër i thoshte të gjitha.

"Kisha shumë për të msu." Çimi nuk guxoi ta ngrinte kokën. Futi lugën e parë në gojë dhe rrufiti lëngun e ngrohtë. Fyti iu çlirua nga ajo shije e hidhur.

"Ato librat kanë për të të marrë në qafë! Ke për të lujt mensh, njësoj si yt atë!" Toni i zërit i Hamdiut ishte bërë akoma më kërcënues.

"Isai nuk u sëmur nga librat!" pëshpëriti Manushaqja, sikur të nxirrte një sekret të mbajtur thellë në zemër për vite me rradhë. Fytyra i ishte skuqur lulëkuq dhe duart i dridheshin. Ndoshta ajo ndërhyrje në bisedë mund të interpretohej ndryshe. Ndoshta si një nostalgji për ish-bashkëshortin që nuk ishte më.

"Po nga se u smun? Pa na thuj!" Hamdiu ndau fjalët njëenganjë, për t'u siguruar që Manushaqja po e dëgjonte mirë dhe se nuk bënte, që të mos i përgjigjej.

"Isai nuk e kishte sëmundje të trashëguar. Kur ishte dhjetë vjeç, u rrëzua nga kati i tretë dhë pësoi një goditje në kokë. U plagos shumë rëndë, por ushtarët Italianë e dërguan në spitalin e tyre ushtarak dhe atje iu bë operacion. Ajo plagë nuk iu shërua plotësisht dhe që atëherë kishte dhimbje pavarësisht nga ndërhyrja e suksesshme." Manushaqja psherëtiu e lehtësuar, sikur të kishte shfryrë një barrë të rëndë. E kishte thënë më në fund. Ta merrnin vesh të gjithë, se sëmundja e Isait nuk vinte nga genet, as nga librat, por ishte shkaktuar nga një goditje e jashtme fizike. Sëmundje e cila rëndohej, sa herë që Isai vuante shpirtërisht. Përgjersa nuk ishte sëmundje e trashëgueshme, nuk duhej të ekzistonte asnjë lloj frike për shëndetin mendor dhe mbarëvajtjen shkollore të të dy djemve që kishte lënë pas.

Pavarësisht nga ndërhyrja e nënës, Çimi nuk foli! Kishte shpjegimin e tij për origjinën e sëmundjes mendore të babait. Një njeri nuk mund të çmendej, sepse lexonte shumë libra. Sëmundja mund të kishte shkaqe të ndryshme: dhimbjet shpirtërore që i ishin shkaktuar nga ndarja me të dashurën në Rusi, mungesa e perspektivës në atdheun ku u kthye, por jo librat, në asnjë mënyrë. Nëse të lexuarit do të ishte shkaku, atëherë do të ishin sëmurë mendërisht shumë njerëz apo jo?! Të gjitha këto hamendësime Çimi i mbajti pas gjuhës, pasi nuk donte të hynte në debat me Hamdiun. Dhe nëse kjo lloj sëmundje ishte e trashëgueshme apo jo, ky diskutim i takonte shkencës mjekësore dhe nuk duhej të bëhej temë për debat. Aq më shumë që atë mbrëmje ishte në faj dhe nuk kishte asnjë të drejtë të jepte mendimin e vet. Mjaftonte ndërhyrja e nënës.

Hamdiu u step disi dhe thellë në shpirt u thye më në fund.

"Unë di të them kaq: Po të pashë ma me romane apo libra jashtë shkollës, do t'i marr e do t'i hedh nga dritarja, e more vesh se çfarë po të them?!" Hamdiu e ngriti edhe më shumë zërin e tij, por toni iu zbut dhe sytë gati sa nuk i ishin mbushur me lotë. Tashmë Hamdiu u ngrit nga krevati dhe i vuri dorën mbi sup dhimbshurisht.

"Për të mirën tane e kam!"

Çimi tundi kokën dhe mbajti sytë përdhe. Nëse Hamdiu ishte vërtet i zemëruar me të, kjo ndodhte sepse ishte mjaft i shqetësuar për fatin e tij si fëmijë. Për aq vjet që kishin jetuar bashkë, Hamdiu kurrë nuk e kishte ngritur zërin karshi thjeshtrit, fëmijës së gruas, por gjithnjë e kishte trajtuar me respekt. Hamdiu ishte një "baba" i vërtetë, që gjithmonë i fliste me shumë dashuri, si ta kishte djalin e vet prej gjaku.

"Fli tani, se do të çohesh herët nesër për në shkollë." Hamdiu i shpupuriti flokët në shenjë pajtimi dhe i ngjeshi një dhjetë lekësh në dorë. "Bli nji bugaçe nesër, meqë kam marrë rrogën!"

XXI.

Zogjtë e korentit

Atë pasdite dikush po trokiste fort dhe pa ndërprerë me një farë padurimi. Çimi hapi me të shpejtë derën dhe çakërriti sytë. Ishte Dini, kushëriri i tij i parë i veshur "beks". Kapelën me yllin e kuq pecëcepësh e mbante disi mënjanë mbi kokën e qethur zero. Xhaketa dhe pantallonat prej stofi të trashë në ngjyrë ulliri të errët e bënin të dukej më i madh në moshë, ndërsa kapota e rëndë i shkonte gjer në fund të këmbëve dhe e tregonte edhe më shtaltartë për moshën 15 vjeçare që kishte. Kishte udhëtuar me tren nga Tirana, ku ndiqte shkollën e mesme Ushtarake "Skënderbej", për t'i bërë një vizitë teze Manushaqes në Elbasan. Dini ishte dy vjet më i madh se Çimi dhe në Shkollën Ushtarake vazhdonte vitin e parë. Këpucët dukej sikur i kishte lyer vetëm pak minuta më parë, aq shumë i shkëlqenin nga pastërtia.

Çimi nuk priti më, por iu hodh në krahë dhe e përqafoi fort. Kishin pothuajse një vit pa u parë, që nga ajo ditë kur Dini kishte lënë shtëpinë e tij në Berat për të vazhduar studimet në Tiranë.

"O ma, ka ardh Dini!" Çimi e shtrëngoi edhe më shumë kushëririn në krahët e vet, ndërsa Dinit i shkëlqyen sytë nga gjithë ajo mikëpritje që po gjente ende pa vënë këmbën në pragun e shtëpisë.

"Uuu, të keqen tezja! Kush më ka ardhur!" klithi Manushaqja dhe iu bashkua me të shpejtë përqafimit të të dy kushërinjve të parë, që nuk po shkuleshin nga krahët e njëri-tjetrit.

"Nuk do të rri shumë, teze! Kam ardhur sa për të të takuar, se e di që nuk ke vend as për vete." Dini ndjehej pak si në siklet, që kishte ardhur ashtu pa pritur e pa kujtuar, por buzëqeshja e tezes ia hoqi atë ndrojtje të fillimit. I zgjati dorën Hamdiut dhe, si një burrë i madh iu drejtua më zërin e trashë dhe të sforcuar, sikur donte të tregonte sesa shumë ishte rritur dhe burrërruar atë vit në shkollën ushtarake në Tiranë.

"Si je, dajë Hamdiu?" Sytë i shkrepëtinin si dy diamante, ndërsa duart i ishin bërë më të mëdha dhe të rënda si darë.

"Mirë, si je ti Dini? Sa mirë bëre që erdhe!" Hamdiu ia shtrëngoi dorën fort nipçes së gruas dhe bëri për nga dera. "Po shkoj të blej nja dy gjana, se na ka ardh nipçja."

"Nuk ke pse, o dajo! Unë pak minuta do rri e do të iki!" tha Dini, por Hamdiu tashmë kishte dalë në korridor. Dini hodhi në krahë Platorin, që po e priste me kërshëri aty pranë. U përkul mbi Alketën, që ishte mbledhur sa një grusht në krevatin e saj dhe i përkëdheli me dashuri majën e hundës. Alketa u kollit fort, aq fort sa iu shkund i gjithë trupi.

"Teze, çar ka Alketa?"

"Është gdhirë pa qejf, të keqen tezja! Po vazhdoi kështu, nesër do ta dërgoj në spital."

"Po pse nuk e dërgon qysh tani?"

"Nuk ka temperaturë. Do t'i jap qumësht të nxehtë pas pak."

"Dërgoje në spital, o teze!" këmbënguli Dini.

"Mos u shqetëso, se e kam vetë merak. Pa na thuaj, si ja kalon andej nga Tirana?" Manushaqja ishte e ndezur nga kërshëria dhe mezi po priste që të merrte vesh sadopak detaje nga jeta konviktore e nipçes në Tiranë.

"Çfarë të them, o teze!? Mure të lartë mbi tre metra. Gjithë ditën e ditës brenda në burg jemi! Zgjohemi me borie në orën gjashtë të mëngjesit. Me vrap shkojmë e dalim gjysëm lakuriq për të bërë stërvitje. Në orën shtatë hamë mëngjesin. Çajit i hedhin shumë klor, aq klor sa na ngec në fyt. Gjatë të gjithë kohës jemi në rresht dhe na bëjnë apel tridhjetë herë në ditë. Dalim vetëm një herë në javë në qytet, por edhe atëherë kur dalim, atëherë e kuptojmë se na mungojnë shumë gjëra!" Dini dukej sikur kishte shpërthyer nga pakënaqësitë. Ajo pyetje naive e teze Manushaqes vetëm sa i kishte ngacmuar koren e plagës që i ishte krijuar thellë ne zemër.

"Ua, çpo na thua kështu?! Pse nuk shikon sesa je rritur dhe zbukuruar! Je bërë një burrë i vërtetë! Ti po bën shkollë ushtarake. Nuk ke shkuar për pushime atje." U mundua ta qetësojë Manushaqja.

"Komandandët janë shumë të egër! Na dënojnë për hiçgjë. Ato dyer me hekura po na marrin frymën! Më mungojnë shokët e fëmijërisë. Më mungon Çelepiasi, lagja ku gjer dje lozja futboll."

"E di ku është Çelepiasi! Ajo shkollë është për të përgatitur ushtarakë për luftë."

"E di, por kam frikë se nuk është për mua. Jemi zogj korenti, që po rritemi artificialisht në inkubator."

"Ku i paske mësuar gjithë këto fjalë të mëdha, more Dini!?"

"Them ta lë shkollën, o teze! Nuk më pëlqen fare. Nuk është për mua. Unë jam zog i lirë."

"Pupupu, se na fëlliqe! Mos ta dëgjoj më atë fjalë. Po për ushqime, kush paguan?"

Dini u zu disi ngushtë, por nuk e bëri veten. Me gjysëm zëri u detyrua të pohojë.

"Shteti paguan! Kush tjetër?"

"Po rrobat, të mbathurat, kanatieret, çorapet, uniformën..., kush paguan për to?"

"Shteti paguan!"

Manushaqja tundi kokën gjithë entuziazëm.

"Çfarë ju japin për të ngrënë? Vetëm çaj për mëngjes dhe fasule për drekë?"

"Ushqimi nuk është i keq, o teze," pohoi me gjysëm zëri Dini. "E di unë, ku do që të dalësh ti, por njeriu nuk jeton vetëm për të ngrënë dhe për t'u veshur!"

"Si nuk jetoka vetëm për të ngrënë dhe për të veshur?! Hap sytë përreth dhe shiko si po vdesin njerëzit për bukë. Mesa kam dëgjuar unë, mish ju japin përditë. Ku ka më mirë, sesa të hash, të vishesh e të edukohesh falas!" Manushaqes po i shkëlqente fytyra dhe me një cep të syrit vëzhgonte Çimin, që gjatë të gjithë asaj bisede rrinte i heshtur.

Ku kishte më mirë: ushqim falas, rroba falas, shkollë falas. Çfarë duhej më shumë? Për katër vjet do të duronte sa të mundte disiplinën e hekurt dhe pa pritur e pa kujtuar do të bëhej burrë. Do të dilte nga shtëpia si një 13 vjeçar dhe kur të kthehej, nuk do ta njihnin dot as edhe shokët e lagjes. Do të ishte pothuajse i pavarur; do të kishte aq shumë kohë për libra, aq sa nuk mund t'ia merrte dot mendja. Kishte vetëm një anë të keqe në këtë mes: do të ishte larg nga Amla! Ndoshta ajo do ta kuptonte dhe do t'i jepte të drejtë. Fundja largësia shuan zjarret e vegjël, por ndez zjarret e mëdha. Ku e kishte lexuar atë thënie aq të mrekullueshme vallë?

Në imagjinatën e Çimit sa vinte e qartësohej një ide e guximshme. Ndryshe nga Dini që donte të kthehej në shtëpi, ai duhej të ikte sa më parë që andej. E ku kishte më mirë, sesa një arsye aq e logjikshme dhe madhore për t'u larguar nga shtëpia?! Do të ishte e dhimbshme në fillim, vërtet, por do të mësohej pak e nga pak. Shkolla në Tiranë do ta bënte të pavarur. Do t'i jepte përgjigje për shumë ngjarje të mbështjella me mister. Largësia nga aty do t'i jepte kohën e duhur për të analizuar gjithçka në detaje. Ndoshta kishte ardhur çasti i duhur për të marrë vendimin më të rëndësishëm në jetën e vet.

"Çarë duhet të baj, që të pranohem në shkollën "Skënderbej"?' pyeti befas.

Dini çakërriti sytë i kapur ngushtë. Nuk ia kishte prerë kurrë mendja që gjithë ai shfrim e vrer kundër shkollës, do të kishte efektin e kundërt tek kushëriri i tij më i vogël.

"Çfarë duhet të bësh? Po ja, duhet të zgjatesh disi, se je ca i shkurtër. Fillo e bëj ushtrime për zgjatje, mëngjes për mëngjes. Kërce sa më lart, sa herë të mundesh e ku të mundesh, por të duhet dhe ndonjë ndërhyrje nga lart besoj." Dini si ndonjë burrë i madh tundi kokën i menduar, duke parë nga Manushaqja gjithë kuptim. "Besoj se e kupton se çfarë dua të them, o teze! A keni ndonjë njeri të afërt që t'ju ndihmojë? Se duhet të jeni me biografi të mirë. Mesa di unë, dajë Hamdiu vjen nga një familje ballistësh."

Manushaqja u shtang nga ai pohim i drejtpërdrejtë dhe naiv i bërë nga një "fëmijë" si Dini. Përpak sa nuk iu mor fryma e duart iu drodhën. Hodhi vështrimin përreth, sikur kishte frikë se mos e kishte dëgjuar njeri, duke harruar për një moment që ishte në atë dhomë me katër mure të quajtur "shtëpi". Ajo "bombë" e hedhur papritur e pa kujtuar në mes të dhomës e shkundi të tërën. Kryqëzoi krahët në gjoks e u përpoq të buzëqeshte, por sytë e zbehtë dhe të trishtuar e tradhtonin.

"Hamdiu është burri im, por jo babai i tij. Nuk ka sesi t'ia prishë biografinë! Nga i ke dëgjuar këto gjëra, mor aman?"

"Kam dëgjuar mamin, kur ka folur me babin!"

"Hm! Paske dëgjuar time motër! Nuk ma merr mendja se e ke dëgjuar mirë!"

"E kam dëgjuar me këta dy veshë! "

"Nuk e ke dëgjuar mirë, se Jakupi, u ka shërbyer edhe ballistëve edhe partizanëve. Jakupi, që ta dish ti, nuk është babai i vërtetë i Hamdiut. Është kushëriri i parë i të atit. Ai u martua me Nazen, të ëmën e Hamdiut, kur vdiq Mirashi-babai i tij i vërtetë. Hamdiu ishte vetëm 12 muajsh. Në atë fshat e kishin zakon: kur burri vdiste, gruaja nuk lejohej të kthehej në shtëpinë e vajzërisë, por martohej sërisht në familjen e burrit."

"Aha! Histori interesante! Këtë nuk e dija, o teze! Domethënë Njerku i Njerkut ka ndihmuar edhe ballistët, edhe partizanët. Ama pushteti i ka shpallur kulakë apo jo?"

"Po! Janë shpallur kulakë për këtë arsye!" pohoi Manushaqja e zënë ngushtë.

"Për mendimin tim, asgjë nuk ndryshon në këtë histori. Jakupi është babai i tanishëm i Hamdiut. Hamdiu është familje kulakësh dhe kjo histori jua prish biografinë, që ç'ke me të. Si përfunduat në këtë birucë atëherë? Më thuaj, a keni ndonjë njeri t'ju ndihmojë?"

"Si nuk kam? Burri i mësuese Vilmës ka qenë shokë klase me Isain. Madje janë ulur në një bankë. Ai është sekretar partie në komitet. Besoj se do të na ndihmojë! Megjithëse është ende herët, do t'i them qysh nesër." Manushaqja mori frymë e lehtësuar disi.

"Tani, po! Ke folur me këmbë në tokë!" Dini tundi kokën si një burrë i madh, ndërsa Çimi rrinte ende i strukur në cepin më të largët të dhomës.

MANUSHAQJA MEZI PO priste që të mbaronte ora e mësimit. Fjalët që nipçja i kishte thënë një ditë më parë, ende i rrihnin si çekanë në rrëzë të veshit. Kurrë nuk i kishte shkuar në mendje se biografia e Jakupit-"babait" të Hamdiut, do të bëhej ndonjëherë pengesë për të ardhmen e djemve të saj. Pikërisht të dy djemve të saj që mezi i kishte rritur dhe i kishte dritën e syve. Nëse do të kishte diçka në jetë më të rëndësishme se vetë fëmijët, Manushaqja as që nuk e merrte dot me mend. Nuk kishte as logjikën më të thjeshtë, që të dënohej për të mos patur të ardhme djali i saj, për shkak se njerku i njerkut kishte qenë korier me ballistët.

E humbur në mes të korridorit, Manushaqja herë humbte në vorbullën e nxënësve e herë ngrihej majë gishtave për të parë disi më mirë, nëse mësuese Vilma ishe vërtet në shkollë. Do të ishte fatkeqësi, nëse syrit të saj vigjilent do t'i shpëtonte silueta e asaj gruaje të bukur dhe plot sqimë, që të bënte për vete me shikimin e parë. Nxënësit, të gjithë të veshur me përparëset e zeza dhe shamitë e kuqe të pionerit rreth qafës, kishin krijuar një oaz të gjallë e të rrëmujshëm. Sikur ndjehej një lloj çlirimi dhe gëzimi spontan për mbarimin e orës së mësimit dhe mbathjes me të katra drejt shtëpisë. Ndjeu një bërryl ta godiste padashur në ije; dikush tjetër, një nxënës gjatosh i shkeli me nxitim majën e këpucës, duke ia hequr disi vëmendjen nga dera e klasës, nga ku duhej të dilte mësuese Vilma. Po i vinte disi edhe pak zor, që duhej t'i kërkonte një lloj favori, kur jeta e kishte mësuar të ishte sa më e pavarur dhe t'i përballonte vështirësitë vetë njëenganjë, pa ia shtrirë dorën askujt. Një zë i brendshëm i thoshte se duhej të ikte prej andej. Fëmijët e gjejnë vetë rrugën e jetës dhe nuk kishte se pse të kërkohej një zgjidhje mekanike nga lart. Një zë tjetër akoma më i arsyeshëm e këshillonte se duhej të bëhej e kundërta. Nëçdo njeri ka dy lloj karakteresh, mbase tre. E njëjta gjë po ndodhte edhe me të, që ishte aq shumë e pasigurt në atë hap që kish marrë për të kërkuar ndihmë atje lart. Ndoshta një shtytje nga jashtë ishte mëse e nevojshme, ashtu si i mbyturi që kapej pas fijes së kashtës me dëshirën e madhe për të dalë mbi sipërfaqen e ujit.

Mësuese Vilma nuk e la të priste shumë. Ja ku po vinte drejt asaj, tërë shend e verë, sikur sapo kishte dalë nga një mbrëmje vallëzimi. Flokët ngjyrë gështenjë dhe me dredha i vareshin lehtësisht mbi supe e sikur ia nxirrnin më në pah sytë e kaltër me atë vështrim të butë. Vilma i mbajti hapat para Manqushaqes dhe i zgjati miqësisht dorën.

"Manushaqe, po ti ktu?"

"Vilma, si jeni?"

"Mirë, po ju? Çar e mirë ju ka sjellë?"

"Të mirat t'u shtofshin! Po ja, nuk di si t'ia bëj për Çimin. Po mbaron klasën e tetë dhe djali ka qejf të shkojë në shkollë ushtarake në Tiranë."

"Në shkollë ushtarake?" u çudit Vilma. "Çimi fare mirë mund të zgjedhë për mjeksi ose për frëngjisht! Ka talent për gjuhë të huja. Ka degë shumë ma të mira se shkolla ushtarake."

"E di! Ty të lumtë goja, por djali e ka vendosur vetë dhe nuk ndryshon mendje. Po të shkojë atje, nuk do të ketë nevojë as për një lloj ndihme, Edhe i ati në shkollë ushtarake ka qenë. Do ta ndjejë veten më të pavarur. Nuk do të ketë nevojë as për ushqime, as për veshje. Të gjitha do t'i ketë të paguara nga shteti. Mendon se do të ketë mundësi të zhvillohet edhe më shumë fizikisht."

"Po mirë! Ta bisedoj me tim shoq Indritin e të shikojmë se çfarë mund të bajmë." Vilma psherëtiu thellë zemërthyer.

"Aman, të keqen! Nuk kam për ta harruar kurrë! Nuk kemi njeri tjetër kush të na ndihmojë. Po ka një pengesë...."

"Çfarë pengese?" Vilma gati i pëshpëriti në vesh dhe u afrua edhe më, sikur të kishte frikë se do ta dëgjonin muret. Muret ishin gjë e madhe. Gjithmonë dëgjonin sekretet më të mëdha. Ishin spiunët më të frikshëm e më të tmerrshëm. Duhej t'ua kishe frikën.

"Po ja, im shoq Hamdiu vjen nga një familje kulakësh. Njerku i vet Jakupi, kur ishte 16 vjeç, furnizonte në atë kohë me ushqime, kushdo që vinte për ndihmë: edhe partizanët, edhe ballistët! E për këtë u damkos i gjithë fisi i tyre."

"Njerku i njerkut? Po ç'lidhje ka djali yt me kët histori?"

"Këtë nuk arrij as unë ta kuptoj! Çfarë nuk na dëgjojnë veshët. Më mirë të sqarohet kjo punë qysh tani, sesa atëherë kur të jetë shumë vonë!"

"Patjetër! Nuk besoj se do të jetë problem. Siç thashë, do të flas me Indritin. Ndërkohë kam një ide. Le të vijë dhe Çimi me Amlën në shpinë tonë. Le të flasë edhe me Indritin. Noshta do të ishte ma mirë që të fliste vetë me djalin, para se të merrte ndonji vendim pa miratimin e tij."

"Ty të faleminderit shumë! Nuk di si të ta shpërblej!" Manushaqja kishte mbetur pa fjalë dhe sakaq e shtrëngoi Vilmën në krahët e saj.

"Nuk ka asgja! Unë jam mësusja e tij dhe e kam për detyrë të kujdesem për të. Si thua për të dilën paradite? Indriti ashtë pushim dhe menoj se ashtë kohë mjaft e përshtatshme për të gjithë."

"Shumë, shumë të falemnderit! Më duket si ëndërr."

"Nuk ka asgja. Pse të mos bajmë diçka që kemi n'dorë?!"

ÇIMI KURRË NUK E KISHTE menduar që do të vinte një ditë dhe do të kishte mundësi të ecte krah Amlës. Ashtu siç ishte vendosur, Çimi atë ditë do të takohej me babain e Amlës, në shtëpinë e saj. Bashkë me Amlën dhe Çimin, ishte dhe Erëza, shoqja e klasës me të cilën bëheshin gjithmonë bashkë. Atë të djelë maji, qyteti dukej edhe më i ndritshëm, me rrugët e pastruara që në pikë të mëngjesit dhe Selvijat e Namazgjasë, që të përshëndesnin, duke tundur krahët e tyre të hollë. Pallati i Amlës ndodhej në krahun jugor, menjëherë pas shkollës. Ishte një pallat pesëkatësh i ndërtuar me tulla të kuqe përballë të cilit ndodhej një shitore vajguri. Amla jetonte në katin e pestë dhe dritarja e apartamentit të saj ishte pothuajse përballë me dritaren e laboratorit të Biologjisë ku shpesh bënin mësim. Ajo dritare kishte një fuqi tërheqëse të mbinatyrshme, sa herë që aty dilte Amla. Kur nuk dilte Amla, ajo dritare ishte kot si të gjitha të tjerat, bosh dhe e vranët. Madje të ngjallte vetëm trishtim.

Ata pesëdhjetë hapa bashkë i dukeshin si një shëtitje në parajsë. Krejtësisht i hutuar dhe i zhytur në botën e vet, Çimi as që nuk po e dëgjonte fare Amlën, që kishte qëndruar në mes të trotuarit dhe po i përsëriste të njëjtën pyetje për të tretën herë. Ishte një nga ëndrrat më të bukura, që po shihte në mes të ditës me diell: Amla vraponte drejt tij e qeshur dhe lozonjare ndërsa ai kishte hapur krahët për ta përqafuar e ngritur në krahët e tij. I skuqur gjer në çaçkë të kokës, Çimi nuk shikonte Amlën, por përtej asaj, me vështrimin krejtësisht të hutuar e të mjegullt, si një natë dimri.

"Çimi, ku e ke mendjen? Ty po të flas!"

"Oh, më fal, se nuk të dëgjova!" Çimi u shkund disi dhe u kthye i gjithi nga ajo.

"Pse do që të shkosh në Tiranë?"

"Po ja, do të jem i pavarur. Do të zhvillohem fizikisht dhe do të kem munsi të studioj. Ktu në Pallatin e Peshkut kemi vetëm nji dhomë e s'dimë ku të rrotullohemi."

"Po si do t'ia bësh pa Amlën?" Erëza ngacmoi me bërryl shoqjen e saj dhe i nguli sytë e saj lozonjarë Çimit, që tashmë kishte ardhur plotësisht në vete nga ajo pyetje shpotitëse që i rrënqethi trupin si një dush i ftohtë.

"Tirana ktu asht! As 50 kilometra larg. Nëqoftëse Amla do që të takohemi, unë do të vij me nji frymë." Tashmë Çimi po dihaste me zor e nuk dinte se çfarë të thoshte më tej.

"Unë nuk thashë gja! Nuk paske shku në fund të botës!? Pastaj kjo ashtë andrra jote. Duhet të ndjekësh andrrën apo jo?!" Tha Amla me shpoti dhe nxitoi hapat. Çimi, nuk dinte sesi t'ia shpjegonte Amlës atë vendim të shpejtë për të vajtur me studime në Tiranë. Donte t'i thoshte se, duke vajtur në shkollë do të bëhej më i denjë për familjen e saj. Më i pranueshëm për familjen e saj intelektuale. E çfarë do të bënte në Elbasan? E shumta do të përfundonte punëtor krahu, pa asnjë lloj të ardhmeje, ndërsa kështu, të paktën do të kishte një mundësi sado të vogël për të ëndërruar për të. Çimi e kuptonte se nuk i përkisnin të njëjtës shtresë shoqërore: Amla vinte nga një familje intelektualësh, ndërsa ai nga një familje punëtore, që mezi siguronin bukën e gojës. Manushaqja punonte në fermë, Hamdiu murator. Babai sapo kishte vrarë veten, pasi kishte vuajtur nga një sëmundje mendore. Ishte jashtë çdo lloj imagjinate që mund të përfundonin bashkë. E mbi të gjitha, ishin aq të vegjël në moshë.

Tashmë i kishin ngjitur të gjitha shkallët gjer në katin e pestë. E skuqur në fytyrë dhe duke marrë frymë me zor, Amla i ra derës fort. Në shtëpi ishte mësuese Vilma, bashkëshorti i saj Indriti dhe motra e vogël e Amlës, Bora!

"Hajde mrena!" Mësuese Vilma e përqafoi ëmbëlsisht dhe e puthi fort në faqe. Indriti, një burrë shtatlartë më flokët e zes dhe të dallgëzuar, i zgjati dorën, sikur të ishte ndonjë burrë i rritur.

"Me sa di unë ti je Çimi! Po sa i ngjan Isait ore?! Sikur të ka bërë nga hundët! Hajde, ulu këtu pranë," e ftoi Indriti dhe ndërkohë i shpupuriti flokët Erëzës, që edhe ajo, dukej sikur rrinte si mbi gjemba. Amla u shkëput disi nga dy shokët e shkollës dhe përqafoi fort Borën.

"Bora, e njeh kush është ky djali? Është Çimi, shoku im i ngushtë. Kemi qenë bashkë që nga klasa e parë." Bora duhej të ishte tre vjet më e vogël se Amla. Kishte sy ngjyrë kafe të errët dhe flokë të zes e të gjatë të mbledhur bisht. Kishte një buzëqeshje të ëmbël që të bënte menjëherë për vete.

"Ti qenke Çimi!" tha Bora shkurt duke rrokjezuar fjalët.

Çimi nuk dinte se çfarë të thoshte. Pra, emri i tij ishte përmendur disa herë në atë shtëpi. Nuk kishte gjë më të bukur sesa kur një ish-shok klase i babait të kujdesej për të, njësoj sikur ta kishte djalin e vet.

"Çimi, çfarë do të studjosh në Tiranë? Më tha diçka mësuesja jote Vilma, por dua ta dëgjoj nga ty." Indriti i zgjati një gotë limonatë për ta pirë dhe u ul pranë tij. Fytyra e tij babaxhane rrezatonte një mirësi të natyrshme, që i vinte nga thellësia e qenies.

"Du të shkoj në shkollë ushtarake!" tha shkurt, duke mbajtur sytë përdhe.

"Po pse në shkollë ushtarake? Fare mirë mund të vazhdosh për mjekësi." Zëri kumbues i Indritit ia largoi disi ndrojtjen e çasteve të para. "Mos harro, se ke mundësi të zgjedhësh për më mirë. Unë kam qenë shok klase me babain tënd."

"E di! Më ka thanë mami! Kam dëshirë të bahem ushtarak si babi! Du edhe të forcohem fizikisht!" Çimi e pa për herë të parë drejt e në sy, por shikimi i tij ishte krejtësisht i turbullt dhe gati gati i përlotur. Donte t'i thoshte shumë gjëra. T'i thoshte se nuk kishte as mundësinë më të vogël për të studiuar në atë dhomë-shtëpi me katër mure. Se e vetmja zgjidhje ishte të largohej nga ai qytet sa më parë të ishte e mundur dhe...të bëhej i pavarur, pa njeri mbi kokë. Se në atë shkollë do të mund të mësonte rreth psikologjisë së njerëzve, të kuptonte më mirë se çfarë kishte ndodhur me babain në të vërtetë. Shkolla Ushtarake do ta ndihmonte të kuptonte shumë gjëra dhe ta përgatiste më mirë për jetën.

"Kush ta ka mbushur mendjen për të shkuar në atë shkollë?" e pyeti befas Indriti, sikur ta kish dëgjuar të gjithë atë ligjëratë të gjatë, atë mori arsyetimesh që bëheshin thellë në ndërgjegjen e tij.

"Kam nji kushëri atje."

"Interesante! Dhe kushëriri yt çfarë thotë? Është i kënaqur?"

"Jo! Fare! Mund ta lej shkollën. Unë jam ma i durueshëm se ai. Ma i fortë. Mund ta maroj shkollën!"

"Në rregull! Nëse mendon se atje do të kesh mundësi të studiosh dhe të rritesh, e të bëhesh i fortë. A je shumë i sigurtë për këtë?"

"Po! Jam shumë i sigurtë!"

"Në rregull! Ashtu le të bëhet. Kam një mikun tim në rreth e do t'ia përcjell atij emrin tënd!"

"Falemnerit!" Çimit mezi i shqiptoi ato fjalë mirënjohjeje, kur kishte aq shumë dëshirë ta përqafonte atë njeri me krahët e tij të vegjël.

"Kështu do të bëhet atëherë! Shpresoj që nuk do të ndërrosh mendje!" Çimi tundi kokën në shenjë mohimi. Nuk do të kishte kthim pas. Befas hodhi një vështrim të shpejtë nga Amla, si për të marrë miratimin e saj.

XXII.

Qerpikët

Manushaqja ishte e mbuluar e gjitha në djersë. Kapakët e syve i ishin rënduar nga gjumi i thellë dhe zemra po i rrihte me një ritëm të çmendur. I dukej vetja si e zënë në një pezhishkë gjigande. Rrotullohej nga të gjitha anët për të liruar disi ata litarë imagjinarë, por fijet e rrjetës së merimangës, sikur ngurtësoheshin dhe i ngushtoheshin edhe më shumë përreth trupit të lodhur. Për t'u çliruar disi, mori frymë me gojë dhe shfryu me gjithë shpirt. Disi më tutje, në një livadh të mbushur me trëndafila të kuq, dalloi Alketën, tashmë jo një foshnje gjashtë muajshe, por një vajzë rreth të njëzetave. Flokët e Alketës ishin në një ngjyrë kafe në të verdhë, që i dallgëzonin mbi supe. Sytë i shkëlqenin nga një gëzim i papërshkrueshëm, ndërsa lëkura ngjyrërozë kishte marrë disi nga nuancat e luleve të atij kopshti lulesh, që dukej sikur ekzistonte vetëm në ëndrra. U përpoq të hapte sytë, si për të kuptuar më mirë e për t'u dhënë përgjigje disa pyetjeve absurde që sapo i kishin lindur në kokë. Si ishte e mundur që Alketa ishte rritur aq shumë brenda një nate dhe çfarë dreq kuptimi kishte ajo ëndërr aq e bukur!? Ëndrrat e bukura janë në antonim me realitetin. Nëse dikush të paraqitet në ëndërr i veshur bukur dhe i qeshur, dije se do të jetë sëmurë ose ka një hall jashtëzakonisht të madh. E kundërta ndodh kur shikon një njeri të vdekur. Vdekja në ëndërr është si një paralajmërim, që ai person do të jetë i lumtur dhe do të jetojë shumë gjatë në jetën reale. Nëse shikon gjak, ëndrra nuk quhet. Të gjitha pamjet fshihen si me buton dhe çdo detaj shumëzohet me zero. Oh zot, nëse kishte, përse nuk po i hapeshin kapakët e syve që të kishte mundësinë për të kuptuar më mirë? Një klithmë, si një piskamë nga fundi i botës, e zgjoi më në fund.

Ishte ende herët në mëngjes dhe dritat nuk ishin ndezur. Hamdiu i kishte kthyer kurrizin dhe flinte ende në njërën anë të krevatit bashkëshortor, me Alketën në mes. Gjithë frikë dhe duke u dridhur pak nga ankthi i ditëve të mëparshme dhe pak nga ëndrra, i vuri dorën të bijës në gushën e vogël dhe të bardhë, për t'i prekur disi damarin e hollë e mavi. E tmerruar u çua këmbëkryq mbi krevat dhe rrëmbeu të bijën në prehër. Me gishtat që i dridheshin u përpoq të kuptonte edhe njëherë se çfarë po ndodhte në të vërtetë në trupin e saj të brishtë. Ia vuri dorën mbi zemër dhe për pak sa nuk u alivanos dhe ra përmbys. Për frikën e saj më të madhe, nuk po ndjente dot atë rrahje të lehtë të jetës, që aq shumë e mbushte me dashuri dhe gëzim. Ndezi dritën, pa u bërë merak për të shoqin dhe të dy djemtë që po flinin gjumë. Hamdiu u rrotullua në krahun tjetër disi i bezdisur dhe pa kuptuar asgjë e detyroi veten të flinte gjumë. Manushaqja hodhi sytë nga djemtë. Çimi ishte kthyer përmbys, ndërsa Platori ishte mbledhur një grusht pranë të vëllait. Edhe ata vazhdonin të flinin. Manushaqja e ngriti vajzën në krahë. Teksa e rrotulloi në ajër, vuri re një njollë të murrme në pelena. Vajza kishte bërë nevojën e trashë, por gjer aty nuk kishte ndonjë gjë të madhe për t'u shqetësuar. Shpesh foshnjet bënin ujët e hollë apo nevojën e trashë në periudha të ndryshme të ditës apo të natës. Sekreti duhej të gjendej aty se, pse Alketa ishte bërë aq meit dhe e zbehtë si një fantazmë. Duart i dridheshin, ndërsa përpiqej me ngut t'i hiqte pelenat që sapo ia kishte ndërruar pak orë më parë. Sapo ia hapi dhe pelenën e fundit, u shtang e gjitha. Dy krimba të mëdhenj e të bardhë ende lëvrinin në nevojën e trashë të foshnjes.

"Hamdi! Hamdi!" Zëri i doli si një klithmë nga trupi i lodhur dhe i këputur, që filloi t'i dridhej nga ai çast tensioni. Manushaqja priti për ndonjë reagim nga i shoqi, por Hamdiu ende flinte si i vdekur pas asaj dite të lodhshme e të gjatë në ndërtim. Manushaqja e la vajzën në prehër dhe tundi Hamdiun nga supi me të dyja duart. Ajo shkundje jo e zakonshme dhe zëri i lartë dhe i mprehtë, e kishin bërë punën e vet. Hamdiu u rrotullua nga e shoqja, duke picërruar sytë.

"Çarë ka nodh? Ashtë shpejt akoma. Nuk ka vajt ora për punë."

"Shikoje gocën. Nuk po merr frymë. Është zverdhur si limon. Ta çojmë urgjent në spital." Manushaqja drejtoi gishtin nga krimbat e gjatë që zvarriteshin në pelenat e ndotura e të kallnin krupën. Kaq mjaftonte. Manushaqja i mblodhi pelenat shuk dhe i futi gjithë neveri në një qeskë plastmasi. E pastroi vajzën me një leckë të pastër dhe me sytë e mbushur me lotë ia ndërroi pelenat njëenganjë. Gjatë të gjithë kësaj kohe, Alketa dukej sikur flinte, me atë fytyrë aq të zbehtë dhe frymëmarrje aq të hollë. Manushaqja e vuri veshin sërisht në hundën e saj të vockël, për të siguruar edhe njëherë që Alketa ende po merrte frymë.

Hamdiu hodhi tej jorganin e trashë prej akllazi dhe u hodh drejt e në këmbë. Pa e zgjatur, e mori Alketën në duart e tij të fuqishme dhe filloi ta tundte në ajër.

"Alketa! Zemra e babt! Alketa! Zgjohu!"

Zëri burrëror i Hamdiut shkundi të gjithë dhomën. Çimi dhe Platori tashmë ishin zgjuar dhe me shikimet e tyre kureshtare po përpiqeshin të kuptonin. Alketa ishte bërë plotësisht e verdhë, si një lule dielli. Kishte marrë pamjen e një kukulle plastike, por që ende merrte frymë. Në një çast puliti qerpikët e gjatë dhe u duk sikur i qeshën ata sy gjysëm të mbyllur. Manushaqja psherëtiu thellë, e lehtësuar disi, por pa ndërruar mendje për asnjë çast se çfarë duhej të bënte.

"O burra ta çojmë në spital, sa nuk është vonë!" Qeskën me pelenat e ndotura i futi në një çantë të vogël, megjithë kundërshtimin e rreptë të të shoqit. "Më duhet t'ia tregoj doktorit."

Hamdiu pohoi me kokë e me duart që i dridheshin ia afroi foshnjën të shoqes. U vesh me nxitim dhe ende pa kaluar pak sekonda qëndroi pranë derës. Manushaqja e mbështolli të bijën me sa mundi dhe hodhi xhaketën e të shoqit krahëve. Pa hapur e mbyllur sytë, tashmë Manushaqja me Alketën në krahë, kishte dalë jashtë. Hamdiu hodhi një shikim qortues nga të dy djemtë që tashmë ishin zgjuar.

"Ça ka Alketa?" Zëri fëminor i Platorit e bëri të dridhej. Në jetën e vet asnjëherë nuk kishte gënjyer. Aq më shumë të gënjente një fëmijë. Duhej të ikte sa më parë në spital, para se të ishte shumë vonë, por një shpjegim të zbukuruar duhej ta bënte. Ishte ende herët dhe djemtë duhej të flinin.

"Nuk ka gja! Do ta çojmë në spital për ta vizitu, kaq!" Dukej se shpjegimi i tij nuk po pinte ujë. Çimi kishte çakërdisur sytë me mosbesim, ndërsa Platori ishte afruar pranë vëllait më të madh dhe e kishte kapur për dore. Ato dy qenie të strukura e të trembura, i futën të rrënqethura në kurriz. Po vraponte për të shpëtuar një fëmijë, por po frikësonte për vdekje dy të tjerët. U kthye menjëherë dhe u ul në gjunjë para tyre, si për t'iu lutur për një favor të madh e sublim.

"Ngjoni! Nuk kam kohë, se mami po më pret jashtë dhe Alketa do të ketë shumë ftohtë. Duhet të flini gjersa të vejë ora shtatë dhe të baheni gati për në shkollë. Po u sollët mirë dhe batë kështu si ju them, do t'ju blej secilit nga një çokollatë të madhe! Si thoni?"

Platori menjëherë nxori majën e gjuhës dhe lëpiu buzët. Me imagjinatën e ndezur përfytyroi një çokollatë gjigande m'u përpara fytyrës: një nga ato çokollatat me katrorë të mëdhenj dhe me thelpinj arre. Tërhoqi vëllanë e madh për mënge dhe shkoi drejt krevatit pa bërë zë. Çimi, si më i madh që ishte, tashmë e kishte kuptuar se diçka e tmerrshme po ndodhte, përgjersa Hamdiu po tregohej aq zemërgjerë. Zakonisht Hamdiu u jepte ndonjë dhjetë lekësh për të blerë panine me bugaçe çdo dy javë, sa herë që merrte rrogën. Çokollatat ishin një përjashtim i rrallë dhe i çuditshëm. Pa e zgjatur, iu bind dorës së vockël të Platorit dhe bëri për nga krevati, pa ia hequr sytë për asnjë çast Hamdiut, që tashmë mbylli derën pas vetes dhe doli jashtë.

ISHTE ORA PESË PASDITE, kur në portën e madhe të oborrit u shfaq Manushaqja. Ajo grua e re rreth të tridhjetave, dukej sikur në atë moment mbante mbi supet të gjitha hallet e botës. Hamdiu e mbante për krahu me të dyja duart, sikur të kishte frikë, se të shoqes do t'i merreshin këmbët dhe do të rrëzohej në pellgaçen e ujit, që ishte krijuar nga shirat e një nate më parë. Në oborrin e Pallatit po loznin një tufë fëmijësh, mes tyre Çimi dhe Platori. Klithma e dëshpëruar e nënës e bëri të dridhej të tërin. Topin prej lecke që i kishte hedhur Platori e la t'i binte në trup. Nuk e kishte parë nënën asnjëherë të klithte ashtu, aq me dëshpërim dhe me një kumbim të mprehtë, sikur donte të çante me thikë kupën e qiellit. Çuditërisht nëna nuk e kishte marrë Alketën me vete. Ndoshta e kishte lënë në spital, pasi Alketa duhej të ishte shumë sëmurë. Po si mund të lihej një vajzë e vogël 6-muajshe vetëm në spital? Aq më tepër që në ditën e parë në spital?

"Ohhh!" Zakonisht nëna klithte sa herë që vinte nga puna në fermë dhe shtrihej e kapitur në krevat për të shlodhur disi. Ajo klithmë ishte ndryshe nga herët e tjera: dukej sikur paralajmëronte fundin e botës. Ishte si e këputur, e dhimbshme, e mbushur me dridhma, me një "o" të zgjatur gjer në amëshim. Manushaqja të jepte përshtypjen sikur zemra do t'i shkëputej nga krahërori dhe do t'i binte përdhe si një zog i vrarë nga ndonjë rrufe në atë qiell të vranët të ngarkuar me re. "Ooooh! Bija ime moj! Po ç'ishte kjo mënxyrë që na bëre, moj zemra e mamit?! Po si na le kështu, moj drita e syrit tim?!"

Më në fund Çimi filloi të kuptonte. Hamendjes së parë ndoshta nëna e kishte lënë Alketën nën kujdesin e mjekëve në spital, po ia zinte një mendim i dytë. Nëna nuk po qante, por po vajtonte. Alketa nuk ishte më!

Çimit iu drodh buza. Lotët iu lëshuan çurk. Iu afrua Platorit dhe ia shtrëngoi dorën e vockël fort, sikur donte t'i thoshte që të rrinte urtë dhe të mos e jepte veten. Platori nuk kuptonte asgjë. Si një ushtar i bindur e la veten të tërhiqej nga vëllai i madh. Iu afruan të dy Manushaqes dhe Hamdiut. Manushaqja me sytë gati të mbyllur, zgjati duart e drobitur dhe ledhatoi kokat e fëmijëve. Ata pesë fëmijë të Pallatit kishin ndaluar lojën dhe të gjithë ishin kthyer me fytyrë nga hyrja kryesore e oborrit. Gratë si me magji filluan të dalin në dritare, për të kuptuar më mirë se çfarë kishte ndodhur. Disa të tjera nxituan nëpër shkallë dhe u dolën përpara për t'i takuar. Disa nga burrat me fytyrat e tyre të vrenjtura dhe duart në zemër, filluan të mërmërisnin fjalë ngushëllimi.

"Të rroni vetë! Na vjen shumë keq! Zoti qoftë me të!" Manushaqes po i merreshin mendtë, por krahu i fortë i Hamdiut nuk e la të bënte. Ato shkallë të pallatit, po i dukeshin si gurë që po i rëndonin në këmbë.

Çimi dhe Platori ndoqën nënën pas, krejtësisht të hutuar dhe të mpirë. Si do të ishte dita pa Alketën, pa buzeqështjen e saj të ëmbël dhe gugitjen gazmore si pëllumb? Psherëtiu si një burrë i madh dhe i la lotët t'i rridhnin çurk në faqe. As që donte t'ia dinte se dikush nga shokët do t'i shikonte lotët. Edhe burrat kanë të drejtë të qajnë. Prej mishi dhe kocke janë edhe ata!

Në familjen Jakupi kishte rënë morti!

XXIII.
Valixhja e babait

Çimit i dukej sikur jetonte në ndonjë planet tjetër, me plot njerëz të dashur, por krejtësisht të padukshëm. Babai nuk ishte më. As Alketa që kishte ikur aq shpejt nga kjo botë. Natyra dhe gjithësia kishin qenë shumë të pamëshirshëm që kishin marrë me vete dy njerëz aq të dashur si babai dhe motra. Rrinte minuta të tëra i zhytur në mendime të zymta, aq sa harronte se ku ndodhej dhe duhej ta kapte dikush nga supi që ta përmendte nga ajo gjendje shtypëse ku kishte rënë. Ndërsa për humbjen e motrës e gjente një lloj shkaku siç ishte sëmundja, për Isain të gjetur të vrarë në rrugë, nuk gjente vetëm një, por dy apo tre. Ishte vërtet vrasje apo vetëvrasje? Çfarë i kishte ndodhur babait në të vërtetë? Apo kishte humbur jetën në mënyrë aksidentale? Dikush duhej të dinte diçka më shumë, përshembull Xhafa, kushëriri i parë i babait. Xhafa ishte njëri nga kushërinjtë më të afërt që Isai e respektonte më së shumti për sa kohë që ishte gjallë.

Manushaqja i hodhi edhe disa lugë me trahana në pjatë dhe priti që i biri të fillonte të hante, por më kot. Skuqi pak salcë në tigan dhe ia hodhi mbi trahana, për t'ia bërë disi më të shijshme, por përsëri Çimi as që nuk e preku me dorë. Kundërmimi i salcës së djegur vetëm sa i ngacmoi flegrat e hundës. Ai mëngjes duhej të ishte si të gjitha të djelat e tjera: i qetë, i mbushur me rrezet e para të diellit, pa atë ankthin e zakonshëm për të shkuar në shkollë. Ishte si një lloj bashkimi familjar pas një jave të gjatë. Çimi futi lugën e parë në gojë, por nuk po e kapërcente dot. Hodhi pak kripë dhe piper dhe e përzjeu trahananë me lugë, por oreks nuk kishte më.

"Po hë mor bir! Fut diçka në gojë!", ju lut Manushaqja, por Çimi shtyu karrigen e drunjtë mbrapsht, sikur ta kishte pickuar grenza dhe hodhi sytë nga dera. I dukej sikur po e përpinte dheu, ndaj duhej të dilte sa më parë që andej. Sikur nuk po mbushej dot me frymë, ndërsa hija e babait zgjatej e zgjatej pa mbarim e gati sa nuk po i merrte dritën. Ngatërrohej me hijen e motrës së dashur që gugiste nga hapësira e bëhej si një vorbull mjegulle dhe tymi.

"Ma, du të dal përjashta!"

"Përjashta në këtë orë? Por është shpejt, mor bir!" Manushaqja hodhi sytë nga Hamdiu si për të kërkuar një farë mbështetje nga ai, por Hamdiu tundi kokën në shenjë pohimi dhe rrudhi disi vetullat e trasha në ngjyrë kafe të errët.

KU DUHEJ TË ISHTE NË atë orë vallë? Xhafa punonte inspektor skene në teatër dhe pikërisht për këtë arsye gjendej gjithmonë aty: ose në skenë, ose në studion e vet të mbushur me portrete dhe skulptura, të cilat i krijonte përditë nga pak dhe me një zell të madh, aq sa edhe harronte se ku ndodhej. Xhafa shpesh gjente kohë të fliste me Çimin, sa herë që vinte "çuni i Isait". Çimi trokiti fort në derën anësore të teatrit, por më kot. Në atë orë të paradites së të djelës, zor se duhej të kishte njeri. Këmbët nuk po e mbanin më. Xhafa ose nuk kishte kishte dalë nga apartamenti i vet në katin e parë pas bibliotekës, ose kishte shkuar për ndonjë vizitë te e ëma, shtëpia e hallë Sadijes që ndodhej përtej Urës së Zaranikës, në rrethinën më të skajshme të qytetit.

Eci me të shpejtë përgjatë kalasë fushore dhe u fut në rrugicën që të çonte në pallatin e Xhafës. U fut nga pas e trokiti fort. Vizitat tek ajo shtëpi ishin bërë më të shpeshta, që nga ajo ditë kur babai ndërroi jetë. Zakonisht në shtëpi duhej të ishte edhe gruaja e tij Xhulja, e për këtë arësye Çimi ndjeu një lloj ankthi dhe zori që kishte ardhur aq herët për vizitë. Ndërsa po bëhej gati të kthehej, dera u hap dhe para syve ju shfaq Xhafa me tërë atë buzëqeshjen babaxhane dhe të ngrohtë, që të bënte menjëherë për vete. Pas shpatullave të tij të gjera u duk Xhulja, me flokët e saj ngjyrëkafe dhe të dallgëzuar. Buzëqeshja e saj e ngrohu disi.

"Prit, ku po shkon?" thirri Xhafa dhe ende pa hapur mirë derën zgjati krahët për ta përqafuar. Vetullat e trasha dhe pis të zeza e bënin edhe më tërheqëse atë fytyrë të rrumbullakët ku lexohej vetëm mirësi. Çimi u kthye i skuqur flakë në fytyrë dhe ndoqi Xhafën nga pas për në dhomën e ndenjes. Xhulja e shtrëngoi fort në krahët e saj dhe nuk vonoi të nxirrte një tabaka me llokume e dy gota me limonatë.

"Hë Çimi, si je? Si po ia çon kto ditë?"

"Mirë!" Çimi uli kokën gati për t'ia shkrepur të qarit. I mbusheshin sytë me lotë, sa herë që duhej të fliste për babain. Xhafa i shpupuriti flokët gjembaçë si për ta lehtësuar disi.

"Ngjo, kam nji palë pantallona të mira, që du të t'i dhuroj. I vishja, kur kam qenë i ri. Thuaji mamit të t'i shkurtojë dhe do të t'bajnë. Xhulja, sillja pak Çimit që t'i provojë." Xhulja la tabakanë mbi tavolinën e vogël prej xhami dhe gati sa nuk fluturoi për në dhomën e gjumit, ku kishin një dollap të madh të mbushur me rroba.

Ishin një palë pantallona teritali në ngjyrë blu të errët, të ruajtura me shumë kujdes. Xhafa i bëri me shenjë të ngrihej në këmbë dhe ia lëshoi pantallonat përgjatë trupit. Me pak shkurtime, patjetër që duhej t'i bënin. I zënë ngushtë nga ajo dhuratë e papritur, Çimi donte t'i thoshte Xhafës se kishte ardhur për diçka tjetër. Xhafa e pyeste për shkollën, pushimet verore, ndërsa ai përgjigjej shkurt me "po" e "jo", duke mbajtur sytë përdhe. As që nuk e kishte menduar, se duhej të vinte aty për ndonjë dhuratë. Ndoshta një kujtim nga babai do të bënte shumë punë. Babai kishte patur një mori librash me tematikë nga më të ndryshmet: që nga poezitë e Sergej Eseninit e gjer tek librat në rusisht që trajtonin shëndetin mendor. Ndoshta do të kishte ndonjë ditar të fshehtë ku mund të kishte ndonjë detaj më shumë se çfarë kishte ndodhur para vdekjes. A mund të kishte pasuri më të shtrenjtë sesa ato poezi, që babai i shkruante dhe i mbante të kyçura në një valixhe prej lëkure në ngjyrë të zezë?

"Xhafë! Falemnerit për pantallonat! Nuk do ta harroj kurrë, që po më jep rrobat e trupit." Zëri iu mek dhe nuk po dinte si të vazhdonte më tej. Duhej të largonte mendimet e këqija. Kapërceu gulçin që i ishte mbledhur në gjoks, por duart po i dridheshin lehtazi. Këto kohët e fundit kishte vënë re se nga hundët kishin filluar t'i rridhnin pikëza gjaku. I ndodhte të paktën dy herë në muaj, sa herë zhytej në dëshpërim të thellë. Nga frika, se mos i dilte gjak përsëri, pickoi veten fort në ije.

"Çimi, mos nuk nihesh mirë?" Xhafa i zgjati gotën me limonatë dhe u afrua më shumë pranë tij në divanin e gjerë, si për t'i dhënë zemër.

"Mirë jam! Më fal! Du të të pys për diçka!"

"Po! Më pyt çarë të dush!"

"Babi më duket se ka pas nji valixhe me libra. Nji valixhe të zezë!"

"Valixhe me libra? Po! E kam unë! E kam rujt si gjanë ma të shtrenjtë."

"A mund t'i hedh nji sy?"

"Po! Qysh tani! Xhulja, sille pak valixhen e Isait!"

Çimi priti me ankth, gjersa Xhulja hyri në dhomën e gjumit e doli prej andej me valixhen në duar. Ishte kaq e thjeshtë: mjaftonte t'i bënte Xhafës një pyetje dhe ja ku ishte, valixhja e çudirave, të cilën e kishte parë kaq herë në ëndërr.

XHULJA U UL PRANË TIJ dhe e vuri valixhen mbi divan me kujdesin më të madh, sikur të ishte prej qelqi dhe kishte frikë se mos i thyhej. Çimi kaloi gishtat mbi të gjithë frikë e ngazëllim njëkohësisht. Seç kishte një fuqi mangnetike ajo valixhe, diçka shpërthyese krahasuar me forcën e atomit. Ku kishte qenë e fshehur kaq kohë? Paskësh ekzistuar vërtet apo u shkëput nga ëndrra dhe ra aty në prehërin e tij, si një meteor që zbriste rrufeshëm nga hapësira? Ai shkëmb i vogël kozmik vazhdonte të digjej nga dëshirat e pathëna, zjarret e vegjël të dashurisë së pashprehur. Kishte pritur kaq kohë. E kish ëndërruar kaq shumë atë çast dhe tashmë kishte frikë, se mos magjia prishej.

"Hape!"' Zëri i Xhuljas e shkundi disi nga ai delir ku kishte rënë. Gishtat filluan t'i dridheshin. E hapi ngadalë atë kuti çudirash. Ç'ishin ato rreze drite që nisën udhëtimin drejt qiellit? Duhej të ishte një vegim i rremë; nuk kishte as magji, as rreze drite. Ishte një objekt i thjeshtë i ngrënë vende-vende nga vitet. Oooh, ja një përmbledhje me poezi e shkruar me një kaligrafi të rregullt, gërma të gdhendura me kujdes e të rrumbullakosura. Ishte një fletore shënimesh, pothuajse e zverdhur nga koha, me disa fletë të fishkura e të grisura. E shfletoi me shpejtësi e sytë iu ndalën tek poezia e bretkosave. I entuziazmuar harroi se ku ndodhej dhe filloi të lexojë me zë të lartë:

Dasma e bretkosave
Bretkosat ekzektojnë
Simfoninë e gjumit
Vetë këndojnë
Dhe vetë duartrokasin:
Nga dasmat e rralla
Ku mblesët s'ndërhyjnë
Ndaj po plasin.

"Kjo qenka nji poezi e përkryme." Çimin nuk po e mbante më vendi.

"E saktë! Lexo këtë poezinë tjetër". Xhafa shfletoi fletoren me kujdes, pa ia hequr nga dora. Këtë herë ishte Xhafa që recitonte:

Prangat
Pranga në tru,
Pranga në zemër
Në pranga hapësira.
Prej tyre
Më çliron
Vetëm dashuria.

"Kjo është poezi për burg!" tha Xhulja.

"E marr me men se çarë do të thush, por nuk besoj se Sigurimi ka pas munsi t'i lexojë këto poezi të shkurtra." Xhafa tundi kokën me mëdyshje dhe u tërhoq në qoshkën më të largët të divanit. Ishte rradha e Çimit të recitonte një poezi nga babai.

Gjethet
Lahem i dehur
Në këtë lumë të florinjtë vjeshte
Nën qiellin e kthjellët
Gjethet-letra dashurie
Dërguar nga pemët.

Çimi ndaloi për një çast si për të rregulluar frymëmarrjen. Nuk po u besonte dot syve që babai kishte shkruar poezi aq metaforike, që të mbeteshin në kujtesë. Ndoshta do të ishte më mirë që ta ruante si sytë e ballit atë fletore dhe një ditë të arrinte të botonte librin e babait. Hovin e mendimeve ia preu sërisht Xhafa me atë zërin e tij bullullues.

"Ka shumë poezi! Do të të duhen net të tana dimni që t'i lexosh gjer në fun. Ja dhe kjo poezi që më ka ba përshtypje," tha Xhafa dhe ia mori fletoren nga duart.

UNË JAM NJERIU
Unë jam Njeriu
Ende i papërfunduar
Nga dora primitive e natyrës
I papërfillshëm ndaj pafundësive.
Rëra e xhamtë e muzikës shkërrmoqet
Mbi lakuriqësinë time
Tinguj të pazakonshëm
Jehojnë nga Pavdekësia
Endrrën shpesh ma prishin meteorë të vdekshëm.
Buzë valësh thërrmuese
Ndanë ftohtësisë tënde

Përpiqem të vetëkuptohem
Të vetëpërmbahem
Të vetëflijohem
Në guackën e dashurisë për Ty!

"Xhulja, çar menimi ke?" Xhafa u kthye nga e shoqja me një shprehje çapkëne në fytyrë.

"I kam lexu me dhjetra herë. Menoj që janë poezi shumë të bukra. Nji qyp plot me florinj, kjo valixhe! Kush tha që babi nuk të paska lanë pasuni!?" tha Xhulja. "Por ka shumë gjana të tjera. Përshemull mu më pëlqejnë kto poezi të Sergej Eseninit. A e di kush ashtë Sergej Esenin?"

Çimi ngriti supet.

"Ta them unë. Poeti ma i madh i të gjitha kohnave. U martu pesë herë dhe ka qenë i shtru në një spital psikiatrik. Del nga spitali për Krishtlindje, dy ditë ma von ban premjen e njanës dorë dhe shkrun me gjakun e vet poemën e tij të funit, e cila përfaqson lamtumirën e tij dhanë botës. I vramë apo i vetëvramë kjo nuk dihet. Ajo që dihet ashtë data 27 dhjetor 1925, kur ndrroi jetë në moshën 30 vjeçare. Xhafë, a nuk menon se ka pak ngjashmëri me fatin e Isait?"

"Besoj se po! Mund të jetë marrë edhe si shembull. Ka qenë poeti i tij i parapëlqym." Tha Xhafa. Papritur Çimit i kapi syri një bllok tjetër shënimesh, ku shkruhej "ditar". E rrëmbeu në duar dhe e shfletoi me nxitim. Kërkoi me ngut në faqen e fundit. Diçka duhej të ishte shkruar në faqen e fundit. Fryma ia ndal për pak sekonda. Bebet e syve iu zmadhuan, sikur po përpiqeshin të zbulonin diçka të tmerrshme të mbuluar nga errësira. Sekreti kishte qenë aty dhe nuk e kishte parë askush: me shkronja blu të errët në fletën e verdhë:

Data 14 Shkurt është dita e Shën Valentinit!
Në këtë datë do të vras veten!

XXIV.

Pushimet verore

PUSHIMET VERORE SAPO kishin trokitur dhe Çimi po mendonte seriozisht sesi mund të shpenzonte ato ditë vere, para se të futej në testet për t'u pranuar në shkollën ushtarake "Skënderbej". Hamdiu vazhdonte të punonte në NSHN-në e qytetit (Ndërmarrja Shtetërore e Ndërtimit), si murator. Rroga e tij ishte burimi kryesor i të ardhurave në familje. Ishte një rrogë e mirë për atë kohë, rreth 5000 lekë në muaj. Manushaqja ishte përsëri shtatzanë dhe për këtë arsye nuk kishte patur mundësi që të punonte në fermë, në detyrën e saj si brigadiere, ku mund të merrte rreth 4000 lekë në muaj. Me kaq pak para mezi u dilte për të ngrënë. Harroje pastaj për veshje, dhe kursime për të ardhmen. Tashmë Çimi po mendonte seriozisht që të jepte ndihmën e vet në familje, qoftë edhe për një kohë sa më të shkurtër. Po të punonte tre muajt e verës, koha do të kalonte më lehtë. Por të gjeje punë, qoftë edhe për tre muaj, ishte mjaft e vështirë.

Atë mbrëmje, si të gjitha mbrëmjet e tjera, ishin ulur të gjithë së bashku rreth tavolinës për të ngrënë darkë. Të paktën dy-tre herë në javë gatuante Hamdiu dhe, kur gatuante ai, dhoma vinte një erë të këndshme qepësh pakëz të djegura. Hamdiu i hidhte fasuleve shumë salcë dhe vaj, për këtë arësye, gjella bëhej akoma edhe më e shijshme, sa që do të kishe dëshirë të lëpije thonjtë. Pale seç i punonte peshkut. E thekëriste aq shumë, sa të të bënte kërc në gojë. Çimi fshiu buzët me picetë dhe nguli sytë nga e ëma. Manushaqes dukej sikur ende nuk i kishte ikur ajo çehre e verdhë në fytyrë, që nga ajo vdekje e papritur e Alketës. Shpesh ngashërente nën zë dhe i linte lotët t'i binin. Atë mbrëmje e ëma nuk e kishte prekur pjatën me dorë, megjithëse Hamdiu i kishte shërbyer, sikur të ishte një princeshë. Mirësia e tij ishte në shkallën më të lartë, por Manushaqja ishte zhytur aq shumë në dëshpërimin e saj të thellë, saqë ato grimca të vogla mirësie nuk i hynin në sy.

"Ma, du të filloj punë," i pëshpëriti në vesh, sikur të ishte ndonjë kërkesë e veçantë rreth së cilës nuk duhej të merrte vesh askush.

Manushaqja nuk lëvizi nga vendi. Dukej si një statujë e lënë në harresë në dallgët e kohës. Hamdiu krruajti pakëz zërin, si për t'i kujtuar se ai ishte aty dhe i kishte dëgjuar të gjitha.

"Mund të të merrja unë në punë, por je i vogël hala. Të bash llaç a të ngresh tulla ashtë goxha e randë për moshën tate. Pastaj dun puntor të kualifikum."

"Nuk jam ma i vogël! Mund ta baj," këmbënguli Çimi. Sytë i kishin marrë një shkëlqim të veçantë. "Me mamin kam shku vjet në fermë, kur mlidhja pjeshka dhe hapja taraca. Nuk ashtë aq e vështirë sa ç'duket."

"T'i them njëherë mësueses tënde Vilmës. Mbase të rregullojnë në ndonjë vend tjetër. Një punë më të lehtë për moshën tënde." Manushaqja tashmë sikur ishte zgjuar nga ai gjumë letargjik ku kishte rënë.

Çimit i erdhi paksa e papritur ai propozim i beftë i nënës. E ëma do t'i thoshte mësueses. Mësuesja do t'i thoshte të shoqit. Amla patjetër që do ta merrte vesh. Çfarë përshtypje do të linte tek Amla, vajza e tij e ëndrrave, që pikërisht Çimi po kërkonte punë që në atë moshë? Fillin e mendimeve ia ndërpreu e ëma, sikur ta kishte kuptuar menjëherë se çfarë bluante i biri.

"Nuk ka asgjë të keqe të kërkosh punë. Meqë i shoqi është sekretar partie, ai ka më shumë mundësi për të bërë diçka," tha Manushaqja.

"As unë nuk menoj se do të jetë nonji problem. O bahet, o s'bahet. Nji punë tre mujore, sa për t'u marrë me diçka. Edhe familjen e nimon!" Hamdiu u ngrit në këmbë dhe filloi të mbledhë pjatat. Manushaqja më në fund e kishte lënë pas ato momente hidhërimi dhe sikur i kishte çelur fytyra.

"Të Hënën që vjen fillon java e fundit e shkollës. Do të vij në shkollë dhe do t'i them Vilmës."

QENDRA E AGRO EKSPORTIT ishte përballë postbllokut të varrezave, në krahë të një pallati pesëkatësh në formë L-je. Aty vinin kamionët e mëdhenj nga e gjithë Evropa Lindore: Gjermania Lindore, Jugosllavia, Çekosllovakia, Hungaria, madje edhe nga Bullgaria e Polonia. Çimi pothuajse kishte vrapuar që nga qendra e gjer në jug të qytetit pothuajse me një frymë. Në ditën e fundit të shkollës mësuese Vilma e kishte thirrur mënjanë dhe i kishte dhënë një letër të shkruar nga vetë shoku Indrit. Porosia ishte që letra nuk duhej të lexohej, pavarësisht se ishte e futur në një zarf të hapur. Me sytë nga ajo ndërtesë e rrethuar nga kamionët që vinin nga qindra kilometra larg, Çimi nuk e kishte vënë re një bordur në trotuar dhe ishte rrëzuar. Letra i shpëtoi nga dora dhe pusulla brenda kishte dalë paksa. Disa currila gjaku filluan t'i binin nga gjuri i gërricur, por Çimit më shumë i tërhoqi vëmendjen ajo pusullë e palosur më dysh dhe e futur në një zarf të thjeshtë. Megjithë porosinë që letra nuk duhej të hapej, Çimi po digjej nga kureshtja dhe nuk duroi më. E hapi dhe e lexoi me një frymë. Ishin vetëm dy fjali të shkurtra të shkruara me gërma të rrumbullakëta dhe një kaligrafi të bukur.

"Është një proletar i Elbasanit! Pranoje!" Letra i drejtohej me emër drejtorit të Agro Eksportit, shokut Betim Lame. Çimi vrau mendjen se çfarë nënkuptonte fjala "proletar". Ndoshta do të thoshte "punëtor" apo që vinte nga nja baba komunist. Hm! Duhej të lexonte më shumë që të merrte vesh kuptimin e asaj fjale. Fjalia tjetër fare e shkurtër "Pranoje", ishte si të thuash një lloj urdhëri që nuk duhej të vihej në dyshim dhe madje duhej të zbatohej menjëherë nga shoku Betim si drejtor. Isai, shoku Indrit dhe shoku Betim kishin qene që të tre shokë shkolle.

Çimi e palosi letrën me kujdes dhe e futi përsëri në zarf. I turpëruar disi nga gjuri i gjakosur, nuk guxoi ta fshinte, duke patur frikë se duart do t'i përlyheshin me gjak. Në oborrin e Agro Eksportit kishte një gjallëri të paparë ndonjëherë. Një maune gjigande nga Çekosllovakia sapo kishte mbërritur për të marrë me qindra arka me domate të mbledhura nga serat e Elbasanit. Në ato sera punonte edhe e ëma e tij Manushaqja për vite të tëra. Për çudinë e Çimit domatet ishin pothuajse jeshile, por mjaft të shëndetshme. Ndoshta mblidheshin ashtu, pasi duheshin ditë, gjersa malli të mbërrinte gjer në destinacion. Ngaqë nuk e kishte mendjen se ku po shkelte, befas desh u përplas me një nga punëtorët: një burrë shtalartë, ezmer, rreth të tridhjetave. Punëtori kishte vënë mbi dhjetë arka me domate sipër njëra tjetrës dhe po i dërgonte brenda në kamion. Ishin ndoshta dyzet punëtorë që ngarkonin pesë kamionë njëherësh.

Çimi ndjeu turp që ishte aq i vogël në moshë dhe në trup. Nuk ishte as një metër e pesëdhjetë i gjatë dhe rreth 13 vjeç. A do të ishte në gjendje vallë që të vinte arkat sipër njëra tjetrës dhe t'i transportonte drejt e në kamion? Dukej sikur punëtorët bënin gara me njëri tjetrin, kush e kush të arrinte i pari. Në fund të ndërtesës stërgjatëse ishin zyrat. Para njërës prej tyre qëndronte një vajzë çeke shtatlartë, e cila ia kishte qepur sytë e saj të bukur përkthyesit shqiptar. Më tutje, një burrë shtamesatar i veshur me kostum se ç'po u thoshte tre punëtorëve të veshur me kominoshe blu. Një tjetër punëtor po shtynte një karrocë të vogël dore, përplot me arka bosh.

"Më falni, kush ashtë shoku Betim?" e pyeti Çimi, ndërsa fytyra iu përskuq nga turpi dhe ndrojtja.

"Ai atje me kostum dhe kollare," tha punëtori dhe shtyu më tutje karrocën.

"Falemnerit," mërmëriti Çimi dhe për një moment mendoi se më mirë do të ishte t'ia mbathte nga sytë këmbët. Po sikur të mos ishte në gjendje ta bënte atë punë? Do të fëlliqej fare. U kthye mbrapsht, por këmbët nuk po i bindeshin. Çfarë do të thoshte mësuese Vilma dhe mami? Po Hamdiu? Do të gjente rastin më të parë dhe do të tallej me të. Më mirë ta bënte zemrën gur dhe ta bënte atë punë. Fundja nuk kishte për të vdekur.

"Hej ti çun! Hajde ktu!" Çimi u kthye dhe kokëulur qëndroi para tij. "Përse ke ardh? A e di që ashtë e nalume të futesh në kët zonë?"

"Më falni! Më ka dërgu shoku Indrit!" Çimi i zgjati zarfin, duke mbajtur ende sytë përdhe!"

"Oh, ti duhet të jesh çuni i Isait!" tha Betimi dhe i hodhi letrës një shikim të shpejtë. "Hm! A ke qef me fillu qysh sot?" Ishte ora tetë e mëngjesit dhe megjithëse fillim qershori, bënte pak ftohtë. "Puno vetëm katër orë sa për ta provu dhe nesër do të punosh tetë orë! Pesë ditë të javës nga tetë orë në ditë. Fillimisht do të spërkatësh domatet me ujë. Punë shumë e kollajt. Si thu?" Betimi i hodhi dorën në shpatull si për t'i dhënë zemër. Çimi sikur mori pak zemër nga ato fjalë të drejtpërdrejta të shokut të babait. A kishte punë më të lehtë në botë sesa të spërkatje domatet me ujë? Fillimisht, se pastaj kur të mësonte, do t'i kërkonte që edhe ai të mbushte maunet e gjata që vinin nga e gjithë bota. Hodhi sytë përreth si për të zbuluar detaje edhe më tërheqëse. *"Eintritt Verboten"- Ndalohet Hyrja. No Smoking-Ndalohet Duhani.* Pothuajse të gjithë punëtorët përtypnin çamçakiza. Çamçakizat ishin gjë e rrallë në vitin 1980. Drejtor Betimi sikur ta kishte lexuar se çfarë bluante në mendje vogëlushi i sapoardhur dhe i ngjeshi në dorë një pako me çamçakiz. "Na, merre këtë dhe shko e merr atë zorrën e ujit atje dhe fillo të spërkatësh me ujë këto arkat e para." Drejtor Betimi fliste me një ton të tillë, i cili as që nuk bëhej fjalë të bëhej dysh.

Epilog

PUSHIMET E VERËS KISHIN mbaruar dhe tashmë Çimi po bëhej gati të vazhdonte studimet në shkollën e mesme ushtarake "Skënderbej. Pallati i Peshkut kishte mbetur po ai, me muret e ngrëna nga lagështira. Tani që do të vazhdonte studimet në Tiranë, Çimit i dukej sikur sapo kishte filluar të shkëputej nga ai qytet i mbuluar nga tymrat e Metalurgjikut. Si në një film bardhezi i kaluan parasysh të gjitha ato grimca kujtese: lodrat që i blinte babai sa herë që dilte nga spitali, lojërat e fëmijërisë me shokët, buzëqeshja e ëmbël e shoqjes së klasës-Amlës, Selvijat e Namazgjasë që sa vinin e përkuleshin nga pesha e rëndë e viteve. Kurrë nuk kishte për ta harruar atë çast, kur i dorëzoi të ëmës rrogën e parë. Dy mijë e pesëqind lekë të vjetra në muaj nuk ishte shaka. Mami i kishte thënë se me ato lekë do të bënin vitin e ri.

"Ik, të keqen mami! Mos e kthe kokën pas! T'u bëftë rruga e mbarë. Mos ki merak për ne." Manushaqja e përqafoi fort të birin në krahët e saj, ndërsa sytë iu mbushën me lotë.

Hamdiu i shpupuriti flokët me duart e tij të ashpra dhe ngriti valixhen e rëndë. Treni për Tiranë nisej për gjysëm ore.

Platori iu hodh të vëllait në qafë dhe nuk donte ta lëshonte. Dukej si një zog i trembur që kërkonte pakëz ngrohtësi.

"Do vijë prapë Çimi! Ja, në dhjetor do të ketë pushimet dhe do të vijë për vit të ri." Zëri i Manushaqes u drodh nga një ngashërim i fshehtë.

"Ohu! Gjer për Vit të Ri ashtë shumë larg!" Platori rrodhi turinjtë. I mbledhur grusht, nuk donte t'i shkëputej nga gjoksi.

"Do të të sjell nji dhuratë shumë të bukur," i pëshpëriti Çimi në vesh dhe e uli të vëllanë në dysheme. Befas u kthye nga e ëma dhe e përqafoi edhe një herë. "Ma, më njofto kur të lindësh."

"Patjetër!" Manushaqjes iu morën fjalët. Tundi kokën në shenjë pohimi, ndërsa sytë e përlotur iu mbushën me dritë.

Çimi nxitoi hapat për të kapur Hamdiun që tashmë po ecte mespërmes oborrit të Pallatit të Peshkut me valixhen në krah. Hodhi sytë përreth, por fatkeqësisht nuk pa asnjë nga shokët e fëmijërisë. Po me Amlën-vajzën e mësuese Vilmës, si do t'ia bënte vallë? Nuk kishte dyshim që do të vinte ta takonte, sa herë që t'i krijohej mundësia. Pushimet e verës do t'i kalonte në Elbasan. Nuk ishte se po largohej përgjithmonë nga shokët e fëmijërisë. Qyteti do të mbetej aty ku e kishte lënë me kujtimet e të gjitha ngjyrave.

"Luji kamët se jemi vonë!" ngriti zërin Hamdiu, duke e zgjuar disi nga ajo kalamendje nanuritëse. Befas dalloi turirin e imët të Kacamiut, prapa koshit të plehrave. Mustaqet e gjata i dridheshin disi, ndoshta nga emocionet që miku i tij i vjetër po ikte për larg.

"Eee, more Çim, qenka dita jote e madhe sot, ë? Po na len lagjen pa gjallëri," tha Kacamiu.

"Duhet të iki, Kacami. Po shkoj për në shkollë në Tiranë."

"Po ne ku do na lesh? Pallati i Peshkut do duket bosh!"

"Do vij prap. Mos u murzit. Do më mungojn edhe kjo lagshtia e mureve, edhe tymi i Metalurgjikut."

"Mos harro, Çim, edhe tymi asht kujtim. Po kur të ngjitesh nalt, në Tiranë, mos e harro rrugicën tonë."

"Si mund ta harroj? Këtu lashë gjithë fëmininë. Edhe Amlën..."

"Ahaaa! Ja ku doli fjala. Amlën, ë? Po ajo të ka për zemër, mos ki marak."

"Do vij prap. Në dhjetor, për Vit të Ri."

"Dhjetori vjen shpejt, po burrat maten me zemër, jo me muj. Rri i fortë, Çim."

"Do përpiqem, Kacami. Falemnerit për çdo kshillë."

"S'ka përse. Hik ime, se treni s'pret. Po kur të vish, sill nonji lajthi apo djath për ne miqt e vjetër."

"Ka marr fun! Mirupafshim, Kacami!"

"Udha mar! Dhe mos harro – kush man kujtimet gjallë, nuk humet asiher rrugën për në shpi," tha Kacamiu dhe u zhduk pas kazanit të plehrave.

Çimi nxitoi hapat për të arritur disi Hamdiun që kishte mbetur i shtangur nga e gjithë ajo bisedë e pazakontë.

Pasthënie

S hkrimtari shqiptaro-kanadez Përparim Kapllani paraqitet
së fundmi përpara lexuesve me një vepër të re letrare, e cila
mban një titull modest "Grimcat". Menjëherë të lind pyetja:
Përse e ka titulluar kështu, me një fjalë që ka kuptimin
"thërrimet"?! Jo më kot. Universi i tërë është i përbërë nga
grimcat, kjo është materja, lënda e parë, atomi prej nga
përbëhet e gjithë bota, universi. Në këtë roman autori ka
zgjedhur fjalën "grimcat" për titull për të na kujtuar se jeta e
shkuar në luginën e lumit Shkumbin dhe pikërisht në Elbasan,
përbëhet nga miliarda grimca jetësore, por ai vetë ka zgjedhur
vetëm disa grimca autobiografike për të na përshkruar e sjellë
para syve jetën dhe historinë e shekullit që lamë pas, sidomos
ngjarjet pas shkëputjes së Shqipërisë nga ish kampi socialist me
në krye ish Bashkimin Sovjetik.

I gjithë romani dhe kapitujt që e përbëjnë atë, rrëfehet sipas
kujtimeve dhe historive të një adoleshenti jetim, me nënë e
baba gjallë, por që atij i duhet të kapërcejë zhgënjime, pengesa,
uri dhe tronditje të mëdha shpirtërore, në një kohë kur duhet
të rrethohej nga lodrat, këngët dhe leximet e librave plot
aventura. Së bashku me vëllain e tij më të vogël, Platorin, ai
detyrohet të jetojë në një shtëpi me mure kallami dhe pikërisht

në një dhomë katër herë katër ku flenë së bashku me njerkun dhe nënën e tyre. Po ku gjendet babai i tij, ish studenti në akademinë ushatrake në Leningrad të ish Bashkimit Sovjetik?! (Petrogradi i sotëm). Shumë afër, në Spitalin Psikiatrik të Elbasanit. Që këtu lindin shumë pikëpyetje. Pse një student i shkëlqyer ushtarak, një ish oficer me biografi të mirë ka përfunduar në Spitalin Psikiatrik?! Pse është ndarë e ëma, Manushaqja me të? Si sillet njerku i prekur nga lufta e klasave? Si sillen me të mësuesit dhe shokët e shkollës? Pra, autori, duke e vënë personazhin kryesor në qendër të kësaj autobiografie kontradiktore, të pazakontë, vetvetiu zgjon kureshtjen e lexuesit. Në këtë mënyrë shkrimtari P. Kapllani ka siguruar epërsinë e parë ndaj lexuesit; duke zgjedhur këtë subjekt shumë interesent dhe origjinal. Me këtë narrativë ai nuk ka dashur të përshkruajë një histori triller, mbytur në varfëri dhe ashpërsi të luftës së klasave, por ai ka dashur të sjellë para sysh vuajtje dhe ngjarje dramatike, therëse deri në kockë.

Nëpërmjet rrëfimeve të Çimit, jetimit me prindër gjallë, ndërtohet e gjithë ngrehina dhe kompozicioni i romanit "Grimcat". Ngjarjet e mëdha politike shkaktojnë edhe drama e tragjedi të fuqishme. Isai, një kursant i shkëlqyer në ish Bashkimin Sovjetik, i duhet të kthehet pa një, pa dy, në Atdhe, medoemos. Urgjentisht duhet të shkëputet me të dashurën e tij, rusen Svjetllana Konstandinova, bijë gjenerali. Ai merr urdhër të kthehet në rastin më të parë në Shqipëri. Vihen përballë njera-tjetrës e dashura e tij, bukuroshja ruse, dhe nga ana tjetër është vetë Atdheu për të cilin ai është betuar të falë edhe jetën. Ai zgjedh të dytën, Atdheun. Isai mendon se nuk mund të jetojë tërë jetën duke mbajtur mbi supe njollën e tradhëtarit. Me shumë dhimbje ndahet përgjithmonë me rusen e bukur. Këtu nis edhe rrënimi dhe shkatërrimi i tij shpirtëror. Llogjikisht nuk mund të pajtohet me zgjedhjen politike të udhëheqjes shqiptare, por urdhëri është urdhër. Dashuria e fuqishme për Svjetllanën e bren, e ndrydh dhe e rrënon pak nga pak, dersa e çon në Spitalin Psikiatrik, duke lënë në mëshirë të fatit, në mes të katër rrugëve, gruan dhe dy fëmijët e vegjël. Bashkëshortja e tij, Manushaqja, një fshatare e duruar, e urtë dhe pa përvojë, nuk mund të përballojë spitalin dhe dy fëmijë jetimë, kështu martohet me një tjetër burrë, punëtor ndërtimi, një njeri kokulur e i nënshtruar për arësye të "disa ceneve" në biografi.

Romani nis me kapitullin "Pallati i Peshkut", përshkruar në mënyrë realiste, deri në detaje të imta. Gra që ziejnë rrobat në kazanë me zjarr e lanin me duar në govata druri, qoshkëza të hirnosura, banja ku gumzhijnë mizat, gjithandej minj të zinj, veshllapushë, radhë për bukë, për peshk, për vajguri, ujë dhe fëmijë që kishin për vakt bukë të lyer me vaj kikiriku e pak sheqer përsipër. Varfëri e tejskajshme. Llampa ndriçimi të djegura në korridor, pasqyra e thyer e dollapit dhe mure të ndërtuara me qerpiç... Pak a shumë kjo është skena ku luhet jeta e një familje të varfër. Si shumë të tjera në ato vite të izolimit të madh të Shqipërisë socialiste.

Shkrimtari nuk ka dashur të mbajë asnjë qëndrim politik duke akuzuar udhëheqjen e Partisë Komuniste. Ai është përqëndruar tek jeta dramatike e personazheve të tij, aq më tepër që rrëfimet e një adoleshenti janë të pafajshme, naive, por të vërteta si drita e diellit, realiste. Indirekt janë akuza për sistemin politik, aventurën dhe vetizolimin që kishte zgjedhur udhëheqja e Partisë Komuniste në pushtet.

Politika ishte shtrirë në çdo qelizë të shoqërisë shqiptare, kishte zgjatur duart gjer në Spitalin Psikiatrik, ku edhe aty të sëmurët mendorë kontrolloheshin dhe përgjoheshin nga policia sekrete se mos "armiqtë e pushtetit" hiqeshin si të çmendur për t'i shpëtuar ndëshkimit. "Disa nga të sëmurët mendorë kanë kërkuar të strehohen në këtë spital për t'i shpëtuar ligjit", thotë drejtori i spitalit, shoku Xhindi. Duket se autori e ka njohur mirë sistemin shëndetësor dhe metodat çnjerëzore që praktikoheshin në këtë spital qendror për të çmendurit. Doktor Xhindi është një diktator i pashprt dhe arrogant, i lidhur me politikën dhe në shërbim të saj, i cili nuk heziton të përdorë në çdo rast shufrat e hekurit dhe elektroshokun për të fshirë memorien e të sëmurëve të irrituar, sidomos ata që shajnë regjimin politik. Ai përshkruhet si një kuadër i egër dhe mizor duke zbatuar me përpikmëri urdhërat që i vijnë nga lart. Në kontrast me të është doktor Arbeni, human, i ditur dhe me shumë kulturë, i cili kujdeset dhe shpëton nga ndëshkimi personazhin kryesor, të sëmurin mendor Isa Vishanji. Ai njeh dramën dhe talentin e këtij pacienti, prandaj e mbron duke rrezikuar karrierën e vet, e fsheh në dollap të zyrës së tij dhe i jep blloqe e laps për të hedhur në letër kujtimet dhe krijimet e tij. Ai e kupton më së miri dramën e Isait dhe pështjellimet e tij mendore. Përdor të gjitha dredhitë profesionale për ta veçuar nga të sëmurët e tjerë, midis të cilëve ka edhe njerëz shumë të dhunshëm e të papërgjegjshëm, deri edhe kriminelë.

Skenat e të sëmurëve mendorë që grinden gjer në gjakosje për një breshkë në oborr, janë sa groteske e të egra, po aq të pështira. Ato janë përshkruar në mënyrë origjinale dhe bindëse. I sëmuri Isa Vishanji, duke përfituar nga maskimi e izolimi, i shkruan disa letra mallëngjyese Svjetllanës, të cilat nuk i postoi kurrë. I shkroi së shoqes, Manushaqes, nënë e dy djemve të tij, si dhe lë amanet një përmbledhje me fjalë të urta që, siç thotë ai, as shiten e as blihen: "Mos u bëj si rrufeja që djeg e shkrumbon çdo gjë që gjen përpara. Lisi rri i përkulur dhe të gjithë gjejnë prehje nën krahët e tij", etj. Ai lë të shkruara poezi me ndjenja të çiltra duke pasur idhull poetin rus, lirikun Sergej Esenin i cili nën peshën e depresionit i dha fund jetës së tij në moshën 30-vjeçare.

Personazhi më i plotësuar i këtij romani është Çimi, (mendoj se portretizimi i këtij heroi nuk është gjë tjetër veçse adoleshenca e vetë autorit). Ai është një fëmijë i pavarur, i zgjuar dhe i shkathët, i pari i klasës dhe njëkohësisht mbrojtje dhe strehë e sigurt e vëllait të tij më të vogël. Mjaft mirë është pasqyruar miqësia dhe dashuria e sinqertë me nxënëse Amlën, tek e cila ai sheh një shoqe besnike të përkryer ndaj së cilës demonstron heroizëm në lodra, shkëlqen për hir të saj në mësime dhe në ndeshjet luftarake me skuadrat "Ilirët" dhe "Romakët". Ai garon dhe lufton dhëmb për dhëmb me komandantin e "Romakëve", derisa e shtrin përdhe dhe vetë ngrihet triumfator në sytë e vajzës së zemrës, Amlës.

Episode mbreslënëse janë edhe ato që i përkasin kolektivit pedagogjik të shkollës, kujdesit të mësuesve dhe gjithë këshillit pedagogjik që punon me përkushtim për të edukuar një brez të ri të përgatitur profesionalisht e moralisht; sa të ditur e humanë. Kolektivi pedagogjik i shkollës është model për nxënësit dhe i lidhur ngushtë me prindërit. Edukatorë shembullorë. Një traditë e spikatur kjo në qytetin arsimdashës, aty ku nisi fluturimin Shkolla e Mesme Normale e Elbasanit, mësuesit e së cilës punuan kudo ku ishin shqiptarët: në Kosovë, Maqedoninë e Veriut e në Mal të ZI.

Çimi, i goditur me plagët që mori nga jeta e vështirë, merr një vendim të prerë. Ndahet me dhimbje nga Amla e dashur, ndoshta përkohësisht; do të jetë edhe ai "zog inkubatori", pra, do të vishet me uniformën ushtarake. Do të vazhdojë shkollën "Skënderbeg" në Tiranë. Ky është një betim përpara kujtimit të babait të tij, i cili nuk la asnjë pasuri veç një valixhe me kujtime, fletore të tëra, shkruar me dorën e tij. Çimi merr në dorëzim gjithë trashëgiminë e të atit dhe premton se do të bëhet një oficer i shkëlqyer ushtarak, pozitë që i ati, viktimë e kthesave të papritura politike, nuk e gëzoi. Babai i tij vetvritet, pëson fatin si e shumë të zhgënjyerëve të tjerë nëpër botë. Duke mos gjetur asnjë rrugëdalje, i braktisur nga të gjithë, Isai hidhet nga kati i pestë i një pallati të sapondërtuar. Sheh të fundit agim që zbret mbi qytet dhe fluturon për disa sekonda në ajrin e ftohtë të mëngjesit, i pafuqishëm të pranojë dramën e tij personale, familjare dhe politike. Kështu jep frymën e fundit të jetës së tij të parealizuar e të dështuar.

Ka shumë shembuj shkrimtarësh të tillë nëpër botë që kanë përcaktuar vetë fundin e tyre; është nobelisti amerikan Hemínguej që u vetvra me pushkë gjahu. Ai luftoi shumë gjatë jetës së tij me alkhoolin dhe problemet e shëndetit mendor. Gjithashtu është shkrimtarja Silvia Plath e cila gjatë gjithë jetës u ndesh me depresionin dhe vdiq nga helmimi me monoksid karboni, shkrimtarja Virginia Voolf e cila u mbyt me ndërgjegje për të mos dalë më nga lumi Quise, shkrimtarja Anne Sexton u mbyt me monoksid karboni në garazhin e makinës së saj për të mos e parë fëmijët, po ashtu shkrimtarja

Yukio Mishima i dha fund jetës me vetvrasje rituale, (seppuku), tradicionale japoneze, etj.

Po personazhi qendror i romanit "Grimcat" i shkrimtarit Përparim Kapllani? Ai u hodh vullnetarisht e me ndërgjegje nga tarraca e pallatit pesëkatësh. Edhe kjo tragjedi është temë e luftës dhe e dëshpërimit ekzistencial. Vetvrasja, duke u hedhur nga lartësitë, është zgjedhje tipike shqiptare. Kështu veprojnë kryesisht të gjithë bashkëkombasit tanë, ata që i mund e i vë poshtë depresioni, dhimbja dhe vuajtja e pameritur shpirtërore. Ata janë delikatë, të brishtë, jetojnë në vorbullën e ankthit dhe është zgjidhja e tyre për t'u dhënë fund vuajtjeve shpirtërore, të pamerituara.

Nëse për një moment ky personazh lirik, Isai, talent ushtarak, do të hapte sytë e do të ngrihej nga varri, me siguri do të shihte birin e tij nën uniformën ushtarake, Çlirimin, i cili vazhdoi me krenari stafetën për mbrojtjen e Atdheut, Shqipërisë sonë të dashur. Bëri atë që i ati nuk mundi të realizojë.

Avdulla Kënaçi

Mississauga, 4 tetor 2025

Biografi

Përparim Kapllani ka lindur në Elbasan, në qytetin e Ditës së Verës, karakafteve plot aromë dhe ballakumeve të magjishme. Vetëm 14 vjeç do të largohej nga qyteti i fëmijërisë, për të veshur kapotën ushtarake të skënderbegasit. Në vitin 1990 diplomohet Oficer i Artilerisë Kundër Ajrore në Universitetin Ushtarak "Skënderbej". Disa vite më vonë diplomohet Mësues i Gjuhës Shqipe dhe Letërsisë, në Universitetin e Tiranës, në Fakultetin e Historisë dhe Filologjisë.

Kapllani ka dhënë kontributin e vet si gazetar në disa gazeta të vendit, duke përfshirë gazetën "Ushtria", të përditshmen "Shekulli", revistën "Spektër", etj. Në vitin 2000 emigron në Kanada, së bashku me familjen. Pesë vite më pas, Kapllani boton romanin e parë "Vizitorë në Had" dhe përmbledhjen e dytë me tregime "Babai në shishe", botime të shtëpisë botuese "Albin". Drama "Mbretëreshë Teuta e Ilirisë" do të përzgjidhej si një nga krijimet më të mira në konkursin mbarëkombëtar të dramës në vitin 2002, konkurs i organizuar nga Ministria e Kulturës e Shqipërisë. Disa vite më vonë Kapllani e rishkruan në anglisht dhe shumë shpejt gjen dritën e botimit. Në anglisht janë botuar edhe romanet "The Last Will",

"The Wild Boars" dhe "The Thin Line". Vëllimi me tregime "Beyond the edge", si dhe libri ilustrativ për fëmijë "Queen Teuta and the little prince" janë dy krijime të tjera të arrira të z. Kapllani. Proza e tij është e përfshirë në njëmbëdhjetë antologji kanadeze. "Genti"- është një tjetër dramë e Kapllanit, e botuar online në platformën më të madhe elektronike Smashwords.com. Romani "Grimcat" është një rikthim në fëmijërinë e tij të vështirë.

About The Publisher

Welcome to "Kapllani" Publishing House, proudly established in Toronto to champion new Albanian voices and stories. At "Kapllani, we believe in the power of words to transcend boundaries and connect cultures. Our mission is to provide a platform for emerging Albanian writers, offering them the opportunity to share their unique perspectives and rich narratives with a global audience.

Located in the heart of Toronto, a city renowned for its vibrant multiculturalism, "Kapllani" Publishing House is dedicated to celebrating and preserving Albanian literary traditions while embracing innovative and contemporary voices. We specialize in a diverse range of genres, from thought-provoking fiction and poetry to compelling non-fiction that explores the Albanian experience in the modern world.

At "Kapllani", we are more than just a publishing house—we are a community of storytellers, readers, and literary enthusiasts committed to fostering a dynamic literary landscape. Whether you are a writer seeking to publish your work or a reader eager to discover new and exciting voices, we invite you to join us on this literary journey.

Discover the voices of tomorrow with "Kapllani" Publishing House at www.kapllani.com.

Did you love *Grimcat*? Then you should read *The Last Will*[1] by P.I.Kapllani!

[2]

The Last Will is the story of Albanian Cham, Muharrem Shahini, who on his death bed, asks his son Zylyftar to return to their homeland in Greece to retrieve twenty hidden land deeds for his fellow Chams, living in exile. During his mission, Zylyftar finds himself at the center of a massive coverup to an ethnic cleansing dating back to World War Two. In the process, Zylyftar reconnects with his ethnic identity, learning about honor and what it is to be a Cham.

Read more at kapllani.com.

---

1. https://books2read.com/u/mlyle7

2. https://books2read.com/u/mlyle7